THE TRANSFER

Thomas Palmer

THE TRANSFER

COLLINS

8 Grafton Street London W1

William Collins Sons & Co Ltd
London · Glasgow · Sydney · Auckland
Toronto · Johannesburg

British Library Cataloguing in Publication Data

Palmer, Thomas
The transfer.
I. Title
813'.54[F]   PS3566.A544

ISBN 0-00-222721-5

First published in the UK 1983
Copyright © 1983 by Thomas Palmer

Made and printed in Great Britain by
William Collins Sons & Co Ltd Glasgow

For My Grandparents

What I write here is the account which I
considered to be true, for the numerous
stories of the Greeks are, in my opinion,
ridiculous.

HECATAEUS

Biscayne Bay

THERE ARE NO CEMETERIES IN MIAMI. Most of the dead are either cremated or shipped away. You could search all day for a headstone and never find one.

There are good reasons for this. First, the water table in Dade County is rarely more than a yard from the surface. No one wants to see a coffin lowered into a ditch full of water. Second, there is very little room to dig, since the soil, where it exists at all, is very thin. Scratch the dust and you come up against a layer of calcified rock, deposited when the whole area was the floor of a shallow sea. This rock extends down hundreds of feet. Shovels and pickaxes are not the answer; even a backhoe can hardly dent the stuff. This situation is not likely to change, and people are going to have to get used to it.

Just as the legal means of disposing of bodies are made difficult, so are the illegal ones. Since it is impossible to bury anyone without investing a lot of time and energy, those corpses that might prove embarrassing are simply dumped somewhere. The nearby ocean makes an anonymous grave, but not everyone has a boat, and the coast is fairly well patrolled due to the level of smuggling activity. On the other side, the Everglades offer miles and miles of near-wilderness, but the very difficulty of access renders conspicuous anyone who ventures out there. Around the city you have plenty of overgrown lots and roadside thickets — these are for amateurs. There remains one other alternative — one that has become more popular recently and that now accounts for nearly a third of the homicide victims discovered by the public — the canals.

Their intent is mostly preventative; they shield the city from disastrous flooding by allowing water to pass easily from the Glades to the

3

ocean. Although they come in all sizes, most are at least twenty feet deep, and there are hundreds of them. A body, properly tied and weighted, has a reasonable chance of disappearing into one of them almost indefinitely. However, since the water is surprisingly clear and the banks are popular with small boys and fishermen, the canals remain only the best of poor alternatives. Many of the corpses that go in there do not stay submerged for long.

So when Ray Hula opened the paper one morning and saw a picture of the police dragging his half brother out of Canal No. 10 he was not especially surprised. He knew that Michael was dead. It was just a question of time.

Hula folded the paper and went down to the corner to get a quart of milk. On the way back he stopped in a phone booth and called the police.

"Hello? I wondered if you have arrested any suspects in the murder of Michael Cruz."

"Who's calling?"

"Arthur Jackson. I'm a friend of the family."

"The officer in charge will release further information as it becomes available."

"What's the cause of death?"

"The officer in charge —"

"Right." He hung up.

Ordinarily, Hula would not have been especially interested in who had killed Michael. He had been expecting it for years. They had met for the first time at their mother's funeral, six months earlier, where Michael had put on quite a display for the police cameras — hunched over the coffin, his hands clutching the rim. When Hula tried to introduce himself Cruz had turned away and said, "I have no brother. I have no life." Then there was a commotion at the door and a girl who might have been a model rushed in and threw herself on Michael, beating him with her tiny red fists. Hula walked out; he didn't know anyone there anyway.

Michael Cruz lived in Newark and their mother had died in Providence. At the time of her death she hadn't seen Cruz for twenty years, and this is what made Hula angry. On holidays there was always an extra place at the table, "for Michael when he comes." All her letters and phone calls went unanswered. She had persuaded Hula to try to find him for her, and he had spent a week in a strange city talking to mailmen and attorneys. On the fifth day he had reached someone who claimed to be Cruz's secretary. She told him to call back in twenty-four hours. The next day she said that Cruz knew what Hula had to say and didn't want to hear it. He went back to Miami.

Although he'd never seen him before, Hula had no trouble recognizing his brother at the funeral. Michael had made a name for himself in Newark and his picture occasionally appeared in the national news. Hula remembered one shot of him crouching outside a courthouse, surrounded by marshals and peering apprehensively into the lens. He was testifying for the Knapp Commission; everyone wanted to be there when he died. His evidence was spectacular — old men went to jail — but for some reason Michael came out of it unscathed. In fact, he was rumored to be even more successful than before at whatever it was he did.

Ray Hula ran a marine salvage business on the Miami River just east of the Twelfth Avenue bridge — a fair operation, since a lot of old boats wind up in south Florida. However, he could see that he'd be forced to sell out eventually, since the small shippers were fading and the big firms believed in tearing down the hulks themselves. Some of them had even opened antique stores to sell the fittings. Hula had tried to start his own construction business, building piers for the rich, but he didn't know the first thing about it. He'd given up on it when one of his foremen punched a hole below the waterline in a forty-foot cruiser. Hula had the equipment to float it again, but the restoration was expensive and his insurance man had to be coaxed back with an incredible sum.

He lived alone in an apartment on the bay at Twenty-fifth Street. His wife had vanished years ago; there were no children. He was solitary by nature. He had a two-inch telescope on his balcony and he liked to spend his free afternoons sitting on a high stool and watching the big yachts push up the channel.

On a hot Sunday in June, nearly a half year after his mother's funeral, Hula was relaxing with a damp towel wrapped around his head when the phone rang in the kitchen. He grunted irritably and went in, his turban dropping to the floor with a slap. He picked up the receiver and grunted again.

"Ray? Ray Hula?"

"Yes."

"This is Michael." There was only one Michael he knew. He might have let it ring, this once.

"Well what the hell do you want?"

"Listen, Ray, I'm sorry if I offended you at Mom's funeral — we just have different ways of doing things — I'm sorry. But I didn't call to talk about that. I'm calling on business — I can make you rich."

"Forget it." Hula nearly put the hook down.

"No, wait!"

"Look, you're the TV star. I'm not interested."

"Ray, that's behind me now. This is the real stuff. I've heard you've been taking some lumps, right? Well, when this is finished you can buy Port Everglades."

"What is it? Dope? Guns? A fortune in diamonds? Don't suppose that you're the first."

"Listen, I'm talking about a half a million dollars. You'll never get a chance like this one."

"So you're a rich man. Do you know what Mom lived on before she died?"

"I don't want to talk about that. There's a lot of things you don't know."

"I guess not. It's a shame, isn't it?"

"Look, Ray, I'm not asking you to marry me. I called because I'm on to something and you might be useful to me. The offer stands — half a million for three days' work. Tax free."

"Bite my crank."

He hung up. Hula stood by the phone awhile, breathing slowly and carefully. The curtains by the window stirred slightly. He could see down into the parking lot, where two Cuban kids were playing with a garden hose. He picked up the towel and went back out to the porch.

Obviously, Cruz was involved in some kind of smuggling operation, probably drugs. It was too much money for anything else. Hula knew a little about the rituals that accompanied the trade — the South American businessmen out on Miami Beach, with their blank faces and their crazy wives; the long-haired drifters that stood around the docks, showing their charts of the Bahamas to the DEA agents; the harried frowns of the customs men while they wrote out their forms; the first-time offenders caught with sixty pounds of marijuana

6

under the living-room sofa, "strictly for home consumption," their names in the paper next day: Arthur Gomez, 32, Harold Crande, 28, Susan S. Willis, 19 — whatever happened to them?

Hula was not interested in staying up all night and making deals with foreigners. He didn't trust his luck. The men who succeeded in the trade were all the same; they acquired expensive wives, moved out to Kendall, sent their kids to private schools, paid cash for a new Mercedes, and spent the rest of their lives worrying about what their neighbor, the osteopath, thought of them. There were easier ways to make a living. If anything, he was a little too stiff about the idea; anyone who wanted to become a foreman for Miami Salvage, Inc., had to serve as an informer first; Hula liked to know in advance which of his crew members were about to leave.

Every six months or so the paper published another exposé of the drug traffic — a profile of a harassed enforcement official, an interview with Mr. Burns, reformed smuggler, and an editorial plea for more men and more federal money. Sometimes it worked, and a few more names were added to the payroll. The trouble with this policy was that it raised the stakes — the war against the importers drove up prices, and profits with them, so that the business became even more attractive to the young entrepreneur. It's possible that a truly massive effort might have had some effect on the trade, driving it elsewhere for a while, but what the paper never said was that if the laws against these substances were ever relaxed, a lot of people would be out of jobs. As it was, the cops worked hard at their trade, weeding out the bumblers, and everybody was happy.

Three days after the call from Michael, Hula was standing by the crane on his small barge in the middle of Biscayne Bay, watching bubbles trail up through the muddy water. He had two divers on the bottom, hooking chains to a light plane that had gone down the night before. The morning was bright and windy, and the sun splintered off the waves, bringing tears to his eyes. To the east the beach hotels stood like broken teeth on the horizon. Beside him a photographer from the *Herald* was fooling with a light meter, his tie flapping in the breeze, and shouting questions into his ear. Hula's socks were already soaked through with spray. He was trying hard to be civil.

"You say it crashed around 2:00 A.M. this morning?"

"That's what they told me."

"Anyone hurt?"

"There were two people in the plane and the Coast Guard took them both to Mt. Sinai."

"Why did it go down?"

"I don't know. Why don't you ask him?" Hula pointed to a man with sunglasses and airborne blond hair standing by the shack at the end of the barge — the insurance man.

"He won't talk to me."

Hula shrugged and turned away.

"Who do you bill for this?"

"Look, I'm trying to get this plane up in one piece. Go bother someone else." He went over to the shack and grabbed the headset. The microphone was loose and banging against the wall.

"PL to One."

"Yeah, One."

"What's the story?"

"Hard to see — there's a lot of crap in the water."

"Is it broken up?"

"Don't think so. Looks like it just sank."

"Good. What about the bottom?"

"More sand than mud. A few rocks. Everything's clear except the wheels. I think we can just yank it up."

"You want the blower?"

"No — I think they'll pull free. Ray, do you want some oysters? They're all over down here."

"I hate oysters."

"Right. How do you want us to set this up?"

"Put a cradle just forward of the tail and see if you can straddle another over the wings. You'll need some more hardware. You want me to drop it down?"

"It's too dark. I'll come and get it. Don't you wish everything sank in fifteen feet of water?"

"You said it."

"That's a roger." He flipped a switch on the box and looked out the door. His tug, an old matchbox he had brought down from Norfolk twenty years ago, rode at anchor a hundred yards away.

"PL to *Anna*." He could see a bright swatch of yellow in the wheelhouse — his captain's slicker. "Wake up, sir."

"*Anna*."

8

"It looks like we'll be getting out of here in an hour or so."

"It's good."

"I want to leave the same way we came in. No sense feeling our way twice."

"OK."

"Go back to sleep. I'll call you." He hung up the mike and stepped out of the shack. The photographer was watching the pelicans bicker over a row of piles. Hula turned around and reached into a greasy locker built against the side of the cabin, taking out a pair of shackles and dropping them into an orange plastic bag. He started to wrap it up, hesitated, and dropped another one in. When he got over to the side his diver was already bubbling and blowing at the surface. The waves slapped at his head. Hula could see that he had to work a little to stay afloat. He slipped the bag onto a gaff and lowered it to the diver, who grabbed it and sank out of sight.

There were five men on the barge: Hula, the photographer, the insurance adjustor, and two crewmen. With the divers and the man on the *Anna,* Hula had five men working for him. Most of them he had trained himself. Although he paid them well and allowed them as much responsibility as they could handle, he was not popular with them. He was distant and irritable; he said no more than was necessary and he kept his thoughts to himself. Oddly enough, his self-control had given him a reputation for having a temper, and some of his crew were a little afraid of him.

The winches were already hot and turning; both cables ran up the crane and down again. On the other side of the barge one of the crew was sitting on a stanchion with a fishline. Hula motioned him to pull it up. Tommy, one of the divers, broke the surface and waved for the hook, then ducked under again. Hula went over to the crane and brought the boom over the side, dropping the cable between the two buoys the Coast Guard had planted the night before.

Two sunfish skated back and forth a hundred yards away, loaded with kids waiting for something to happen. Hula waved and shouted at them, to no effect. He decided they could be ignored. The two divers breached together and headed for the ladder at the end of the barge. Hula started the crane. The cable tightened and rose, quivering. The winches hummed against the weight. Something huge and dim stirred in the murky water, sending little shocks up the line; the droplets leapt off in bunches. The two sunfish had dropped their sheets, sails flapping idly. Now the hook was breaking through, the chains running out taut to either side. The water flattened, enormous shapes rose out of nothing, and for a moment a great white bird glowed just beneath the surface. Then the tail cleared with a rushing sound, and the sun gleamed along the length of a wing; the sea let go and water spewed out of a thousand apertures, pounding the bay into foam. The plane hung in the air like a jewel, swinging gently. Hula shut off the crane and gaped. Everyone on the barge was looking at him. In big black letters, standing out against the white of the fuselage, someone had written: TO RAY — FROM MICHAEL. The photographer went to work.

Hula at Sea

HULA'S OFFICE was a tiny box bolted under the roof of an old shed on the river just east of Twelfth Avenue. He had a broom in the corner and a dirty pool of water under the air conditioner. From his seat by the window he could see his tug squeezed in alongside a couple of rotten hulks that he had never bothered to tear apart — the owners had refused to pay, their promises notwithstanding, and Hula liked to keep them there as reminders of his own stupidity. When the Port came around and told him he'd have to get rid of them, he threw up his hands and said they didn't belong to him, what could he do? Sooner or later, he told himself, someone would pay him for the job.

Across the river, only about two hundred yards wide at this point, there was a small marina with a row of finger piers loaded with sports-fishermen, and beyond that a couple of businessmen's hotels and the great massy heap of the civic center — ten hospitals and a few city buildings, a pile of bricks dropped from an airplane. Though most of the cargo traffic had moved out to the Port of Miami — a man-made coral platform in the middle of the bay — some of the smaller freighters still crept up the river, halting traffic on the Twelfth Avenue bridge and providing plenty of excitement for the taxpayers, who were waiting for a nervous tug captain to let one swing wide and poke its way into their waterfront condominiums. On a quiet Sunday Hula liked to watch the greasy water slide back and forth and listen to the crowds at the Orange Bowl five blocks away.

On this particular afternoon he had other things to do; the insurance man was sitting on a carton of outdated forms and asking questions. Hula had known him for five or six years, and they had an unspoken liking for each other. The adjustor looked like a crack shot with a blow dryer; tall, lean, sunburned, tending toward bright blue vested suits and dark glasses. This was the first time Hula had been forced to lie to him.

"OK Skipper, what you want to say is that you don't know anyone named Michael and you don't know who decorated that plane. Is that it?"

Hula creaked back in his chair and stared at the ceiling. "Look, what can I tell you? You're the one who's supposed to investigate these things. All I know is that I got a call to pull up a wreck and my name was on it. I didn't ask for the job, the city gave it to me. If someone named Michael did want to leave me a message, how could he be sure that I'd be there when it was raised? Tell me that."

"I'll say this — you get a feel for the odd apple, and this is about as odd as they get. I'd be a whole lot more comfortable if you could explain it to me."

"Why don't you ask the people who own the plane — the people who were *in* the plane?"

"I just did."

"Well?"

"I believe them. They're still too shook up to lie about it."

"So tell me."

"Don't get excited. You can read about it in the paper tomorrow."

"Tell me now."

"They said they were sucked up in midair into a spaceship. People from the planet Michael. Green, with no eyeballs."

They sat staring at each other for a moment before Hula turned away. "Look, I've got better things to do."

"I'll tell you. It was a young couple in the plane, just going out for a ride. He bought it six months ago and keeps it at Opa-Locka. They were in evening clothes. He said he didn't know anything about the message on the plane. I think it could have been there without them noticing it — on the side away from the door. The engine cut out right after takeoff and he was too low to do anything but dump it in the bay."

"You think someone fixed it?"

"I'm going to have a look at it later. By the way, the first name of the guy who owns it is the same as yours."

"Well all right. Does he know anyone named Michael?"

"Loads of 'em. For what it's worth, he thinks the guy who did

14

it — wrote the message — is his father-in-law, whose name is George, but who likes pranks."

"What do you think?"

"I think you know more about this than you say you do."

"What do you want from me? Don't I always cooperate with you? Believe me, I'd love to be able to clear this up."

The insurance man stood up, dropped his clipboard on the desk, and moved to the window, his hands clasped behind his back. "OK. I can understand why you wouldn't want to tell me anything. It doesn't make any difference to me — no matter what happens, we'll probably have to pay the claim. And you'd be stupid to tell me anything you didn't have to. But since I think you should know, I'll tell you why I thought you might be involved in this somehow. This morning I heard that we won't be seeing much of each other anymore, because you won't be getting any new contracts from the city. Don't ask me why — that's just what I heard. I'm a long way from the people who decide these things. But you see if I'm right."

Hula sat up straight and blinked.

"And another thing. I don't know how long this is going to stick, but I think you better try and do something about it. Good luck. If you ask me, you should have taken some time to make a few friends in this town. Nowadays you have to pay for every cent."

Without looking at Hula he turned, grabbed his clipboard, and walked out the door. The whole office shook; he took the stairs two at a time.

» » »

Michael Cruz slept later than usual. The sun slanted through the window blinds, embossing a bright rectangle on the head of the bed. Cruz — a small, rabbity man with dark hair cut short, short enough that you could see the whorl on the back of his head — twitched from side to side and lashed out viciously at the sheets, which were creeping up the bed in order to smother him. He was vaguely aware of the heat on the back of his neck and he tried to ignore it. Earlier, when he had rolled on his side to investigate, the sun had burst through his eyelids like a bomb, shocking them open, and he didn't want that to happen again.

A young girl in a bathrobe appeared at the door. She had long, glossy, dark hair and a narrow face. She watched him, sipping on a cup of coffee and leaning against the doorframe. She placed the cup on the dresser, circled the bed, and yanked up the shade. Cruz jerked violently and lunged for the pillow, knocking it onto the floor. She ran out, giggling.

Cruz rubbed his eyes, lurched up from the bed, and wandered into the bathroom.

An electric hair dryer hung from a bracket by the shower. Someone had installed a lock on the medicine cabinet. Cruz found a hairpin and pried it open. It was nearly empty — just a few prescriptions, years old, and some vitamin pills. He opened some of the bottles and sniffed them, then turned away, leaving the pin in the lock and the cabinet open. He walked to the door and shouted down the hall.

"Hey — you got any aspirin?"

"The bedside table, in the drawer."

He sneezed and crossed the bedroom, scratching his head. Without clothes to disguise it, Cruz's body looked pale and undernourished — his skin the color of cardboard and the muscles clinging to his bones like tar. He brought the bottle back with him and shut the door. When the hot water hit him he began screaming obscenities, and he went on long after the pain had stopped.

The girl stood by the kitchen counter, measuring coffee into the basket of a percolator. Her robe was short and hung open slightly, so that she could look down and see a band of tawny brown skin extending all the way to her ankles. She was proud of her body — the taut skin between her breasts, the angular swell of her hips, her long runner's legs. There is a close relationship between mind and body, she was convinced, and she thought that if you took care of your body, which was easy enough, your mind would take care of itself. She was beautiful, and she was twenty-two.

Cruz found another bathrobe in her closet and strolled into the kitchen. She handed him a mug of coffee and pointed to a table on the terrace by the pool. It was shaded, and there were fresh flowers in a bowl in the center.

"Do you want any eggs?"

"No."

"Toast? Orange juice?"

"I don't want anything."

She poured herself a mug and went out to join him. Cruz peered

16

narrowly at the opening in her robe as she sat down. She watched him, smiling, and pushed the robe off her shoulders, letting it fall to her waist.

"Is that better?"

"Suit yourself."

She laughed and pushed her hair back. "You know, that rag fits you pretty well. You're no bigger than I am."

"So what do you want, a medal?"

"Look at you — you're all skin and bones. Do you think the girls like you that way?"

"I don't care."

"The hell you don't. What were you shouting about in the shower?"

"Nothing."

"Nothing?"

"So where are your parents?"

"They're spending the week at Marathon. They may stay longer — Dad can do business on the phone. Isn't our house nice?"

"What does he do, print money?"

"I don't know — a lot of things, I guess. He used to be a developer."

"You still in school?"

"I graduated last month — from Barnard. I was in the city all that time and I never told you. Will you forgive me?"

"No loss. You couldn't have reached me if you tried."

"Well aren't we mysterious. Here's a question for you — where was it that we first met? And what was I wearing?"

"That's easy. The bar at the Royal Biscayne. You were in a green dress and you nearly knocked me over. I never made anyone easier than you."

She laughed and dipped her fingers in the flower bowl, throwing water in his face. "Why thank you — I don't remember myself. So what brings you to Miami?"

"Business."

"Drugs? Gambling? You look like a crook to me."

"Never mind."

"Why don't you carry a gun? Aren't you supposed to?"

"It's unlucky."

17

"I thought that maybe that was why you wouldn't dance with me last night — you might have dropped it. Who told you about the Forge?"

"I've been here before."

"I don't go as much as I used to. Too many cranks. It's the same everywhere on the beach. Alton Road isn't the cozy address it used to be."

"People don't want to fight the city traffic."

"That, and all the undesirables moving in — like yourself."

"They were always here. You got a lot to learn, Miss Titty."

"Well." She made a face. "That's what I'm talking about. You have bad manners." She tood up, threw off her robe, and leaped into the pool, pinching her nose between her fingers. Cruz grinned, almost involuntarily, and watched her slither through the glassy water.

Some hours later, Michael Cruz emerged from the front door and walked to his car, a black Thunderbird with New York plates. The girl was still in bed, rubbing cold cream into her neck and chest. She groaned and wrapped her arms behind her kness, stretching the muscles in her lower back. She was still there a week later when her parents came home. Her skin had turned pale and bluish. The police said someone had torn a hole in the porch screen and smothered her, probably with a pillow. A neighbor enabled them to trace the car that was parked outside that day. It was registered to Michael Cruz in Brooklyn. They never found it.

» » »

From the balcony of his apartment Hula could see his barge moored just west of the channel down near the public marina. It was too big to drag up the river. In the middle of the deck an object wrapped in dark canvas stood out against the horizon. Hula had been staring at it all morning. Heavy high-topped clouds floated overhead — tropical clouds, moving in from the gulf, with their bottoms cut off evenly, as if they were sliding on a sheet of ice. In the afternoon they would close up and drop some rain. By the seawall a pelican swayed uncertainly in the crown of a diseased coconut palm, drying its wings in the breeze. Hula had tried to phone the Port earlier in the day, with no success — it was Sunday. He wanted to know how soon he could take the plane off his barge. That could have waited, but he also wanted to know how much truth there was to what the insurance man had said

the day before. Of course no one would tell him anything — they
preferred to communicate by deeds — but he hoped the fact that he
seemed to suspect something might have a good influence. The har-
bormaster, who had inherited Hula's phone number and the habit of
calling him from a predecessor, was not a friend. Soon after he took
office he had called Hula and asked him to consider moving his operation out to some city property at the Port of Miami, since he was trying to cut down on river traffic. That way, he said, Hula would have a
permanent berth for his barge and could make a nice profit on the sale
of his waterfront land. Hula replied that there were less boats on the
river every year and that rents at the Port were too high. They had
rarely spoken since; they had never met each other.

Although most of his bills went out to private addresses, Hula was
dependent on the Port. Whenever a vessel sank or was abandoned,
the Port was the first to know, and they usually called up Hula and
told him to clear it away. If the owner was reluctant to pay for it the
Port could be persuasive. For years Miami Salvage had received most
of this work; there was not enough to attract competitors. Hula only
missed out on the largest jobs. He didn't have the resources to work
offshore or to mount a big effort, so that kind of thing went to the
local marine construction firms, which could handle them. They had
dredges that could put up a new island in three weeks.

However, Hula did not do so poorly that he went unnoticed; given
the chance, the giants would have been glad to absorb his business.
They certainly didn't need to buy any more boats to do it. If he was a
little more quick off the mark than they were, it was only because he
was rarely tied up in any long-term commitments. So he needed a little good will at the Port. He had always assumed that prompt action
and the ability to wait for his money were enough. For the first time,
it occurred to him that he had nothing to guarantee those phone calls.
And if he had to fight he was bound to lose.

Hula's apartment was painfully small. Add a dog and it would have
been crowded. He kept the bedroom shuttered and dark — there was
no room in it to do anything but sleep — and the living room looked
like a hallway in disguise. A deep leather couch sat along one wall,
across from the TV, and a lacquered pine table with two chairs occupied the bright spot by the doors to the balcony. In the kitchen, which
was more or less built around the dishwasher, he had to keep his arms
at his sides and move deliberately. In the icebox he kept a bag of

apples, a quart of milk, a few pounds of cheese, a head or two of Homestead lettuce, and a case of beer; the freezer compartment was jammed with turkey pies and frozen pizzas. Although he was a fair cook, he was too lazy to eat well, and if there were too many dishes in the sink when the evening news ended he would often forget whatever it was he had planned to make and have another drink instead.

Built over an entryway, his apartment was the smallest in the building, and he could easily have afforded a larger one. But he didn't like to clean and had no use for the extra space. On one side of him lived a retired ice-cream salesman from Michigan who had once had a name as a prizefighter; on the other, a young cabdriver named Norton, who had visions — late at night he would call on Hula in order to tell him about the young girl he saw in the mirror or the man that sat beside his pillow. Hula never ventured to question their existence, but the whole thing got boring very quickly and he stopped inviting Norton in. Norton moved on to the ice-cream salesman, and they apparently had something in common since Hula sometimes heard them murmuring well into the morning. Occasionally they would argue over something and start a fight. Since the salesman was barely sixty and kept in shape, and Norton was 6'2" and very energetic, they could do some damage to each other. For a week they'd repair themselves in private, and then it would begin over again.

Downstairs there were a couple of Cuban families, some young hospital workers, and a widowed real-estate saleswoman, Lisa Bishop, who Hula sometimes had up for a drink. They made jokes about the cracked plaster and the landlord's teeth. Once in a while Hula would take her out to dinner. Lisa Bishop was a tall, wary native with a gift for self-mockery and an obsession with her figure, which was nothing to be ashamed of, and they were comfortable spending the night together, if only because they had grown up in a different time, and so discovered that they were equally ill at ease with the freedom they allowed themselves. Her skin was permanently brown and seamed from years of Florida sun, and she converted Hula to gin and grapefruit juice. They were agreed to be married as soon as it became respectable again, but they were each a little too grown into their independence to live in the same room, and it was only luck and proximity that kept them together.

Hula was more or less content with the particular beach where he had crawled ashore. Whatever ambitions he once had were long since faded; he had tasted money and power, to some extent, and they were not the drugs they claimed to be. He was not overly proud of his record as a human being; he considered himself no better or worse than most. In fifty years God had never spoken to him, and he didn't bother to listen anymore. Almost by default, he had achieved a kind of balance. But though he believed he was a free man, and that he'd long since shed the passion and prejudice of his youth, in reality his time on earth had crusted him over like salt, and each turn of the wheel left him a little further behind. So when the force of circumstance began to nip and bind, he was not entirely ready.

He spent the morning thinking of the events of the day past. All of them seemed to lead to his brother. From what he had seen of him at the funeral, he guessed that Michael was capable of anything. And unless yesterday's shocks were the result of a fantastic coincidence, Cruz must be behind them, because no one else Hula knew could have either inclination or resources to put them together. That afternoon Cruz appeared at the apartment. Hula was nearly expecting him.

At the door he looked out of place in his dark business suit, a black coat on his arm — the Long Island Railroad rather than Biscayne Boulevard. He stood erect and stared up at Hula, breaking into a smile after a moment. Hula stepped aside without a word and ushered him in. Cruz threw his coat on the table and looked around. His movements were precise and theatrical; he was evidently enjoying himself.

"Don't you have any place to sit down?"

Hula pushed the coat away and seated himself at the table. Cruz dropped into the couch.

"Raymond, you don't look too happy to see me. Why is that?" He lit a cigarette and tossed the match out onto the balcony. "Not talking. OK, let me fill you in. That plane you pulled up yesterday? I put it there. Also, I've been talking to some people I know and they said business is off and they won't be calling you up much. Do you know what I'm saying?"

Hula picked up a bottle cap and dropped it on the table. "What did they charge you?"

"Hell, it was free. I'm a rich man, so people treat me different. Whenever I open my mouth people sit up straight and listen. It's weird, if you just have a little money you can say the stupidest things

21

and they act like it was the word of God. Hell no, it didn't cost me anything."

"I don't believe you. I've been here too long. It won't work, Michael."

"What won't work?"

"You're a loser. Even if I did want to try something like this I would never do it with you. I can smell the shit sticking to you."

"Huh. Tough guy." Cruz fingered his moustache thoughtfully. "Look Ray, I'm not asking for any favors. The fact is you don't have any choice."

"What do you need me for?"

"I'll tell you later." He stood up and undid his tie. "Right now, will you turn on the damn air conditioner? It must be eighty-five in here, and I hate to sweat."

Hula sat motionless. "You should learn to dress for this weather."

Cruz turned and glared at him, his eyes bulging. The shirt clung to his back. "Move, would you please! I'm dying!"

Hula reached up and twisted a dial on the wall. A faint stream of cool air blew noiselessly from a vent in the ceiling. Cruz stood under it and pushed his hands through his hair.

"Thank you. You know, brother, you live like a pig. Look at this place. What a dive. How much do you weigh, 220, 230? You're a pig in every way. I don't know why I'm bothering with you."

"So get out."

"No — you've got something I want. First, I'm going to tell you why you have to listen to me." He returned to the couch. "It's very simple. Unless you're with me on this, all the way, I'll ruin you. You know I can do it. If you don't please me, I will personally see to it that all your boats rot away at the pier. And if you try and sell out, you'll find that nobody wants your business. Is that clear?"

Hula looked again at the man on the couch — his brother, with whom he had nothing in common. "All right. You expect me to believe, number one, that you can reach into the Port — you, all the way from Newark — and persuade them to drop me, no matter what I have to say about it; and number two, that if I were to decide, God knows why, to sell all my boats and tackle, you could keep every pile driver from Norfolk to Texas from making me an offer. Did I get it right?"

"You got it."

"Then the answer is no."

Cruz got up and stalked around the room waving his arms in the air. Hula sat back. Someone began pounding on the wall.

"Who's that?"

"My neighbor. He likes his nap in the afternoon."

Cruz rushed to the wall and began beating it with his fists. "Go back to bed! Sleep it off, moron!" The pounding stopped. He stood in the center of the room, breathing heavily, sweat running down his temples. "I hate this goddamn place!" He collapsed on the sofa and glared at Hula. "OK, that won't happen again. Strictly business from now on." He sat up and straightened his tie. "I've already shown you what I can do, am I going to have to give you another demonstration? Got anything in mind?"

"I don't think you've got much credit. Didn't you put all your friends in jail a few years ago?"

"That thing was planned from square one. Just cleaning out some deadwood."

"If you say so."

"Look, brother, you're just not in a position to argue with me. Do you know what this is?" He reached into his pocket and threw a small plastic bundle onto the floor. Hula could see it was filled with white powder. "That's pure cocaine. I put three more like that on the desk in your office this morning. You can see them through the door. Now either you go along with me or I'm going to call the cops right now and tell them where they are. They know who I am. They'll get there before you do. That's the way it is — I'll buy you one way or another. This is the biggest deal I've ever seen and I'm not going to let you spoil it for me. Your share is half a million, cash. I'll be back tonight to talk about it. By the way, don't leave here until then." Cruz got up, mopped his face with a handkerchief, and walked out the door. He left the packet where it fell.

After a while Hula picked it up and sniffed it. He brought it into the kitchen and put it behind the toaster. Out on the balcony, a lizard was chasing flies up and down the rail. When Hula arrived it leaped into space, falling to the grass below. He put his eye to the telescope and looked at the barge. The plane was still there; the canvas was speckled with the first few drops of rain.

» » »

It was dark when Cruz returned to Hula's apartment. He found the door wide open and the lights out. The mercury lamps in the parking lot shone into the first few feet of the entryway — beyond that, nothing. Cruz approached to within a step or two of the door and stood beside the wall.

"Ray."

"Yeah?"

Cruz was relieved. "Can I come in?"

"Door's open."

"Turn on the lights. I might trip over something."

In a moment there was a bright square on the landing and a glow from the window. Cruz turned and walked inside, shutting the door behind him. Hula had returned to the couch. He was about halfway through a large sandwich. Cruz pointed at the entrance.

"What was that all about?"

"I like to sit in the dark — it makes it seem cooler."

"You should know better."

Hula shrugged. Cruz pulled out a chair at the little table. There were two empty beer bottles in the middle. He wore the same heavy dark suit as before — it looked as if it was almost too much weight for him, dragging down his shoulders and binding his arms to his sides.

Michael leaned back and tapped a cigarette on his heel. "What have you got to tell me?"

Hula sighed. "First of all, I want to know exactly what it is you want to do and how you're going to do it."

"Then you're in? Do I hear you correctly?"

"I didn't say that. If I like your project and I think it stands a good chance of succeeding, then maybe I'll go along. I don't know yet."

Cruz lit his cigarette and smoked quietly for a few minutes. He already knew what he was going to say. "Ray, look — you have everything backwards. This is not the way I like to operate. There ought to be another way — but there are problems. First, this plan of mine is very illegal and I can't go spreading it around. Second, I need your help — nobody else will do. So you can see the kind of jam I'm in."

"What does that have to do with it? I don't owe you anything."

"That's right, you don't. All all I want is a yes or no." He was watching Hula very closely. "But if you think about it, I think you'll see that a yes would be better for both of us." He leaned forward and stubbed out his cigarette. "Don't let me rush you — take your time."

24

He was a different person — cool, patient, relaxed — than he'd been that afternoon. Hula was unprepared for this side of him. "Look," he said, "I'm not asking for much. Just tell me what you want to do. Save your threats for when I turn you down." The even, steady note in his own voice was just as surprising.

Cruz frowned. He took off his coat and laid it carefully over the far arm of the couch. He had the grace of movement typical of many small men.

"OK — no more, no more. Let's talk. Tell me something — what do you know about me?"

Hula couldn't resist. "She used to talk about you a lot. I think you were about four feet high."

A wry smile. "All right. What else?"

"Just the usual stuff. Police informer, two-bit hood, criminal conspirator, loudmouth, traitor, and so on."

"So you've been keeping an eye on me."

"I was always interested."

"Do you think you're better than I am?"

"I never saw you before in my life."

"Sounds good to me." He scratched his ear deliberately. "Ray, you run a payroll in your business, right?"

Hula nodded.

"So you know what I mean about protecting the amount."

"What?"

"You know — when you write up your paychecks, the first thing you do is fill in the numbers, so if something goes wrong nobody else can fill in their own."

"Yeah."

"Well, that's more or less what you're asking me to do for you. You want me to fill in all the facts on this job before you do anything else."

Hula sat back and crossed his arms on his chest. "I'm not asking you for anything."

"OK, right. But you have to understand — once I tell you what I'm looking into, the check isn't blank any more. You become a person to me. You see what I'm saying?"

"I already told you what I think."

"All right. What I mean is that I've got a lot riding on this thing — it's very important to me. You should know that by now."

He settled into the couch and puffed out his cheeks. "You may not think you need to know everything I'm going to tell you, but just bear with me and you'll see why."

If he'd been looking at Hula while he said this, Ray might have tried to stop him. But he wasn't, and Hula didn't.

"I guess you know that a lot of drugs come through Miami. Most of them come from Colombia. All of the coke comes from there — some by mail, some by commercial freight, some is carried in by airline passengers. It's very light and compact, difficult to detect. That bag I showed you — two hundred grams, worth two thousand dollars in Colombia, worth twice that over here.

"I didn't know anything about it until last winter, when I was asked to go to Colombia to take part in a series of meetings. I wasn't going to move anything — I'm too well known for that. In fact, I think one of the main reasons they asked me was because I have a name. Anyway, while I was there a lot of money fell in my lap." He talked in a lunging, headlong rhythm — sudden spurts separated by brief pauses, his momentum sparked by sharp flourishes of his small, delicate hands.

"There's no amateurs in the coke business. You need a hell of a lot of cash — for bribes, for salaries, for security, and for the coke itself. The big shots in Colombia will ignore you unless you have a lot of money to spend. And you need a lot of connections to lay off the stuff over here — you have to keep it moving and you have to get out of the way. What it means is that nearly all the coke coming into the U.S. is handled by only three or four large organizations, mostly naturalized Colombians.

"Of course they all want to be number one. It's not just greed — they all think they have to move first before the others get a chance to put them away. So it didn't take much to get started.

"I was working for the main New York group." He turned his head and looked out the glass doors to the balcony, his hands folded in his lap. Hula began to realize that this man had a life independent of his hatred for him, and it made that hatred seem uncomfortably shallow and limited. Like he said, he'd never seen him before in his life.

"As of last year, the only part of the business that they didn't own was the far end — the farmers. They had signed up the smugglers, the Colombian wholesalers, the refineries — everybody but the farmers. Most of the coke is grown in Bolivia and Peru, in the mountains, and is carried through the jungle to the Colombian border. The farmers chew the leaves all day long. They eat up a thousand dollar's worth of coke a week, but they don't have enough money to buy a pair of sneakers. Anyway, to buy the farmers they had to crawl back over those mountains with lots of money and guns — hell, they had to send a small army. And as soon as the other big traders found out what was happening, they had to try it themselves.

"I don't know much about what happened up there, but I hear there were lots of fun and games. They were all trying to tell the farmers what to do. It lasted for six months, and towards the end nobody — not even the guys in Bogotá who were supposed to be running the operation — knew what was going on. They just kept pumping in more men and guns. Then Peru and Bolivia sent in troops and cleared up what was left. The survivors crawled back with the bad news and a general truce was called. That's what those meetings were for — to let everyone cool off and try to decide how to split up the dust in the future. Everyone saying '*Qué barbaridad*' and trying to blame it on the other guy. I didn't have much work to do — they were all tired of fighting and wanted to get back to business." He sniffed and rubbed his nose with his knuckle.

"One of the guys who didn't make it was a friend of mine. He was a Cuban from New York and he'd been recruited to lead one of the groups going into the mountains. After he got there he was chosen to herd a big load of coke back down again, by an alternate route, since by that time the fighting had spread to the trails leading out and every move was a shot in the dark. It was the last sizable shipment that came down to Colombia — the farmers started hiding their crops and smuggling them out by way of Peru and Ecuador — the Colombians had stopped paying for them.

"They didn't make it. On the way back they were shot up by soldiers or police or maybe even their own relief crew — nobody knows. But by that time they had already cached the load. My friend was the only one who came away from it, and when I heard he was at the state hospital I went to see him. He was in pretty bad shape — he had an infection in his leg and he wouldn't let any of the doctors near him. He said they'd tried to poison him once already. They didn't care — nobody knew who he was — my bosses said he was permanently cracked and forgot about him. But he had enough life to be mad as hell about what they'd done to him, and the second time I went to see him he told me what had happened and where the stuff was hidden. He said he had to tell someone. He also said that if I had any brains I'd take the stuff out myself, because if you're going to risk your ass for something, he said, you might as well do it for yourself, and not for some clown who cuts you off as soon as he's finished with you. He was dead a few days later.

"I kept my mouth shut about the whole thing. At first I thought I'd go up and check out the story myself, but I wasn't in a position where I could just disappear for a few days and I didn't know shit about taking care of the stuff. I thought about passing the word on, but I couldn't see how that would help me. If I was wrong they would all start looking at me funny, and if I was right they would try to sign me up for keeps, which I didn't want. So I forgot about it."

"Wait a minute," Hula said. Cruz stiffened. Hula got up from the table and went into the kitchen, returning with glasses and two bottles of beer. He waved one at Michael, who shook his head. He looked unhappy at the interruption. Hula went back and put one of the beers back in the icebox. He felt very uneasy; he hoped the alcohol might bring him down to earth. When he came back he started drinking immediately. "Are you ready?" Cruz said. Hula preferred not to answer. He took another swallow.

"Well, as the meetings went on, I began to learn something about the way they do business down there. These Colombians — the ones who'd never left Colombia and were standing on top when the war was over — they said things were going to be different. They changed their shirts every half hour and drank scotch like water, but they knew what they were doing. They said that our guys had been away too long and had forgotten their manners. From now on the American interests wouldn't be allowed inside the country — they said we'd proved we couldn't handle it. They laid down the law about how the coke was going to move and they wanted their bite all at once. From then on we were supposed to come in, pay our money, and leave. In return they said they would police the network inside Colombia and guarantee good stuff at a good price. They also promised we wouldn't have to pay anything extra on the way out.

"There was a lot of grumbling and delays, just for effect, and eventually the bosses agreed. They had all got burned and were ready to try something new. So they shook hands and we all went home.

"After I got back I started thinking about that story again. No one had seemed to notice the coke that was missing — it looked like they never got word of it at all. From what I had picked up at the meetings, I figured it just might be possible for me to take something out myself, since I knew where to go and might be able to bluff my way through. And since I wouldn't be actually buying the stuff, the guys on top might never hear about it. I decided it was worth a look. I told everyone I was going to be out of town and I left.

"The stuff was buried beside an old railhead in the jungle. It was already refined — pure gold. I had figured that I'd put it in a suitcase and carry it back to town, but it would have taken a dozen suitcases. That's when I began to see the possibilities in the situation. I covered it up and came back to New York to think about it.

"A week later — this was about two months ago — I went back. I brought a friend who knows about boats. We looked around and found an old sailboat we could have — we spent the next few weeks fixing it up. Just inside the hull, up under the floorboards, we put in a series of watertight plastic boxes — big ones. Then I rented a truck and went and got the coke. I brought it back and we loaded it into the boat. We had a couple of visits from people asking questions — if I hadn't known a few things we never would have made it. We took off the next morning.

"Right now that boat is just over the horizon, in a small harbor in the Bahamas. My friend is watching it. There's nearly two thousand pounds of pure dust buried in it. Right here in Miami it's selling for about twelve hundred an ounce. If I can get it over here safely, I know more than one person I can offer it to — I should be able to ask two and a half million. They'll scream like hell — they'll figure out where I got it from — but there's no way they'll be able to say no. Then I put my money away and disappear. It's a one-shot deal — all or nothing."

Cruz got up and stretched, his arms held high, his suit bunching at the shoulders. He let them fall.

"Now," he said, "I guess you want to know what I need you for."

» » »

Three days later Hula was lying in the dark, wide awake, wondering what time it was; irritated, because he was no closer to sleep than when he'd started. It was after midnight, judging from the traffic noise. He could hear the bay water muttering along the seawall. Next door Norton was arguing with someone, probably himself. Hula rolled over and planted the pillow on his head. It cut off Norton but it cut off the air too. He pulled it aside and turned onto his back. If he concentrated he could make out a word or two coming from the next room, but nothing more than that. There was another noise, too — closer, and very familiar, though at first he had difficulty identifying it. Someone was knocking on the door. He got up and moved silently into the hall. The night air was moist and cool — he noticed he was shivering.

"Who is it?"

"It's me — open up."

Without thinking, he obeyed. Lisa Bishop stood there in her bathrobe, watching him closely.

"Am I welcome?"

"Yeah, sure." He moved aside. She sat on the couch and leaned back, crossing her legs. When he joined her she was staring at him again, her long fingers pushing through her hair.

"Ray, I don't mean to be nosy, but you've been acting a little strange lately — for instance, you just answered the door in the nude. You said you wanted to go to dinner tonight — you said you'd call. Who needs to call — I live two steps away? And then you didn't anyway. What did I do?"

"It's not you. Don't worry about it."

"Tell me. I'm curious."

"I'm just tired."

"All right. What next — do I get up and leave? Come on, Raymond, take a chance. You owe it to me. You were going to take me out tonight, remember?"

He got up, fished his bathrobe out of the closet, and tied it loosely around his waist. He sat down next to her in the dark.

"Lisa — it has nothing to do with you. You should keep clear of me for a few weeks. It'll all blow over."

She stiffened. "That does it. Either you tell me what this is about or you'll never get another moment of peace. Don't say anything more — I'm not kidding."

"Nope," he said. "Some other time."

"Why do you think I'm here? Who else can you talk to?"

"It's nothing. Let's just forget about it, OK?"

30

After a moment she leaned close to him, grabbed him by the ears, and shook his head gently. "Ray, Raymond, Hula, Hula, Hula." He laughed and she pushed him away. "You want me to go?"

"Right."

They sat there for a while, not looking at one another. Ray stood up. He turned to her, his body huge and insubstantial.

"You want something to drink?"

"Uh-huh."

He moved into the kitchen and worked in the dark, quickly and noisily. Lisa wasn't quite comfortable; she took a few deep breaths. When he returned he had two small glasses full of rum and ice. He handed her one and sat down at the table a few feet away.

"I have a brother who wants me to help him bring in some drugs. I can't say no."

She put her drink on the floor and ignored it. "I didn't know you had a brother."

"Not many people do. He's not the kind of person you'd brag about."

"But I thought your father never married again."

"He didn't. My mother did — not legally, I guess, since they never got a divorce."

"How did you find out about each other?"

"When I went north to see Mom for the first time he had just left home. She could hardly talk about anything else. His father was a Portugee named Cruz. He was lost at sea a few years after Michael was born."

"Your mother didn't have much luck with husbands, did she?"

"No." Hula picked up a dime and started rapping the table with it. "The reason I never told you about Cruz is because he embarrasses me. In New York he's a well-known figure in organized crime. From what I've seen of him, I'd never guess he'd made it that far."

"How long have you known him?"

"I never saw him until Mom's funeral. That was the first time he'd seen her since he left. For years she begged him to come home — but he never did, not for an hour. I spent a week in New York looking for him once. He finally showed up when she died."

"Nice."

"I was hoping I'd never see him again. Now he's got me tied up in this deal and I don't know what to do."

31

"Was he the man who was over here last weekend?"

"You saw him?"

"He was on the balcony when I came home from work. I wondered who he was."

"That wasn't the first time I heard from him. He's got other ways of communicating. He told me that if I didn't go along with him I would lose my business and go to jail."

"So what did you tell him?"

"I said yes, of course. What else could I do?"

"Can't you go to the police?"

"He knows them better than I do."

"Then you're going to do what he says?"

"I don't know."

Lisa finally got started on her drink. Hula looked at her face in the dark. It troubled him; her features were tilting oddly toward the edges. He felt cheated, relieved, and a little guilty. She took another swallow.

"What if you say no?"

"I tried that. He'll take my business away. He already showed me he could do it."

"I don't know — it sounds crazy to me. I think you should tell him to get lost. That's what you want to do, right?"

"You don't understand. He can ruin me, and he will."

She shook her head. "I don't believe it. Why should he bother with you?"

"He says I can help him."

"Do what?"

"Smuggle cocaine."

She put her glass on the floor and looked at him. "There's nothing he could do to you that'd be worse than that. People get killed every day."

"Lisa — you don't know him. I do."

"Ray listen to yourself! Do you know what you're saying? Look, I've got plenty of money — I'll bail you out." She sat up suddenly, knocking over the glass. "I won't let you do this to me."

"I'll do whatever I goddamn want!"

Next door, Norton groaned in his sleep.

She collapsed back into the couch. For the moment, she had nothing more to say.

Hula's anger gradually left him. He rubbed his bare feet together and looked out onto the porch. He could see a long way. The lights of the beach hotels shone over the water — a cool, illegible glow. He could identify them by color; pale blue for the Roc, aqua for the Bleu, green and orange for the Holiday. I shouldn't have told her anything, he thought.

"Ray, I know I forced my way in here — I'm sorry. But I meant what I said."

He got up and sat down on the couch beside her. She didn't shrink away but she didn't relax either. "You know," he said, "if I was going to sneak something through on a boat I'd pack it into the keel. I'd risk the Miami customs but I wouldn't unload it here — I'd cruise up the Intracoastal for a few days and take it off where you have a little privacy — at Fort Pierce, maybe."

"If you were going to." She sighed and let herself go, rolling her head back on his arm. "Tell me that you won't."

"All right. Let me show you something." He walked into the kitchen and returned, tossing a plastic bag on the low table in front of the couch. "Cruz left me this. I've been wanting to try it out. OK?"

"Why not?"

He sat down. "From what I've seen you're supposed to lay out a little bit and snuff it up your nose."

He pinched open his pocketknife and dipped the blade into the white powder. It showed up well in the dark. When he was finished he rolled up a dollar bill and leaned down to the table. "Your turn," he said. She inhaled sharply and coughed. They were done in a moment.

"I think we messed up," he said.

"Why?"

"We only made two piles — one for each of us. You have to take it all at once. So we only got it in one side of our noses."

She nodded. "It probably won't make any difference. How fast does it start working?"

"I don't know. It must be pretty amazing stuff, considering what people are willing to pay for it."

She shivered and pulled her robe tightly over her shoulders. Before she spoke again she hesitated, as if she were afraid of being interrupted. "Ray — do you believe that if you love someone then you owe them something?"

33

"I don't know. Like what?"

"Well — suppose none of this had happened. Suppose you had locked the door tonight. Suppose you disappeared."

"I'm not going anywhere."

"If you did. And I didn't know where you'd gone. Would I owe it to you to find out? Would that be my responsibility?"

"I hope you would, whether you owed it to me or not."

"But is that why I'd do it? Would that make it right?"

"I couldn't tell you. I think most of what people owe, they owe to themselves."

"But I'd only do it for you."

"True." He looked at the ceiling. "But you'd be the one that was doing it."

"We're talking about the same thing." She shook her head. "This isn't what I wanted to say. I'm worried about you, can't you see that? I don't want anything to happen to you."

"Neither do I." He laughed. "I promise you I'll do everything I can to keep myself in one piece for as long as possible. I owe you that much, right?"

"Don't make fun of me. I know you, Ray. This is a lousy time to turn away from me. Don't think I'm going to be grateful if you cut me off, because you don't want me to get involved, or some crap like that, just when you need me most."

"OK. I'll keep you informed. I'm glad you came over, Lisa — I feel a lot better."

"Do you?"

"Let's forget it. What's done is done. Let's think about something else."

"Don't leave me, Ray."

She laid her head in his lap and wrapped her arms around his thighs. He reached down and brushed her hair back from her forehead. She wore it long for her age. The heat from his legs was pleasant and she opened her robe. In a little while she began to relax. Ray had got his fingers under her head and was stroking the furrow that ran up the back of her neck. She was quiet, and she was smiling, but she was still unsatisfied — she wanted to say something more, but she didn't know where to start. Though she concentrated for a minute or two, she couldn't make up her mind. Meanwhile her hand had crept under him and was caressing him lazily. She knew what he liked without thinking. Before long Hula stood up and followed her into the bedroom. You might say they gave up too easily.

» » »

If there was another way to earn a million dollars very quickly, Michael Cruz didn't know what it was. According to the IRS, he worked for Aurora Northern, Inc., a business-consulting service with offices on Grand Avenue in Brooklyn, and he made about twenty-five thousand a year. Oddly enough, this was a fairly accurate assessment of his situation; he never stuck with anything long enough to make it pay as well as it might, and the people he worked for were happy to relieve him of responsibility whenever he got bored with what he was doing. He had managed loan banks and discotheques, trucked cigarettes from North Carolina, rented gambling tables in Manhattan, and once in a snowstorm, he had held up the tollbooth on the Tappan Zee Bridge, driving away with about two hundred pounds of quarters. He was well known for his luck and skill, but he didn't have the patience to operate on a large scale. He couldn't hold onto the money that came his way, and had learned from necessity how to get along on almost nothing. However, he never remained out of work any longer than he wanted to, since he could travel fast and he wasn't greedy. Hundreds of people knew his name and face; very few knew where he lived or how to get in touch with him.

On Monday morning, the day after his visit to Hula, he moved out of his room at the Du Pont Plaza and checked into the Omni Hotel. The last time he had stayed there someone else was paying his way. He had liked what he saw and decided he was worth the extra fifty dollars a night; it made him feel better. From the sixteenth floor he could see over Key Biscayne and twenty miles out to sea. The door to his room was heavy and well balanced; he spent a few minutes shutting it and listening to it click. He slept most of the afternoon. When he got up he took a small packet of cocaine out of his bag, examined it, and put it back. As soon as his suit came back from the cleaners he dressed and went out.

Cruz drove west on LeJeune to a barbecue pit on the edge of the city. It was popular with businessmen from south Dade. The parking lot was dusty and unpaved; the dining room was like a barn, with saddles hanging on the walls and low picnic tables in rows on the floor. At one end there was a long counter, where the heat from the pit was sensible. Young girls in tight dresses and leather vests carried the meat from the counter to the tables. The stink of roasting flesh and hot sauce made their eyes glisten — on a still night you could smell it three blocks away.

The parking lot was full of expensive cars. Cruz pulled into a spot with plenty of room on either side, turned off the engine, and waited. There were no valets by the door — unusual for a Miami restaurant. It was about eight o'clock.

Within a quarter of an hour he saw what he was looking for. A sky blue Lincoln pulled up in the space beside him and three men got out, laughing and joking. Cruz sat quietly and watched them. It was nearly dark and none of them saw the man in the adjacent car. When they disappeared into the building he got out and followed them. Inside, he ate a half chicken quickly, ripping paper napkins out of the box by the fistful. The three men were on their second pitcher of beer; all of them had removed their ties and jackets. They were obviously enjoying their meal. From time to time Cruz looked up from his plate and glanced in their direction.

As soon as he was done he paid his check and left. The parking lot was dark. When he got to his car he unlocked it, reached in, and turned the headlights on. There was no one else in the lot. He returned to the building. The hostess was on the phone and he waited for her to finish. She turned to him, smiling, and he whispered in her ear. She nodded and he left.

In a moment the three men looked up from their plates. The hostess was standing in the center of the room, banging on a tray with a serving spoon. It made a clean ringing sound. The buzz of voices quieted.

"Please excuse me, folks. There's a sky blue Lincoln with a vinyl roof out there with the lights on. Thank you."

The crowd resumed talking and eating. One of the three men got up and wiped his mouth. He put on his jacket. The other two jeered at him. On his way out he smiled at the hostess and gave her a dollar bill. She tucked it inside her dress.

Cruz was sitting inside his T-bird. He saw the man stride purposefully out the door about six steps and hesitate, as if he had to stop to remember where his car was. The man spotted the Lincoln and made for it. Cruz crouched down across the seat, his head next to the wheel. The man stopped again, about five yards from the Lincoln's rear plates. He walked around to the front and looked at the headlights, which were dark. Then he looked at the lights of Cruz's car, shining into the long grass behind the lot, and he noticed that the driver's door was unlocked. He went over and opened it.

Cruz grabbed the stranger's collar with both hands and yanked his head down. In an instant he was holding a gun to his ear.

"Move and you're dead. Put your hands in your pants, under your belt." With one hand Cruz touched the muzzle to the man's temple; with the other he rifled his clothes. The wallet was in the inner breast pocket. He pulled it out, squeezed it open, and glanced inside. He threw it on the seat and went back to work. In the right pants pocket he found a set of keys. He took them.

"You're going to fall. Don't get up." He placed his palm on the crown of the man's head and gave him a shove. The man landed on his back in the coral dust. A knot of people emerged from the restaurant. Cruz sat up, shut the door, started the car, and screeched across the lot and onto the highway. When he was a half mile away he checked the wallet — about three hundred dollars. Not much, considering he would have to get rid of the car now. He knew someone in Hialeah who would buy it. They might give him another in exchange. Even so, he decided it was worth it. His luck was running good.

» » »

The boat was due to cross over from the Bahamas on Saturday night. Hula got a phone call late Thursday.

"Hello."

"Ray. This is Michael."

"Michael."

"Listen, something's come up. I have to talk to you."

"Oh?"

"Not now. Meet me tomorrow morning at the seawall in Bayfront Park, just south of the marina. Make it about 9:00 A.M."

"What's the trouble?"

"No trouble. No change in plans. But it's important that I talk to you. I'll see you there."

He hung up. Hula put down the phone and returned to the living room. Norton, his neighbor, was sitting on the couch. Hula reached up and clicked off the TV.

"I don't mean to kick you out, but I have to go to bed. You can take another beer with you if you want."

Norton kept staring at the darkened tube, his hands clasped across his stomach. He was tall and loose-jointed, like a basketball player, and his bushy red mustache muffled the relationship between himself and the world. Hula was in no mood to argue.

"Did you hear me?"

Norton looked up. "Yeah, OK. Hey, before I go let me tell you something. It happened last night. I was — "

"What did I say? I said you could come in and sit around as long as you wanted, provided you didn't tell me any ghost stories. I'm tired of your ghost stories — so is everybody else."

"Are you calling me a liar?"

"No. I'm just throwing you out."

The tall man stood up and moved towards the door. "Fine. Fine. But I thought you might be interested — since you were there. That's right. I was wide awake, and I heard a bubbling noise — I looked down, and there you were, lying on the bottom of the sea, drowned, with fish swimming all around you. You didn't see me. Then I heard the noise again and this big wobbly bubble came out of your mouth and started up towards me. I looked away — I couldn't take it."

"And then what?"

"Don't mock me! I know what I'm talking about!" Norton seized the doorknob and glared at Hula. "All right, I'm leaving." He turned and walked out. Hula heard him banging on the ice-cream man's door. He had another beer and went to bed. He didn't dream about anything.

In the morning the air was clean and bright and the wind was out of the northwest. Soon after he got up Hula hung his clothes over the balcony. Dry shirts were a luxury in June. At eight-thirty he got into his car and started down the boulevard. He drove badly, jumping out at the lights and burning up the brakes in between. Around him the commuters were testing each other's reflexes, quickly annoyed and quick to punish.

He parked in the center island on the boulevard, crossed into the park, and headed for the water. A few winos sat in the shade on the library steps and yawned. Hula looked carefully at everyone he saw, not wanting to miss his brother. He walked past Ponce's statue and out under the ficus trees. The bay gleamed in front of him. He was less curious than he might have been about what Cruz had to say — in the last few days, as the time for action drew near, Hula had become oddly indifferent toward the shape of his future. Though he realized that there was plenty to worry about, he just couldn't keep at it all day long.

Cruz was not behind the library, or anywhere in sight. Hula started north along the water's edge toward the marina. There was no beach — just a pile of coral rubble and the seawall. The bay was dirty here, so close to the river, and the rocks were stained dark below the tide. The sun barely penetrated the surface; it seemed to Hula that most of it was bouncing up in his face.

As he approached the margin of the marina parking lot Cruz stepped out into his path.

"Let's go this way." They headed back the way Ray had come. Cruz was wearing a light suit — for once — dark glasses, and conservative leather boots. He looked like a Cuban businessman. They hadn't gone more than a few yards when he sat down on the seawall, facing the park. "Have a seat. I'm tired of standing. We get a good view from here, too."

Hula joined him. "What is it you wanted?"

"Like I said before, something has come up."

"Well?"

"Two things. Number one, I'm very glad that we'll be moving the stuff the day after tomorrow. It's important that we get this over with as soon as possible. Two, a little advice. Between now and then you're going to have to be very careful. Stick to your daily routine — don't do anything unusual. It could make a lot of difference. And one more thing. Since this job is going to be a lot more dangerous than I thought it would, I want to give you the opportunity to take a walk. If I knew what was coming I never would have forced you into it."

"What are you talking about? How could it be any worse than it is already?"

"Believe me. Even if you drop out now, it won't be as if nothing happened. You'll have to sign over your property to a friend and leave for good. You better go far away. If you don't, I guarantee that someone will be shooting at you pretty soon. This is for real. It's just possible that I'll draw an ace and we won't have to worry about it anymore, but don't count on it."

"What is this crap?" Hula discovered he was shouting; he lowered his voice. "First you go to the moon and back to get me into this thing, and now you're suggesting that I drop it. Since when do you care? What about your money?"

"I'm not suggesting anything. I'm giving you a choice. If you want to leave, OK, I'll try it by myself. If you don't want to go, that's all right too. All I'm saying is that things have changed. If you stay, you'll be risking your skin every minute — not that it was all roses before, but it's a lot different. You're 90 percent dead already. That's all I'm saying."

"How did they find out?"

"Who?"

"Your friends — whoever it is that's coming after you."

"I'm not going to tell you any more because it wouldn't make any sense to you. All I want is a yes or no. You have to decide — I don't have time to mess around."

Hula leaned back and stretched out his legs on the walk. He shaded his eyes with one hand. "How about this. Suppose you tell me everything you know about this new threat, or whatever it is. In return I'll allow you to make the choice you just offered me — about whether I stay in or not. Is that fair?"

Cruz turned to look at Hula. "Listen, brother, don't talk to me. I know what I'm doing — you don't. I swear I'm not trying to hurt you. Sometime in your life you're going to have to trust someone — why not do it now? Make up your mind."

"I could always count on you, Michael. That was never a problem."

"Have you decided yet?"

"Nothing's changed. I've come this far."

"Good. Then it's Saturday. Remember what I said." Cruz got up and started across the park, scattering the pigeons before him. Hula called after him.

"Michael!"

Cruz stopped and came back, visibly irritated. "I thought we were through."

"I nearly forgot. What do you want me to do with all that stuff you left in my office? Do you want it back? It's sitting in my desk and I'm worried about it."

"I don't care. It's only sugar."

He turned and went off in the same direction. Hula watched him until he disappeared, then counted the days till Saturday. He might have felt a lot better, and the waiting might have been much easier, if there were any way he could prepare himself. As it was, Cruz had told him very little and there was nothing for him to do. He had hoped that Michael's summons this morning would introduce him to an active role, and now that the meeting was over, Hula suspected that it was partly his own disappointment that made him refuse to drop out. Would it have made sense? Cruz said he would have had to go away immediately.

Maybe Cruz was scared — maybe he thought his partner wasn't going to bear up and wanted to cut him loose. Hula decided against this idea — if Cruz wanted a professional he could have gotten one. Then Michael's warning was real? Was he really concerned about Hula's safety? He had to be, because he needed him — perhaps Cruz was telling him that if he dropped out he would have to leave because Cruz would withdraw his protection. Or maybe it was just as dangerous to stay, or more so, but Cruz was implying that half a million dollars was worth the extra risk. What extra risk? What the hell was going on?

Hula picked up a handful of pebbles and began tossing them into the greasy water. A rotten grapefruit floated by; without intending to, he became absorbed in trying to hit it. As each throw missed, some by a wide margin, he threw harder, feeling the muscles in his arm stretch and wobble. When the pebbles were gone he brushed his hands on his pants and looked around. An old man with a stick and a bucket wandered by, looking for choice bits of trash. In the parking lot by the marina two kids were playing Frisbee. Every time a bad throw bounced off a car they stopped and looked around guiltily. Down the walk an elderly couple were arguing noisily about something. Hula quietly hated them all. They would never be punished for their innocence. He had been given the chance to go back and he had refused it. He was glad that he had no children.

He got up and started across the park; in a few minutes he was gone. A man approached along the seawall and sat down where Hula had been. He was a large man, solidly built, wearing a flowered shirt, khaki trousers, and sneakers. He looked off in the direction Hula had gone and glanced at his watch. There was something unusual about him; he was absolutely bald.

» » »

At 8:00 A.M. on Saturday Cruz was sitting alone in his hotel room, looking out over the ocean. When the phone rang he leaped for it.

"Michael — this is Wally."

"Right."

"Can I go?"

"It looks good. Maybe a little rain tomorrow morning."

"Well all right. When do I get paid?"

"As soon as I do. Does your radio work?"

"It does now. I've been talking to some boats out of Freeport. One of them wants to race me back."

"Don't do it. Then we're all set — if there's any trouble call me first. You'll have plenty of time. I'll be listening."

"No problem."

"We'll see. I'll be in touch tomorrow." Cruz hung up the phone and gazed out the window. To the east, beyond the beach, the sea was blue and empty. A low haze clung to the horizon. He wished that he could be with the boat where he could see what was happening.

Many miles away, Wally Liberty tipped his cap to the girl at the desk as he walked out of the hotel where he had made his call. The hotel was still going up and Liberty had to pick his way through the workmen and piles of brick on his way to the dock.

He was young, handsome, and energetic. The sun had bleached his blond hair and eyebrows, and his tanned face and arms stood out against his light clothes. If he seemed to be right at home here, it was partly because he was the kind of person who can shine in any setting. The men in the trenches, their skins streaked and dusty, stopped to look up at him as he went by.

He hopped into the dinghy, set the oars, and shoved off. He stopped to look at the anchor when he reached the boat. The water was clear and the chain showed dark against the white sand twelve feet below him. Off to the west the lagoon was milky green and a row of feathery pines ran out along the neck — beyond that, the booming reef, and the deep water.

When he got aboard he dragged out an old foresail and draped it over the boom, making it fast to the stays on either side. It shaded most of the cockpit. The crossing to Florida would take eight or ten hours; if he was to be there at 10:00 P.M. he didn't have to get underway until later in the morning. At this time of year the breeze would be steady all night. He spread a towel over his air mattress, stretched out, and fell asleep.

» » »

On Saturday morning Lisa Bishop got up at nine o'clock, two hours later than usual. She put on her bathing suit and took her coffee out to the terrace by the pool. No one was swimming. She dropped into a plastic chair and put on her sunglasses. The warmth felt pleasant on her skin and made her drowsy. Somewhere behind her she could hear the maintenance man pushing his broom.

She hadn't seen Ray for three days. They had stopped talking about his predicament, as he had insisted, and it had left a vacuum in their relationship. As much as she liked him, she was a little angry; she felt that he didn't want to see her. There was little for her to do. But she was not so helpless as he supposed.

"Excuse me."

She blinked. Someone was standing over her.

"Excuse me."

She cocked her head forward and shaded her eyes. "Yes?"

The sun darted out from behind his shoulder, blinding her. "Do you know a man named Ray Hula? Does he live here?"

She could make out his basic shape — he was big. She sat up. "Say that again?"

"Ray Hula. Does he live here?"

"Not that I know of."

"These are the Blossom Apartments, aren't they?"

"Yes."

"His name is on one of the mailboxes over there. He lives in number twenty-three."

"Oh."

"He's not there. Do you know where he is?"

"I don't know everyone who lives here. I'm visiting some friends."

"Your name is on one of the boxes too."

"You must be mistaken. Excuse me." She dropped her head back and shut her eyes.

43

"Why lie to me? What's the point?" He didn't wait for an answer. "Is this man Hula in some kind of trouble?"

Lisa began to feel that the silence was working against her. She sat up and nearly shouted at the man. "I told you, I don't know him. What's more, I don't know you. To tell you the truth, I don't enjoy your company. You don't belong here — get out."

"Could I take you to dinner some night, maybe? You're a lovely woman, Mrs. Bishop."

Her hand tightened on the chair. If he didn't leave, she decided, she would get up and run.

The man stepped to one side, letting the sun drop full in her eyes. "When you see Hula, tell him that I'm looking for him. He'll know who I am." He turned and walked off towards the parking lot. She got her first look at him; he was tall, heavy, and bald. She reached for her coffee, shuddered, and gulped it down. It was cold.

In a few minutes she got up and knocked on Hula's door — no answer. His car wasn't in the usual spot. She put on a skirt and a T-shirt and left.

When she got to the yard she asked the first man she saw where she could find Hula. He pointed to some dirty windows over a shed. She hurried inside and stopped, momentarily frustrated by the dimness. Great piles of wood and rotted iron towered over her, blocking her path, and the air was unbearably close and still. She looked behind her, saw the stairs, and headed up. The heat was even worse at the top. She knocked on the door and pushed it open. Hula was sitting at his desk. He flinched when the door banged against the wall. The breeze from the air conditioner was ruffling the hair over his ears.

"What do *you* want?"

"I'm so glad you're here. I was just back at the apartments — it was horrible. There was a man there who was looking for you. He knows something. He knew who I was. He asked me where you were — I didn't tell him. But it won't be long before he finds you — and then what? What are you going to do? Have you got any idea?"

Hula stared at her hungrily, as if he had been waiting all day for her. "Don't you think I have enough things to worry about? What's wrong with you? I've got just about all I can handle without you tearing in here telling me I'm in trouble. Don't you think I know?"

"But — "

44

"Shut up!" Someone knocked on the door. Hula shook his head and snorted.

"Come in."

A tiny dust-blackened man poked his head in. Lisa jumped; he looked like he had crawled out of an ashpit.

"Say boss, do you want to take out that screw? It's in pretty good shape."

"Forget it — it's not worth it. Tomorrow's Sunday. I want you, Silva, Geronimo, and Murphy on call. Tell everybody they can knock off after lunch. It's too hot."

"Right." The tiny man flashed a smile, looked at Lisa, and disappeared. It was quiet again. Hula held up his hand. "Let's start over. Who did you see? Don't rush it."

She pulled up a deck chair and told him her story. "I was scared," she said.

"It doesn't matter. I don't think he was trying to learn anything from you. I don't recognize him from your description — I probably don't know him."

Hula sighed and leaned back. There were dark stains under his shoulders. "I hope — and this is no more than a hope — that he was one of Cruz's flunkies — though I thought he had already called them in. I don't know."

"Who else could he be?"

"Could be a cop. Could be worse."

"He wasn't a cop. He told me to tell you he was looking for you — as if you would know who he was."

"And that's just what you did, didn't you?" He looked away. "Don't worry about it. I don't blame you for anything. Thanks for trying to help out."

Lisa sat up. The chair was too small — she was all arms and legs. "What are you going to do?"

"Nothing. As soon as I see Cruz I'll tell him. It's almost time now — I can't afford to think about it."

"Shouldn't it make a difference to you if this man knows something? Hadn't you better find out?"

"What can I do? I don't know how to reach Cruz. He doesn't tell me anything."

She nodded. "Wait a minute. If someone wanted the drugs why

would they go after you now? You haven't got them yet. I'd think they'd stay out of sight until then."

"There's no sense in talking about it. My role in this thing is entirely unclear. For all I know Cruz could be just playing tunes in his head. There might not be any coke."

"What are you talking about?"

"Nothing in particular. What do you think?"

"What?"

"The guy you met — was he a killer or a mailman? Am I going to make it through the weekend?"

"There must be something you can do to protect yourself."

"There is. I cleared some space out of my bottom drawer here — now there's room for two guns. Before there was only room for one. The other day Cruz told me it was going to be twice as dangerous in this office so I figured I ought to be twice as prepared. Of course I haven't got any guns. It's a good thing, too, since if I shot everyone who came in here today I would've run out of bullets long ago." He pulled a rubber band from a bundle of letters and snapped it across the room. She watched it hit the wall.

"I'm sorry Ray — I don't understand any of this."

"That's a good start. Keep it up, and you may have a future. Look at me — I refused outright and here I am running the whole operation."

"Ray —"

"I know, I know, don't tell me. You think I'm taking the wrong attitude about this. You're absolutely right. If I had any sense I'd be out there threatening strangers and being as mysterious as the rest of them."

"Are you finished?"

"Sure I'm finished."

She got up and bolted the door, testing the handle once or twice. Hula smiled. "So you're the assassin."

"For my sake. I feel better."

"If we wanted to we could go downstairs and weld ourselves into a couple of diving suits. They'd never recognize us."

She dropped into her chair and sighed. A fly crawled into a candy wrapper on the desk.

"You know what my men are thinking, Lisa? They're thinking, why does the boss bring his piece up to that office where there's not even a couch, or a rug on the floor? A man his age? They won't bother us now. If someone comes to the door it's going to be somebody else."

"Stop it! What's wrong with you?" She shook her head. "Do you want to get hurt? Just stop it!" She ransacked her bag, her eyes dropping tears. By the time she got the tissue out she was all through. Hula had swiveled his chair around to face the window behind him. He creaked gently back and forth.

"You never met my husband, did you?"

"No." He turned back to look at her again. "What does that have to do with anything?"

She looked away. "I don't know. I just thought of him."

"What, do I remind you of him?"

"No." She didn't sound too sure of herself.

Hula took a deep breath and blew it out. He wasn't going to pretend that he had anything to say.

"I lost him, you know. I wish I knew whether or not I've lost you."

Hula suddenly became interested in her dead husband. "How long ago was it?"

"Eight years."

"I was married once myself." He had a brass paperweight shaped like a sailboat on his desk. He pushed it along the top and showed it going over the edge. "On the rocks." They had been over this ground before.

"You know why I don't talk about him?"

This was new. He sat still and shook his head slightly.

"Because I wanted him to die."

The remark hung in the air. Hula decided to handle it head on. "Why?"

She leaned her face to one side and ran her fingers along her hairline. "I wasn't strong enough, I guess. He had stomach cancer — they were keeping him alive with drugs and electricity."

It took him some time to absorb this. "It's not good, the way they make people hang on forever."

"That's not why I wanted it."

She said it without feeling or emphasis. Hula felt as if he was being pushed along. "If you've got something to say, go ahead. I won't stop you."

Lisa collected herself and looked at Hula carefully. "We had a big

47

house out in Miami Shores. I used to drink a lot then — I used to start with scotch and hot water in a coffee mug at breakfast and by 10:00 A.M. it was just scotch." She glanced around the room. "Anyway, he wasn't much like you. He was a real driver — on the phone day and night, shouting and scheming — his company built the main terminal at MIA. When we were first married, he used to come home. sometimes and take me on a little inspection tour of the house, to see how well I'd done the cleaning. He'd sniff the shower curtain and make a face. He liked to eat peanuts and he'd leave the shells around in odd places — he tried to tell me it was a joke. Sometimes I think it was just me, sometimes I think he really was a monster."

Hula waited for her to continue. He had no trouble imagining the situation.

"I was about to sue him for divorce when he got sick and they put him in the hospital. They didn't think it was serious and I hoped maybe it would slow him down — neither of us had had any peace for a long while. But when I found out what was really going on I began to sink. Friends and relatives started crowding around, making sympathetic noises. I got frightened of sleeping alone in that huge place. His partners began sending me letters about 'hard decisions' and 'the best interests of everyone.' I hadn't loved him for years and I was terrified that I was going to lose him. I almost wished that it was myself and not him. It took me a while to figure out that I didn't want him to die only because I had wanted it so many times before.

"Every day I went to the hospital and there he was, stretched out, roped together with tubes and meters, and looking at me as if he never expected to see me again and didn't particularly care. There was no flesh on him. I could see right through. He was already dead — and however much I wanted him to live, I just wished he would go one way or the other, because I couldn't stand to look at him."

She paused thoughtfully and wetted her lips. "Of course he didn't live. I'm not trying to make excuses for myself — but I want you to know that I've been through this kind of uncertainty before and it's not any easier the second time. I feel as if you think I'm being too pushy, and that you wish I'd get out of the way and leave you alone. Maybe I will. But there's nothing worse than having to wait around like this. I just want you to understand my attitude. It's not easy for me."

48

They were silent for a while. Hula looked around himself — the dusty cardboard cartons, the curling photographs of old wrecks taped to the wall, the heaps of dead flies on the windowsill — and across from him a dark-haired woman of some years in a T-shirt, watching him, with the fluorescent light shining on her forehead. He couldn't keep his eyes on her.

He took a deep breath and blew it out. "Eight years ago, huh."

"I'm not looking for sympathy. Actually, it was the perfect solution — I never should have married him in the first place."

"You complain about uncertainty. Well, all the uncertainty should be over with by tomorrow night."

"Why is that?"

"I'll tell you how this is supposed to work." As he saw it, he had to either tell her or deal with more difficult questions. "I don't think it will, but then Cruz doesn't seem to value my advice. Tonight, shortly before midnight, there's going to be a wreck on Otter Reef, north of Elliott Key. A forty-foot sloop. The man on board will radio for help and someone will arrive to take him off — whoever's in the area. Tonight, or maybe tomorrow morning, the Port will call me up and give me the job of bringing in the remains. There'll be a lot of cocaine aboard that boat, and it'll be up to me to get it all in here to the yard intact. Then Cruz takes it away and my troubles are over."

"A shipwreck," she said. She was quiet for a moment. "That seems like an awful risk.

"No — the point is that Cruz is trading on my reputation as a friend of the feds. It's a lot more risky to take a ton of coke past the entry officials than it is to put a boat on Otter Reef. I'll be standing right there when they find it. I wonder what I'll tell them."

"Will they search the boat?"

"It depends — every vessel that comes in from abroad has to report to the customs agency. Nowadays they look at practically everything. Of course, my barge is a little clumsy for that type of maneuver and Cruz is hoping that they'll wave me in. He's also hoping that when they find out I've been hired by the owner to put the boat back together at the yard, they won't bother to send a man to check it out, because they'll figure that I'll be likely to turn up anything that might be in it. I've done it before. They know how I am about that kind of thing. They'll figure I can do the job just as well as they can."

"Is that how it usually works?"

"Cruz is right — they trust me to keep an eye out for them. It's in my interests to do so. But the fact is, it doesn't matter whether they trust me or not."

"No?"

"These inspectors are no different than anybody else. They get a little bored over at the Port. When something like this comes up, it gives them a chance to get away from the docks and go for a ride. Also, if you're at all interested in boats you might want to see what one looks like after going up on a reef. It's simple curiosity. They're getting paid for it — why not? I guarantee they'll send somebody over here. Maybe two or three. They have a full shift on Sunday."

"Did you tell your brother all this?"

"Sure. He told me don't worry about it. He said they'd have to look hard to find the stuff and he was sure I could distract them, if they came. Sure. You have to look real hard to find a ton of white powder." He unbuttoned his shirt down to his waist and slouched backward, his belly a pale mound in his lap.

"Isn't there anything you can do? I'd think —"

"I'm not totally helpless. If I wanted to, I could tie the boat alongside the barge and keep it half full of water. That would make it hard to search. Also, I could splash a little grease around on the decks, so the customs men might think twice before going aboard. They hate to get dirty."

"Would that work?"

"It might. Trouble is, these guys aren't stupid, and if they decide that I'm trying to make things difficult for them, they'll impound the boat and take it apart themselves. They wouldn't hesitate. They're determined little turds."

"Oh."

"And besides, I'm going to have to yank the boat eventually. Cruz wants his stuff. And that's another problem."

She watched him for a moment. "Go on."

"I can't do all this work by myself. I'm going to need a full crew. I'm going to have four or five men crawling over this wreck at one time or another and they're going to do it with their eyes open. If they see anything I guarantee they're going to get curious."

"Where's the coke hidden?"

"It's fastened under the deck at the edge of the hull. You probably can't see it from anywhere but the bilge, but I'll bet you can sure as hell see it from there. Maybe I'll tell them it's some new kind of flotation material. That should be good for a laugh."

"I guess you'll just have to keep them out of the bilge."

"That might work. Provided the hull isn't so banged up that the coke is running down the side of the boat. But it's white, isn't it? Maybe white powder won't show up against white paint."

Lisa had run out of questions. Hula was shaving the hair off his knuckles with a penknife. He was breathing slowly. "Tomorrow night Michael is going to come in with a truck and take it all away. It's as easy as that."

"It might work, you know. There must be a lot of successful smugglers somewhere."

Surprised, he glanced up at her. "You're right. Have you ever heard of the *Cimmerian?*"

"No."

"It's probably the largest private yacht on the east coast. Like something Onassis might have built. Panamanian registry. What's special about it, though, is not the size. It's equipped with three or four million dollars worth of the most advanced computer tracking systems anywhere. It's a floating antenna. If it had an armament to match, it could take on the Panamanian Navy."

"Who owns it?"

"I don't know. But it probably has something to do with smuggling, because it spends most of its time standing well offshore and listening. I heard it's been searched, at sea, more than once. Probably just harassment. If it ever was carrying any contraband they'd have time to dump it before the patrol boats got within thirty miles."

"But what good is it, if it only draws attention to itself?"

"Exactly. It's completely useless for moving anything. Some people say it monitors all the federal boats and broadcasts their location to the small craft that actually do the smuggling — a kind of early warning system. But I doubt it. That would be too risky. I think it's just a gigantic toy — some guy who dominates the trade decided to build this thing and have a little fun with the DEA. It probably drives them up a wall."

Hula leaned down and pulled open a small refrigerator beside his desk, taking out a bottle of beer and a sandwich wrapped in waxed paper. He waved them at her. "Hungry? There's more."

"Well — I don't think so." She stood up and looked around the room, as if searching for a way out. "You know — there's no reason for any of this. You don't owe him anything. All you have to do is make up your mind — call him up and say that you've had enough — you don't have to go to the cops."

He stared at her. "I can't call him up. I don't know his number."

"For God's sake, Ray, listen to me! It won't work! You said so yourself! Then do something about it!"

Hula pointed to the door.

"Ray — you know that farm I have, out in west Dade? Let's go out there for the weekend. If your brother gets caught, you've got nothing to worry about. If he doesn't, then he won't bother with you. Can't you see?"

He rose from his seat, shivering with anger. She flinched, forcing back the tears — he was shouting at her. She saw him start toward her.

"It's not that easy, Ray. I'm not afraid of you."

She didn't have time for more than that. The chair fell over as he kicked it aside. She reached up for his face but he batted her hands away. Seizing her narrow body by the shoulders, he reached back, opened the door, and hurled her onto the upper landing. The wooden rail shook and nearly gave way as she crashed into it; nothing else kept her from going over the edge. The bolt clicked in the door behind her.

After a few minutes Lisa got up and walked carefully down the stairs. A deep bruise was forming on her wrist. When she got to her car she looked back at the small window high up on the wall of the shed. The sun was too bright — there was nothing to see.

» » »

Krome Avenue — like any other south Florida country road conceived on paper and built to specifications — mathematically proportioned, true as a beam of light, consistent from beginning to end. Dade County is entirely two-dimensional, flatter than Kansas, and lends itself perfectly to the pet geometries of the civil engineers. Theoretically, it would be possible to set the steering wheel on a compass point and leave it there for thirty miles.

The road is a foot or two higher than the land. Just two lanes, no shoulders, and a 45-mph limit combine to demand some attention from the driver. It runs north to south, crossing the canals, and passes near a buried-missile site and an abandoned blimp base. There is not much to see. Farms border the road on either side, each looking exactly like the other. In dry weather the jet sprinklers crawl over the fields like great mechanical grasshoppers, shooting their snowy arcs high in the air and scattering tiny rainbows. Between the farms there are open woods of slash pine and palmetto, and cooters sun themselves in the ditches.

But the road divides as well as connects; it discriminates between worlds. To the east are the trailer camps, the U-Pik-Em pole beans, the mango plantations, the bulldozers, the suburbs, and the city. To the west a few dirt roads stretch out to a few more farms, where the migrant workers' buses bake in the dust, and then the tracks sink into the earth, and there is nothing. Anyone discouraged by the flatness and monotony on the eastern side of Krome had better not cross over to the west — for here is the edge of the Glades, a near-wilderness of oceanic proportions, and conventional ideas of time and distance do not apply.

It is a land without scale. There are vast thickets where the lush grass is eight feet high, and grows so densely that it blocks out the world two steps away. There are forests where the tallest of the ancient, knotted trees barely reaches shoulder height. There are large animals here, but they are never seen. The horizon is low, regular, and unbroken; the sky overhead is huge and empty. In every direction the plain dwindles to infinity without relief. A single tree, a clump of bushes — anything that displays the slightest trace of individuality — assumes here the status of a landmark, like a mountain or a river, but there are too many trees, and too many clumps of bushes. Travel is slow and pointless. The grass clutches and hacks at the ankles, and the limestone floor is pitted and treacherous. In the wet season the water rises a few inches above the ground, not high enough to float anything, and brings forth masses of mosquitoes. Here you'll find no precipices, cataracts, or rock canyons; this is nature without scenery, committed to its own ends, following the old cycles beyond limit.

Under pressure from white expansion, the Miccossuokee Indians fled to the Glades before the Civil War, and have been there ever since. There was no way to dislodge them. After a few costly attempts the army threw up its hands and said that the land was worthless anyway. Now they are clustered along the two routes that cross the

53

Glades, the Tamiami Trail and Alligator Alley, at Pinecrest and Frog City; hunting, fishing, and selling a version of their past to the road-weary tourists.

The Glades are drier toward the eastern edge, and a few good tracks lead in from Krome Avenue. When her husband died, Lisa Bishop inherited an old farm that lay along one of these trails, built before it became clear that the soil, even when drained, was too poor to grow anything. Mr. Bishop had put a pump over the well, brought in electricity and a phone line, and built a new floor about a foot higher than the old one, which was nearly rotted away. He used the house as a hunting camp, bringing his friends out to drink and play cards on weekends. It was a low, rambling place, built on the edge of a hammock and shielded from the afternoon sun, with a brick hearth and some bleached, papery rattlesnake skins that still nailed to the wall of the ell.

When he died Lisa decided to sell it as soon as possible. She wanted too much, and there were no takers. Since she showed it occasionally, she had to keep it reasonably clean, and she spent some time fixing it up in March and October. She discovered that she enjoyed the work — the planning, the tools, and the solitude — and she removed the house from her listings. She now referred to it, ironically, as her vacation home, and whenever she grew tired of the city she would head out with some wine and a portable TV. The memory of her husband was strong there, and she liked to sit back in the stout wooden armchairs and dream about the past — it was a kind of pilgrimage. Alone, feeling the empty miles around her, she imagined that her life was a separate, distinct, and personal enterprise, connected to the lives of others by a slender thread, which she herself had measured. She ate bananas and figs, and was sometimes overcome by a mysterious tide of affection for the people she knew, which she could not explain.

She had taken Ray along two or three times. He said he couldn't sleep there, for all the noise — when he was trying to go to bed, the whole swamp was just getting started for the night. Lisa conceded that the Glades were an acquired taste and didn't invite him anymore.

She drove rapidly south on Krome Avenue. The radio was turned up high to a rock 'n' roll station. The sun was long gone, and the headlights of the oncoming cars exploded in her face. The local men liked to install special high-intensity bulbs in their trucks, and she despised them for it. For the moment, she was finished crying and her anger had subsided; she was concentrating on getting where she was going. She wanted nothing more to do with Ray Hula.

In the backseat she had her traveling bag and a carton of groceries. The windows were open a little and the moist breeze flattened her hair against her temples. She felt free and capable; proof against any further shocks. She slowed down for the turnoff, then rumbled away into the Glades. Out here the night was deep and quiet. The city glowed on the horizon. From Krome Avenue you could have watched her red taillights bob and blink for miles before they disappeared.

» » »

The U.S. Coast Guard, Liberty decided, had taken the fun out of making harbor. From where he was, a few miles east of Elliott Key, he could see no less than four lighted buoys, of varying colors. There was no need to learn the shoreline, or even hold a compass bearing. It might just as well be broad daylight.

Although he was not sentimental about boats, Liberty was a little sorry he was going to have to wreck this one. Much of the wood on it was hand-tooled mahogany — he had never seen anything like it. The most he could say was that it had probably been built on the west coast, maybe as far south as Chile, and that whoever had put it together had known what he was doing. The seams were still tight after years of neglect. He had counted six layers of paint on the bottom, pimpled here and there by a stray barnacle. It was a heavy, solid, and graceful piece of work, and it inspired confidence.

Liberty had not been ashore in the United States for over five years — one of the reasons for his success. Soon after he began hiring himself out to smugglers he had insisted that a boat be provided for him well out in the water, or that he be allowed to keep the one that made the move, so that he could return to the Bahamas without entering the U.S. customs zone. This meant that some kind of transfer had to be made offshore. Not everyone was willing to meet these conditions, but those who were had no complaints about his performance. When he was involved things tended to work out properly. Between jobs he skippered for a few rich yachtsmen out of Nassau, and he had a house on North Bimini where he spent the slack time.

Money occupied a small but influential orbit in Liberty's private universe, and he was well aware of the value of the load he was carrying. He guessed that boat and contents were worth about three million dollars. Cruz had initially hired him for the safe work in Colombia and the voyage to the Bahamas, and it wasn't until they were nearly done that Cruz suggested he stay on for the actual move. Liberty was doubtful.

"Do you know how I like to work?"

"I heard — you don't come ashore and you get a ride back. That doesn't fit in with my plans."

"Too bad."

"I can't pay you in advance. What do you usually get?"

"Ten thousand."

"I'll give you two hundred. Two hundred. And you don't have to take the boat through customs. All you have to do is come and get your money."

"How do I bring a boat in without taking it through?"

"You're not going to bring it in. You're going to wreck it."

"I am?"

"That's why I can't let you take it home. Someone will pick you off and bring you into Miami. You're a British yachtsman and you got confused. Don't worry, I'll have papers for you."

"What about the cargo?"

"You're going to wreck it, but you're not going to drown it. I'll handle it from there."

"You should have told me about this earlier. You're going to have to find another man."

"I was hoping you'd agree."

"Not a chance."

Cruz shrugged. "Have it your way."

Nevertheless, here he was, crossing the stream in a loaded boat, headed for one of the most heavily policed ports in the world. Liberty gave Cruz little credit for persuasion. He also doubted that the enormous fee had been a factor, since he never expected to see it. Possibly the sheer size of the move and the attendant risk appealed to him, he thought — he wasn't in this business because he craved security. Maybe he just liked the idea of coming home again after a long exile. But ultimately, try as he might, he couldn't discover to himself the sources of his apostasy.

Liberty tied the helm and went below. He put on a sweater and

56

unfolded a chart of the approaches to Miami. The main channel was wide and well marked; it passed between Key Biscayne and Miami Beach. Elliott Key was about ten miles to the south. There was a wide gap between Elliott and Key Biscayne, but it wasn't dredged anywhere and most of it was shoal water. The federal government owned Elliott and used it as a park, accessible only by boat. It was long and narrow — nothing more than a breakwater, really — and there was a small harbor on the bay side. Liberty guessed that his rescuers might arrive from there.

Otter Reef was a pile of rocks just off the north end of Elliott, marked by a red gas buoy, visible at night from four or five miles under good conditions. The marker was not intended to warn boats off the rocks themselves, which were nearly inaccessible, but rather to keep them out of the general area, which was unsafe for some distance to the north. If Liberty succeeded in putting the boat on the rocks he would probably be the first man in history to do so, since there was barely enough water around them to keep the mud wet. He had decided to wedge himself in the bottom about a mile north of the reef, in about five feet of water, where a small boat could reach him fairly easily, since the water dropped off from there in the direction of the bay. The tide, such as it was, would be full, and there was little likelihood he would be dragged away. His chief concern was with the breakers; the breeze he was riding in would be piling up three-foot waves on the bars, and it was essential that he get beyond them somehow. If he got caught in the surf they would take the boat apart.

Liberty returned topside and flipped the chart overboard. He unlimbered the wheel and sat down behind it, settling his back on the cushion.

The breeze had faded and swung around to the west, off the land; the surf on the bars would be a little flatter. An hour ago the other traffic had veered away to the north, headed for Virginia Key and the ship channel, and he had the coast to himself.

The boat glided easily across the wind. It was too early for the moon and the sea was dark under the stars. The Milky Way arched over his head like a web of jewels, cut in half by the pale wing of the sail. In the bow wave millions of diatoms glowed briefly and went out. Sailing at night often gave Liberty a weightless feeling, as if all his organs had left their moorings and were drifting into random constellations, while his soul expanded into a thin cloud, intensely silent and aware. Fish nibbled at the edges of his consciousness, their dim brains drugged with sleep, and the salt air wetted his skin. Ahead, the coast was low and distant, pricked with lights and stretching away as far as he could see in either direction. Dead ahead there were no lights at all; this was Elliott Key, uninhabited, blocking out the shore behind it. He fell away a few points to the north, steering for a cluster of tall buildings on the mainland.

He could feel the waves shortening under the boat as he left the deep water; the rigging creaked, adjusting to the new rhythm. Liberty imagined that the craft sensed the danger, and its own helplessness. The sounding line lay coiled on the deck beside him. He threw it over, counting the tapes as they slithered over the gunwhale. At six fathoms he stopped it; there was still plenty of water. He knew that the bottom shelved gradually, and that there shouldn't be any surprises. When he finished bringing in the line, he reached inside his sweater for a cigarette and huddled away from the wind, protecting the match. He seldom smoked, and as he lit this one he wondered if it was the right time for it now, before the job was finished — perhaps his luck required that he make no concessions to his own nervousness. And he was nervous. Five years since he had last stepped ashore on the continent. Five years of remarkable success, all based on the idea of avoiding that place where he was headed now. Things must have changed since he'd left. He was curious, and he wondered how it would feel to enter his home as a stranger.

He was glad that there were no other craft in the area. He had his running lights burning, for appearances, and anyone could see that he was going up on the bars. The north end of Elliott was now clearly visible, silhouetted against the mainland; he saw the last fingers of mangrove pushing out into the water, and a weak surf bubbling over a bank just this side. Otter Reef should be less than a mile away. He was nearly past before he saw it. It was tiny, a few clumps of pioneer weed, showing black against the dark water behind it. Liberty looked at his watch. He would sail north for five minutes, then cut toward the shore, close to the wind. He should catch the shoal within ten. It struck him how painfully easy the job had been thus far — no time problems, no weather problems, no meetings or transfers. He turned and glanced at the water trailing under the stern. He could see the surface dimly. It was seamed and flattened, retaining only the larger contours of the swells passing underneath. He looked more closely. Beyond the outer skin there was nothing, no hint of depth or clarity, no suspended lights, no signals at all returning — not an inch down, not five miles down — it was the sea at night. He sat up quickly.

The hull scraped bottom once or twice, like a plane making a clumsy landing. Each time the bow pitched forward and the sails snapped flat. It occurred to Liberty that turning back was no longer an alternative. The keel caught for the final time, ploughing deep into the substrate, sending a mild shudder through the deck. The wheel twisted out of his hands and locked tight. Liberty let go the sheets, jumped up, and pried open the bilge, shining a flashlight among the timbers. He hadn't heard anything; he couldn't find any damage. He guessed that the keel was mired in mud or soft sand. The water nearby was quiet. He hadn't crossed the breaker line, if you could call it that. Fifty yards ahead the low seas were foaming gently on a narrow bar. There was no force to them at all. He guessed they would have to rise another two feet, at least, before they started breaking on the boat. Of course the tide would make a difference — as it went out, it would draw the line back towards the boat. If the seas rose, it would probably draw the line well astern. All in all, Liberty decided, it was a pretty good job.

It was time to practice his role. He retrieved the ignition key from his pocket and started the engine. At first the prop spun vigorously, gathering sound, building to a roar. Then after too long, something jammed somewhere, a cracking noise, while a rising whine vibrated the floorboards. He noticed a harsh odor. Then a handful of pebbles rattled on an aluminum roof, and it was done. Liberty was neither sorrowful nor relieved; he didn't particularly like engines.

He was in no hurry to be rescued. The boat was angled perfectly into the weather, and it hardly rocked. He walked forward to the bowsprit and leaned his weight over the edge, feeling for motion. The hull stuck tight. Satisfied, he returned and stretched out behind the wheel, enjoying the quiet. He was well north of Elliott, and had an open view of the mainland coast, above five miles away. It was brighter than he remembered it — a narrow, continuous glimmer stretched taut against the darkness. He guessed that he could see up and down the shore for thirty miles, and he knew that what he saw was only a fragment. There was an enormous gravity generated in that vastness, and Liberty imagined he could feel it on his skin, drawing dollars, words, and people from the far places of the world. He thought about the cargo under the deck and wondered how long he would stay.

Something woke him from reverie. He sat up, scanning the sea around him. To the south, shining through the thick growth of Elliott, he saw a group of lights moving. A party from the yacht harbor, stumbling in the bushes. They certainly had plenty of lanterns. But the lights were moving in concert, steadily, at the same speed. The first ones emerged from behind the Key and moved out over the water. Others followed, suddenly bright. It was a ship, an enormous one, steaming north along the edge of the deep water. Liberty reached under the seat for his binoculars, knocking the lens caps onto the deck. He couldn't see much. It was bigger than anything he knew from the Coast Guard, and built like a liner, high off the water, with at least three decks all the way back. He was sure he had never seen it before. Now the tangled shadow over the bridge was visible — a mass of antennae. There had been pictures in the newspapers. The odds were too long. It had to be the *Cimmerian*.

Liberty sat very still for a minute. If he got on the box, they would come for him. They had nothing better to do. If he kept quiet they might pass him by. However, the ship was bound to have some kind of official company, and they were sure to see him and investigate. On the slight chance that they didn't, the ship would broadcast his position. God help him if the *Cimmerian* took him off first. So quickly, it had all gone to pieces. Everyone was going to be very curious. Well, if he wasn't going to leap off and swim away, he had better get started. Liberty went below and picked up the microphone. He flipped through the bands once or twice, trying to make an impression. No use bothering with the distress signal — he knew they were listening.

"Hello, this is the yacht *Dart*, out of Freeport. Can anyone hear me?"

"Come in, *Dart*."

"Yes, well I seem to be stuck in the mud and I wonder —"

"Acknowledged. This is the *Cimmerian*, KXE49292. We have your location. We are sending a boat."

"Why thank you. I'll just wait here then. I suppose I'll see you later." He put down the mike and waited. He didn't have to wait long.

"This is Y district patrol twelve. *Cimmerian,* come in."

"*Cimmerian,* KXE4292. Go ahead, twelve."

"You've received a distress signal?"

"Roger — a small yacht, the *Dart.* Grounded just north of Otter Reef. We're sending a boat."

"Don't bother. We'll get him ourselves."

"I think the boat is already gone."

"Acknowledged. We'll be in the area."

"*Cimmerian* out."

Liberty clicked off the radio. There might be more, and he didn't want to hear it.

Topside again, he saw the pale launch moving towards him. Over the buzz of their engine the roar of the patrol boat somewhere behind Elliott grew louder. In a few minutes it was clear of the Key, and the main lamp was sweeping across the dark water, catching and examining the upper decks of the *Cimmerian* like a collector studying a recovered valuable. Liberty freed the main halyard and began wrestling with the damp sail.

Two hours later he was sitting in a small room on the third deck with a sun-reddened man of about fifty in khaki fatigues. There were shelves full of technical manuals along the walls. Everything was painted a dull aqua and there were rivets in the floor. Over the desk in front of them was a large black window, in which nothing was visible except their own reflections. They were drinking coffee.

"I didn't expect to be retrieved so promptly. For that matter, I never imagined that the need might arise."

"This is a busy coast — there's a lot of small-scale smuggling activity, and the police are suspicious. That's why they kept the lights on you while you were leaving your boat. Since you came from abroad, we'll have to leave you at the entry office tomorrow. I hope you took your papers off."

He nodded. "Sorry for all your trouble. It's embarrassing. The weather could hardly have been better."

"It happens every day. The bottom shifts all the time, with every storm. Charts are obsolete by the time they're printed. Unless you know these waters, it's risky to travel at night."

"Yes — well, the forecast was good for two days and I thought it might be fun — an adventure, you know. I thought I could hardly miss Miami."

"They're going to come down on you tomorrow. If your papers are good, they might believe you."

Liberty appeared surprised. "Oh? Have I broken a rule of some kind?"

The man in khaki was tall and spare, with a two-day beard. He wore his uniform like a challenge, stiff and spotless, as if to make obvious his loathing for it, and to dare anyone to share his contempt. He had a bright hard shell over his eyes, and a deep alertness which he maintained without effort.

"No, you haven't broken any rules. Not that I know of. You're just a victim of poor planning, that's all."

Liberty smiled. "That much is evident, I think."

The man turned to him suddenly. "Don't expect me to believe you — piling up on Otter Reef — hell, you couldn't have been more than a yard or two from the bar. That place is lit up like a Christmas tree. I suppose you're going to say you thought the buoys marked the channel."

"I don't understand."

"Forget it. It's none of my business."

They were quiet for a moment. Liberty looked at him curiously. "About my boat. Do you think it's safe where it is? I don't think there's any major damage."

"It'll stay till it sprouts. The Port will probably send someone after it in the morning. They'll hold it for a day or two. You can expect a big bill."

"Is that regular? I might prefer to make my own arrangements."

"They have authority over all wrecks and groundings. You can bet they'll be interested in this one. Everything's going to be done for you."

"Why is that?"

"First of all, because you're not a local boat. You haven't even been checked through. That makes it likely. Second, because you're sitting with me right now. They'll want to know all about you. It would be better for you if you were still on the reef."

"Do you really think so?"

For the first time, the man in khaki smiled. "Don't worry about it. You'll find out." He placed his hands flat on the table and stood up.

"Come on. You're a guest. I have orders to show you around." He walked out of the room.

Liberty caught up with him some distance down a dim corridor. Exposed pipes and wiring snaked along overhead. The way was narrow; he had to follow behind, trying to match stride.

"The hull is Japanese — a wartime escort. A little armor along the waterline and under the turrets. It survived, somehow. Handed over in Singapore at the end. It sat and rotted for years. Rebuilt in Tokyo and brought over here." The man ducked through an entryway and started up a tiny staircase. Another corridor and another stair. They had seen no one. The steel walls sang faintly. "We have a fueling agreement with a yard in Tampa. It wasn't easy. They tell everyone we're doing contract work for the Cubans — the ones from Cuba — air speeds, ship movements, stuff like that. 'We have reason to believe.' It's not true." Now the rooms on either side were lit and open. Liberty glimpsed a nondescript man at a large table, annotating charts. They squeezed past a row of file cabinets.

"Looks like an insurance office, doesn't it? This way." He turned sharply, and they entered a spacious, dimly lit room with a row of windows along one side. They looked out onto a larger area, nearly as dark, and filled with rows of steel computer boxes. A few men sat at consoles, punching buttons. "This is the reason for it all — a goddamn weather bureau. Have a seat."

Liberty sank into a foam chair under the window. The officer sat beside him. A few darkened screens were set into the counter in front of them.

"How do you like these chairs? You feel like you're about to have a tooth pulled, don't you?" He looked away and began playing with a panel of illuminated switches. One of the screens came to life — a grid glowing yellow against the dark, broken here and there by islands of flashing green. "Do you know what you're looking at? This is the short radar."

He seemed to expect an answer. Liberty shook his head.

"Here — I'll give you a hint." Another grid floated into place over the original, marked with soundings, buoys, and land outlines. It seemed to be based directly on the CGGS charts. Liberty could see the tip of Elliott Key at the bottom of the screen. "Well? Any better?"

"I'm afraid I'm not familiar with this sort of thing."

63

"I didn't think so. Look — you see those green blotches in the center there? That's Otter Reef. That bright speck a little way to the north — yes, that's it. What was the name again? The *Dart*."

"That's my boat?"

"Exactly. Just where you left it. OK, let's move on." His hand wandered among the levers. The screen went dark and jumped to life again — this time the yellow grid and the chart appeared together. A series of blue dots crept slowly from right to left. Liberty recognized Key Biscayne, the southern end of the beach, and the harbor islands. "This is a much larger scale. You can see a good part of Miami. Those blue lights are commercial jets — the approach path to the airport stretches out to the east, over the water." He turned it off. "This high-altitude stuff is marginal. It's not necessary for our purposes. Let's check up on our friends."

This time the map overlay did not appear. "Station — that's us — is at the center there. You see the contact — that little blue bastard? That's the patrol boat. He's always tagging along. Sometimes they board us and make a search. You can bet they would have tonight, if we had picked you up before they arrived. They think we're involved in smuggling operations. This is the same game they play in the eastern Med with the Soviets. It gets boring after a while."

He leaned forward and started fiddling with a new bank of dials. Liberty clapped his hands to his ears. Out of nowhere, a great echoing roar shook the walls, like a blow on the head. The officer lunged and it was gone. Faces turned in the room below. "Sorry. I'm not used to this yet. Listen." The noise returned, softly now; a low, regular thrumming sound.

"Those are our engines. When navies first had to deal with submarines, they tried towing microphones in the wake, since sound carries so well in water, and no sub can travel silently. The trouble was, it was almost impossible to hear anything over the sound of their own screws, and the problem was intensified when you had ten or twelve convoy ships nearby, all grinding away. And even if you did pick up the sub, you couldn't locate it — you could only guess at distance and direction. So they went to echo-location systems, and tried to bounce signals off the sub's hull. It worked, just barely. Since then, the principle has been exploited in various gadgets — most depth finders work that way.

"However, these machines can't distinguish between a sub and a

64

large fish, and they are confused by special hull materials. Ideally, a good ear can do the job better, and since the invention of computers and directional microphones, it's become possible to abandon sonar. Listen to this." The engine noise subsided. In seconds a new sound appeared — a higher, more insistent throb. On the display screen, the patrol boat began flashing red.

"I set the machine to locate and amplify the strongest signal within a certain radius. As you can see, it picked up our shadow right away. This ship has thousands of tiny microphones mounted underneath, each directed at a few arc seconds. The computer makes it possible to sort out and integrate whatever noises they pick up. They tell me the system is something like an insect's eye. The other day we were well offshore south of here, and one of the engineers tuned in on a whale's heartbeat. In other words, this is the ultimate ear.

"You can't buy this kind of technology — you have to build it yourself. The tracking systems we have here are more advanced than the Coast Guard's. Frankly, I don't understand why we need them. It's not as if we're at war." He stood up stiffly. "That's all. If you wait here, a man will be by to show you to your quarters. There'll be a message for you there. We'll probably have you ashore by noon tomorrow." He turned and walked out, vanishing into the dark corridor.

Liberty settled back and stared through the thick glass in front of him, watching the myriad lights of the electronic city below. He had earlier thought it might be possible to negotiate a return trip to the Bahamas; a deal for his cargo and a few names. It was now apparent that the owners of the *Cimmerian* didn't need that kind of assistance. Apart from original cost, he guessed that operating expenses for this vessel ran well over ten million per year. Rumor maintained that the boat was used to monitor and protect a large-scale entry network. However, Liberty had always believed that the most vulnerable stage of any move was the actual landing. No amount of listening gear could make it any less dangerous — there were too many things that could go wrong. He had privately believed that the *Cimmerian* was an expensive toy, purposely uninvolved with any aspect of the trade. Who owned it? A wealthy citizen who liked to play games at sea. Had it been financed with drug money? It hardly mattered. All it could do was draw flies.

But everything looked different from inside. The lightning "res-

65

cue," the sparring on the radio, the grand tour, and the threat of special treatment ashore; the fact was, the whole operation had been jeopardized by the bare presence of this ship. Was it possible that the *Cimmerian* worked with the police, pointing out targets which it believed worthy of attention? How many sailors had sat in this chair? Liberty saw that, regardless of its value as a carrier, the boat might be quite effective in shutting down a piece of the business in the area. Good publicity for the authorities, and good prices for the market. They had plenty of chances to talk. Some kind of arrangement was not unfeasible. He looked up. His escort had arrived.

"Follow me." They moved down a long hallway toward the rear of the ship. He was young, bony, and expressionless. Again, the khaki uniform. The boy walked a step or two ahead, the back of his skull bobbing high in the air. More than once, they had to crouch to pass through a fire door. He stopped abruptly and turned, indicating a door. "Please remain here. If you need anything, pick up the phone. The deck officer will answer." He started back the way they had come.

The room was small and windowless, like a cell, with a sink and a john in one corner. There was an envelope on the bed. He picked it up; there was a handwritten note inside. "Please excuse me for any inconvenience we may have caused. You'll be served breakfast at seven, and a launch will take you to Miami directly." Liberty crumpled it and tossed it on the floor. No more surprises. Cruz had said he had the salvage wrapped up tight. He hoped it was true.

» » »

Raymond Hula was born in Providence in 1930, son of an electrical parts salesman and his wife of two years. Her name was Lucy Pratt, and she had met her husband on a streetcar in the summer of 1928. At the corner of Olney and Thayer her car had jumped the tracks, thanks to a worn shoe on one of the wheels, and rammed into a dry-goods store. Hula senior was inside at the time. He pulled Lucy out of the car and sat her down on the sidewalk. Her eyes popped open (she was unhurt) and she smiled vacantly into his great, red, ungainly face. They were married three weeks later.

By the time Raymond arrived they had grown tired of each other, and not without reason. Gregory Hula was not the kind of man that Lucy Pratt had hoped he was; he didn't seem to understand what she expected of him. They bought a sooty brick house on the north end of town and he got her a job as a secretary at the Foremost Switch Company. She kept it long after he was gone.

When Ray was six years old his father made up his mind that he was through with Providence. He told Lucy that he was going to head south and he wanted to take their son with him, if it was all right with her. Hula could still remember that day — a gray, rustling evening in November, the mud by the stoop brittle from the first frost, and the coal truck rolling down the hill to the city. After dinner his father stood up from the table; erect, polite, and deferential. Lucy turned from the sink and the remaining dishes, burying her hands in her apron; she was troubled, but she was smiling. Ray sat at the table and played with the saltshaker.

"If you want to go there's little I can do to stop you. And if you want to take our son, well . . . you're a good father, Gregory. Promise you'll take care of him."

"Lucy, I most solemnly vow — "

"And you, Raymond, must make me a promise also." She leaned over and knotted her hand in his thick hair, pulling his head back. "You must promise to come back and see me, when you can." He looked up into her face, his eyes wide and strangely placid. His father coughed nervously. She kissed the boy once and went back to the dishes.

They traveled a long way that winter, stopping for a week or two in New York, in Baltimore, in Washington. The hotels where they slept had bellboys in uniform and glittering lobbies where Ray first encountered the smell of cigars. Mr. Hula taught his son how to play cards, how to tell jokes, and how to buy a ticket at the railroad station. The boy was often nervous and uneasy; day after day he saw nothing but strangers. It didn't occur to him to ask his father why. Often they ate breakfast on the train, and he didn't respond when the waiter flourished a bottle of ketchup over his eggs. "Your stomach's still asleep," his father would say, and clean his son's eyes with his handkerchief. "Take a look at them now," he said.

So Gregory Hula arrived in Miami in the spring of 1937 with a young son and six hundred dollars. As soon as he got off the train he went directly to the First National Bank and deposited the balance, reserving only fifty dollars, which, as he explained to the boy, they would need for expenses. Ray was extremely attentive; the city was utterly strange to him and he was eager to learn whatever tricks were necessary to survival. The sun was smaller and hotter than he ever remembered it, the earth was flat as a griddle, and the men hurried from shadow to shadow. Miami is the City of Cats; that morning the boy saw at least fifty of them — dozing on stoops, poking through the gutters, chewing on scraps and sprawled, dead, on garbage heaps. The coral rock crunched under his feet and he squinted doubtfully at the dark birds soaring high in the sky. Women and children were unnaturally scarce. His father dragged him around for what seemed like hours, shouting and pointing, till the boy lost all track of himself, and was close to tears when they stopped in the deep shade of a spreading tree by the edge of the docks.

"What's wrong?"

The boy sniffed. "Nothing."

"What do you mean? Everything's wrong! Out with it, kid."

"I don't know."

Mr. Hula unbuttoned his son's collar and pushed the hair out of his eyes. "Hell, it's just another town. Only this time we're staying. You'll get used to it — you'll see."

The boy stretched out his legs and began picking at the bark of a tree.

"OK, be a grouch," his father said.

Ray managed a weak smile; seeing it, his father laughed. "You let me do the worrying from now on. In case you're wondering about our stuff, I sent it to a hotel downtown. We'll go over there later."

The boy got up and walked around in circles, kicking at pebbles. Mr. Hula watched him for a moment and then pulled out his wallet. He rummaged through it idly, taking out papers, crumpling them, throwing them away.

Among cities, Miami has the shortest of memories; it has never learned to look backward. By 1937 the boom of the twenties was forgotten, though its wreckage lay everywhere. Henry Flagler was gone, his daughter lived alone in Rye, New York, and his railroad was broken in pieces. The bridges to the Keys were useless. George Merrick, the man who built Coral Gables, was long since bankrupt, and his ideal kingdom available for rent. The colossal hotels — some of them only half-finished when construction stopped in 1926 — had never fallen down, but their failure was only dimly remembered, and the local people never stopped assuring each other that there was big money in the hotel trade. One of these giant skeletons currently housed eighty thousand chickens; most of them were empty. But even at the height of the boom, when money, real money, was as common as dirt, when the railroad couldn't handle all the shipments from the north — even then prosperity was a dream, an article of faith as much as a reality, and the man who had a million put away was not considered so rich as a young salesman with a vision of paradise. Everyone was hooked, and when the money ran out nearly everyone went bankrupt, but it was a failure of statistics, rather than imagination, and no one doubted that the city in their minds would grow up even stronger. In September of 1926 a hurricane roared out of the Gulf and took hundreds of lives, destroying half of Miami. In the north the public abandoned Florida and applied their energies to the stock market. In Dade County people looked at the ruins and saw the foundations of grandeur.

Ray and his father settled into a boardinghouse — previously a hotel — in North Miami near the bay. Their room had palm trees painted on the walls and the handles on the faucets were modeled on starfish. The man who owned the place rarely made an appearance; all responsibility lay with Mrs. Harken, a bloated old woman who cooked the meals, distributed the mail, and threw out the trash. She was stubborn, arthritic, and often pretended forgetfulness, but no one dared argue with her — her power was comprehensive and absolute. When the dinner bell rang, anyone who came down the stairs and went directly to the veranda, without stopping by the kitchen to carry something out, would be sure to suffer her displeasure, one way or another. When they first arrived, Mr. Hula, always polite, made a habit of tipping his hat to Mrs. Harken as he went by her chair on the porch. She ignored him completely; after a while he began to feel a little ridiculous, but by then it was too late to stop. Ray was also afraid of her, but whatever little mercies she permitted herself went out to the children in the house, and she sometimes called him into the kitchen to give him a stalk of cane or some bread and butter.

Apparently Mr. Hula could sell himself as well as anything else; before the week was out he had a job downtown and a suitcase full of electrical hardware. He did his best to ingratiate himself with the other tenants. He learned all their names, inquired about their health, told stories, spoke glowingly of their hometowns — regardless of whether he had ever heard of them — and in general applied himself so diligently that they asked each other what he was trying to hide. Prevailing opinion judged that Mr. Hula and his son did not belong at Mrs. Harken's. Most of them lived there by necessity, since they couldn't afford places of their own — widows, invalids, retired laborers, seasonal resort help — and they couldn't understand why a successful businessman like Mr. Hula wouldn't try and do a little better for himself. So Mr. Hula, who was looking for their goodwill, became a figure of mystery, and his son, who wanted nothing to do with them, was petted and worried over.

On a close, steamy day in July Mr. Hula returned from his office at lunchtime. The tenants were lined up on the porch, motionless, waiting for a breeze off the water. Ray was behind the house with a magnifying glass, trying to burn a hole in a clam shell. He looked up, startled, when his father came around the corner.

"Son, it's too hot to sit still today. Let's go down to the beach and get wet." He turned and went back to the front of the house. The boy hid the glass under a shingle, grabbed a towel off the line, and followed him.

The bay water was warm and dirty; Mr. Hula suggested that they go out to the ocean. His son nodded and they set off for the boulevard to catch the streetcar.

Though there were plenty of seats available, they stood all the way down, and Mr. Hula pointed out the sights. Most of the hotels were shuttered up for the summer. They caught an occasional glimpse of the bay down the streets to the east. The homes along the route were like nothing the boy had ever seen — large, grim, and fantastic, with tremendous awnings staked out everywhere, and sidewalks meandering to the front door. Further along, the buildings grew together and the power lines crossed overhead in bundles.

The ride across the bay was a little cooler. Mr. Hula stuck his head out the window to catch the air. He pointed to a gull gliding alongside the car. Ray nodded and waved at it. The gull veered away, heading back for the city.

Old black men with hand lines stood like dead trees on the bridges. Off to the south a freighter steamed down the channel, long streaks of rust dropping from its scuppers. A white haze obscured the horizon in all directions and the sun gleamed like oil on the water. The other passengers slouched in their seats, their knees swaying gently.

By the time they got to the beach Mr. Hula was worn out with talking. His son had hardly said a word. They trudged across the hot sand to the shade of a fishing pier and spread their towels among the pilings. Even the ocean was quiet; it swelled almost noiselessly at their feet. The boy began picking barnacles off the wood and throwing them in the water. His father sighed and stretched out on his back, hands under his head.

"Son, you don't look too excited for someone who's never been here before. This is a famous place. People up north save up for years just to come and see it."

"It's OK."

"Yeah." He slapped at his leg. "You know, when I was your age I used to scream and carry on like a red Indian. Is there something bothering you?" The boy continued work on the pilings. "You always did hang back a little, I know, but ever since we left you've been tight as a clam. Am I doing something wrong? Hell, I don't mean to criticize you, or embarrass you — I just want to know how you're feeling. Are they giving you a hard time at the house when I'm gone? Is that it?"

"No."

"Well that's good. You know, we can go somewhere else if you want. Some of those people are sort of a nuisance. It wouldn't bother me a bit."

Mr. Hula sat up and wrapped his elbows around his neck. Someone was walking on the pier overhead; he waited for the footsteps to recede.

"It occurs to me, Ray, that when we left Providence I never asked you whether or not you wanted to come. I didn't even think of it. You could have stayed at home with your mother, if you liked. That's me all over, son — I don't think before I do something. It gets me into hot water every time." He coughed nervously. The boy had nearly stripped the piling of barnacles; he ran his hand over the far side, searching for more.

"Anyway, I can see my mistake now and I thought I'd better try and fix it. Better late than never, right? What I'm saying is, if you want to go back north, to the old place, or if you want to get out of Mrs. Harken's, or anything else you can think of — just tell me, OK? Do it for my sake, son, because if you're not happy I'm not going to be happy either."

He might have been talking to himself, for all the interest the boy showed. He had abandoned the barnacles; at the moment he was pushing the damp sand into mounds over his feet. Mr. Hula moved on.

"I know it must have seemed strange to you — just picking up and leaving like that. Maybe you couldn't see the reason for it. If we had stayed you would have seen it soon enough. Your mother was a good woman — I never saw a better — but she and I didn't belong together, and sooner or later we all would've had to pay for it. When things go wrong there's no sense in trying to pretend that they haven't — you've got to admit it and then see what you can do. That's what we did, and I don't apologize for it. But I know it must have been tough for you and I'm sorry I was too ashamed to talk about it sooner. I'm getting off the track a little here — I meant to ask you whether there was anyplace you wanted to go, including back to your mother. Remember, it's what you want that counts. What do you say?"

The boy turned and looked at his father blankly. He had been listening intently, all the time. The confusion on Mr. Hula's face startled him. He turned back to the water and began carefully scraping up piles of sand with his heels. They sat there together a long time without a word. Shortly before they left they went swimming, and the tide carried them a good way down the beach. The ocean was dark, almost black, in the lowering sun. Mr. Hula tried to teach the boy how to float on his back, though as it happened, neither of them had much talent for it.

The Snowbirds

RAY HULA WOKE UP at seven on Sunday morning. He passed quickly out of sleep, as if something had disturbed him; a presence, a signal, that he had prepared for and recognized. He looked around the room; nothing was happening. Satisfied, and with an odd sense of relief, he sank back into the pillow and enjoyed a moment of remarkable ease and quietness, until the phone rang again and the last three weeks came back in a rush.

"Hello?"

"Hula? This is Rawden, at the Port. Sorry to wake you. We've got a job."

"Urgent?"

"Not really. A small yacht, stuck in the mud just north of Otter Reef. On the ocean side."

"How much water?"

"I don't know — maybe six feet. It's a keel boat."

"No brains at all."

"Less."

"Can he pay?"

"I don't know. The *Cimmerian* took him off last night. They said they'd bring him in this morning."

"What?"

"You heard right. They were in the area."

"Goddamn Boy Scouts."

"He grounded at about eleven — he was coming from across the way."

75

"So what's the hurry?"

"No hurry. I thought you might like to know. It'll probably take a while to get out there."

"All day. I'll see what I can do. What's the forecast?"

"Southwest, ten to fifteen, I think. Rain tonight."

"Right. It may have to wait till tomorrow. I can't do it myself. Cubans are probably at church already."

"Monday's OK. Listen, check this one twice, would you? We're curious."

"Oh yeah?"

"You know what I mean. It's not local. Call us on the way in."

"Right. See you later." He hung up. All you have to do, Cruz said, is do what you always do. Except hide it from them. Don't let them see it. Don't let them even imagine it.

He sat up heavily and groaned, surprising himself. It came from deep in his chest, a mortal sound, his two lungs rasping together. There was no longer any question of turning back, of taking any path but the simplest, pursuing only those objects which presented themselves clearly.

He picked up the phone book. Inside, stapled to the front cover, he had a list of numbers. Many were crossed out; others were smudged and barely legible. What did he say yesterday? Alante, Silva, Geronimo, Murphy — he would need all of them. Silva was the one to watch. Put him on the tug, out of the way. That was the best he could do. They all had good eyes and none of them were stupid. "Remember," Cruz had said, "if anyone sees it we might as well start over. You'll have to bring it straight to the Port and that'll be the end of it. In a few weeks they'll know everything. So don't let anyone see it."

A woman answered, shouting over a clamor of children.

"Silva. Hector Silva."

"*Quién es ese?*"

"Hector Silva."

"*Está durmiendo. Quién es ese?*"

"Mr. Hula — Miami Salvage."

"OK." He heard the small voices quieted, one by one, and then Silva, groggy and amiable. "Hello?"

"You're asleep. I'm amazed."

"I have practiced."

76

"A yacht grounded near Otter Reef last night. I want to pull it up today. Do you want to do it?"

"Where's Otter Reef?"

"A long way — just north of Elliott. Eight hours at least."

"Why not?"

"I'll meet you at the yard. If you get there first, start up the boat. I have to get a crew together."

Hula was surprised to find them all at home and willing. On the other hand, he remembered that he hadn't had much for them to do lately. It wasn't for lack of work; there were still a few jobs on the list. But he hadn't begun any new projects in the last week or so. Another sign of his lagging will, he thought. It would have been better if they were bored and tired.

The sky was clear, and the light slanted into his pitted windshield, scattering in all directions. He could feel it on the back of his neck as he pulled into the street. In June the sun was tiny, fierce, and ambitious; turning the rain to vapor before it hit the ground. The boulevard was nearly quiet this morning, and he waited patiently at the lights, listening to the engine and wondering where the life of the city had fled. The parking spaces were empty and without value. On either side, an unbroken row of cracked pastels and palm litter; travel agencies, nameless motels, surgical supply centers, minor public offices, and the deserted oases of the fast-food industry. Hula remembered the street as it looked forty years ago. It was still the same.

Crossing the Twelfth Avenue bridge, over the dark rooftops and the chalky river, he could see south to Flagler Street and east to the towers downtown. Another minute and he was at the yard. Silva's rusted station wagon was pulled up out front alongside a Japanese compact. He nudged the gate open with his fender and parked by the main shed. The smaller car was new to him, and he walked over to investigate. He stood just inside the wire, leaning on one of the support posts.

There was a man in the car. He had a large, blocky head, massive shoulders, and a straw hat. His head hung forward, and his chin flattened the collar of his rainbow-dyed sport shirt. Hula was curious. He stepped around the gate and took a closer look. The hat was a necessity; the man had very little hair, just a sparse stubble back of his ears. His skin was smooth and thick, allowing no wrinkles. Hula guessed

77

late forties. He was about as much as the car could hold. His knees were jammed under the wheel and his hips obscured the seat. He was breathing slowly and evenly through his nose. Hula wondered how long he had been asleep.

A door banged in the yard and he saw Silva coming out of the main locker, starting towards the slip, moving with that wobbly stride of his. When he looked up Hula waved him over. He dutifully changed direction, head down, his silver hair still wet and glistening over his wine-colored face. He had two gold teeth which he claimed to have stolen from his mother. He stopped at the gate, looking out.

"Morning, boss."

"Silva. Did you see this guy?"

"Been here since I came. Maybe he sat there all night. Don't wake him up now."

"You've never seen him before?"

"Not him, not his car. What about you?"

"No. That's why I'm asking."

"Well, I'd say he was drunk, since last night was Saturday, but he doesn't stink. I checked."

"He must have got here since sunrise. His shirt's dry. The car's dry."

"Boss, I got to hand it to you. You're pretty sharp for 8:00 A.M."

He looked up. Silva was grinning at him, his teeth shining through the fence. Hula spat in the dust. "Fuck him. He'll wake up when the sun hits him. Let's get going." Silva waited for him to get around the gate, and they started toward the back of the lot. The smaller man was mumbling and chuckling.

"It don't surprise me. I knew you'd want to know about him. I knew as soon as I saw him. It's because he looks just like you, boss. More hair, that's all."

By the time the last man arrived they had all the gear aboard the tug and were ready to go. The younger men were still groggy; they loitered on the forward deck, passing a thermos. Hula walked back to lock the gate. The car and its occupant were still there. He wondered how anyone could sleep so quietly, like a stone. Hula held up his key ring and rattled it against the fence. No reaction. He turned and started back.

Though the wheelhouse of the tug was Silva's private preserve, Hula joined him for the swing down the river. As soon as the lines

78

were off, the crew collected on the main hatch, settling down for the
ride. Later they would move back behind the cabin, taking whatever
shade they could find. Even now the sun had started to shed fire,
pounding the city flat, driving the shadows underground.

Silva backed swiftly into the channel, just kissing the edge of the
slip as he made the turn. Hula gazed at the back of his foreman's
head, envying him. He might as well be a million miles away. His
small hands held the wheel lightly; this was the way he cradled a
woman, or lifted his son into bed, a careless solicitude, the kind of
grace that Hula had cast away. He looked at his own hands. They
were stiff and nerveless, blunt clubs and shields, apt instruments of betrayal; they no longer belonged to him. He shoved them into his
pockets and looked out over the water.

They slid around the last bend; in a moment they were steaming
into the milky blue water of the bay. Silva called over his shoulder.

"We going to need the barge?"

"I don't know — what do you think?"

"It's a grounding, right? How are we going to get close?"

"Tell me."

"We'll take the barge. Go away, don't bother me."

Hula turned and pulled a chart out of the bracket behind him. He
stepped down into the after cabin and spread it out on the table.
There was no point in looking at it; a week ago he had printed it on
his retina. He took out a pencil and drew a circle around Otter Reef,
with an arrow pointing north along the bar. How many other maps
were marked like this? From the first, Cruz's plan had struck him as
painfully obvious. Cruz said that the most straightforward moves
were often the most successful, and that there was no way to avoid
suspicion — the trick was to escape detection. "And that," he said,
"is why I'm counting on you — your special relationship with the authorities." Hula wasn't impressed; he couldn't make planes fall out of
the sky, for instance. "That's a point in your favor, Ray. They think
they know you. You shout at them over the phone, you don't send
your reports in on time — they know all about you."

Concentrating, he bore down on the pencil until it snapped. He
slumped into a chair and pulled out his pocketknife. Silva was whistling loudly and tunelessly. Cruz had asked if he had ever told anyone
he had a brother. No, he had said. That was the truth. Though Cruz
seemed convinced, he had made him repeat his answer, as if he en-

joyed the sound of it. He said that anyone who linked them could easily blow the entire scheme. "You never told a soul, did you? I knew the first time I saw you, at the funeral. You hated me for what I did to Mom, right? If you talked about it you couldn't hate me as much — that's the way you are. I wouldn't worry about it if I were you. I didn't tell anyone either." Hula hacked at the pencil with his knife, exposing the lead and breaking it again.

Silva stayed aboard the tug, while Hula and the crew stepped down onto the barge. Hula took a deep breath; the familiar stink of hot tar and resin bit the skin around his nostrils. Murphy already had the tow cable off the tug and was poking around the end of the barge, looking for the place to secure it. He was new and eager to please. The other two let him fumble for a while and went over to help. Hula climbed into the crane and waited. In five minutes they had slipped the moorings and were underway, pushing dutifully after the tiny, high-decked tug.

They passed the Cape shortly before eleven. Hula was in the shack, sitting motionless on the stool beside the radio. The heat and the rich salt air had made him drowsy; the throb of the tug's engine seemed far away. Up forward he could see the crew scattered across the deck like toys. On the Cape, the feathery pines leaned away from the breeze, and the wake of the tug pushed against the narrow beach. The sea was green and clear over the sand, darkening into blue along the horizon, where the blue of the sky was deepest. On the shore, near the lighthouse, a few bright towels shone like flags; the black specks in the water were the heads of swimmers. Hula watched one of them emerge. She was tall and brown and straight, with a dark strand of hair running down her back. Her legs carried her steadily up the beach, working smoothly against the grade. She bent at the waist and seized a towel. Hula wondered how she looked at close range, her body wet and gleaming. Geronimo, more alert than usual, was sitting up and pointing. Now the others were rubbing their eyes and peering into the distance. For a moment Hula forgot himself and smiled, thinking how easy it was to dream of heaven. The radio crackled into life; Silva was calling him.

"Wake up, boss. Take a look."

Hula grabbed the mike. "She's mine. I saw her first."

"Not the girl, you jerk. Around the Cape — look."

Hula looked. Some miles to the north, standing out to sea, a snowy white hull, like a cruise ship in miniature, pointed toward the land — the *Cimmerian.* Silva was talking again.

"That's the goose. Four decks, hidden stack, shallow stern — that's the one we hear about. How'd you like to strip that mother?"

"Stick with me, Silva, and you can buy one yourself someday. I'll see to it."

"Say that again?"

"Watch your course, please."

» » »

It was a small room, windowless, with white scuffed walls and a gray metal desk in the center that was obviously public property, since it was too old and banged up to merit the attention of any of the people who might have claimed it. The linoleum was dirty and the wastebasket was empty; this office belonged to nobody. On the rear wall, slightly above eye level, a framed photograph of Ronald Reagan hung on a nail. A few battered folding chairs waited at the desk. There were footsteps in the hall and Wally Liberty entered, glancing around quickly before taking a seat with his back to the door. He had a tissue and was wiping ink from his fingertips. More footsteps, and two older men walked in and sat behind the desk. One of them — he had stained teeth and a graying mustache — was whistling and carrying a large folder. The other appeared grim and preoccupied, a thoughtful man with large, bushy eyebrows and a vaguely exotic way of combing his brown hair straight back from his forehead. Liberty, dressed neatly in white jeans and a striped shirt, wondered if most arrests began like this. Mustache started the dialogue.

"So you're Mr. Ralph Richmond. You're the owner of the *Dart,* right?"

"Yes. Perhaps I should say I was the owner of the *Dart.*"

"I think the boat can be recovered. We should be getting word on it later."

"Is there any way I can arrange to have it brought back? I'm willing — "

"It's happening right now." He opened the folder. "British citizen — vacationing in the Bahamas. How long were you in the Bahamas, Mr. Richmond?"

Liberty waited before answering. "This would be the eighth week, I think. Yes, that's right."

"On your passport, you state your occupation as 'business agent.'
Who do you work for? How often do you get eight-week vacations?"

"It's an importing firm. I'm a partner. We handle Oriental manu-
factures — Hong Kong, Singapore, Korea. We've done quite well
lately."

"Do you travel a lot?"

"No more than necessary, I hope." He smiled. The silent man was
watching him closely. Mustache shifted in his seat.

"How much did you pay for your boat? Who did you buy it from?"

"I paid five thousand to an old Bahamian. He said that none of his
sons would take it."

"Five thousands dollars?"

"It was less in U.S. dollars, of course."

"Where was this?"

"Freeport."

"Is that where you sailed over from?"

"No — I stayed a few weeks in a small harbor to the north. James
Harbor, it was."

"I see." Mustache began flipping through some of the other papers
in the folder. Liberty's heart began to race; he allowed himself hope.
If they knew anything they were keeping it to themselves. "Mr.
Richmond, these questions are purely routine. It's our job to monitor
all the incoming traffic here in Miami and we do the best we can,
under the circumstances. Our work makes us suspicious, and we can't
let anyone by. It's nothing personal. Now my colleague, Mr. Rawden, is especially interested in the boat that picked you up last
night — the *Cimmerian*." He pushed the folder to the other man and
whispered something in his ear. Rawden looked up and stared at Liberty — his eyes were small, green, and angry.

"You're one hell of a sailor."

Liberty looked at his hands. "Yes — well, I must admit that I'm
none too proud about all this, and I — well — what's done is done, I
suppose." He could feel those eyes feeding on him. Welcome home,
welcome home.

"When they took you on board, what did you think?"

"I was quite grateful, of course. Who knows — "

"What did you *think?*" Rawden was leaning forward, glaring.

Liberty smiled. "I don't think I understand."

"Who did you think it was? The U.S. Navy? The searchlights, the

82

engines, the fighting on the radio — it must have been like an air raid out there. Didn't you wonder what it was all about?"

"As a matter of fact — "

"Did it occur to you that it was as if they were waiting for you? As if you had tripped some kind of alarm?"

"I called for help on the wireless. I thought — "

"Forget it. How would you know? You were sitting on the big ship the whole time. Did you ever get to see the man they took off the *Dart?*"

"What?"

"How about this — how many men were on the launch when they picked you up? That should be easy."

"Three, I think. They — "

"Listen, Hollywood, you shouldn't believe everything you're told. When they're through with you they feed you to the sharks. We're the sharks. What did you do to make them so angry?"

Liberty sat up. "I don't know what you're talking about."

" 'I don't know what you're talking about.' Perfect." He turned to Mustache. "Where have we heard that before? That's our cross, isn't it? That's what makes our job so difficult. No one understands us." He looked at Liberty. "The sad thing is, it's true. You really don't know what we're talking about. But you have to behave as if you do. The same goes for us — we don't know either. We know, but we don't know. God, I hate Sundays." He slumped backward, one arm crooked over the chair. He looked unhappy with himself. "OK, let's hear all of it. What happened after you went on board? You'll notice that my partner is taking notes. Be careful what you say."

Liberty looked at the picture on the wall. "I'm sorry if — "

"No apologies. We don't allow them. We'll do it the easy way — questions and answers. Who, in your opinion, was the highest-ranking officer you met on board?"

"He was a tall man, gray-haired, middle-aged and fit. I don't think I got his name."

"Was he cold? Sarcastic? Had a bitter streak?"

"Rather."

"Rather? That's a British expression, isn't it? Write that down, Charlie — 'rather, a British expression.' Where did you see him?"

"I was taken to his office."

"You were taken to his office. Then what?"

"I was taken on a tour. He showed me some of their electronic gear."

"What sort of gear?"

"Radar, a sort of listening device . . . a computer."

"Did he give you that story about a whale's heartbeat?"

"Yes — he said something about that."

"Then what?"

"He told me a boat would take me to Miami in the morning. Another man showed me to my room."

"Did the old crank have anything to say about what would happen when you came ashore? About your reception here, for instance?"

"Yes — he said you people would be very interested in me."

"Why?"

"He wasn't explicit. I assumed he meant the circumstances of my rescue."

"Anything else?"

"He said that I was a victim of bad luck."

"Write that down, Charlie — 'victim of bad luck.' He pulled a roll of candy from his pocket and ate one. "Were you carrying any contraband aboard the *Dart?*"

"No." Liberty had answered without thinking; he was glad.

"I can generally spot a lie when I hear one, Mr. Richmond. Remember that we are in possession of the boat. Were you carrying any contraband?" He ate another candy.

"No."

"And yet your friend on the *Cimmerian* said that you were a victim of bad luck. What do you think he meant?"

"I think he meant that since I would be arriving from his ship, the customs officials would take a special interest. From what I've seen this morning, I think bad luck sums it up quite well."

"I'd say it's a little too early for you to call the toss. Tell me this. Do you think there is such a thing as luck?"

"Excuse me?"

"You heard me. Do you believe in luck?"

Liberty looked at Mustache, who didn't seem bothered by the question.

"I don't think I understand."

"All right. What were you doing on Otter Reef?"

"Otter Reef?"

84

"The place where you left your boat."

"Yes, well I ran out of water. I was stranded."

"You were on your way to Miami?"

"Yes."

"From the Bahamas?"

"Yes."

"What schools did you go to in England?"

Although a few names popped into Liberty's head, he didn't make the mistake of saying them out loud. "I don't see any point in reviewing my academic history."

"No?" The look on Rawden's face parodied surprise and innocence. "Simple — we call up the schools and ask if you ever went there. We could do it right now." He nodded at the phone.

Liberty didn't answer.

"Have you ever been to Miami before?"

"No."

"Never?"

"I think I should know if I had."

"You want to know what I think? I think you're lying." He turned to Mustache. "Charlie, do you think he's lying?"

Charlie, or Mustache, was noncommittal. He bobbed his head slightly to one side.

"Write that down, that I think he's lying," Rawden said.

Charlie did as he was told. Rawden returned to Liberty. "Do you know who I am?" Liberty didn't respond and he went on. "I work for the DEA — that's the Drug Enforcement Agency. I'm supposed to net a few bodies out of all the tourists, exiles, and felons that come through here. Some I like, some I don't like. Some are guilty, some are innocent. Some get caught, some get away. It's all up to me. I've been at it for a while, and I won't deny that it's changed the way I look at people."

Liberty was impressed. He could see that this speech was just a screen Rawden had thrown up, a mask to peer at him through. He tried not to listen too closely.

"It's made me skeptical — I've been fooled too many times. So now I just naturally assume that everybody's hiding something, and that all I have to do is find out what it is. Secrets. You know what I mean? I'm paid to be paranoid — it's part of the business. Look at the *Cimmerian,* for instance. The whole ship is nothing but peepers and

85

beepers, and they think that just because they have all this expensive stuff they know what's going on."

He smiled. Mustache was sitting quietly, twirling his pencil, as if he'd heard it before. Rawden's bad temper had given way to a brisk expansiveness; his face was flushed and he was cutting the air with his hands.

"Why am I telling you this? Because I think you're a smuggler and you ought to be concerned with these things. Why do I think you're a smuggler? Because you look like one. You might take comfort in the fact that half the people who come through here are carriers and it would be stupid to arrest them all. I know what you're thinking — it's the question they all ask themselves in this room — will I get caught? I don't know yet. We're still working on your boat. That's all — if you wait outside, Charlie will bring you your papers in a minute."

As Liberty walked out the door he wished he really was someone named Ralph Richmond.

After he was gone Charlie started doodling on the outside of the folder. "Ten-to-one he's going to make a stink. I think you went overboard a little."

"Maybe. But I know he was lying about something."

"Like what?"

"I don't know." The question irritated him.

"It's this *Cimmerian* thing. I think you should leave it alone."

"Yeah." He didn't sound convinced.

"They've picked people up before. It never comes to anything."

"Uh-huh." Rawden wasn't listening any more. "Look, can you sub for me this afternoon? I want to check out this boat as soon as Hula brings it in."

"You don't think Hula can do it for us?"

"I'd rather see it myself."

"All right. I'll write this one up." He opened the folder.

"Thanks." Rawden scraped back his chair, got up, and left the room. The other man watched him go.

» » »

By noon the clouds had started piling up in the east and moving out over the water, and the sea was gray and dull in their shadow. The last ice had melted in the cooler by the shack. As Hula moved around the barge he could feel the sweat forming on his neck and shoulders; the wind dried it almost instantly.

The boat was about two hundred yards away, wallowing in the muddy water at the edge of the bar. Tiny waves rushed past it and broke. A slack anchor line ran over the bow. The sloop was tubby and broad-beamed, with a rudder that extended well above the waterline and might have been carved out of one hunk of wood. Plenty of room for cargo, thought Hula. He guessed that it could carry more sail than most boats its size. It would go over big at an antique show; he wished Cruz had found something a little less obvious. Beyond it, off toward the mainland, the Sunday crowd was swarming out of the basins, their sails like bits of colored paper.

Up ahead in the tug Silva blew the horn and backed water. He had gone as far as he would go. Hula saw him leap down from the cabin and loosen the tow cable. He was shouting and holding his nose. He ran back to the wheelhouse and swung the tug around sharply, bringing it back to the deep water. No longer taut, the cable sank out of sight.

The crew had gathered by one of the cranes, talking and pointing. Hula walked to the rear, by the outboards, and called them over.

Alante was frowning and looking over his shoulder. "Are you sure that's the right one, Ray? It looks like a shrimp truck with a flat tire."

Geronimo shook his head. "I'd say it's probably a bus stop. Hell of a place to put a bus stop."

Hula waited for the laughter to die. "All right. We'll do it this way. There's no point in waiting around — the tide's as high as it's going to get. I don't know how much water we have. If we're not careful we may have to get towed off ourselves. The way the boat's listing, it doesn't look like it's dug in very deep. We'll come up on the lee side and put some lines on. Don't be afraid to cleat them tight — if we're lucky the weight of the barge might drag her free.

"I don't think she's holding water but we'll have to check anyway. Murphy, you're going swimming. Watch what you're doing and don't get in between — you're not worth it. Right now, get the tow cable off the bow and set it up back here. Alante, you open up the bin and get a couple of slings ready. Geronimo, see if you can get these outboards started. Don't anybody rush — we've got plenty of time. No one goes aboard until I tell them to. Let's go."

They went off to their work. Hula crossed his arms and wandered up and down the barge. He dropped a lead line over the stern and tried it again at various points forward. Silva was in the wheelhouse of the tug, chewing on a sandwich and watching through a pair of binoculars. The rich, muddy odor of mangrove arrived on the wind and made Hula think of mosquitoes. He heard the outboards mutter into life and hurried back to talk to Geronimo.

"Got those steering cables matched?"

"That's what took me so long. Pain in the ass."

"This thing doesn't handle like a sports car, so watch what you're doing. Try and get it straightened out early. I'll direct you from the bow. When I drop my hand, cut the power. If we start to bump, don't worry about it — I'll scream at you if I want reverse."

"Right. How much water?"

"We've got eight feet now — we can float in three. Don't start until I tell you." He turned and walked forward. Alante was standing by the door of the shack.

"I got those slings mounted."

"Good." Hula brushed past him and picked up the microphone. Silva answered immediately.

"That's me. You look pretty busy over there."

"We are. Listen — since we've got less water than most bathtubs, I want you to keep that tow cable extended and be ready to pull us off any time. Leave the radio on and hold your piss."

"You can count on me, boss. I hope you know what you're doing — this trip isn't worth more than a dollar and change. I think you should call up the blimp and — " Hula clicked it off and walked to the bow, signaling Geronimo to start moving. The other two were standing next to him, looking down into the dim water. He glared at them.

"Get some lines ready under the crane. Put them on as soon as she's alongside." They went off.

The barge began to creep forward, slowly, almost imperceptibly; drawn toward the wreck by an unseen strength, and fighting a massive inertia. Hula stood with one foot on the low rail, the lead line dangling from his hand. The barge floated like a compass needle in heavy oil, the earth turning beneath it. On the *Dart,* a pair of gulls leaped out of the cockpit and stood on the deck, watching. Six feet of water. Now Hula could see the lead hit bottom. It bumped and fell flat, stirring a pale ring-shaped cloud. Just yards ahead, the bar rippled

88

and splashed as the waves slipped over; he was close enough to count them. On the other side, out of reach, the green skin of the bay stretched off toward the distant mainland. Geronimo had judged the angle perfectly. In thirty seconds the forward edge of the barge would scrape the yacht. Hula raised his hand and dropped it. With the engines quiet, he would hear the great rafted bulk of the hull grind into the bottom and stick. He dropped the lead on the deck and waited.

A minute later they were still afloat. The barge had stopped right alongside the *Dart,* with four feet under the bow. Murphy and Alante were dancing furiously in the shadow of the crane, tossing lines and pulling them tight, like spiders wrapping a fly. Hula stood beside them for a minute, watching, and walked to the center of the barge, disappearing into the shack. He emerged with a diving mask and a flashlight. The men had finished when he rejoined them.

"OK, first thing we do is check for damage. Murphy, as soon as you catch your breath, get under and see if you can find any holes." He tossed him the mask. "You'll see better if you stay off the bottom and don't stir up the mud. Watch yourself. I'll open the bilge and check it from the inside. Alante, you and Geronimo hook up the pump — we probably won't need it, but do it anyway. And watch the boat — if she starts to work free, give a shout."

Turning, he stepped onto the yacht and looked it over. The deck had a slight list toward the barge. He usually left the dirty work, crawling under decks, to the crew; he wondered how many would ask themselves why today was different. Silva would definitely notice. It didn't matter, he didn't care, it wouldn't make any difference — there was no time. Behind him, he heard someone pounding the hose collars into place.

He stepped down into the cockpit. The gulls had left a mullet's head behind, probably discarded bait. The remaining eye was glazed and puffy. He picked it up and threw it overboard. Whoever had grounded the boat had pulled the sail down and left it there; it flooded the cockpit to knee level. Hula kicked his way to the cabin and looked inside. Then he backed out and started shoving the sail into it, out of the way.

The bilge cover was large, about the size of a card table, and recessed into the floor of the cockpit. There were no hinges. A few cutouts were scattered along the edge of the frame; Hula discovered he could get four fingers into them. Squatting on his heels, he tried the rim of the cover. It would come up easily. If Geronimo and Alante were through with the pump, they would be standing at the edge of the barge and watching him. He wanted to look and see, but he avoided it. Finally he jerked his head up and stared. There they were. Geronimo was sucking on a cigarette.

"Either of you noticed any motion in the hull?"

Alante answered, grinning. "Not enough to move her. It's not as if you don't weigh anything, boss."

"Call up Silva and tell him to drop a hook. I don't want the tide taking us any closer." Grunting, he forced up the cover and thrust it aside.

The engine sat directly under the hole, an old and fatty heart blackened with age. It had no more shape than a lump of tar. A narrow plank was laid along either side. Apparently the hull was still solid; the pool of sludge at the bottom was shallow and thick, with a glossy blue film of oil and gas floating on top. Hula eased himself down on the planking and switched on the flashlight. A wooden crosspiece mounted just forward of the engine obscured his view. Crouching, he crept toward it. Someone had hung a fire extinguisher on one end, bulbous and green with age. The stink of fish was as thick as smoke.

Beyond the crosspiece, total darkness. Peering over, he shone the light on a wide cargo platform built well off the bottom and awash with crushed ice — a thin layer of fish scales. Here, where the bulk of the cabin squeezed it, the hold was low and cramped, but Hula could see that there was much more space beyond. He shone the beam directly ahead; the heavy column of the mast broke it in two.

Tilting the light upward, he examined the seam where the deck met the edge of the hull. Turning, he scuttled to the opposite end of the crosspiece and studied the other side. Like a string of lanterns, a row of blue boxes had been bolted into the seam as far as he could see. Amid the stained timbers and dirty joists they shone like diamonds. He shut off the lamp. It was useless; he could still see them. They gathered whatever light remained and flung it back at him. He shut his eyes. As if we are dying for recognition, he thought, as if our stupidity is our most sacred guarantee.

What could he do? He could flood it to the waterline — too bad there wasn't any dynamite on board. He could murder all the crew, make a deal with Silva, and head for the open sea. Or he could raise the alarm, right now, and later claim he had only gone along out of fear. That was not so bad an idea.

Something dropped through the hatch behind him. He pivoted, catching his knee on a nail. Geronimo was crouching on the plank on the other side of the engine. He wasn't looking at Hula; he didn't seem to know he was there. Eyes shaded, he was squinting into the darkness over the crosspiece. A cigarette burned in his hand.

Hula could see the tip of the cigarette glowing red. The fire extinguisher was right beside him. He snatched it off the hook and shouted.

Something slipped; the handle came off in his hands. He just had time to catch a glimpse of Geronimo's distorted features before a screeching geyser of yellow foam exploded in his face. Masses of mustard-colored suds bloomed in midair. Hula turned and tossed the squirming canister over the crosspiece. It bounced once and rolled down the platform toward the mast, spinning pale clouds in the dark. The foam had buried the engine; when he turned around again he could still hear the canister hissing. Geronimo rose out of the oily bubbles and wriggled through the hatch, the cigarette still in his hand.

Now the foam was flooding over the crosspiece behind Hula, wetting his shoulders and rising over his waist. It was as light as air; he barely felt it. He watched the bubbles surge up the walls of the hold. The sunlight shone right through them. In another moment they were piling up over his head. The light faded and the hissing was far away. The hatch, he thought — where was it? Suddenly troubled, he felt dizzy and began to move.

» » »

At five o'clock Hula was alone again. Silva had been the last to leave. The *Dart* floated quietly beside the tug, her decks shining in the rain. After mooring the barge in the bay, they had towed the *Dart* up the river and roped her into the slip. Hula stood under the overhang of the rear shed, watching the water come down and waiting for Rawden to arrive. There were large patches of red on his neck and forearms, where the foam had touched his skin.

Geronimo hadn't said a word on the journey back. Before, when they finished dragging Hula from the bilge, Murphy had popped out of the water, full of news, and seeing Hula on his hands and knees, retching, had demanded to know what had happened. No one answered him. All recovered very quickly, but the earlier mood was gone, and Geronimo's silence was not unwelcome. When they got back to the yard they exchanged a few remarks about the weather and dispersed singly. On his way to his car Silva stopped to talk to Hula.

"If I were you I'd let him go. You can't afford to keep him around. Not after what happened"

"You think he'll show up tomorrow?"

"I'd call him up tonight. He won't complain."

"I'll think about it."

Silva nodded and left. He ran across the yard, leaping puddles, holding his slicker over his head.

The rain had stopped and the sun had broken through under the clouds when Rawden drove up to the gate in his blue Nova. He didn't wait for company; he heaved himself out of the car and walked directly through to the river, stopping in front of the *Dart*. He was carrying a carpenter's rule and a small plastic hammer. He had left his jacket in the car and his tie, narrow and black, was loose around his neck. Hula had been waiting for him in the shed; he stepped out and joined him. Rawden put one foot up on the railroad tie at the top of the embankment. He had a dour, sun-reddened face; the sort of face you might see in a planeload of business executives coming back from a conference at an island resort.

"That's the one," Hula said. "Hardly scratched."

"I saw you come in with it. I didn't call you in because I was busy and I wanted to see it myself."

"So you're curious?"

Rawden reached into his pocket and produced a small square photograph. He gave it to Hula. "Ever seen this guy?"

Hula returned it. "No. Who is he?"

"Got me. He claims to have been aboard when the boat grounded. The *Cimmerian* brought him in this morning."

"The *Cimmerian*. We saw it this morning, off the beach."

"Does that surprise you?"

"If the sun came up black, that would surprise me."

"Well I don't believe in surprises. So we're keeping an eye on this guy. If we can get something on him he might talk to us. By the way, what happened to your face?"

"Chemical reaction. I set off a fire extinguisher under decks. It got out of hand."

92

"Any damage?"

"There wasn't any fire. One of my crew jumped down the engine hatch with a cigarette. I didn't have any choice."

"What is he, stupid?"

"You can't count on any of them."

"Well." Rawden squinted and looked up at the sky. "What about the boat?"

"I haven't had a chance to check it out properly. There's a lot of space on it."

"Show me."

Hula grabbed a stay with one hand and stepped down onto the deck. Rawden followed, placing his feet carefully. Hula pushed the doors to the cabin aside and Rawden poked his head in. He stood up quickly. "Stinks like hell."

"I guess so. This boat's been through a lot of fish."

"Got a flashlight?"

"In the shed — I'll get it."

"Don't bother." Rawden hiked up out of the cockpit and walked forward, his eyes traveling along the edge of the coaming. "This isn't exactly your marvel of engineering."

Hula remained aft and watched him. "It floats. Reminds me of my youth."

Rawden stopped in front of the mast. "You want to come up here a minute?" Head down, Hula made his way up the deck. "Help me open up this hatch." Stooping, they lifted it and forced it aside. Hula bit his lip to keep from smiling. In a better world, he might have pushed Rawden into the hole and replaced the cover. It irked him that there were any limits at all on what he could do.

There wasn't much to see. An oil mass of gray bubbles filled the hold to within a foot of the deck. Rawden muttered an obscenity, brief and noncommittal. He looked at Hula. "This is how you put out fires?"

"I know. You like it?"

"All I know is that I was planning to have a look down there and now I can't do it. This is awfully inconvenient, if you know what I mean."

"I'm going to fire the kid with the cigarette. But I don't think he could have planned it. He didn't know the extinguisher was down there. Except for him, I'm the only one who's been on board."

"What are you going to do?"

"I'll wash it out in the morning and see what I can see."

"That could take a while. Tell me, Ray — did it ever occur to you that we don't pay you for the work you do for us? We ask you to take apart these boats piece by piece and we don't give you a thing."

"I put it on the bill anyway. It's a cost. And you guys have helped me collect."

Rawden reached up and tugged on the fleshy tip of his nose. "I see. Well don't spare yourself on this one. Get on it right away and call me as soon as you're finished. And don't let anyone else do it for you."

"What am I looking for?"

"Whatever you can find." He turned, stepped ashore, and walked off across the wet gravel of the yard.

So I did it, Hula thought. It was easy.

After Rawden left, Ray climbed the stairway to his office, halting momentarily when he put his hand on the rail and remembered how close Lisa had come to going over. It didn't matter; the important thing was that she hadn't fallen and that she was gone. He unlocked the door and settled in the chair behind his desk. A scrap of greasy paper reminded him that he hadn't eaten for ten hours; there was plenty of food at the apartment. He turned to look at the old boat outside his window. The puddles on the deck were rosy in the afternoon light, and a couple of loose lines lay draped over the bowsprit. He was proud of it. More valuable than any other ship on the river, more valuable than any five of them put together, yet the money didn't matter so much — that was Cruz's business — but it was I, he thought, I who dragged it off that stinking mudbank, where the next storm would have pounded it to bits, and carried it to safety, intact, in spite of what anyone could do. It was too early to leave. He decided to walk up to Flagler and get a sandwich.

When he got back to the office Cruz was sitting in his chair. There was a gun, black and shining, on the desk in front of him. Hula tossed the sandwich on the desk. He pointed to the gun. "What's that for?"

"I'll explain. You want to share this with me?" Cruz unwrapped the package and held out half of the sandwich. Hula shook his head. "Not now."

Cruz shrugged and began to eat. "Have a seat. We've got a lot to talk about. So who was that guy who was here earlier?"

Hula pushed the door closed and lowered himself into the deck chair. Cruz in his seat and a gun on the desk; Hula felt like an intruder in his own office. "A man came from the Port to look at the boat. I had to show it to him. I said I'd check it out thoroughly in the morning."

"Why did he come?"

"Routine, maybe. I didn't have the boat inspected on the way in. They told me to go on ahead, they couldn't handle it right then. So he came out later."

"Did he tell you anything?"

"He said the boat was mixed up with the *Cimmerian* somehow, and they were interested."

"That's what I heard. What's this *Cimmerian?*"

"It's a giant radar platform. It looks like something the navy would buy if they had the money. I don't know who runs it. Nobody knows. It's around here most of the time."

"Then it's privately owned?"

"A lot of people say some rich Cubans built it to help get their relatives across. I don't know."

"This guy who came over — what did he see?"

"We just walked around on the deck. He couldn't go underneath because the hole's full of chemical foam. I set off a fire extinguisher down there while we were still out at Elliott."

"Why?"

"Why?" Hula leaned forward. "Because you're an idiot! Because anyone with half a brain would open up those damn boxes! I'll tell you something — as soon as I went through the hatch and saw what I had to work with, I promised myself I'd blow this thing at the first opportunity. I mean it was no contest. What the hell's the matter with you?"

Cruz pushed what was left of the sandwich away. "We did what we could. There wasn't any time."

"You don't know how lucky you are."

"You're the one who got lucky. It could have gone either way. But I thought you could handle it. Was I right?"

Hula felt his anger fading, against his will. "Is that how it works? I take all the risks? When something goes wrong you walk away?"

"Look Ray — you should know by now how much I've got riding on this thing. What should we do — sign a contract? Besides, I forced you into this, remember? You didn't have any choice. You ought to be pleased that we've come this far. The way I see it, I trusted you, and you came through." After a moment he looked away and wiped his forehead with his sleeve. "Now let's go on. Did this guy tell you anything else?"

Hula slumped back. "He showed me a picture. Said the man had been picked off the yacht last night. Young, blond, healthy-looking."

"That's Liberty — my pilot. I talked to him an hour ago."

"Well, I don't think Rawden believed —"

"Who's Rawden?"

"The guy who came over — he's a senior inspector at the Port."

"Go on."

"Well, he said this guy had come off the *Cimmerian* this morning and claimed he was wrecked on the *Dart*. Rawden wasn't even willing to give him that much."

"Anything else?"

"No. He never has much to say. He asked me why I was always so glad to help him out — checking over the boats. I said I did it because I got paid for it."

"Why would he ask you that?"

"It's typical. He doesn't trust anyone. More than once he's asked me to take one of his men on my crew. I always say OK, but he never does anything about it. Just fishing. If he ever did put someone in with me, he wouldn't tell me about it. Maybe he has already. Sometimes I think he doesn't even know which side he's on himself."

"Then he seemed about the same as always?"

"A little more suspicious, maybe, but I don't blame him."

Cruz looked at his fingernails "So now what?"

"What do you mean?"

"How is he going to follow this up?"

"He'll expect a call from me tomorrow, after I've gone over the boat."

"That's all he'll do?"

"He may send someone down in the morning to help out. Or he may come himself — I don't know. But it doesn't make much difference. If you want to get that stuff out you'd better do it tonight."

"I agree. So you don't think he knows anything?"

"I couldn't tell. He always looks the same."

"Suppose he did. What would he do?"

"Well — he would want to make sure he could hang me along

with the rest. Probably — probably he'd do just what he's done so far. Act like it was any other time, and keep an eye on the boat until something happened. That means he would be watching us tonight." Hula found Cruz staring at him. "What's the matter?"

Cruz shrugged. He picked up a pencil and started scratching on the edge of the desk. "I don't know. Thought I heard something. I wish there was another way."

"I'll tell you another way. If that stuff had been hidden properly, I probably could have got it past my crew and whoever else shows up tomorrow. If it was found, I would say I didn't know about it. But it wouldn't be found — I could steer them away. Then you could take that boat wherever you liked and unload it in private.

"Impossible." He tossed the pencil on the desk. "In two days this town is going to be swarming. You're right, though — what you said. It would be a lot better if we could clear the load before we took it off, and wait a week or two before we touched it. If I was going with the percentages I'd drop the whole thing — let them find the stuff tomorrow. You'd have to be pretty stupid to try and operate like this day to day. But this is different." His gaze fell on the table before him; he appeared to be lost in thought. His cheek bulged as he tongued his teeth clean.

"Ray, sitting in your chair here, in your office, I can kind of get a feel for you, you know? I mean I can understand your attitude. You've got your own business here, that you built up yourself — not that big really, but it's all yours — and you don't owe anyone for anything. And then here comes this piece of shit, your brother, from New Jersey, who gave Mom so much trouble before she died, and now he wants to fuck you up too, with his dope and his guns and everything else. Your asshole brother, who you could never find when Mom was alive, and now you can't get rid of him. But you're a little afraid of me too — and so you do what I say, and as time goes on you realize that all this is for real, and that nothing's going to be the same again. Now you hate me even more, because you thought I couldn't touch you, and now I've taken everything away. But listen to this — I don't feel sorry for you — if you want my opinion, there was nothing to take."

Cruz glanced out the window. He made a face and shook his head. "Anyway, you're not the only fucking professional in this world — we could talk all night and it wouldn't make any difference. If we get

out of this, it'll be because we had the guts to do it right, not because
we sat back and got lucky. So let's count up our hands and see what
we have. Is that all right with you?" He stared at Hula. Hula's face
was closed, expressionless. He hurried on.

"All right. The way it stands, we don't know what Rawden will do.
This is a problem. If we try and take the stuff off tonight, and he's
waiting for us, we're dead. So we'd like to find out what his plans are
for the evening. Got any ideas?"

"It wouldn't help any — to know what he's doing tonight."

"Why not?"

"He wouldn't come along. He's strictly nine to five."

"Not even if he thought he might pick you up along with the
rest?"

"No. He'd stay home and sleep."

"What else?"

"Huh?"

"What else can we do to find out?"

Hula blinked slowly, like an owl. "I don't know. There's a chance
they might call me. A couple of times, when I've located something
for them, they've asked me to leave it where it was and keep my
mouth shut. They were watching it. One time they caught someone."

"So they would call you tonight?"

"Probably not. Why should they tell me? I haven't reported anything."

"No — but they'd want your permission to put a man inside the
yard, right? They wouldn't want you running into each other in the
dark."

"Yeah. If they put someone in here, they'd call me. But they
wouldn't have to. They could watch the boat from across the river,
and they could watch the gate from the street. It's not that easy to get
in and out of here."

"Listen, Ray, this is no time to get negative — your ass is on
parade. If we get hurt they're not going to care whether you had one
leg up or not. If there's any way around this you'd better figure it out
right now."

"I think Rawden would tell me if I called him up and asked him.
But I've known him for fifteen years and I've never tried to do his job
for him. I can't start now. Like I said, if they're watching the boat
they might call me. They might not. I don't know."

98

Cruz pulled open the top drawer of the desk. He rummaged through it, now and then looking up at Hula. "All right. So what you're saying is that there's no way we can find out whether the boat's being watched. If it is, they might give you a call tonight. All right. I can live with that. We're not totally helpless. I'll take a walk later on and see what I can see. Unless they're really on the ball around here, there's a good chance I'll pick something up."

"What if you do?"

"Then we'll let them have it. Tomorrow you'll find the load and report it — by then Liberty and I will be gone. Anything else is too dangerous." He pushed the drawer shut and opened another one. "OK. Good. Now what about tonight? We have to get the load out of the boat and into one of your sheds — it has to be one that you can drive a van into."

"We're sitting in it. This is the closest."

Cruz turned to the window and looked down. He pointed. "Hell, what about that one over there? To the left?"

"It's not safe. It's falling down. No door for a truck either."

"This is lousy. There's about twenty yards to cross here, with no cover. Anyone could see."

"Not really. The sheds block the view from the yards on either side. You can't see in from the street. All you have to worry about is the other side of the river."

"What's over there?"

"A marina — nothing going on at night. The manager lives in one of those apartments behind it. Those two big buildings are offices."

"What about the bridge up there?" He pointed to a high concrete span arching over the river a few blocks to the west.

"That's right. Anyone crossing over at Twelfth Avenue can see down in here. It's a long way, but you can see. But it would just be a glimpse. People move pretty fast over that bridge."

"This really stinks. Any cop driving over there would see for sure. Not to mention the clowns in the apartments." He shook his head. "I'll bet you got sixteen dozen floodlights scattered around too, that you keep lit all night. This is the middle of goddamn town, you know?"

"I've got three six-hundred watt lamps back here. One of them's over this window. I could leave them off tonight."

"No way. Everything's got to be the same as always. Just have to wait till early morning and do it very quick. Once we get down in the hold we can unfasten all the boxes and stack them in the cockpit without being seen. You've got some kind of handcart or wagon, right? We'll throw them on the cart and drag them into the shed. It shouldn't take more than a minute or two. Do you know the cops around here?"

"No. I never have any problems. I keep the place lit up and there's not much worth stealing."

"OK. All right. Next item — it's too late to bring in the van now, and it would be stupid to do it tonight. So I'll drive it in here tomorrow morning, early — seven o'clock — load it, and get out. What time do your men show up?"

"Not before eight."

"Good. Let's hope we get that far. Be in this office, alone, at noon tomorrow. I'll call you then. The same for the rest of the week. If everything goes right, we'll be through by Thursday." He rubbed his eyes with his knuckles. "Thursday. Thursday, my ass. Well, I think we've done what we can for now. You better get going — you have to be at your place if that call comes through. You don't have to come back tonight if you don't want to — I could do this job by myself. It doesn't make any difference to me. If you decide to come, get here at quarter, after ten and don't park right out front. Leave it down the street a little way. You'll have to stay here all night."

Hula shook his head. "Wait a minute. How do you know I won't pick up the phone and call Rawden and tell him to come and get you? Why should I go through with this if I don't have to?"

"Don't ask me. I couldn't tell you. That's something for you to think about tonight. Keep this in mind — there are a lot of things that could go wrong."

"What's that supposed to mean?"

Cruz's face stiffened. "Just forget it, would you? We don't have time for this crap. I can take care of myself, understand?" He turned away and looked at the floor. "Now, is there anything else you can think of? Take your time — we've got all night."

"The hold is still full of chemical foam. We won't be able to work down there."

"We won't be there long."

"It'll take our skin off. Before I leave I'll wash it out. It's still early — there's plenty of light. Nothing unusual — I've stayed later than this lots of times."

"OK. Anything else?"

"Yes. How are those boxes attached? If Rawden goes through the hatch tomorrow, is it going to be obvious that something was taken out of there?"

"I don't think so. Four screws on each box. All that'll be left is the holes, and the wood's so dirty and banged up — no problem. You might show them to him, though. Remind him that he was too late."

Hula pointed at the gun on the desk. "What about that?"

"That's for you." He picked it up and tossed it in Hula's lap. "Have you ever used one?"

Hula turned it over in his hand. It was heavy and cold, and the barrel was slick with moisture. "No — well, once or twice. A long time ago."

"It's very simple. Just point it and shoot. It's an automatic. The safety's in back there — leave it on."

Hula eased the gun back onto the desk. "Keep it. I don't want it."

"No?"

"I'm too old for this stuff. Anything could happen."

"The only reason I'm offering it to you is because I think you're steady enough to use it right. I thought you might argue — I respect you for it. But you're going to need something like this. I guarantee you, if you don't take it now, very soon you're going to wish you had. And chances are I won't be around to help you."

"I said no."

Cruz smiled. "Let me tell you what we're up against." He picked up the gun and examined it. "First, the cops. That's including your friend Rawden. Rule one — you never, never, show it to a cop. You're pretty safe as long as you don't. If you do, they start shooting, and they don't miss. I don't think I have to tell you this.

"Second, there are the people I'm going to do business with. They think I hurt them, hurt them bad, and they're looking to punish me for it. I don't really blame them. Those are the rules. They'll kill me if they get a chance — you too, if it's necessary. They're in a bind — they can't afford to pass up what I have, but they can't stand to pay me for it either. Anyway, it's not a good idea to shoot at them, either, because our job is to keep them as cool as possible, and once the shit starts to fly they're going to have everything on their side. So don't do it unless I tell you." He put the gun back down.

"I told you I don't want it."

"I'm not finished." Cruz pulled out his wallet and laid it flat on the desk. On one side, behind a piece of cloudy plastic, there was a photograph of a man from the shoulders up. "That picture's ten years old, but it's all I have. Look at it." He picked up the wallet and tossed it to Hula.

A head like a block of beaten clay, massive and hairless, the bones hidden deep in the flesh, the eyes large, clear, and little too widely spaced; it was the head of a forty-year-old fetus. Hula closed the wallet. "Who is he? I know this guy."

"What? You know him?"

"No — I saw him this morning."

"Where?"

"Just outside the gate. He was sitting in a car, asleep, when I got here. Who is he?"

Cruz'd head was thrown back, his chin pointing at the ceiling. He had his hands over his eyes. He sat up slowly and gazed at Hula. "It's too bad, Ray. If I was with you we could have done something."

"Who is he?"

"I don't know. I've never seen him. I got that picture from a friend. All I know is that he's been trying to find me for nearly two years and that he's shot at me twice, in crowded places. He killed the guy who gave me the picture. I think he killed a girl I knew out on Alton Road, just because I spent the night with her. He had more than one chance to kill me, but he didn't. I don't know anything about him. Up until now, I didn't know for sure that he was here. It's like he's waiting for something. I can't sleep at night thinking about him." He fell silent.

It seemed to Hula that Cruz expected an answer, or a question, or any sort of response that might be interpreted as reassurance, as if he, Hula, had access to knowledge that had been withheld from Cruz. He didn't know what to say. "You must have made lots of enemies in New York. Maybe they hired him."

"Impossible. I would have found out, sooner or later. This guy is a stranger — he doesn't stick anywhere. Nobody knows who he is. I even got his prints to the police. They didn't know."

"Maybe he's after the coke."

Cruz laughed. "I wish he was. I'd give it to him. You know, it's not that easy to keep track of me — you found that out for yourself, right? — especially when I'm making an effort. But here he is, a year later, right behind me. He knows about you now, and what we're doing together. If he wanted to he could take it to the cops and finish us. Or he could try and deal himself in for a buck or two. Only he won't; it's not his style. All he ever does is kill people." He looked directly at Hula. "In fact, I wouldn't be surprised if you were next in line."

"So? I'm supposed to shoot him first with this?" He held up the gun.

"That's right. I can't protect you. It's your choice, of course, and maybe you don't want to start blasting away at strangers, but it's my opinion that it's the only chance you'll have — unless he decides to go straight to me. Then you'll have other things to think about."

Hula put the gun on the desk. "No."

"What — do you want to die?"

"If he was going to murder me, why didn't he do it this morning? And if he's so worried about being seen, why did he fall asleep in my parking lot?"

"I don't know, goddammit! If I was there I would have fucking asked!"

"I believe you, Michael. I just don't want it."

Cruz wasn't listening. He was mumbling and holding tight to the arms of the chair. He sat up, jerked open the top drawer, and shoved the gun inside. "I'm going to leave it there. You may change your mind. Enough of this crap." He slammed the drawer shut. "It's getting late. You better wash out that boat. I'll stay here. If I don't see you at quarter after ten I'll know you're not coming. Wear something dark, and don't sneak in — walk in like you own the place. And if you see that clown again, tell him hello for me. Tell him I'm waiting for him. Tell him anything you want."

Hula stood up heavily. "The lights go on automatically. Around eight-thirty."

"Right. Go on, get out of here."

Hula left the door open behind him. Outside the shed, the sun had dropped below the rim of the horizon and blue shadows were gathering in the low places. There were headlights crossing the bridge up the river; darkness was no more than ten minutes away. He dragged the hose to the edge of the water. At the marina he could see some people in bright windbreakers standing at the end of a pier and drinking. A girl's high laughter floated across the channel. It seemed like it was coming from a long way off. He went back to turn on the water.

» » »

A man sat uneasily in one of the hundreds of plastic shell chairs that are bolted, row upon row, down the center of the main concourse at Miami International Airport. Like so many others that sit in those chairs, he had absorbed the anonymity of his surroundings. He was between worlds, deprived of a context, and no one stopping to look at him could have told you more than the bare facts of his appearance. If the airport had not been so empty that night, he might have vanished altogether.

He wore a young man's business suit, a light gray, at once neutral and stylish, and the coat over his arm indicated a northern origin. An expensive leather suitcase occupied a pair of seats beside him; the tag on the handle said JFK. His hair was thick, black, and glossy. It was parted in the middle and pushed back over his forehead. Somewhere between twenty-five and thirty-five, he might have walked out of an ad in a magazine, an ad directed at the millions who could aspire to his vague aspect of wealth and mobility, except for the black stain that darkened the area of his right temple. It was as if a vein full of ink had burst under the skin and seeped outwards. A janitor coasting by behind his large carpet machine turned to look at the stain, his face empty and slack.

Another man, dressed like the first, a little younger and with lighter hair, approached and sat down beside him.

"Forget it. They're all closed."

"You sure?"

"It's Sunday night — they close early. We'd have to go out."

"No wonder there's no one here."

They sat quietly for a moment. Up and down the concourse, all the ticket counters were dim and empty. The escalators were frozen in place, the shops were dark behind their steel grills, and the noise of the blowers in the ceiling dominated the stillness. Here and there a few reddened vacationers sprawled atop their belongings, waiting for an early flight. The younger man rubbed his eyes.

"So what are we doing here?"

104

"Jack is due in at midnight."

"Who's Jack?"

"You'll see."

"So what are we doing here?"

The older man crossed his legs irritably. "We're looking for some-one. Do you know Michael Cruz?"

"Everybody knows Michael Cruz."

"Have you ever met him?"

"No."

"Don't underestimate him. He's not stupid."

They fell silent as a security guard strolled by, his keys clinking. The older man's eyes followed him. "Fucking brand new .45. Opens his beer with it."

"Why Michael Cruz?"

"He wants to make a sale. I'll tell you, they're pretty hot for him."

"Where'd he get it?"

"I don't know. None of my business."

"What are we up against?"

"Not much. All we have to do is find him."

"How soon?"

"Right away."

The younger man lit a cigarette and dropped the match on the floor. "Sounds to me like somebody fucked up somewhere. Somebody who should've known better."

"Sure. For somebody who doesn't know shit, you know plenty."

One floor beneath them Jack was standing by a baggage conveyer and watching a row of suitcases push their way through a rubber-skirted hole in the wall. The crowd was small and quiet. Jack was having a little trouble with the moist Florida air; he seemed to think he had to chew each mouthful thoroughly before he swallowed it. So he wasn't getting nearly enough, and you could see the irritation in his face as he struggled to keep up with his need. At last, when disaster was imminent, Jack discovered the key, or the secret, or whatever it was; his jaw dropped open, his chest expanded, and a great quantity of air rushed down his throat. By that time his suitcase had already gone by. He watched it drift down the line away from him and exit through another hole. He was a small, shrunken man, probably in his sixties, and his various qualities did not quite match one another, as if they had been borrowed from other people. His hands were smooth and knobby; his hair was pale, gray, and wispy, like an old man's; and his putty-colored suit might have originally belonged to someone three inches taller than himself.

A few minutes later he appeared in front of the two men sitting upstairs. His hard-shell vinyl case was heavy and his face was darkened with exertion.

"Let's get out of here," he said.

Import Duty

IF YOU HAD BEEN STANDING on the bridge at Twelfth Avenue at about eight-thirty on Monday morning, and if you had looked down the river to the battered collection of sheds on the shore opposite the apartment building and the tiny marina, you might have seen Ray Hula emerge from one of those sheds and walk out to the edge of the water with a folding chair under his arm. The sun was low and dazzling in the east, and he intended to catch some of it before the heat began. He pulled open the chair, bent down, and planted it carefully in the dust. Then he positioned himself in front of it and sat down slowly, like a man getting into a bathtub. It was something an elderly man might do, a man whose blood is cold and watery, so that he spends much time adjusting himself to sources of warmth, and if you had been standing on the Twelfth Avenue bridge you might have guessed that Hula was much older than he was.

At about 4:00 A.M. Cruz and Hula had descended into the stifling hold of the *Dart* and pried loose all twenty-eight boxes of cocaine. They reopened the hatch and stacked them on the floor of the cockpit. Cruz leaped ashore; he drew up the hand truck and Hula passed the boxes over the side. When they were done they went back to the shed, pulling the truck after them. For nearly two minutes they had been fully visible in the strong lamps suspended over that end of the yard. They might have been figures on a lighted stage. But the theater was empty; no one had seen them.

Inside the shed, Hula leaned against the wall and coughed violently. Cruz buried his nose in a handkerchief. In the hold, the fumes of old fish and chemicals had combined to nearly overpower them, and the stink still clung to their bodies. When Hula had recovered sufficiently to stand up straight, he pointed to his office.

"I've got some spare clothes. There's a hose down here. We can douse ourselves and change."

Cruz shook his head. "The ones we have — we'd have to put them somewhere. And then you'd have the water on the floor. Rawden will be here in a few hours."

"I'll think of something."

"No. We have to wait it out." He sat down on an overturned oil drum in a corner. He was wearing a black sweatshirt and sneakers. "If a cop saw us, or someone else reported us, they should be in here in ten minutes. If we were set up, they'll wait till we make the exchange." He was breathing heavily.

In the twenty years that he had owned the yard Hula had never spent a night there. It seemed to him that this omission represented a real failing in him, of one kind or another. He heard a rat scratching under a pile of rubbish. Two or three large birds were evidently roosting over his head; he heard a squawk and the sound of claws on the roof. He picked his way over to the stairs and sat down. Even at this hour the darkness was by no means complete. Streaks of brightness showed at the base of the walls, where the metal edged the rough oolite, and a meager glow crept in at the eaves. The piles of scrap in the rear of the shed towered over the shadows. Cruz's face, disembodied, shone like a dirty rag ten feet away. The sound of Hula's own breathing seemed much too loud.

It was his first opportunity to talk to Cruz. There was a lot that they might have discussed, starting with their mother lying in bed in that old brick house in Providence. But Michael wasn't interested in conversation.

As the night gathered towards morning Hula sat perfectly still and watched the first glimmerings of dawn sift through the wall of the shed. Objects revealed their textures — the corrugations in the roof, the pitted rock on the floor, the scarred steel housing of his power plant in the corner. Color returned to the yellow drum of fiberglass by the door. Within minutes the first shaft of sunlight brightened into being, shining between the blades of the fan in the uppermost vent and touching the far wall with a spot of gold. Cruz groaned and stood up. Bending over, he massaged the joints in his legs. When he was done he walked over to the stack of blue boxes on the cart and laid his hands flat on top of them, seeming to draw strength from their solidity. He looked at Hula.

"Six-thirty. Time to move." He peeled off his sweatshirt and dropped it on the boxes. The shirt he'd arrived in, pale blue and cotton, was hanging on the stair rail. Hula grabbed it and tossed it to him. Cruz pulled it on and stuffed the tail under his belt. He carefully placed his gun on top of the boxes. "That'll stay here for now. Go outside and open up the gate for me — leave it wide open, remember. When you come back I'll go and get the truck. While you're at it, look around — see if you see anything unusual."

Hula stood up and quickly sat down again. He had forgotten that his legs were asleep. He grabbed each one in turn and shook it. His feet dangled nervelessly from his ankles.

"Wait a minute," Cruz said. "Don't go out there till you're ready."

Hula went out anyway. He found that he couldn't slide the door shut behind him; he was weak as a child. He abandoned it and moved off. Turning the corner, headed for the gate, he saw his shadow leap out in front of him. It must have been thirty feet long. When he looked up at his destination he became immediately dizzy. He stopped, shook his head, and tried again, with the same result. It was a fact. He couldn't raise his eyes without losing his balance. For the rest of his march he kept his eyes fastened on his shoes.

The gate was a large rectangle of talon fencing about eight feet high, with a few slack strands of barbed wire strung along the top. It had a makeshift hinge which did nothing to support it. A loop of heavy chain secured with an outsized padlock held it shut. The key turned easily. He wiggled the bolt free and started tugging at the chain. It slipped free all at once and dropped to the ground like a leaden snake. He dragged it out of the way. The gate moved more readily than he thought it might. His strength was returning. Crouching, he grabbed the iron pole that stood at the free end and backed away to one side, pulling it behind him. By the time he started back for the shed his head had cleared.

Hula found Cruz standing just inside the entrance. "Gate's open."

Cruz nodded and put his hands on the edge of the sliding door. As it rolled out of the way the light fell cleanly on the stack of boxes. They were out of place; they didn't belong among the heaps of discarded wood and iron. Hula turned and looked at the marina across the river. The white-hulled yachts sparkled beside the narrow piers. A few sleepy gulls hopped from boat to boat, their wings half-spread for balance. There was no one in sight.

"I'm going to get the van." Cruz pointed at the boxes. "Keep an eye on them, would you?" He walked away.

In five minutes Hula heard the truck rumbling into the yard. Cruz wheeled around onto the apron in front of the shed and backed up to the door. The van was a tall and flimsy steel box with "Southwest Pest Control" painted on either side. Below the legend there was a simple drawing of a round-headed bug with a worried look on his face. Cruz stepped down from the cab and joined Hula in the building. He produced a key and opened up the van. Smiling, he looked at Hula. "Shall we?" he said.

He stood inside the truck while Hula handed him the boxes. Cruz was stacking them faster than Hula could bring them in. As he waited for the next one he snapped his fingers and drummed the walls. "Come on, old man. You're dreaming. What is this, slow motion?" The cases mounted higher behind Cruz's back. "You think it takes brains to load these things? Put your ass into it." Now Hula stood back by the wagon, heaving the boxes through the air. One of them caught Cruz full in the chest, nearly knocking him over. He staggered back, smiling.

When they were done Cruz stepped down from the truck and quickly shut the doors. He plucked a rag from his back pocket and dusted his hands. "Well," he said, "that was easy." He walked around behind Hula and snatched his gun from the wagon where it lay. Hula turned to find it pointed at him. "Bang," said Cruz, and kissed the barrel, murmuring a word into the chamber. He wrapped it in the rag and stuffed it in his belt. "OK. I'll call you here at noon. I may need some more help. Don't forget what I said about that piece up in your desk — it might come in handy. And you better get out a hose and wash down that boat again before Rawden gets here. He'll want to know why you stink so bad. The boat's yours, if you want it — a present from me. I'm proud of you, Ray. You've been good to me. So far, anyway." He reached up and laid his hand on Hula's cheek. Then he slipped out the door and climbed up into the van. He slapped it into gear and drove away, the limestone rubble crackling under the wheels.

Hula stepped out into the sunlight and blinked. The day was warming and he could smell the thin, acrid odor of the river. It re-

minded him of a thousand other mornings. In the still air he heard
trucks wheezing up the freeway ramp, the traffic honking on Flagler
Street, all the noises of the awakening city. Across the water, the
yachts at the marina were still gleaming with dew. He was tired; the
day before him seemed impossibly long. The one thing he didn't want
to do was to get down in the hold of the *Dart*. As he understood it,
the crisis of the last few days had ended when Cruz drove out of the
yard. He doubted if he would ever see his brother again. Michael had
come and gone like a ghost, and now that he was gone, Hula wanted a
chance to sit back and enjoy the feeling of relief and exhaustion that
was properly his. Certainly he was free to choose; he could ignore this
last hurdle, just as he could have ignored any of the others. But whatever he did or failed to do, the moment had been spoiled. He went
into the shed and dragged out the hose. It was heavy, cracked, and
obstinate. Twenty minutes later, when the job was done, he was sitting at the edge of the water in his folding chair with a disgusted expression on his face. He had lost part of a meal aboard the *Dart* and
the taste in his mouth had survived his attempt to wash it away.

Within a short while his nausea had given way to a profound leth-
argy, so that when someone came up behind him and tapped him on
the shoulder he took a little extra time to react. He twisted his head to
one side.

Silva walked around to face him. "Morning boss." He was smiling,
his red-brown face wrinkled as a dead leaf.

"Oh. You."

"You been rolling in something, boss?"

"What time is it?"

"What time is it? How long have you been sitting here?"

"I must have fallen asleep."

"It's about eight-thirty. Excuse me, sir, but you stink."

"I just washed out that boat we brought in yesterday. God, what a
job." Hula was dimly aware that he had to be careful about what he
said. He wasn't exactly sure why. His head began to ache.

"I think maybe you should see a doctor about that smell. When
you smell like that, you need a doctor."

"I want you and the rest of the crew to check out that boat this
morning. Pump the bilge, check for leaks, try the engine."

"I guess you're in some kind of hurry. That was nice of you,
cleaning it out for us like that."

"I get nicer every day."

Silva took a step back and looked across the river. "I hope you don't mind sir."

"Mind what?"

"It's not that I wanted to do it, or anything, but I thought that maybe I should be the one. I thought it might make things easier. He understood — you don't have to worry about it any more."

Hula sat up and grabbed Silva by the wrist. "What the hell are you telling me?"

The little man turned, obviously alarmed. "Geronimo. I called him up last night and told him he was through working for Miami Salvage — he said he was quitting anyway. It's all over with. I thought it would be easier for me — that's all." He looked down at the white fingers wrapped around his arm.

Hula let go. The blood thickened in his head. "OK. I'm glad you did it. Thanks."

"Any time. Any time at all." Silva was himself again, smiling and opaque. "Like I said, about that doctor. If you and a skunk had the last seats on the bus, I'd sit next to the skunk. And you know about skunks." He turned and walked away.

It doesn't matter what he thinks, Hula told himself — the coke's gone, it's all over. The sun was warm on his skin and it melted the knots in his muscles. He smiled and shut his eyes. How nice, he thought, how nice to be sitting in the sun and not rushing off after white powder and other obscure objects.

When he woke up he was warm and beginning to sweat. Silva, Murphy, and Alante were crawling over the deck of the *Dart*, their fists bristling with screwdrivers, tape measures, scrub brushes, and putty knives. There was someone standing beside him. It was Rawden.

"Hard at work, I see."

Hula rubbed his eyes. There was something on his knuckles that made them sting. "I was wondering when you'd get here."

Rawden's black, rubber-soled oxfords shifted as he looked at his watch. He had his jacket folded on his arm. "I didn't expect to find you. There's a scrap auction at the Port at eleven — an old lightship from up north."

"I can't compete for that stuff. I couldn't even get it up the river."

"Too bad." He looked across at the marina. "Well. What have you got for me?"

"Nothing. The boat's clean. Of course, we still might turn up something. We're not through with it yet."

"Clean, you say. I'd say it was pretty dirty until you cleaned it out."

"Yeah." How long had he known this man? "Someone had to do it."

"You've been through a lot on this one, haven't you? First you play fireman in the hold, and then this morning you go back down and wash out the mess. Aren't you the boss of this outfit? Can't you get someone else to do the shit work?"

"I can do whatever I like."

"Oh."

Hula noticed that some of the crew had stopped work and were looking at him. Silva's head popped out of the cabin. He shouted at the others. "Get moving, you scum! Show me some muscle!" He wielded an imaginary lash. In a moment he disappeared below again.

Rawden ignored him. "Why are you so sleepy on Monday morning? Have a big weekend?"

"The fumes in the hold — they took my wind away. I thought I'd sit down for a while."

"What did you find?"

"Some old tar buckets and fishbones. It doesn't look like anybody's been down there for years."

"I can see why. Let's check it out, all right?"

Hula heaved himself erect and made his way to the edge of the water. Rawden came up beside him. The *Dart* floated quietly at the slip. Murphy and Alante were in the bilge scraping grease from the engine block, their brown backs shining with sweat.

Hula pointed. "The hull is a single shell and the ribs are exposed. So everything between the hull and the deck functions as the hold. There's a platform built over the ribs starting just forward of the block. It's pretty cramped under the cabin but it opens up more beyond the mast — you can almost stand up down there.

"That collar halfway up the mast," he said, pointing again, "it probably supported a short spar at one time, that they used to drag the nets aboard. There's another hatch under it — they may have culled and boxed the fish topside and lowered the boxes into the hold. This boat obviously wasn't built for fishing — they had to adapt it."

Rawden turned and looked blankly at Hula. "Just tell me what you know."

"The hold is the only thing I've examined personally. Like I said before, it's wide open — there's practically no concealed volume. I didn't see any new wood down there. If I was going all out I'd tear up the platform and I'd drill some of the joists under the deck. I'd also check the floor of the cabin. As for the rest of the boat, I haven't looked at it yet. It takes a little time."

The customs man chewed thoughtfully on the edges of his tongue. "That's it?"

"So far, anyway. I'll know more after I talk to the crew."

Rawden put his hand around Hula's elbow and led him back toward the shed. Hula didn't try to shake loose; he was glad they were getting away from the boat. Rawden stopped just inside the door, out of the sun. He forced his hands into his pockets and cleared his throat. "Ray, I'm a little disappointed in you. Do you know why?"

Hula was suddenly very uncomfortable. He felt threatened by the dimness in the shed. "No."

"I'll tell you why. There's something about that boat that you should have noticed right away. Maybe you already did. Do you know what I'm talking about? Something about the waterline."

"No. I haven't had much time — "

"It's too obvious. You should have seen it."

Hula was quiet.

"All right. I'll tell you. You had three men aboard that boat, right? Say about five hundred pounds. But even then, you could see a little haze of algae just above the waterline. A quarter inch, maybe a half. Not much, but it was there — green, healthy stuff. In other words, that boat recently weighed a lot more than it does now. In the past week or two, someone did something to make it ride higher. I don't know what it was — could have been anything. Maybe the owner took some lead out of the keel. Maybe it had a leak. You pumped it out yesterday, right? Maybe that was it. Or maybe somebody jettisoned a good-sized cargo out on Otter Reef."

He coughed discreetly and went on. "When I was here yesterday I don't remember seeing that algae. I was tired, the light was bad, maybe there was still a lot of water in the hull. But this is the kind of thing you should notice. The newest man at the Port would have picked it up right away. We can't have someone over here all the time. That's why I depend on you to notice these things for me. But you didn't."

There had been time to prepare a response. "OK. I should have noticed. But when I check out a boat, I look for contraband, I don't look for waterlines. If it's there I usually find it. I know where to look."

"I thought you might say that. It's about the only thing you could say." Rawden coughed and shook his head. "I'll tell you something, Ray. We don't like to press each other too much at the Port — this business is nervous enough as it is. Just remember this — I'm your friend. You need me. With a little good faith, we can accommodate one another. I sit in an office all day, writing reports, and I don't get enough time to see what my people are doing. I don't have much confidence in a name on a piece of paper. Sometimes I get an order to let something past, or to yank one of my own men. I don't ask questions, I do it. There's only a few people left that I know well enough to listen to, and you're one of them. So when I come to you and I find that you're looking the other way, I feel like I'm starting to lose my balance. I've been around awhile, you know? I can't do it all by myself."

Hula was relieved. He took aim and kicked a pebble out the door and into the sun. "I'll do what I can. I like to think that I'm pretty good at it."

Rawden took a little while to answer. "Algae. Sometimes it's nothing more than that. You know, if I were starting over in this business, I think I'd work for the other side. I could have retired by now."

"It's not too late."

"That's what you think. You're either odds or even." He turned and looked at Hula in the face, his eyes jiggling a bit in their sockets, as if he were focusing too hard. "I've got to get back. I don't expect to hear from you. But call me anyway." He struck out into the light, his neck, hands, and ears instantly bleached by the glare.

At noon Hula was in his office above the shed, waiting for Cruz's call. It was right on time.

"Ray?"

"Whenever you're ready."

"How'd it go?"

"I didn't find anything. Looks like the boat is clean."

"What?"

"Don't laugh. It's a joke, but don't laugh."

"Let's take it easy, all right? Tell me what happened."

"He came and looked at the boat. He noticed that it was floating high — he said that someone had taken some weight off it recently."

"What'd you say?"

"I agreed with him. You could tell just by looking at it."

"What else?"

"Not much. I think he was suspicious, but he didn't push it. He only stayed a minute."

"OK. It sounds like we're clear. If they saw us last night, they probably would have squeezed you. I'll bet that guy is already thinking about next time. He knows how helpless he is."

"So it's done. I'm glad it's over."

"Not quite. For you, maybe. Call me around this time the day after tomorrow and I'll tell you what's happening. Hell, we're on our way."

"Think so?"

"Remember what I said about that gun. That hasn't changed."

"All right."

"Don't forget."

That was it. Hula sat and listened to the dial tone for a few seconds before he hung up. It had been a long time since he felt so free. Let Cruz and Rawden and all the rest fight it out among themselves. It didn't concern him anymore.

He turned and looked out the window. The crew had broken for lunch and had left their tools scattered over the *Dart:* drills, hoses, a mallet, a chrome-plated tape measure. That boat is an egg, Hula thought, a precious sea egg that has failed to hatch. For the rest of the afternoon his men would tap the shell and listen.

At this moment there was something that held him apart from his surroundings, a weightless transparency of feeling, nourished by silence and the discipline of inaction, which, as the light from the window flooded his head, he saw no reason to interrupt. So he wasn't thinking about the future, about the hours and days that lay ahead. It would be quite a while before he reviewed his conversation with Cruz. When he did, he would remember that Michael had told him to call in a day or two, and that this was impossible. Why? He didn't have

Cruz's number. And at that time he would discover in himself neither anger at his own stupidity nor relief in his inability to act. He would find, instead, something painful and unexpected. He would find that he wanted to see his brother again.

» » »

The Seahorse Motel had been recommended to Liberty by Mustache, the customs officer. "Not too swank," he said, "but convenient to downtown and the yard where your boat will be." It was on Biscayne Boulevard, a few blocks north of Bayfront Park. Liberty remembered watching the Orange Bowl parade from someplace nearby when he was eight years old.

Swank or not, the motel hadn't done much to improve his sense of security. The door to his room, for instance, had less wood in it than an average-size walnut. Just a light frame, warped inward at the top, surrounding an enormous shutter panel that shook whenever anyone walked by; he judged that it might be very difficult to knock on it without breaking it down.

The manager had a jowly bulldog face and red rubbery ears. There was a Russian calendar tacked up on the wall behind him, along with some prints of snowy landscapes full of horses and chimney smoke. Liberty was sitting in a plastic chair beside a dusty philodendron and a rack full of faded leaflets. About an hour earlier he had called Cruz from a phone booth down the street.

He had called Cruz to ask about his money. According to Michael it was still a few days away. Liberty had avoided any suggestion of trying to pressure Cruz, simply because there was no way he could do it. What did he have? A bogus passport, a new police file, about seventy dollars in cash, and a phone number. No guarantee that he would see any return on his work. Not even enough money for a ticket home. Above all, no control — no names, no goods, and nothing that might be traded away. He was at the mercy of events. Any further interest Cruz showed in him would be purely charitable. The obvious move, the move that Cruz probably expected, was to hang around the marinas until he could bum a ride back to the islands, where he could forget about the whole thing. He wasn't particularly angry at Cruz for dropping him; anyone who couldn't protect his own interests deserved to be abandoned.

But he was still here, still waiting. He knew perfectly well that if the *Dart* was searched they would find the coke and cart him away. At his interview on Sunday they had almost promised him as much. It was as if he wanted to make it easy on them.

Liberty got up suddenly and left the motel. Two blocks away he stepped off the baking rock of the sidewalk and into a phone booth. He pushed the door shut and the air in the booth, unnoticeable at first, began to press in on his eardrums. The quarter sounded wooden and distant as it stumbled through the machine.

It only rang once. Silence.

"This is Wally."

"You just called an hour ago. What is it?"

"Listen, I've had about as much as I can stand of this. I want to know what's going on."

No answer. Liberty waited. The less he said, the better.

"I thought you didn't want in on it. That's what you told me."

"I changed my mind."

"Look, I already set up the transfer. It's for Thursday. If we all start moving around we might miss each other."

"We might miss each other anyway." The heat in the booth made Liberty say things he hadn't planned on saying.

"Wait a minute. You know what we're dealing with. We're better than that."

"OK. It's your move."

"We're through negotiating, you know. We already did that, remember?"

"Did you unload the boat yet?"

"Yes."

"That's not why I called."

"All right. I could use you tomorrow. Meet me at one o'clock."

"Where?"

"Right where you are now. I'll fill you in then. Satisfied?"

"I need to know, Michael. You can understand that."

"You're going to be right out there where everyone can see you. Is that what you want? It's not as if you're a brand new face."

"Let me worry about it."

"One o'clock, then. If I'm not there I'll be here, where you can call me. We've come a long way."

"Me especially." He hung up and pushed his way out of the booth. I could still change my mind, he thought. I could leave right now.

» » »

Although the big house in Miami Springs looked like many others on the street, all you could see from the gate was a long driveway curving around behind a tall row of palms.

Inside, Jack was handing out bottles of beer at the head of the dining-room table. The clear green light of watered foliage just penetrated the curtains. The man with the stain on his temple was there, walking down the hall with a telephone. Jack snapped his fingers and pointed at someone, ordering him to go and find another ashtray. A small dog with a narrow face peered out at them from under a low chair. It pulled its lips back from its teeth and growled silently. No one went near it.

When they were all seated, excepting himself, Jack moved to the head of the table and looked at them. His eyes rested on a large, young, and muscular man who, like most of the others, had blue black hair and olive skin.

"Who are you?" he said.

"My name's George. I work for Mario."

"No. You're working for me." Jack sat down.

He was wearing a loud green suit and a striped tie. His head was wrinkled and nearly spherical, perched rigidly on his narrow neck, and tufted around the ears with clumps of colorless hair. He had an intensity that must have come from the green rims of his pupils, since the rest of his face was so dried and leathery that it could support no more variety of expression than a reptile's. His voice was as wizened and raw as his body. He pointed to the small sprightly man with the white jacket. "Peanut," he said.

"I got nothing."

"Tell us what you did."

He sat up and looked at the men around him. He was obviously uncomfortable. "Well — the main thing, like I said, is that nobody knows anything. There's nothing new coming in. Usually, at a time like this, you start to hear all this crap about a big load that's just about to hit, and there's always lots of stories. That's what it's like now. A lot of talk and nothing happening."

"What kind of stories?"

"You know — the Arabs bought all of it and they're waiting for a price, or the caterpillars ate the crop, or some jerk took the stuff and ran. You can listen to it all day long."

"So nothing's moving. And nobody's taking advantage of it?"

He shook his head. "Hey, it's worse than you think. For the first time in my life, these guys are glad to see me. They're sitting me down and pouring me drinks, as if I'm supposed to have something for them. The ones that think they're being cut off are trying to apologize, and the ones that are still getting a little are shaking my hand and saying they knew they could count on me."

"Do you know Michael Cruz?"

"No."

"Never heard of him?"

"Nope. What is he, Colombian?" The word escaped too quickly. Jack leaned forward. "Colombian. Why Colombian?"

The man's face was limp and sullen. "Just curious. It's a Latin name."

"You have a Latin name. Ramón has a Latin name. Everyone in this goddamn city has a Latin name. Why Colombian?"

"It's not what you think."

"Don't tell me what I think. Answer the question."

"Well — everybody's got the idea that the Colombians are holding out. That's what everybody says."

"You know as well as I do that the Colombians run this business."

"I just thought that maybe if you were looking for one of them — a Colombian — then maybe the trouble was starting over here. Maybe the city would change hands. I just wanted to know."

Jack had closed his eyes and was tracing circles on the table with his forefinger. Someone coughed. The man called Peanut was beginning to look smug, having found refuge in the banality of the truth.

Jack roused himself. "All right. You don't know Michael Cruz. That's what you said, right?"

Peanut nodded, a little reluctantly.

"In the next twenty-four hours I want you to find out everything you can about him. That means going to see all your friends again. Make it clear that we are very interested in this person. Call here every few hours and tell us what you've got. Anything that might lead us to him, call us right away. Someone give him the number." A man sitting next to Jack scratched on a piece of paper. It traveled quickly down the table. "If you don't have anything for us we'll know that you're not trying hard enough. It might affect your future. So don't waste any time. Any questions?"

"Yeah. Who's Michael Cruz?"

"He's just a name. Now get out of here."

Peanut got up slowly, encouraged by his own boldness. "How do I get back to town?"

"Call a cab. Take the bus. Walk."

When he was gone some of the men stretched out and crossed their legs. Jack's voice lost its edge of irritation.

"OK. We've all been here a few hours and we've all had a chance to learn something. Before we start I want to hear what you've done so far. Arthur." He turned to the man beside him, the man who had written the number.

Arthur, who looked as if he'd done it many times before, wiggled his jaw and cleared his throat. He was wearing expensive gold-rimmed glasses.

"He wasn't stupid enough to stay at any of the houses down here. No one's seen him for months. So I've been checking the hotels. About a week ago, someone calling himself Michael Cruz moved out of the Seventy-ninth Street Holiday. He'd been there four days. Turned out it was probably him. No one remembers him having any guests or talking to anybody. At the time he was driving a black Thunderbird with New York plates. I don't know where he went from there. I'm still looking."

Jack turned his gaze on Arthur for a little while. "Not good enough," he said. "From now on, concentrate on the five or six best hotels in town. Put a man downstairs in each of them. If I know Michael, he wouldn't settle for less." He looked at the man with the stain next to his ear. "Ramón. Tell us about the Thunderbird."

"It's sitting in a garage in Hialeah. It belongs to a guy named Stanley who runs a body shop. He's done work for us before. He said the cops are looking for it and he's going to take it apart. Cruz brought it in six nights ago and wanted another car — he gave him an old Camaro. Dark green, two-door, Florida license 83LOP."

"Wait a minute." Jack looked at the ceiling. "I want all of you to remember that number. 83LOP. Think about it for a minute. Write it down." There was a brief rustling of paper. "Now. If Cruz had money to burn, he wouldn't have wanted a trade. He would have bought a car somewhere else. So there's a good chance he's still driving this car.

"The police are looking for the Thunderbird because it was seen at a house on Alton Road a week ago, about the time a girl was murdered there. It doesn't sound like Cruz, but it's a possibility. I've know him long enough to know that he likes to screw around wherever he is. So any of you that know the local girls, call them up and see what you can find out." He smiled bleakly. "Jamie. What have you got?"

He was the best-looking man at the table; healthy, tanned, and boyish in his vested suit. His face might have lacked character without that hint of ironic glee he had picked up by loitering outside courtrooms.

"The police have been looking for him for a week and they don't know anything. There haven't been any big arrests for coke lately. Not very surprising, considering."

Behind his glasses, Arthur looked particularly sour.

"Anyway, given the size of the move, I had to assume that it came in by water. So I got a photocopy of the register at the Port for the last week and a half." He reached into a briefcase beside his chair and tossed a heavy sheaf of paper on the table. A whiff of chlorine momentarily sharpened the air. "The DEA codings are on the left-hand margin. Morons take note — any number over thirty-three indicates special interest, and a possible followup. Anything over forty-three and the boat is probably clean. Not much gets by at that level. I think we can disregard the commercial entries — from what I hear, Cruz doesn't have the connections, and a load this size would attract too much interest. Of course, I'm assuming that he's not the leading edge of a group of Colombian bureaucrats and fruit shippers." He paused a little longer than was necessary. He was waiting for Jack to say something. Jack, however, was not given to speculation.

Jamie continued. "So what we're looking for is a private yacht, twenty-five feet or larger, entering from the Bahamas or points south. As you know, it's very risky nowadays to run a boat of any size past the Coast Guard, and I'd say the one we're looking for is probably on that register." He nodded at the papers. "It's possible that a transfer was made at sea, and the load was brought in on a local boat — in that case, we probably won't find it. But that means he had to hire somebody in the area. So we might hear about it that way.

"Coming from the other end, we know that Cruz has been absent from New York for about eight weeks. We're assuming that he spent part of that time in Colombia. However, our friends tell us that no American named Michael Cruz has entered Colombia since last winter. Therefore it's likely that he was moving under another name, and I have a few people checking out the paper mills to see if they remember him. If any of you have ever picked up passports on your own, come and talk to me later. I don't want to miss anyone." He fell silent as an old man with a bad cough entered from the next room — the housekeeper. When he got to the head of the table he handed Jack the folder he was carrying and shambled away. Jack glanced inside, laid it down in front of him, and looked at Jamie. "Go on," he said.

"That's about it. Unfortunately, a search like this takes a lot of time. The feds have already been after him for a week and a half."

"What you mean to say is that you haven't got anything."

"Nothing yet."

Jack reached out and thumped the pile of documents with two fingers. "No one has time to read that crap. Put it away." Jamie held his briefcase up to the desk and slid the papers inside.

Jack settled back in his chair. He had taken off his zippered nylon jacket and his thin, white, and freshly ironed shirt did nothing to conceal his frame. His forearms were sticks of dried kindling, yellow where the bones of wrist and elbow rubbed his skin. Up close, the healthy reddish tones of his face separated into tiny clots of gray, pink, and blue purple.

At the other end of the table the man in the lime polo shirt was fidgeting. He had wrapped a rubber band around the stem of his thumb and was watching it swell and darken. He wasn't listening very closely; he had delivered the folder that the housekeeper had brought in and his responsibility was ended. When he glanced up and realized that Jack was speaking to him he answered without missing a beat.

"Yeah, I know him."

Jack had opened the folder and was holding up a large black-and-white photograph. "Who is it?" he said.

"It's Michael Cruz."

Jack shoved the folder into the middle of the desk. He waited until everyone had a copy of the picture. "All right," he said. "It was eight years ago when I first met him and he hasn't changed much since then. He's not a good businessman. He's half PR and he doesn't feel comfortable anywhere. I'm not going to go into the whole thing with the Knapp Commission. I'll just say that the cops knew even less about him than we did and he came in handy at the time." Jack didn't enjoy speaking at length. He let the words fall without emphasis.

"Cruz was never given any real responsibility. And since they didn't have anything on him he was always on the outside. The point is he liked it that way.

"So all this talk you've been hearing about Colombians is pure crap. He'd be the last guy in the world for something like that. Too many people, too much work, too much attention. Forget the Colombians. We're not going to learn anything from them.

"We're working on the assumption that he has exactly what he says he has. If he didn't, he'd have no reason to make this kind of offer — he knows we won't pay him for nothing. So the hardest part of his job is over. He's got the stuff, and it's safely inside the country. Now listen very carefully. We are not interested in Cruz. The only reason we're here is that we want very badly the stuff he's offering us, and we'll gladly pay him for it if we have to. Got that? He's not our enemy. This is no scalp hunt. We're ready to give him everything he wants." He looked around the table. "Do all of you understand that?" His eyes rested on the other end. "George, you look confused. Do you understand it?"

George returned Jack's stare. He nodded.

"Then you understand it?"

"Yes."

"What? What do you understand?"

"That our job is to make sure Cruz gets what he wants."

"Exactly." He leaned forward and whispered. The men had to strain to hear him. "Anyone who makes problems at all for Cruz is going to suffer for it. I'll see to it personally." He sat back and rested his arms on the chair.

"OK. I can tell you a little about Michael from my own experience. This picture we have is pretty good. He's got that stiff black hair, narrow face — he looks about thirty. He's about five-nine, maybe one-fifty. He likes to dress well. Don't expect to surprise him. He knows what we're doing — he knows as much as if he were right here listening to me. Look what he's accomplished already — he stole a ton of coke, got it out of Colombia, across the ocean, and into Miami. He can do a lot of things.

"I believe that Cruz is working alone — not just because it's the safest way, but because he never would have considered anything else. If you knew him you'd know what I'm talking about. You may have heard that he never got anywhere with us because he's a PR. That's garbage. Or maybe because he was always talking to the cops. Hell, we loved it when he talked to the cops. We knew that he was giving them the same brand of shit that he was always giving us. They've been listening to him for years, and now that they're looking for him, they can't do a thing. So take my word for it. He's got maybe two or three people working with him. No more.

"Up until a day or two ago he was still able to use our name and our resources. This guy Stanley, for instance. But now that the word is out he's lost all his flexibility. Anything could trip him up — a parking ticket, a flat tire — he's already made his plans and he's got to stick to them. This is going to make him very nervous. Whatever we do, we've got to avoid making trouble for him, because if he gets spooked and starts to run there's no telling what'll happen. I don't want to hear that one of you has got him shut up in a hotel room, or that you ran him off the road on 95. It would be better if you never found him at all, than if you found him and he knew that you found him." His eyes, bright and sharp, traveled around the table.

"Later on, after the transfer, there'll be plenty of time to cut him. Until then you better keep your hands to yourselves. If you don't you're going to wish you had.

"That's all. We've got no more than forty-eight hours until the exchange — probably less. Now get out of here."

If Jack's speech was intended to inspire the men with enthusiasm and desire, there was no sign that it had succeeded. After a brief interval they struggled out of their chairs and passed quietly from the room, their shoes leaving streaks in the carpet. Jack remained seated and watched them go. He might have been an old judge exiled to traffic court; aware that his powers had waned, but determined to hold tight to what was left. When they were all gone he took up the picture in front of him and examined it. Opening his mouth wide, he reached in and stratched at a back tooth with a fingernail. His brow furrowed momentarily. The sound of the cars starting up in the driveway barely penetrated the foliage and the heavy curtains.

More than ten years ago he had recommended that Michael Cruz be taken on as a courier for the bachelor circuit. At that time Jack had been impressed by his alertness and reserve. Within six weeks Cruz had thrown a network onto the island and was drawing fire from three directions. Though it was another year before Escobar finally gave up on Cruz, Jack had already started to speak out. It would be inaccurate to say that he disliked Cruz, and Michael had never tried to blame his eventual fall from grace on anyone but himself. But Jack had noticed that recent events were having a queer effect on his state of mind, beyond the natural increase in tension; he was floating on a high of oddly vindictive anticipation, broken here and there by fits of drowning melancholy. His equilibrium was threatened, and he discovered that the cool place at the center of his head demanded a lot of fuel for maintenance. He opened a newspaper someone had left and started doing the crossword puzzle. In a little while the calls would begin to come in. They were bound to turn up something.

Bad Sleepers

Rᴀʏ Hᴜʟᴀ — citizen, businessman, and high-stakes smuggler — spent most of the next afternoon sitting in his office and listening to the rain pound the roof over his head. The uncertain light outside the window, the water trickling from his slicker by the door, and the cool, humid air in the room combined to give him the impression that he inhabited a small and somewhat leaky bubble.

The storm had begun at midmorning and he had sent his crew home at lunch. The pile of papers on his desk received no attention; their significance eluded him. All the excitement, he decided, had ruined him for any real work. Real work. Real life. The real Ray Hula was long gone, leaving no instructions.

By two o'clock the rain on the roof had drummed his brains into a sweet and pliable slush. The footsteps on the stairs failed to alarm him; he was vaguely curious. A large pale shadow appeared behind the frosted windows of the door. Pale knuckles rapped the glass. "Come in," he said.

He had seen this man before. An expensive, light-colored raincoat hung from his monumental shoulders. He was wearing a white shirt, khaki pants with cuffs, and safety shoes. It was the man he had seen sleeping outside the gate. His head was as large as a basketball and had even less hair. Drops of water gleamed as they ran down his brow and temples. Hula couldn't think of anything to say, or of any reason to say it. For the moment he was content just to stare. Whoever this is, he thought, he is impressively packaged. He made the office seem very small.

"Ray Hula?" Though the man's smile was broad and triumphant, there was something painful about it, as if the necessary muscles were a little stiff. Hula nodded. He tried to smile also.

The man took a step forward, swung the deck chair around behind him, and sat down. It didn't make him seem any smaller. "I've been wanting to talk to you," he said.

"Who are you?"

"My name's Apnes." He shrugged his way out of the raincoat and gazed eagerly at Hula. His wrists and forearms had a swollen, pickled look; they were too big for his hands. "I want to talk about Michael. Michael Cruz."

"Who's he?"

"You know — your brother. You helped him unload all that coke the other night. I've been looking for him for some time."

"I can't help you."

"Maybe not." He seemed pleased with himself. His body radiated heat and humidity. He was slowly coming to life. "Why did you do it? What did he tell you?"

Hula said nothing. His stomach started to gurgle.

"You don't have to tell me. It's none of my business. He probably threatened you, waved his hand in your face. I know him a lot better than you do. Don't look so surprised. Don't you know who I am?" Hula's silence didn't seem to annoy him. He had plenty to say.

"My real name isn't Apnes, of course. Just like your name isn't Hula, and Michael's isn't Cruz. That's one of the things we have in common — we don't have real names. It's not our fault, but we have to suffer for it. I'm not complaining." A drop of water ran into his eye. He rubbed it away. "He told you about me, I guess. He told you to watch for me, right? He doesn't trust me — he thinks I'm trying to kill him. So it's hard for me to get in touch with him. But I think I've done pretty well. Here you have the police and his friends turning over the whole city looking for him, and I'm the only one who knows about you. Why is that?"

He didn't wait for an answer. "You'll have to admit that this gives me some kind of advantage. Certain questions don't bother me any more. Michael has finally gone in way over his head — he won't be able to avoid me any longer. All his strengths have become weaknesses. You must have talked to him recently — does he seem like a man who knows what he's doing? Just looking at you, I can tell how desperate he is. You're afraid of me. You think I'm dangerous. All these lies he told you — I can see them in your face. Michael has never been able to tell the truth about anything. He's made a life out of dodging it." He smiled at Hula, capping his knees with his wide hands. "I can tell he's been here. Something about this place — do you mind if I ask you a question? What did he say about me?"

Hula studied the man's flat, smooth forehead, his dark-pupiled eyes, the dry, bloodless ridge of his nose. The image of the gun in his desk kept floating into his head. He tried to force it away. No one was going to be shot. The rain above his head soothed him. Hula decided not to answer any questions; the man seemed happy enough talking to himself.

"Don't look so gloomy. You know, I feel comfortable with you. This is the first time I've been to Miami and it's just like I expected it to be. Your cruddy apartment, this office, all those boats rotting at the pier — I could swear I've seen it all before. If you knew what I know I think you might have come to the same conclusions. Whatever Michael told you, it's all wrong. We've got nothing to argue about. He probably said that I've been hunting him down for years. That I've tried to take his life. That's what fear does to you. I'm not denying anything — if Michael wasn't so frightened of the truth, this would have been over long ago. You know what I mean? Your opinion matters to me, Ray. I have a lot of respect for you. What I have to do isn't easy, but somehow I know that whatever happens, we will always agree on one thing. I won't tell you what it is." A sly grin; Hula got a good look at it. The man went on.

"Did you know I met your friend — your friend Lisa? She seemed like a nice woman to me. If I had the choice, she's the kind of person I could live with. I only talked to her for a minute, but I could tell she cares about you. But not too much — that's the important thing. She would rather lose her lover than give up her sense of perspective. That takes a lot of courage. Hate, war, disease — all the forms of evil — they're everywhere because people can't see outside themselves. They do whatever their chemicals tell them. They get inside their cars, roll the windows tight, turn on the AC, and smash into each other. They think they're good at what they do. I see it happening all the time and it's just like a silent movie — everybody's talking at once and you don't hear a sound. They lie in bed at night and manufacture enemies. 'I don't smoke or drink,' they say, or 'I will never wear polyester,' or 'Our African policy must reflect certain responsibilities' — they'll do anything to set themselves apart so that their anger won't go to waste. When they get tired of punishing themselves they're ready to punish someone else. When it's all over it's time to make excuses. 'We had bad advice,' they say, or 'We were mistaken.' But they hate to make excuses. They make them for each other, not for themselves. Somehow they remember everything."

Hula discovered himself nodding in agreement. The man had been speaking rapidly and was out of breath. This is easy, Hula thought, I just sit here and listen. "Who are you talking about?" he asked.

"You and me. People in general."

"Then what do you suggest?"

"I don't suggest anything. I know what I have to do."

"What's that?"

"Murder Cruz."

Hula twitched. "Are you serious?"

"I'm determined, if that's what you mean."

"But why? You were just saying —"

"I don't have to explain myself."

"This doesn't make any sense. If I —"

"What did Michael tell you about me?"

"He said you'd been following him. For a long time. He said that —" Hula cut himself short. Cruz's story had sounded so ridiculous. Now, for the first time, he was ready to believe.

"So he told you. I thought so." The man was speaking very quietly. "And did he offer an explanation? Did he say why? Why I would want to kill him?"

Hula locked his teeth together. He was through talking. Something in the man's manner convinced him of the extremity of his situation.

"He didn't tell you? I didn't think he would. You've got enough to think about already." He smiled; he'd become aware of Hula's distress and it seemed to please him. He drew his chair up to the desk and rested his chin on the edge, cushioning it with his hands. When he spoke his jaw remained in place and his face bobbed up and down. Hula had trouble listening to what he said. There was a jar full of pencils at Hula's elbow and he wanted to feed them to him.

"I'm not going to tell you why either. I'll leave that to Cruz. Of course he may be dead before he gets the chance. I've been waiting a long time for this opportunity and I won't let it escape. As a matter of fact, Ray, I'm a little surprised at you. I thought you'd be grateful."

Hula had opened the drawer, taken out the gun, and was pointing it directly at him. The barrel trembled an inch from his nose. The man was cross-eyed from looking at it. When he glanced up at Hula his expression was heavy with remorse and sympathy. He sat up quickly and twisted the gun away. Hula's finger had been caught behind the trigger; he winced. At the same time he looked a little relieved.

"I suppose Cruz gave it to you," the man said, "a sop for his conscience. I'll tell you something. Never pull a gun unless you intend to use it. Now let's just forget that it happened." He held out the gun across the desk. Hula stared at it stupidly. "Go ahead, take it — I'm not a thief." His eyes narrowing, Hula accepted the offer, like a dog taking a morsel from a stranger. The gun was heavy and uncomfortable in his lap. He put it back in the drawer. "What do you want from me?" he said.

"Nothing, really. I just wanted to meet you. Also, I wanted to find out what Cruz had told you about me. He seems to have made a convert out of you. Well, now that you've had a look at me you can judge for yourself. If I were you, I wouldn't go out of my way to do him any favors. They'd all go to waste. Like I said, he's going to die. I'll kill him with my own hands. And I'd appreciate it if you did nothing to interfere — you'll only make it worse. You've been working with him on this big drug marketing project, very dangerous and illegal and so forth, and you're not really prepared for what I have to say. But my advice to you is to sit tight and wait it out. When Cruz goes he's going to take all your problems with him."

The phone rang. Hula snatched it to his ear. "Miami Salvage."

"Ray, this is Michael."

Either the man heard Cruz's voice, or something in Hula's expression informed him of the fact, but he seemed to sense immediately what was happening. He leaned forward and wrenched the receiver from Hula's grasp. He pinched it between his head and shoulder.

"Hello, Michael," he said. "Good to hear your voice." Meanwhile he was waving wildly at Hula and pointing at one of the desk drawers.

Hula, still wondering what had happened to the receiver, did not respond. The man half rose, clenched one large fist, and again waved at the drawer.

"That's right, Michael," he said.

135

Hula shrank down in his chair. Then at last he understood. He brought up the gun and put it on the desk. The man seized it and a look of impossible glee spread across his face.

"Michael, don't plead with me," he said. "I've got only one thing to say to you." Turning, he held the receiver out from his body, aimed, and fired. Splinters of black Bakelite snapped against the walls and dropped to the floor. Hula's ears rang. A gash on the man's forearm oozed red. He examined the mouthpiece; a few scraps of bright metal. Smiling, he put it back on the hook. It slipped off; he had to balance it more carefully. "Looks like I'm going to get wet," he said. He laid the gun carefully on the desk.

As he was turning to go out he stopped flat-footed halfway through his motion. His eyes opened wide. He swiveled his head around and looked at Hula, or at least in Hula's direction, because all his senses were concentrated on an inward shock that was moving swiftly toward his brain. His eyebrows traveled up his forehead and apprehension constricted the muscles around his jaw, so that his mouth vanished into a dark and irregular hole in his face. He lunged at the pistol, held it up, aimed it directly at Hula, and fell to the floor like a rotten tree.

After a moment Hula leaned forward and looked over the edge of the desk. The man's eyes were shut and his expression was peaceful and composed. His chest rose and sank evenly. A ball of dust was pasted to his lower lip. The gun still lay in his hand, his finger jammed against the trigger. The most remarkable thing about him, Hula decided, was his sheer size; his thighs were as big around as telephone poles. Hula sat back and stared at the space where the man had stood, trying to absorb the fact of his absence. The phone rang again. It was Cruz.

"Hello Ray? This is Michael. You all right?"

"He had some kind of fit. He's on the floor."

"Answer me. Who is this? What the fuck is going on?"

"I'm all right. I'm OK." There was no response. An electrical storm was somewhere in progress; he could hear it crackling on the wire. Then Cruz's voice again, spent and empty, one word at a time.

"So it's you. Stay right where you are. I'll be right there."

"Michael — wait a minute!" Hula nearly cut himself on what remained of the mouthpiece. He heard the dial tone buzz. He listened to it for a while and hung up.

In a minute or two Hula got up slowly and walked around to the front of the desk. The man was still stretched out on his side, exactly as before. Hula bent down, grasped the pistol firmly by the handle, and yanked. There was a very loud noise and a window in the door shattered. Hula jumped back and sat down hard on a pile of cardboard boxes, banging his head against the wall. Suddenly the man was on his feet again, looking at Hula. Ray was too scared to move. The man glanced down at the gun in his hand, threw it in a corner, grabbed his raincoat, and rushed out of the office. Hula heard him running across the floor of the shed. The back of his skull was beginning to throb and he barely managed to get up and make his way to the chair under the window. He felt the pain as a kind of relief. Only a few minutes of rest, he told himself — that's all I need. He tried to shut his eyes but the lids kept flying upward.

By the time Cruz arrived at the yard, a half hour later, Hula was gone.

» » »

The chief offices of the Drug Enforcement Agency in Miami now occupy one of the upper floors of the justice building, an aging skyscraper built before the advent of the glass box, when a squared column of stone could still inspire a sense of the weighty presence of a national government. Today, forced to look at its own reflection in the massive sky-colored planes of the downtown banks, the building's willingness to reveal its form seems almost innocent, and the terraced pyramid that caps the structure is a childish denial of necessity. A good-sized flock of vultures inhabits its uppermost ledges and cornices, having resisted all attempts at removal, and they glide in slow circles around the higher floors, while the people in the outer offices point them out to visitors. Rawden knew all about them and he didn't bother to look up as he got out of his car and crossed the wet street to the main entrance.

He had to examine the directory by the elevators to confirm his destination; behind the glass, the movable white characters reminded him of the ease with which entries could be juggled and dropped. Rawden hadn't been to the eighteenth floor for quite a while — he had reached that point in his career where his superiors were no longer particularly concerned with his activities, and on those few occasions when they had something to discuss with him, they usually did it over the phone. Typically, the bloodhounds at the Port viewed the DEA leadership as an irritating but necessary buffer between the real working edge of the agency and the media playground in Washington. If Rawden's intelligence did not allow him to share this prejudice — he refused to consider some activities more "real" than others — he was still quite aware that the officers in the justice building recognized a different set of signals and procedures than that to which he was accustomed. Here the filaments of power were less obvious and more flexible, and he knew that if he held up the rulebook, as he so often did at the Port, it would be snatched out of his hands. Of course, in his current situation, the rulebook wouldn't have helped him anywhere.

There was no hallway; he stepped out onto a dazzling blue carpet about the size of a squash court and bounded on two sides by a pair of nearly identical secretaries sitting behind highly polished desks with chrome legs. They looked a bit embarrassed, as if he had interrupted a conversation. One of them yawned self-consciously and the other started a dictaphone and turned to her typewriter. Rawden became aware that neither of them were going to acknowledge his presence and that there was no point in remaining any longer. He walked down the carpet between them and passed through a narrow doorway. As soon as he was gone one of the secretaries looked at her watch and made a note on her blotter.

He remembered that the office he was seeking was in the southwest corner of the building, and he had to force a route through a few empty conference rooms and auxiliary kitchens before he found it.

"Come in, come in. Have a seat." Big smile, outstretched hand. Rawden dropped into a bottomless vinyl chair that squeezed his knees together and pointed them at the ceiling. It was quite a while before he felt safe enough to loosen his grip on the arms. He was looking up at a corner window, whose purplish tint gave the rainy sky more color than it deserved. The door shut behind him and a tall graceful man sat down at the desk beneath the glass.

"So how's everything?"

"Excuse me?"

"So how's everything? Enjoying the weather?"

Rawden recalled that this man had made a career out of youth and optimism. He didn't answer. A large acrylic painting on the wall diverted his attention. The surface was covered with bright rings and circles; some of them round, some of them not quite as round.

The young man coughed. "Look, I don't mean to ignore the critical nature of this meeting. We've got a lot to discuss. I've been hearing about you ever since I got here and I never thought I'd have to call you in. You're the best we have. So tell me what happened — I want to hear it from the source."

"I acted within my authority. I did what I had to do."

"Hey, relax — I'm not here to take evidence. We can get this straightened out very quickly if we're frank with each other." He had a boyish, engaging smile that was the object of much grumbling and resentment. "Can I get you something? Cup of coffee?"

"No."

"I guess you heard about that garage sale we broke up in Hollywood. Four hundred pounds, Jamaican. They were so scared they were giving it away. It was Howard, one of your old trainees, that made the buy."

"So what?"

The personnel director inclined his head and scratched his eyebrow with his thumb. "Well — what I'm trying to say is that we've always been happy with the way you bring up your agents. They've got an outstanding record. So we've always accepted your recommendations knowing that your advice is better than anything we could come up with ourselves. Maybe we gave you a little too much freedom. I'll say this — whatever the result of our discussion, it's very unlikely that your decision will be allowed to stand. We can't afford to demoralize a whole generation of our people. In other words you better have something good."

He took out a yellow legal pad and put it on the desk. "This morning you tried to dismiss eleven men, all junior inspectors working under you. Your entire staff. So who bought them? How'd you find out? Whether it's true or not, you picked a hell of a way to break it to us."

"Nobody bought them."

The director didn't conceal his relief. An hour earlier he and the other division heads had agreed to keep a lid on this thing for as long as possible. "Nobody bought them, you said?"

"I don't think so."

"Then there's no argument — we can't fire them. They've all got five years."

"I don't care what you do with them — I just don't want them working for me."

"But you're the senior inspector at the Port. Who else can they work for?"

"It's your job. You'll think of something."

"Of course." The director smiled. A recent political appointee, he was having trouble being as severe with Rawden as the situation required. With proof of corruption, Rawden was a dangerous insider; without it, he was no threat at all. "So what happened? Why did you do it?"

"I didn't trust them."

"Then you should have tried to collect some evidence. Now they know what you think."

"That's not what I mean."

"Then what the hell do you mean?"

Rawden had a lot on his mind. "I'll tell you why," he said. "But really, all you have to do is look at them. Watch them practicing their tennis strokes in the break room. Watch them sniffing up a yacht full of girls. Go to the airport and watch them pulling out some poor slob with a half ounce of dope in his shoe. They look pretty grim, but they don't care. This morning I was sitting in the office with a pile of reports and one of them comes in and asks me if he can be photographed for some consumer drug magazine. He was out of breath — he'd just run in from the gate. He was ready to stand on his head for this guy.

"You don't know what's going on out there. I send in my totals every week and what do I hear? We're running ahead of last quarter in X substances and we beat out New Orleans and Jacksonville for the regional lead. We turned over eighteen cases to the prosecutors and we've already got half a dozen pleas. What does that have to do with anything? There's so much stuff coming in that we could arrest just the grandmothers and do just as well. You can't turn around without tripping over a felon — we wave them in and they laugh at us. There's no relation —"

"Wait a minute. I don't want to hear this garbage. You better have something better than this."

Rawden ignored him. "It's just a game for them. They'll pass up the obvious one to get at some guy who's got a gram of coke packed against his eardrum. The law doesn't mean anything — it's just a tool. Now that the volume of trade is hitting the roof, they're having a field day. They can pick and choose. Take this new man Lutz, for instance. He doesn't like Puerto Ricans. I've been watching him. It's been weeks since any Puerto Ricans got through. The last guy was a rich tourist who came in on a chartered fishing boat — he didn't even have to stop, he'd never left the coast — but Lutz spent all morning tearing up that boat until he found a couple of joints the guy's son had dropped down the sink. It doesn't make any sense."

Rawden knew that he was talking too much. He could tell that the young man wasn't listening anymore. But Rawden hadn't expected to be taken seriously. He took a strange sort of pleasure in trampling on what remained of his credibility. He was absolutely sincere.

The director shook his head. "Then why are you complaining to me? Shouldn't they be the ones to hear all this?"

"You can't tell them anything. I've tried. They know how secure they are. Last week I called them all together and said I wasn't happy with the way they were choosing their targets. Since they were allowing their prejudices to influence the spread, I told them that we were going to start distributing the intensive searches on a random basis, keyed to the number of letters in a vessel's name. They didn't like it. They said it took away their freedom to follow up on their nonevidentials. That's just the point, I said.

"So we tried it for a few days. You'd be interested to know that in spite of their gripes, our discovery totals shot up during that period. But they were against it from the start, and after a while I learned that the timesheets they sent in didn't have much to do with what was actually going on out on the dock. They were picking and choosing again — jumping on this one, waving that one through. So I canned it."

The young man nodded. "I sympathize with them. It seems to me that this random system of yours deprives them of those skills you went to so much trouble to teach them."

"Yeah — I was aware of that. It was only a temporary thing. But don't you see? The point is that they defied me. I wasn't able to guide their decisions at all. They followed their own noses. That means that anyone who becomes familiar with their habits, in one way or another, will then be able to cruise through the Port as if it was the goddamn Bahama customs. And anyone who has the bad luck to trip over one of their specifics is going to get held up over and over and over. Those traders aren't amateurs. Any edge we give them, they're going to take advantage of it. Unless we come up with some system that distributes the spot checks more evenly, and unless I have the authority to maintain that system, the Port is going to get so leaky that they'll make a point of entering here."

"I don't agree. Our totals have been very good lately. I don't see any sign of slippage."

"Totals don't mean a hell of a lot — not in the long run. The only reason we're finding so much is that they're piping it through here like water. All we get is the accidents. I'd say our percentage of total traffic is lower than ever."

The young man started writing on the pad in front of him. "It's a matter of opinion." He dropped the pen. "So far you haven't told me a thing. Everybody has complaints. Yours sound reasonable enough. But it's not reasonable to use them as an excuse to fire eleven men. Is there anything more I should know? Anything more substantial?"

"Yes," Rawden said. "We're not accomplishing anything out there. We're just playing with ourselves — we're a bunch of freelance bloodsuckers. All we do is work off our own bullshit fantasies — lick my boots, we say, and maybe we'll let you go. And we're supposed to be the law."

"Our resources are limited — we can't get everybody."

"No — just the ones that ask for it. The ones that look at us funny."

The young man waited for a minute before he spoke. "I hope you're not waiting for me to drag out the official cynicism. I believe in what you're trying to do. I also believe you can overcome this problem if you consider it sensibly." His voice was calm and soothing. He sat up and looked out the window. A vulture soared in close at eye level, brought its legs forward, and flapped out of sight over his head.

Rawden stirred. He was extending his arms and tugging at his sleeves. It was pointless, he realized, to expect this boy wonder to understand what he meant. How some went to jail, some were shot to death, some were commended by Washington. More grist for the mill.

"I want to ask you a question," he said. "How much do we know about the *Cimmerian?*"

The director frowned. "I don't want to talk about it."

"It's been a year and a half since we started watching it. That's a long time."

"I haven't been involved in the project. I'd say you know more about it than I do."

"Doesn't it seem odd to you that it's still out there? They keep telling us that they think it's involved in the trade, and every chance they get they search it top to bottom. They keep a detailed record of its movements, they take photographs of everyone on board — but none of it seems to have any effect. If they were really that eager, don't you think they would have come up with something by now?"

"The thought's occurred to me. Maybe they're building a case."

"Do you really believe that?"

"I don't believe anything without proof."

"Then I don't suppose you believe all this crap about a billionaire smuggler or Cuban exiles either."

"It's an unusual ship. There's probably an unusual explanation for it." A wan smile.

"Right," Rawden snorted. "Did you hear about this character the *Cimmerian* took off Otter Reef the other night?"

"I just got back from Washington yesterday."

"They brought him into the Port the next morning. I thought he deserved some attention. But your friend Joshua told me to let him alone — he said that their work on the *Cimmerian* had priority. That was OK with me. But I was a little curious and I said that I didn't give a damn about the *Cimmerian* and that I was going to hang this guy if I could. Joshua suddenly got very mysterious. He said that it wouldn't be a good idea. I said why not. He said it wouldn't be a good idea. So we danced around a little more but he didn't have anything else to say. He's your boss, isn't he?"

"That's right."

"Was it his idea to have me come in and talk to you?"

"As a matter of fact, I volunteered."

"Why?"

"Because I wanted to hear what you'd have to say. And I was the logical choice."

"You and he work pretty closely, is that it?"

"You guessed it. We conspire against everybody else."

Rawden was feeling a little light-headed. "I could tell you more," he said.

"You've told me a lot already. Have you reached a decision?"

"About what?"

"About those eleven men that you tried to fire this morning, every one of whom was hired on the basis of your advice."

"What do you suggest?"

"I don't suggest anything. It's up to you. Maybe you can persuade them all to quit."

A long pause. Rawden had been acting on impulse all day; now he began to realize the fact. An idea suddenly occurred to him. "Look, what you want me to do is rescind my order, right?"

"I think that would be the best thing for both of us."

"OK, I'll do it — provided you do something for me."

The director looked as if he'd just noticed an unpleasant odor. "I'll consider it. Don't expect any miracles."

"I want a transfer to the section that's working on the *Cimmerian*."

He stiffened. "That's impossible. I don't have the authority."

"Like hell."

"You'd have to put in an application. You'd need a full security check."

"That's bullshit. You know it, I know it."

The young man wished he had asked Joshua to this meeting. But it was too late now. It would look like he was running for help. "Face it, Arthur, you're already hanging on by your fingernails. You're in no position to make terms." He tried to sound mild and impersonal but his nerves kept creeping through.

"No," Rawden said. "You don't understand. Eleven men fired at the Port — that's big news. It could be embarrassing."

"Not eleven men — one man. Everyone knows that the pressures here are intense."

"They'll know a lot more when I'm through. There's a lot to tell."

"If you read the papers, you'll remember a few criminal indictments at the CIA for just that sort of thing." This is wrong, the director thought, all wrong. You're letting him get to you.

Rawden returned to his point. "I made you an offer. Are you listening or not?"

The young man took a few moments to think it through. It doesn't matter, he reminded himself, whether Rawden is bluffing or not. What matters is whether I can keep him happy. "I have too much respect for you," he said, "to make promises I can't deliver. But misunderstandings like this happen fairly often. Don't kid yourself — there's a place for everybody."

"You said it. Even the jails are crowded."

"Look — we both know that you've earned your pension and you only have a few years left anyway. You can do what you like. But don't suppose that you're going to persuade me to fire you, because I'm not going to give you the satisfaction. This is all your show, and you're going to close it out." He shook his head. "I wish I knew what you want. Since you —"

"Tell me about the *Cimmerian*."

"Not that again. You're dreaming."

"Tell me about it."

The young man abandoned his cool manner. "You think you're missing out on a lot — that nobody will tell you what's really going on. I'll give you a little advice. Don't go around trying to unmask people all the time. I get the impression that you're convinced there's some big secret up here — you think it's being hidden from you. But you'll find that things often make a lot more sense if you're willing to accept them at face value."

"I asked you about the *Cimmerian*."

"Use a little common sense. If they were anxious to get rid of this boat, don't you think they would have succeeded by now? They have a lot of cards they can play."

"So you're saying that the boat is government owned?"

"You're damn right I am. I generally like to keep my notions to myself, but I feel safe telling you. You won't believe me anyway."

"How would they fund something like this?"

The young man laughed. "That's too easy. Why don't you ask me something difficult."

Rawden noticed that one of the bulbs over his head was buzzing faintly. "If you put me in the section I'll find out for you."

The director decided he'd held out long enough. "All right," he said, "I'll give it a try. I'm doing it because I think you deserve a second chance — you've been around a long time. We'll meet with Joshua and the others and I'll take your side. But I'll need something

145

from you in return." He had no intention of lending Rawden any real support — the man was obviously unbalanced. He didn't expect to deceive Rawden either. However, he didn't know what else to say.

The conversation was losing its interest for Rawden. He realized that the die was already cast; there was nothing left for him at the DEA. His decision to fire his entire staff that morning, which had seemed so petty and melodramatic even as he did it, now made perfect sense to him. He had needed to free himself for action. The man calling himself Ralph Richmond was still in Miami. There was no time to lose. "OK. I want a two-week leave."

"We'll call it a vacation."

"Right."

"What about the firings?" The young man was reviving.

"A mistake. I'll see them when I come back."

"Can I issue a retraction in your name?"

"Go ahead. Schaedtzer can take over for me."

"Whatever you say. I'm glad you're beginning to develop a reasonable outlook on this. I really am." He was standing up, his hand extended across the table, but Rawden was already at the door. As he went out he banged his hip against the door frame. The elevator was waiting for him in the outer office, and when he stepped inside he thought he felt the floor give a little under his weight.

» » »

"Why are you looking for him, anyway?"

She was leaning over a black formica table in a booth at the Sheraton Four Ambassadors bar. The room was cushioned in darkness, sealed in vinyl, and haunted by the scented passage of cocktail waitresses in sheer dresses. It was the kind of bar that tries to create an atmosphere of eternal night, totally removed from the progress of time, and since the bar was located at one of the newest and most expensive hotels in town, where the insulating properties of money are well understood, the effect was largely successful.

She was pushing her hair back and shaking her head. "I couldn't say. I'm not here that often." There had been a moment, about a minute previously, when Jack might have said something better than "You wouldn't understand." Something equally disingenuous, but also bearing a spark of sexual tension; something she could react to. Now it was too late. She was trying to look bored.

Jack was aware of his age and appearance. He knew that the women who found him attractive were guilty of unusual tastes. So it was hard for him to recognize those few occasions when he was required to play the wolf. He could still do it if he made the effort, but what irritated him was the realization that there had been a time when it had taken no effort at all — when he hadn't even known he was doing it.

"Any more questions?" Jack flinched, his head snapping erect. In the process of uncrossing her legs she had kicked him, not gently, on the knee. She smiled and pushed herself to her feet. The bartender watched her go, fading around a screen of thick greenery, and looked at Jack. Jack was ordering another scotch from the waitress.

He didn't enjoy showing photographs to women in bars. He would much rather have been out in the lobby, where he could see something, but he couldn't afford to have Cruz run into him. On the other hand the lounge, dark as it was, was really no better — here there were so few people that, if Cruz walked in, Jack could hardly have gotten out unnoticed. When his drink arrived he wasn't thirsty anymore. He was trying not to be too angry at himself. He knew that he belonged at the house, taking the calls, watching the bank, and keeping everyone informed. The excuses he had made up on the ride into town no longer impressed him, and now he took the opportunity to demolish them at leisure. The lack of time before the transfer, for instance. It put a premium on immediate action, and he had allowed himself to think that if he went out and added his own skills to the mix it might be just enough to make a difference. Now it was obvious to him that the lack of time could queer any information they might find unless he acted on it instantly. And if he was sitting in a bar next to a pay phone he was a long way from the center of things.

Jack buried himself a little deeper in the shadows along the wall and started in on his drink. There wasn't much hope. It was going to come down to a free-for-all after the transfer, like the old days, and someone was bound to get his picture in the papers. The Colombian treaty would crumble under the pressure — everyone in Cartagena would want to know where all this coke had come from — and the reaction against the remaining American partners would make him into a fat target for some ambitious young man. Maybe even Ramón — Ramón would have to prove his loyalty somehow. Jack knew that he had missed his own chance long ago. If he had looked ahead in the late sixties and married into one of the families, he might have had some kind of a future. Now he was caught in between; his standing with the Colombians would evaporate, and his friends from the old days had been calling him a traitor for years.

Cruz was sitting on what was probably the largest single shipment of cocaine ever to enter the U.S. There was no mystery about where he had got it. One of the chief topics at the winter negotiations in Bogotá had been how to deal with the loss or disappearance of most of the export crop, a result of the mountain war. Since no one had any real knowledge of where it had gone, the various parties agreed to make public the extent of their inventories, in the interests of detente, but these totals had amounted to less than a third of a normal year's production. The figures naturally bred universal suspicion. Everyone privately believed that much larger supplies had survived the conflict and that some of the people who were complaining loudest had managed to quietly put away large portions of the missing balance. In the U.S., where demand was still climbing, the shortage could possibly double wholesale prices, and even a relatively small cache might be worth a fortune. But as the year progressed it had become apparent that few outside sources were bleeding into the new system, and the conviction spread that very little hoarding had actually taken place. In a few months the effect of recent crops would reach the American market and prices would stabilize. By that time the release of a large stock would not be especially rewarding.

Although Jack's bosses made a point of telling him no more than was strictly necessary, it was easy enough to guess what had happened. Cruz had called someone, probably Mario, and managed to convince him that he had X hundred pounds of cocaine hidden away somewhere. Mario went to Escobar and repeated the story. Escobar, for once, had looked beyond his own immediate advantage; he had realized that as far as this deal was concerned, he could afford anything but success. If he suddenly appeared on the dry market with an enormous pile of coke that he had bought or stolen from Michael Cruz, all the other hidalgos in New York would cordially agree to tear him to pieces. After thinking it over he had decided that the most attractive alternative was to ignore Cruz entirely. But the coke was too valuable, and Michael wouldn't go away, so he had picked up the phone and started calling his rivals. They had a meeting soon afterward. It was the first time they had seen each other since the winter talks.

Subsequent events gave Jack a reasonable picture of the compact they had arranged. Since he was still taking orders from Escobar, they must have decided that they didn't have the time to coordinate a large common effort — petty jealousies would cripple it anyway — and they had appointed Escobar to handle the mechanics by himself, using his own soldiers and having the right to draw on their resources when necessary.

As for the money, Jack could tell by the way the bank was being handled — four men, each responsible for his own security — that the funds had been raised by subscription. It was likely that the coke would be divided on the basis of the individual contributions, whether or not the cash was actually spent. The large sums involved were making everybody very nervous. Right now, in New York, Escobar was probably peeking out the curtains and telling his kids to shut up. There would be at least six different people watching his front door.

The only thing that puzzled Jack was his own selection as head of the search and transfer. Though he was the logical choice, as Escobar's longtime chief advisor, they might have been expected to find someone whose loyalty was less strictly professional. Jack was aware that he'd always been regarded as an outsider, even within Escobar's own circle. He could imagine what Surtano and some of the rest thought of him. The only explanation was the overriding influence of that fact that had undoubtedly been introduced first as the prime objection to his appointment — the fact that he knew more about Cruz than any of them. In their temporary rearrangement of priorities they had put the chastisement of Michael Cruz first and banished all other considerations to the periphery. They all knew that Jack had spoken against Cruz's admission to the winter talks. They also knew, from hard experience, that increasing isolation had hammered Jack's pride into a formidable dedication to results. A good part of their resentment was due to his habit of making everyone else look unprepared. Jack had lately begun to realize that his value to Escobar, however great, might eventually be outweighed by the bad blood he seemed to engender between his boss and the rest of the community.

So they had chosen Jack because they thought he could do the job.

Jack himself wasn't so sure. He could finish the transfer smoothly enough, if it came to that, but they wanted more — most of all they wanted to prove to everyone concerned that Michael couldn't wholesale Colombian products to Colombians. They were willing to take some large risks in order to demonstrate it conclusively. Jack didn't look at it that way; in his opinion, Cruz had taken advantage of a unique situation abroad and had succeeded in bringing into Miami some highly valuable goods, which he was now willing to sell at a reasonable price. The set of circumstances that allowed him to do this would never recur, and no one would profit by his example. It made more sense to pay him his money and let him disappear than to chance loss of the coke and widespread exposure by hunting him down with a private army. Cruz was wanted by the police and they could be relied upon to keep him quiet.

These thoughts led nowhere and Jack suddenly got tired of them. He got up quickly, flipped a bill on the table, and left. In the lobby he called the housekeeper and told him he was coming. There was no news.

When he got back to the house, his nerves pulled taut by the rush-hour traffic, he found the front door locked. George, still wearing his lime polo shirt, answered the bell. He'd worked with Cruz in New York; Jack had grilled him about it the day before. The man didn't move out of the way when he saw who it was. So he's still hurting, Jack told himself.

"Thanks," Jack said. "What was your name again?"

"George. My name's George."

"OK, George, thanks for answering the door. Can I come in?" George stepped back and Jack brushed by him, headed for the kitchen and a cold drink. The housekeeper was standing by the counter, where he had laid out a row of scraps of paper. When he saw Jack he picked one out and handed it to him. Jack studied it for a minute and went to the phone. The housekeeper had missed his afternoon nap and was moving slowly. He wrapped his cloth robe tight around his shoulders and made his way out of the room, sliding one foot after the other.

Jack dialed the number on the note. It rang once and Escobar answered.

"Go ahead."

"This is Jack. What's up?"

150

"Where were you when I called?"

"Out. I'm back now."

"Have you found him yet?"

"No."

"Why not?"

"A lot of reasons. Is that why you called? To ask me that?"

"They remembered him in Cartagena. They said he left the country in an old fishing boat about ten meters long."

"Wait a minute." Jack laid down the receiver and crossed to the other side of the kitchen, grabbing a yellow pad and a pen off the counter by the sink. As he picked up the phone with one hand he was scribbling with the other. "Go ahead."

"It was old and wooden and painted white. It was a sailboat. It was crudely made and very ugly, they said. Nobody remembers the name."

"Can't they get it from the customs record?"

"The people who remember him aren't customs. They're local police."

"What else?"

"He had one companion. They say he was young, very fair, and very handsome. They both had American passports."

"When did this happen?"

"About one month ago."

"We need a picture of this boat."

"They're sending someone on a plane to Miami tonight. He'll have a drawing with him. He's going to arrive on Pan Am flight 502 at 11:00 P.M., wearing black sneakers and a T-shirt with Muhammad Ali on the front."

Jack didn't answer until he had finished writing. "Good. We'll get him. I wish I knew who this other guy was."

"They said he looked like an American."

"I'd say he was someone Cruz hired to help him with the boat. A professional, probably — a pilot from the dope trade."

Escobar said something unpleasant in Spanish.

Jack looked at his watch. "Are we going to get this other guy's name from the police in Cartagena? He might have used it again."

"I think I would forget about him. It would surprise me if he entered this country at all. The boat is more important — a boat like that is difficult to hide."

"You're right. This is just what I needed. You haven't heard from Cruz yet, right?"

"Nothing."

"That's good also. No distractions."

Escobar grunted. "What have you learned? Are you making progress?"

Jack wished he had looked at the other notes before he made the call. "We're about a week behind him. We've got a license plate."

"One week? He was in Miami a week ago?"

"That's right."

"No. He would not have waited five days before calling us. He must have brought it in more recently than that."

"Maybe he did. But who says he did it himself? This other guy — that was probably his job."

Escobar was quiet for a moment. "This is all the news I have. As you know, we sent down this American, George, with the pictures — he once worked with Cruz. I don't think he knows anything."

"He's an idiot."

"I hope you'll find some use for him. Is there anything else I can give you?"

"I could use Roberto. He could do a lot down here." Roberto was Escobar's son, the heir apparent.

"Impossible — he must stay with me."

One more guarantee, Jack thought. "That's too bad."

"Yes. We'll learn what we can about Cruz from here. But I expect you to perform in this situation with the excellence and skill you have shown in the past. I expect you to win."

"Of course." Jack was a little startled. Escobar had never threatened him before.

"You must have seen that they're watching you as closely as myself."

"They can do what they like. I know what I'm here for."

"I'll call again tonight."

"Right." Jack hung up the phone.

The other notes were disappointing. Ramón had checked the garages at the Plaza, the Omni, the Sonesta, the Royal Biscayne, the Americana, and the Diplomat in Hollywood — all negative. Arthur reported that he had put a man in all of these and a couple of others.

Arthur himself was downtown at the motor vehicle office. Jamie said
he was talking to some friends at the Port. Jack guessed that Jamie
had already tried to sell Cruz's old license number — the number for
the T-bird — to the police, to see if they knew anything worth
knowing. Of course they already had that number. Jack was aware
that the cops would hear about the search very quickly — it was unavoidable — but he wished Jamie wasn't so eager to deal with them.
They rarely gave anything away.

Jack raked up all the messages and logged them in order on the
notepad. When he was done he crumpled them together and glanced
around the kitchen, looking for the garbage pail. Seeing none, he
snapped open the cabinet doors under the sink. The housekeeper was
tidy; there was a large roll of paper towels mounted on one door and
the trash can had a fresh liner folded over the rim. Jack's mind was
elsewhere and he acknowledged these facts without actually noticing
them, but as he leaned down to drop the wad of paper he saw that the
can was half filled with beer bottles, and he stared at them for a moment before straightening up. They hadn't drained nearly that many
at the meeting. So George's belligerent stance at the front door had
been reinforced by a couple of quarts of Budweiser.

Jack found the key in his pocket and unlocked the liquor cabinet.
Though there was no guarantee that the boat would lead him to Cruz,
Jack was pleased that he at last had something to work with. He
would call the men back to the house as they phoned in, all of them
except Arthur's plants at the hotels, so that they could all see the
drawing tonight and get some rest for tomorrow. Jamie knew a lot of
people around the Port; he'd be particularly valuable.

He could hear the TV going in the office at the other end of the
house — George again. Even though he'd never met him before,
Jack knew George pretty well. George was slouched in an armchair,
the lights off, gazing glumly into the tube, not really watching it, but
grudgingly accepting its attempts to distract him, while he nursed his
wounded ego.

Underneath his contempt, Jack concealed a mild and ironic affection for George; not so much for George himself, but for the type he
so dependably represented. George was proud, stupid, greedy, violent, and totally predictable. Jack knew he couldn't count on George's
loyalty — he would fall away immediately if Jack's authority lapsed —

but since George had no will of his own, and reacted only to the most unambiguous signals, it was impossible not to know the point at which he became no longer reliable.

Thinking about George led Jack right back to Cruz — the contrast was unavoidable. Cruz had always made Jack nervous. His meaningless jokes, his predatory weakness for girls, and his sudden anger had alarmed Jack from the beginning. Jack had tried to ignore these signs because he recognized Cruz's ability and he hoped that gratitude would make him a useful ally. Cruz had quickly divined the terms of this bargain and he lost no time in stepping all over them. By the time Jack withdrew his support it was already too late. Cruz had a gift for skipping rungs; when Jack told Escobar, in passing, that he had decided to drop Michael Cruz, Escobar said that it was a good idea, because he needed Cruz for a couple of jobs that would take up most of his time. Jack didn't say a word. He never found out how Cruz had contacted Escobar; there were other men in the network who had worked for him for years and never learned his name. Cruz didn't last very long with Escobar either. Jack was now and then tempted to ask Escobar how useful his Puerto Rican had been. He never did. They both knew what had happened. There was no point in talking about it.

If Cruz now and then proved, as in his appearance before the Knapp Commission, that his talent was much larger than the demands he usually imposed upon it, this never resulted in any real alteration in his status, because word had gotten around by then that he was only good for a couple of weeks at a time. But Jack had seen something else in Cruz, something visible only at close range. It was a variety of fear, Jack had guessed, that made him suddenly get up and walk out of a room in the middle of a sentence, or lie compulsively and at length about trivial events. He was constantly in motion — shaking his head, abandoning one chair for another, picking up and handling everything within reach. Jack remembered a visit to a bar in Englewood where Cruz had ordered a hot cheese and pepper sandwich, and instead of eating it he had spent twenty minutes rearranging the contents according to some private system that he was apparently unable to satisfy, because he had finally abandoned the effort and pushed it away. In the meantime he had devoured five or six small bags of potato chips.

Jack had finally concluded that Michael was just too unsteady to be offered anything more than an occasional odd job. But to satisfy his own curiosity, and to give Cruz a chance to make a case for himself (or at least to make up some excuses of his own), Jack had decided to ask him about it. They were sitting in a car outside an apartment block in Jackson Heights, waiting for someone who probably wasn't going to show up. They could both stand to sweat a little, Jack had thought — it was after dark in January and there was ice in the streets.

"Why do you want to be in this business? You like freezing to death?"

Cruz expelled a little air to indicate amusement; a puff of vapor whitened and vanished.

"If I were you I'd try something else," Jack said. "In a few years the Colombians will have it all. Most of it, anyway."

"So what?"

Jack let the remark hang for a moment. "Where'd you say you were from again?"

"Boston."

"What's wrong with Boston? They don't like Puerto Ricans?"

"They can have it."

"Not big enough for you, I guess. I'll ask you again — why do you want to be in this business?"

"I want to be like you, Jack. You're my hero."

Jack would have to push a little harder. He didn't mind; it was like dangling yarn in front of a kitten. "You'll probably have to spend a few years locked up. When you start out, they get something on you right away and then they send you up two weeks later — just to see how you'll take it. You think you can handle that?"

"I've been there before."

"For what?"

"For getting caught."

"I'm not interested in your sense of humor. If you don't want to talk to me, just say so."

No answer. Cruz seemed preoccupied. Jack wondered just how much more obvious he could be. He was convinced that Cruz knew how his silence would be interpreted; the problem was to make him admit it. Jack took a pair of soft leather gloves out of his pocket and started putting them on.

"Those tricks you pulled last week brought us a lot of grief. Everyone wanted to know who you were. We said you were right off the boat and didn't know any better."

Cruz dipped his head graciously, like someone acknowledging a compliment. Jack ignored it.

"I'm not saying ambition is a bad thing — you've got to have it, no question — but you also have to have the confidence of the people you're working for. If they don't know how long your string is then they're going to cut it and see." He was watching Cruz's face closely and getting a little irritated. Cruz was acting as if Jack had already made up his mind and there was nothing to be gained. Although this was indeed the case, Jack didn't like to have his decisions anticipated. He decided to finish it quickly.

"It's too bad, Michael. You looked pretty good to me."

Cruz put one foot up on the dash. "Jesus Christ, where the fuck is this guy?"

When Jack learned, a few days later, that Escobar had recruited Michael for private use, his surprise was tempered with a small degree of satisfaction. For one, it was now clear why Cruz hadn't bothered to talk to him in the car. Jack was also certain that Escobar would can Michael in no time at all; Escobar demanded absolute loyalty and respect from a new man, even in appearances, and Cruz just wasn't the type.

Jack still remembered the touch of pleasure he had felt upon hearing of Cruz's fall from grace. "Bad luck," Cruz might have said; Jack called it stupidity. To suppose that recklessness, presumption, and the deliberate cultivation of ambiguity might lead quickly to the top was naive, and to try and put that belief into practice was a solid gold guarantee of failure. At least that's what Jack told himself. The fact was, if Cruz had succeeded he would have shown that all Jack's concessions to the hierarchy of power were self-defeating — that his long service to Escobar, for instance, had earned him nothing but contempt — and that the only index of authority was the number of men you could afford to throw away. And although Jack thought of himself as an impartial scourge, a public prosecutor, an instrument of a larger purpose, and was determined to observe the law in his pursuit of the lawbreaker — this is why he put retrieval of the cocaine before the punishment of Cruz — in the furnace of his will another picture was forming, a picture that included only Cruz and himself, as everything else had become abstract and burned away. Without Jack's knowledge, this picture was seeking to reproduce itself in actuality. If it ever succeeded he would know what to do.

The last man to call in was Jamie. He said that the police didn't have Cruz's new plate number yet and that no tickets had been issued to it. "Forget it," Jack said. "Get back here right away. I've got something to show you."

» » »

Tuesday night. Hula is stretched out naked in his bed with his head on the edge of the sheet. The material is cool and dry; he has spent the evening going back and forth to the washing machines at the end of the building. Earlier he had phoned Silva and told him to take over at the yard for the next few days. He didn't offer any explanation. The only person he will talk to is Michael, and Michael hasn't called.

He now realizes that he should have stayed in the office until Cruz arrived. It's obvious that Michael is through with him and is solely interested in the large-headed man. The next place he'll see Michael, Hula decides, will be the six o'clock news.

It's after midnight and he is thinking about what happened at the office. None of it makes any sense. Like Cruz, it's just one of those things he's going to leave out when he starts his life over again in the morning. His difficulty in falling asleep doesn't bother him. He's very comfortable on the clean sheets in the familiar room and he wants to savor his rest. His mind travels aimlessly among the events of the past few days and he smiles at the embarrassing moments. All in all, he didn't do so badly. He hopes Michael will escape from the mystery man. He wishes he could do something for him. The last of the three Libriums he borrowed from Norton dissolves in his stomach and he begins to snore.

A few miles away, on the sixteenth floor of the Omni Hotel, Michael Cruz is still fully dressed. He has been in his room since 7:00 P.M. He twists the dial on the TV, adjusts the curtains, and chronically examines himself in the mirror. There's a pile of newspapers on the chair by the bed. On top of the dresser is a large pencil diagram he has drafted on the back of a shirt cardboard. He has just shined his shoes and he wants to go down to the bar, but he settles for a magazine and a glass of ice water.

He undresses slowly and gets into bed. He is wide awake. He plays absently with the remote switches for the TV, noticing that the volume doesn't go nearly as high as it should. He clicks it off, pushes himself forward, and lowers his head slowly back onto the pillow. Although the sheets are cool and dry, the air almost chilly, his feet are beginning to sweat. Something Jack once said returns to mind: "Waiting is the hardest — if you can teach yourself to wait, you can teach yourself anything." Cruz has been waiting for sleep since Friday night, and his body is as exhausted as his mind is active. Sparks, images, and faces shiver and bolt across his consciousness faster than he can recognize them. After a while he stops trying. His arms are at his sides and his backbone is as brittle as ice. Just after he drops off his muscles suddenly relax, but he remains absolutely still. He won't move again until morning.

When Cruz drove to the yard late in the afternoon, looking for Hula's visitor, he didn't stay more than five minutes. If, after leaving the office, he had decided to search the area, he might have found the bald-headed man sitting behind a stack of mushroom anchors in one of the rear sheds, where he was resting after his recent encounter, since the excitement had made him as sluggish and secretive as a wounded animal. He remained there until well after dark. At about 10:00 P.M. he got up and felt his way to the door. For the next couple of hours he occupied himself with a leisurely tour of the yard, taking care to stay away from the lights and out of sight. Every room without a lock, he entered; he identified and examined every length of fence along the perimeter. He got into Hula's office by knocking out the broken pane in the window and reaching in for the doorknob. Ray's personal possessions seemed to have a special interest for him. He tried on a nylon windbreaker he found on a hook — he could barely get his fists through the sleeves — and he thoroughly excavated the confused mass of papers on Hula's desk, even though there was too little light to read. A peculiar caution showed itself in his determination to leave everything as he found it. He came upon a couple of curled snapshots in the back of the middle drawer, held them up to the weak brightness by the window, and blew the dust away. One of them he recognized as Lisa Bishop; the other, also a woman, was new to him. The file cabinet by the door was locked, and he ran his fingers over every horizontal surface in the room, in seach of the key, but he didn't find it. No loss — he didn't seem to care. He was like a man who's been kept waiting too long and who, out of boredom and impatience, begins to catalogue every detail of his surroundings.

When he was done he sat quietly behind the desk for a while. Now and then he squinted at the electric clock on the wall. At 2:00 A.M. he got up and left the office, making his way carefully down the stairs in the dark. He stood just inside the door of the shed, blinking at the bright circle of light in front of him. The floods brought out all the whiteness in the limestone. Several puddles, like pools of gray paint, were left over from the storm. Outside the circle, in the apartments across the river, a few windows still glowed orange, or green or blue, depending on the curtains inside; otherwise there was no sign of life.

He stepped out of the shed, walked quickly to the edge of the water, and jumped down into the cockpit of the *Dart*. The rim of the embankment cut off the light from the yard and he was nearly invisible. Crouching, he felt the floorboards with his hands; they were dry. He turned and stretched out on his back. Seeing that a corner of the sail stuck out under the cabin doors, he yanked them open, swept up an armful of damp synthetic, and matted it under his head for a pillow. He still wasn't comfortable; he grabbed some more of the sail and spread it over his body. The cockpit was just large enough to accommodate his entire length. The level floor beneath him enforced a kind of symmetry in his posture, and his chin and toes pointed directly upward. He laid his arms at his side, palms flat against his legs, and took a deep breath. Arching his neck, he could see where the mast ran out of the shadow and into the strong glare from the yard.

After a while his pupils ceased moving and centered themselves on the uppermost points of his eyes' circumferences, as if someone had attached weights directly below them. His mind, like an overturned vessel, slowly emptied itself of thought. He knew better than to expect sleep. Sleep could be neither anticipated nor invoked; he had learned to live with substitutes. Towards morning he slipped away for an hour or two, but by then he had so entranced himself that he never knew it happened.

The city itself passed the night quietly, a few sirens advertising the maintenance of vital functions, and the ubiquitous rumble of the freeways as steady as the surf on the outer beaches. The individual liable to accident, the group defined by statistics, and the total population of

Miami, inhabiting a platform that is really the burial monument of a trillion ancient sea creatures — they were all part of a larger identity that none of them could envision in its entirety, but which was visible from high in the outer atmosphere as a small blur of light surrounded by thousands of square miles of swamp and salt water.

Shore Liberty

At about 8:00 a.m. on Wednesday morning Michael Cruz stepped out of the whispering doors of the Omni Hotel and stood, blinking, on the edge of Biscayne Boulevard. He was dressed like a golf pro, in a knit shirt and beltless white trousers, and he might have been a businessman on his way to an early round. He had a flat manila envelope under one arm.

His car was parked a few blocks away outside a peeling bungalow with a *For Sale* sign tacked to the porch. As he got inside he took the ticket off the door and threw it on the seat.

He drove back to the boulevard and headed north. In a few minutes he turned right onto the road leading to the Blossom Apartments at the edge of the bay. The lot was half empty and he parked under Hula's door, nudging a stray shopping cart out of the slot. In a minute he was examining the courtyard from the top of the stairs. He knocked twice and waited.

Hula answered the door in his pajamas, leaning on the knob for support. The sudden light made him turn away. Cruz glanced at his watch.

"Morning, Ray. Remember me?" The stale air in the apartment was sweetened by the odor of fresh coffee. Cruz counted to ten and scanned the parking lot a second time.

"Did you find him?" Hula said.

"Find who?"

"That guy — the bald guy."

"No. He's still around."

"Who is he?"

163

"We'll talk about that later." Cruz walked past Hula into the apartment. "You have to get dressed and ready to go."

"What? Go where?"

"I've found a place for the transfer and I'm going to need some help. Your choice, of course."

Hula shut the door, went into the kitchen, and turned off the flame under the coffee. He poured himself a cup and splashed in a couple of spoonfuls of sugar. It was too much; it wouldn't all dissolve. He dumped it in the sink and poured another one. His voice sounded hollow in the narrow space. "Today's Tuesday. I've got to be down at the yard in half an hour." This was a lie.

"Call them up and say you're not coming. You're in charge, right?"

Hula had already made up his mind. He had to go with Michael — it was the one thing he most wanted to do. He tilted the cup and nearly burned his lips. "Give me a few minutes," he said.

"Good. I'll be out in back." Cruz unlocked the glass door, pushed it aside, and stepped onto the balcony. There was a breeze off the water and the rail was still slippery with dew. The smell of the bay reminded him of wet plaster. Cruz generally didn't like the morning hours — the clarity of light and sound was too much for his head — but there was something invigorating about this particular place and time. It had to do with his dry clothes and the full day ahead.

In a few minutes Hula appeared at the door. He was in his standard weekday clothes: old jeans, a paint-speckled shirt, rubber-bottomed pancake shoes. His sparse hair was damp and flattened against his head. Except for the eyes, he resembled a stuffed animal; the thick hair pushing out of his collar, like frayed kapok, might have been a sign of excessive wear.

"Got your keys?" Cruz said.

Hula nodded. "Why?"

"We're taking your car."

"All right."

Cruz led the way through the apartment and out the other door. If he was pleased that he'd had so little trouble in recruiting Hula, he gave no indication. "Don't you have to call your place?" he said.

"It's too early. Besides, I told Silva I might not be in today." Hula had reached a point where he was willing to improvise facts whenever convenient. He didn't care how obvious it was. The truth had become so obscure that one lie was just as good as another.

The car was in the shade of the building and the interior was still cool. Hula opened the passenger door, tossed the keys to Cruz, and got inside. It felt odd to be in the right-hand seat of his own car. He noticed that the springs had a lot more life in them.

Cruz slid in and started the engine before he shut the door. He backed into the sunlight. Within a minute they were back on the boulevard, headed south, and mired in the commuter traffic.

Hula rolled down the window and rested his elbow on the ledge. "Where are we going?"

"Way down towards Kendall."

"You should have crossed over on the airport connector."

"We have to stop first."

The logical rejoinder, of course, was to ask where they were stopping, and then maybe why, but Hula said nothing, and ended the exchange. He sacrificed these questions because he wanted to introduce a more interesting subject and he didn't want Cruz worn out with explaining beforehand. "About yesterday," he said. "Sorry I couldn't wait around. I couldn't stand it in there any longer."

"We have to talk about that. That guy — he was gone by then, right?"

"That's right."

"What happened to the phone?"

"He shot it when you called. He just lost it completely."

"He·brought a gun?"

"No. Well — I don't know. But he used the gun you gave me."

Cruz didn't seem surprised. "How did he get it? I thought you left it in the desk."

"I did — but he took it from me when I threatened him with it."

"You pulled it on him? Why?"

"I don't know — I was scared. He was talking about how he was going to kill you. He knew everything about me — where I live, my friends, the coke."

"You pointed it at him and he took it away. Then what?" Cruz kept his eyes fixed on the car in front of him. People in the adjoining lanes looked at him twice. He seemed to have the terrific powers of concentration typical of the worst drivers.

"He told me not to interfere. That was when you called. By then he'd given the gun back to me — he made me get it for him and then he shot the receiver."

"Where were your guys while this was going on?"

"I sent them home at eleven, because of the rain."

"What about the blood on the floor?"

"A piece of the phone cut him on the arm, I think. It wasn't much."

"Wasn't there another shot? I saw the window was broken."

"I tried to take the gun away from him after he passed out. I was going to —"

"He what?"

"He fainted — right after he shot the phone. He was about to leave."

They were waiting at a light. Cruz shut his eyes, leaned forward, and rested his forehead against the wheel. His head was still down when the signal went green. The driver behind him honked. Cruz sat up and the Toyota snapped out like a billiard ball, forcing them into their seats. Cruz had already hit forty before he jumped on the brake for the next light, a block away. Before Hula had a chance to complain Cruz was talking to him. More accurately, he was talking to himself, but Hula was listening.

"You didn't do anything. You had him right there, helpless, out cold, but you didn't do anything." When the light changed he roared up behind the closest jam of cars and forced his way through.

Hula turned in his seat. "I tried to take the gun away from him — that's when he came out of it. The gun went off. I fell —"

Cruz was shouting now. "Why didn't you tie his hands? Why didn't you roll the desk on top of him? Why didn't you beat his fucking brains out?"

Hula started to say something and abandoned it. There was obviously no point. He tried to collect himself. Michael pulled out of the traffic and onto the apron of a boarded-up gas station. He switched off the engine. "Done," he said. "Over with." He bounced the heel of his palm off the dashboard, an oddly fastidious gesture; the blow landed with none of the force that it started with. "I should've told you before. He's a cataleptic, cataplectic, something like that — I think. It means that when he gets excited he falls asleep — not all the time, but when it happens there's nothing he can do about it. Remem-

166

ber when you found him in the car outside your place? Same thing."
Cruz rolled down the window and hawked on the pavement.
"Now — how long did it take him to wake up?"

Hula had to stop and think. "Five minutes. It couldn't have been
any more than that."

"That's why he's so big. It's a disease, it makes you fat."

"Why didn't you tell me? If I'd known what was happening —"

"No. You're better off. Besides, I was hoping you'd use that gun I
gave you."

"You think I'm going to shoot someone just because you tell me
to?"

Cruz didn't answer. He started the car and pulled up to the edge of
the traffic. As he turned his head to watch the oncoming stream,
leaning over the wheel, Hula noticed he had a small cut under his ear,
probably from a razor. Hula had done the same thing a hundred
times. The sight of it was painful — it reminded Hula that trivial
human accidents like this were the most that they had in common,
and though he couldn't explain the distance that separated them, he
knew it was there. He had always known. The more he saw of Cruz,
the greater it became.

They ducked into the street and rolled away. Hula tried again.
"How can you expect me to help you out if you won't tell me anything? Who is this guy? What does he want?"

Cruz turned on the radio and lit a cigarette. Hula heard his question vanish into an ad for motor oil. He reached up and clicked the
radio off. "Who is he?"

Cruz pinched the cigarette out of his mouth. "He must have been
looking for me. If he wanted to kill you, he would have done it already. I was wrong about him — you should be glad I was. So he
doesn't concern you anymore."

"I want to know."

"Look — rule one is that nobody gets told any more than he absolutely has to know. It's the only way. So just shut up and relax. You
already showed me how much help you can be."

Hula dropped it. He realized that he'd gone as far as he could go.
They drove the rest of the way in silence.

The spell broke when Cruz swerved into the turning lane and
slapped the signal up. Hula looked across the street and saw a couple
of old two-story motels, one chalky blue, the other faded orange.

He'd driven past them daily for years. He now learned that the blue one was called the Seahorse, according to the name on the awning above the office. The other remained anonymous, because the day-light made the clear neon tubes on the roadside sign impossible to read.

There were only a few pedestrians on the sidewalk, nearly motion-less old people with plastic bags, and so Hula noticed the small and youthful man who left the bus stop on the corner and walked briskly back to the door of the Seahorse, where he stopped and looked around. The hotel facade — the watery pastels, the seahorse cutouts in the shutters, the palm-trunk columns supporting the balcony along the side — looked ancient beside him.

A moment later Liberty angled past Hula's bulk into the back seat of the Toyota and saw Cruz's dark, brown-rimmed pupils studying him in the rearview mirror. When he finally got settled in the tiny space, he saw Cruz was still staring at him, so he reached up from be-hind and put his hands over Cruz's eyes. "Guess who," he said.

"That's poor," Cruz said. "Really poor."

Liberty dropped his hands and sat back. He was wearing a tur-quoise Hawaiian shirt, gray corduroys, and sneakers. He stuck his arm between the seats, where Hula could see it and reach it. "My name's Mr. X. Are you Mr. Y?"

Hula smiled uneasily. He reached up and pumped the hand once. "Pleased to meet you."

"Don't mention it." He sat back again.

In a few minutes they had looped through the soaring aerial curves of the downtown highway terminus and were traveling west toward the airport and the suburbs. The squat, nearly flat-roofed houses that lined the freeway on either side, each centered on a half acre of undif-ferentiated plain, managed to convey the idea of motion without ac-tually fulfilling it, since they slipped past and behind at a rapid, con-tinuous rate, refusing to give way to anything but themselves. Cruz leveled off at sixty-five and was ready to talk.

"OK," he said. "You've both said you want to help me with the transfer. Today I'm going to show you how we're going to do it. If either of you are thinking of backing out, this is your last chance — in a few hours there won't be any time for a change in plans. That's about it." He waited half a minute, and chose to interpret the result-ing silence as acquiescence.

"Second point. They're going to see all of us tomorrow. They're going to have six guys out there with Nikons and telephoto lenses. Once they know who you are — they don't know yet, I don't think — they're going to keep looking for you until they find you. I tried to set it up so they won't get a chance to take pictures, but I'm not making any promises. Whatever happens, they'll be looking for you for a long time. Of course they already know who I am." The hum of the wheels on the roadbed beneath them emphasized the silence between Cruz's words.

"Third. When we're through tomorrow — if everything goes right — I'm going to give each of you two million dollars in cash. The coke is easily worth ten times that, or more, but the fact is there's not that many people who I could sell it to and there's no way I could get full value for it. Forty, fifty million — it's funny money, as far as I'm concerned. If you're wondering what you're going to do with the two million after you get it, I have a suggestion. The Palm National Bank gives no interest on special deposits and so isn't required to report them. You can walk in there, hand them the money, and they won't say a word. The only thing they'll answer to is a court-ordered subpoena, and even then they'll drag their feet. But if you'd be happier keeping it somewhere else, that's fine with me — just don't get caught."

They rode down the tight inside curve of the southbound exit onto the Palmetto Expressway, heading off toward Kendall and Cutler Ridge. They were nearly ten miles inland from the bay — the last time Liberty had been out here, west of the Gables, it was mostly scrub pine and dusty roads made out of fill. In the meantime the contractors had been very busy. The shiny, sprinkler-fed exotics — forty-foot Norfolk pines, casuarinas, paperbarks — concealed the homes and shopping centers and made the land look lusher and wilder than it ever had before. Liberty tapped Hula on the shoulder. "What about that big toll road they were going to build west of here — did they finish that yet?"

Hula was taken by surprise. He'd been thinking about other things. He wanted instructions — he glanced at Cruz and looked away; his dependence was becoming reflexive. "The turnpike? Oh yeah, they opened that a few years ago — takes you all the way to Homestead. You don't have to beat your way down Dixie Highway anymore. Costs you plenty, though — they really soak the tourists."

169

Liberty was trying to sort out the relationship between Cruz and the older man. He could see constraint on one end, condescension on the other. There was definitely a lot more going on than the basic quid pro quo. Two million — he must have earned it somehow. What Cruz needed was a veteran utility player, but the guy in the passenger seat looked more like a chief clerk at a hardware store. What was he getting into? He pushed it a little further. "You lived in Miami long?"

"Forty years. That long enough?"

The young man saw Cruz's black eyes looking at him in the mirror. "I grew up in the city," Liberty said. "In 1959 we elected a Cuban president of our high-school class. That was before they swamped us."

Now Hula was on familiar ground. "They couldn't get Castro, so they made us take everybody else."

"You're a Cuban, aren't you, Michael?" Liberty had never inquired about Cruz's origin.

"I'm a goddamn Rockefeller — can't you tell?" Nobody knew whether or not Cruz was trying to be funny. Hula laughed anyway.

They passed a tiny old man with a wedge-shaped head who was nearly buried in the upholstery of a maroon Cadillac. He had to extend his arms fully to reach the upper half of the wheel.

"I haven't driven a car for nearly two years," Liberty said.

Cruz didn't take his eyes off the road. "That's too bad," he said. "Because you're going to have to drive one tomorrow."

Quickly, Liberty said, "For two million dollars, I can drive a car."

"It's not a car — it's a van, standard. We'll start a little earlier so you can practice."

"Probably a good idea."

Liberty had discovered that he couldn't concentrate on watching Hula. He'd been shut up in the Seahorse Motel for three days and there were too many things he wanted to talk about. "This is Florida," he said, nodding out the window at nothing in particular. The morning sun penetrated under the first row of pines and flashed white and yellow against the rough bark of those set farther in, so that the speed of the car generated a brilliant coruscating light. Now and then a white steeple, sharp and geometric, broke through the sparse canopy — the suburbs are full of churches. "This is Miami," Liberty said, "this is where I was born and raised — I spent most of my life here. But if I tried to come back they'd put me away. I can't be the person I am and live in my own town without them catching up with me — they would, somehow. I don't belong here, I don't belong there — what I am is a goddamn refugee. It's all here, everything I wanted, and I can't touch it." He threw his head back, exposing the long, unblemished line of his throat, and sneezed. "Allergies too," he said, laughing. "It's all here." He pulled a Kleenex out of the plastic box between the seats, mopped his nose, held the tissue up to the window, open an inch, and let the suction pull it away.

Nobody said anything for about five seconds. Then Cruz nodded once, deeply, a mock acknowledgment. "They'd get you for that, too. Littering."

Hula twisted his neck to one side, so he could look at Liberty. "Were you the guy that grounded the boat on Otter Reef? That was some kind of job you did."

The young man's face was flat, moist, and expressionless.

"That's wrong," Cruz said. "It wasn't him."

Now the road, pared down to a nearly shoulderless two-lane strip, sprouted legs and left the ground, stalking high over Kendall Drive in a soaring curve, dizzy as a child, before it descended and spilled them out onto Dixie Highway: a wide, six-lane, ground-level strip repeatedly interrupted by traffic lights, with just enough distance between them to allow more ambitious drivers to reach sixty or seventy before they have to depend on their brakes. The road had originally served as the main artery between Miami, Homestead, and the Keys; south of Homestead, where they still call it U.S. 1, it remains the most direct route. In that area you can see what it must have looked like forty years ago — just a dike, actually, with a heavy inlay of tar and crushed aggregate, doggedly crossing the canals on reinforced concrete, and sloping down on either side to swamp, scrub, or cultivated fields.

Wally Liberty, sitting quietly in the backseat, discovered that the nervous, uneven rhythm of riding in traffic was making him a little nauseous. He'd never spent much time this far down the highway and the effort to place himself was a little too difficult to hold interest. There was never anything here, according to his recollection. The distant, whitewashed bunkers of the chain stores occluded the horizon without asserting an individual identity; out of habit he tried to fix the route of his journey, watching the mileage signs and studying the faces on the billboards.

So now I've done it all, he thought, everything that I've forbidden myself since I began — I've ferried a cargo into Florida waters, landed it, come ashore, been examined by the DEA, showed myself in Miami, and agreed — not agreed, but demanded — to take part in a high-level exchange well away from the coast and without any sort of backing or guarantee. He couldn't deceive himself about Cruz any longer; Cruz was clearly an amateur, and a plunger besides — no money behind him. It had probably taken everything he had just to pay Liberty's initial fee. It was one thing to join in on a quick day-night affair on the Colombian side, where Cruz had proved he had the right connections, and where a solid credit line could get you out of just about anything; it was another thing entirely to jump into Miami, the snakepit, with a shipment that would light up the whole East Coast.

But Cruz had a powerful ally — Liberty's own cooperation. For weeks Liberty had been carrying on a secret war against his own integrity, and his old self had definitely had the worst of it. In a few hours the entire American coke establishment was going to take sides. He was looking forward to it — he liked to have his antagonists out where he could see them. No more fine distinctions, no more compensating falsehoods; just a limited set of reflexes and the necessity to act. For all the crimes he had committed on his own person, Liberty set himself a simple penance. He was going to make it back. Whatever else, he was going to survive.

Liberty suddenly noticed that Cruz had floated into the left-turn lane. He sat up and looked around. It was just like all the other intersections they had passed through — a string of lights, a narrow road entering on either side (here cutting between, on the left, a supermarket and a flaking aqua wall of plywood surrounding a drive-in theater), and a few cars zipping through the parted seas of idling machinery. A green arrow appeared on the signal above their heads and Cruz stepped on the gas. Before Liberty had a chance to wonder where this road led to, Cruz turned left again, into the supermarket parking lot. He quickly cut across the near corner and bounced back onto the highway, heading back the way they had come. It was a little disorienting. If he hadn't been paying attention, Liberty might not have noticed that anything had changed, because they were still traveling along the same crowded conduit, with the same fast-food franchises repeating themselves at regular intervals — the only difference was that the sun had leaped across the sky and was shining on the other side of Cruz's face.

Michael pulled into another parking lot, drove alongside the highway a few hundred yards, and nosed into a space that looked diagonally across the traffic. The shopping center behind them was a quaint relic of underdevelopment, just fifty yards from the road, so that there were only three rows of parking spaces from which to choose. The stores themselves — a hardware store, a hairdresser, a stationer's, a few others — were small and unambitious and they looked as if they were suffering from their need to share an average of a dozen parking spots apiece — in fact, Cruz had taken one of the few slots remaining at 9:00 A.M. "I realize it's cramped in here, but there's nowhere else we can sit and talk." Michael had to turn up his voice a little so they could hear, and it took some effort.

"The whole point of this location is that it allows us to divide the transfer in half. Tomorrow afternoon, you and I" — he looked at Hula — "will be sitting right about here, while you" — he looked at Liberty — "will be across the road. We'll be able to see each other, but nobody will be able to get from here to there in less than fifteen minutes. This whole area freezes up at about four-thirty and it stays that way for over an hour."

Liberty was hunched over in the backseat, looking out the windshield and across the highway. There was only one store over there. It was sufficiently large, far off, and isolated to assume the character of a traveler's mirage — a square-cornered, talc-colored mesa in the middle of the parking lot. The name on the facade — Jefferson's — meant nothing to him. The black motes moving around by the doors, just visible over a carpet of automobiles, were the heads of shoppers; not that they were recognizable as such, but it was unlikely that they could be anything else.

"We're about a half mile from the entrance to that store," Cruz said. "The quickest way to get there is to walk. Look up and down the road — you see how far away those lights are?" To the north, towards the city, Liberty could see two black cables crossing the road — it was impossible to tell which was closer, and he couldn't see any part of the intersections they controlled. To the south he saw no lights at all. Perhaps they were hidden under the curve in the earth.

"If we tried to drive over there now, with the traffic tailing off, we could get there in just under five minutes — if everything went right. We'd either have to hit the left-turn green — it stays that way for about twenty seconds — or just after the green, when the crossing road has the signal. That's another forty seconds — in between there's about four minutes when the highway traffic has the green. We could try and cut over then, but you can see how fast the cars move along here, and we'd have to wait for a break or we wouldn't have a chance. Once we turned around, we'd have to come back this way until we reached the parking lot entrance. Right now, that wouldn't take much time at all, but late in the afternoon that far lane slows down to ten or twelve miles an hour. And that's the only way to do it. Those trees over there, on the far side of the lot — there's a big condo development over there, with a gate and a guard and a chain-link fence around the whole thing — it comes right up to the edge of the road, and you can't drive on the shoulder because of the bill-boards. To come back this way, you have to stay on the highway. If we were really eager, we might try and crash straight across right here — but there's that steel rail running right down the middle.

He cracked his knuckles and drummed the wheel with his finger-nails. "I'm not counting on them to stop for traffic lights. But no matter what they do, they're not going to be able to get from here to there tomorrow afternoon fast enough to give us any trouble. Especially since they don't know the area.

"OK, here it is. I pick up both of you around two tomorrow. The truck with the coke isn't too far from here — we get it and come this way." He touched Liberty on the shoulder. "Across the road — do you see the Fotomat by the main doors?"

"Fotomat?"

"That little thing with the yellow roof — looks like a shithouse with windows."

"To the right of the doors?" Liberty's vision was nearly perfect.

"That's it. There's a phone booth right behind it — you can't see it from here. We park the van with the coke as near to that thing as possible. Then we leave you there. As soon as we get over to this side we call you, just to get the line straight. You're going to have to stay close to that phone until we're finished. Stand right here, sit in the van, do what you like — but you have to be where you can hear it.

You won't have any competition — there's eight or ten of them just inside the store, where it's cool — people use those.

"Right after I call you I'm going to call up the bankers and tell them to be down here within one hour, with their money. If they don't come by then, I call again and tell them the price has gone up fifty thousand. They'll get here in time — they just may not want to show themselves. I'm going to call them at 3:15 — they get here by 4:30 — that gives us an hour and a half of rush-hour traffic — until 6:00 — to get the job done in. That'll be plenty. If they try and stall us too long I'm going to kill the whole project — I'll donate the coke to the PBA — I'd rather lose the cash than get held up too long. But as bad as they want us, they want the coke more. They won't touch us until they've got it."

Cruz lit a cigarette and shook out the match. "As soon as they get here I'll ask to see the money — then I'll call you and tell you what's coming. They're going to send one man across the highway, on foot. I'll make sure he's unarmed. You should be able to see him coming across the lot. I'll tell him to stand in front of the Fotomat. When he gets there, take him over to the van and show him the coke. Don't give him more than a few minutes.

"When he's satisfied, take him to the phone booth and give him the number over here and the keys to the van. He's going to call his boss and say the coke is ready. Make sure he also says that unless I'm seen driving away from here he's not going to get near that van again. After he hangs up, tell him to stay in the booth. Wait there — if they give me the cash, and I'm happy about the way things look, I'll ring the number twice. That means you're ready to go. Tell him that you're leaving, and that it's time for him to take possession of the van. Tell him also that if he tries to do anything else, such as follow you, then someone else is going to take the van away from him.

"Give me five minutes after he makes his call. If I don't signal by then, something's gone wrong. It's up to you after that — whatever you want to do. You might get the van yourself and drive it away, so you don't have to leave empty-handed. I'll have a gun for you tomorrow, if you want it. This guy may be easier to handle if you've got something to point at him.

"After the signal, all you have to do is walk into the store, go straight through, and walk out the back. There's a cab stand outside the door — wait there. We'll pick you up as soon as we can get around. If we're not there in thirty minutes, we had problems, and you better get in one of those cabs and go back to the city, because that's about how long it'll take them to find you."

Liberty was slow to notice that Cruz had stopped talking, because his imagination was treating him to a picture of what could happen if the buyers found him before he got away. They weren't lacking in imagination either, he supposed. "What if it rains?" he said.

Hula considered this remark for a moment before he realized it was funny. He started to laugh; even Cruz was smiling. Michael pushed his hand through his hair. "More on this later," he said. "While you're sweating it out over there, my friend and I will be planning our escape. We're going to have two cars here tomorrow afternoon, not counting the van — this one, and another I'll rent in the morning. The rented car is a dummy. We'll be sitting in it when they arrive, and you" — he looked at Hula — "are going to stay in it the whole time, in the driver's seat. Before I call over with the signal, I'm going to put the money in the rented car with you. You're going to take it out of the case it comes in and put it in something else — just so we won't be embarrassed if the case is bugged. I'll give it back to them before we leave.

"It's very important that we park the rented car in one of the three spaces just in front of that flower store back there. Turn around and look at it." Everyone obliged. It was a tiny shop, with a white scalloped awning shading the door. They could see the FTD label on the black-misted window. The fluorescent lights in the orchid boxes glowed pink in the darkness. One of them went out; someone must be standing in front of it, Liberty decided.

"The worst part of the transfer is going to be the five or six steps from the rented car to that door. If they're going to start shooting, that's when they'll do it. We walk past the counter, through the store-room, and out the back door, which is where this car will be parked. I'm counting on the fact that none of them will know for sure that the coke is safe, and so they'll hesitate — let somebody else take the risk.

"You can see that it's a good two hundred yards to either end of this line of stores. In the late afternoon this lot and the even smaller one in back are filled with old ladies cruising around and looking for a space. It gets pretty well gummed up. There's only three exits from the back lot — two lead around the building to this side, and the other goes straight out from the rear of the flower shop. This third one cuts between a couple of ball fields and into a residential area — one-family homes — lots of stop signs. We can get out that third exit before anyone else can come around from the front lot.

"Once we're out, it's about two miles south to the first road that crosses the highway. There's a road on the other side that leads right into the back of Jefferson's. It's twice as far as going up the highway and back, but it's a lot faster too. And we don't have to go back to the highway after we pick you up — we drive west to the turnpike and take the long way around to the city. And we live happily ever after."

Cruz turned in his seat and looked first at Hula, then at Liberty, his stare hard and unblinking as a lens, though not nearly as remote. "I know there's a lot of things that could go wrong," he said. "No shit, some of them will. But I think this setup shaves our risk about as far as possible, and before you start to complain I want to talk about some of the problems and advantages." He settled himself again, slouching low in his seat until his knees touched the bottom of the dash. He grabbed one leg, pulled it towards him, and draped it over the steering column.

"First of all, there's the possibility that they won't want to deal at all. That'd be very bad news. When I call tomorrow, they might tell me the boss isn't in, or they might not show up at the site. They're not hurting — they could afford to ignore me. I need them a lot more than they need me. And they know the longer they put me off, the stronger they are, because it gives them more time to hunt me down."

It dawned on Liberty that Cruz wasn't talking to them — he was talking to himself. Why did they have to know all this stuff? And it bothered him a little; maybe Cruz was trying to shift the burden.

"So I'm going to have to convince them that I'm willing to blow the deal if they don't follow my schedule. Either we sell it or we don't. Whatever happens, that'll be the end of it.

"Whether we sell or not, they're going to come after us. We're each going to become celebrities. If they don't find out who you are tomorrow, there's a decent chance they never will — the problem is that you can't tell how much they know. The safest thing for both of you would be to leave the country and not come back. That says to them that you're very sorry for what you did and you won't let it happen again. Then if they find you, they might let you go — after all, they don't want to seem like total pricks." Cruz paused, waiting for a laugh. He didn't get it.

"I tried to set up the transfer so they won't get a chance to recognize you. For instance," he nodded at Hula, "you'll be sitting in the dummy car nearly the whole time. Before they arrive, I want you to tie a stocking around your head and put on a hat. I'll get a car with tinted glass. They'll get a lot of pictures, but they won't do them any good. Whatever you do, don't get out of the car until the time comes. They're going to try pretty hard to upset me, one way or another, but it's not going to get them anywhere. As long as we have the coke, they can't touch us — remember that.

"As for you" — he blinked at Liberty in the mirror — "whoever they send over the highway is going to get a good look at you. If we do it right, nobody else will. You might want to disguise yourself, but you can't do anything that'll freak any strangers — that means no nylon, no ski mask, nothing like that. You can take it from there. You ought to screen yourself from the highway — they may have a camera over here that can close the gap — not to mention a high-powered rifle. I wish there was some way you could dump the man they send, when you're through with him, but it's just not possible. He'll remember your face — he'll do nothing but look at photos for the next week and a half.

"That takes care of the basics. I'll have new plates for this car tomorrow. We'll put them on before we leave the city."

He sat up and took a deep breath. "They'll definitely try and follow us out of here. If they do it, we're dead — it's that simple. I realize that this stampede through the flower store doesn't make a hell of a lot of sense. The whole area will be crawling with them tomorrow — who says there won't be two or three of them waiting inside? Also, it won't take them long to find out about this exit from the lot in back and they'll probably put a car nearby. In the whole thing, there's not one point we can depend on.

"Once we start to move, we can't stop for anything — the thing I'm counting on, the only thing that'll save us, is that they won't know what we're going to do until we've already done it — done it and finished and moved on to the next. By the time they figure out that we ran into the flower store we'll be out the other side, and by the time the guys in back figure out who it was that got into the

Toyota we'll be halfway out the exit. They won't have time to concentrate their strength — anyone who tries to stop us will be acting as
an individual. I can handle the individuals."

A heavy woman in a faded housedress was trying to get a large box
into the car beside them. She had pushed it in the driver's side and
now it was stuck between the seat and the steering wheel. Liberty
turned his head and watched her. The loose flesh on her upper arms
flapped and reddened; her smock bellied like a sail. Close up, her body
seemed even more substantial than it was. In the movies he'd seen as a
child, death was always abrupt and violent — motion arrested, crumpling, maybe some blood on the chin. He'd been shot at more than
once since then, but always at sea, where tilting decks made guns into
toys. It was just that kind of death that would be denied him here, he
knew. Instead it would be something as slow, fleshy, and unpalatable
as this old woman, with her colorless hair and her silent cough — her
struggle with the box was as mortally strenuous as anything he had
ever seen. Finally she straightened up, grabbed the corner of the
door, leaned back, and delivered a powerful heel kick to the center of
the near face of the carton, shutting her eyes at the moment of impact. The cardboard tore inward in a half circle; the box itself didn't
move.

Ray had been watching her also. "Too much sweat, not enough
brains," he said. He started to open the door. Cruz's hand jumped out
and caught him just above the wrist.

"You can't get out of the car tomorrow. You might as well start
practicing now."

The woman managed to get one arm around the box and she
pulled it out behind her. She hugged it to her chest and plodded off
towards the line of stores.

"She's going to try and return it," Hula said. "Goddamn."

"There's a few precautions I want you both to take tonight," Cruz
said, ignoring him. "But before I get into that I want to hear your re-
actions. Do you understand how this thing is supposed to work? Do
you see any problems?"

Hula answered immediately. "What do you need me for? As far as
I can tell, all I'm supposed to do is sit and watch."

"That's right."

"So what's the point? What am I here for?"

"If you didn't want to come, you should have told me earlier."

179

"I didn't say that. You wanted to know my reaction — that's my reaction."

Cruz shook his head "It's very simple. When they get here I'll be standing on the sidewalk, you'll be in the car. They'll see you watching and they'll guess that you're involved. When I bring you the money they'll know for sure. And they'll naturally start to think I'm planning to ride away in the car. They won't be sure, but they'll have to deal with the possibility. If I was standing there alone, with no help in sight, they'd have to think harder about what I was going to do, and they might spend more time thinking about the back lot. Just by being there, with the cash, you're going to tie down a lot of their attention."

Hula had never intended to resist; he only wanted to assert his presence. "Makes sense, I guess," he said. "Something else —" The seat behind him suddenly jerked forward, pressing him into the windshield. Liberty was opening the door. He squeezed out of the car, turned, and walked off toward the stores behind them. The seat fell back into place and Hula straightened up again.

"Wait here," Cruz said. He got out of the car and followed Liberty across the lot. Hula pushed his door open and got out too. He leaned against the fender, arms crossed, and gazed fixedly at the block of stores, like a man whose wife is eating up his Saturday morning at the pharmacy.

Cruz and Liberty were standing under the flimsy promenade by a coin-operated ice machine. Hula could tell they were arguing about something; neither was using his hands, but it was clear that they were restraining themselves. The traffic roared in his ears and there was no chance to catch what they were saying. Suddenly Liberty looked up and pointed at him. Hula became resentful; he knew the accompanying remarks weren't complimentary. He was tempted to go and join them, but he didn't want to appear foolish. From what he could see, Liberty was complaining about something and Cruz was hearing him out. He guessed that Liberty's brusque exit was intended to gain a private audience. Right beside them, the heavy woman emerged from the store with another cardboard box; this one was a lot smaller.

". . . Because that's the way it is. Look, you're going to be sitting over there with all that coke — you could just drive it away. You could even call up the Colombians beforehand. But I'm trusting you not to do that — is that so hard to understand?"

"But why do I have to wait for you? Why don't we get another car? I could leave right away and we'd meet somewhere else. This way, I have to stand over there and watch them coming. You think they don't know me? Bullshit they don't! Suppose you get stopped? Suppose you're a few minutes late? Then what?"

Cruz scratched his nose and watched the heavy woman lumber off toward Hula. "One car is always better," he said. "That gives them only one chance to find us. If all they have to do is get one out of three, then we're making their job easy for them."

"All right! But not unless you get another car for me tomorrow — we'll put it in back and I'll use it if I have to. Better yet — when you get over there we switch everything to the other car — so if they make you on your way out of here it won't matter. Didn't you think about that? They could pick us up anywhere from here to the city. The tollbooth on the turnpike — did you think about that?" Liberty's eyes turned carnivorous and he was leaning forward from his ankles. This posture disturbed Michael's concentration; he placed his hand flat on Liberty's chest and gently straightened him up. They stared at each other for a moment.

"You're totally right," he said. He said it with a rising tone, as if he found his own dismay at being corrected a little humorous. In the ensuing pause Liberty could see Cruz studying his reaction. He didn't answer. The dregs of his anger still obstructed his thinking and he waited for them to drain off. His demands had been met; was that what he wanted? He had noticed this abrupt sensation of absence at other times in Cruz's company — you thought you were communicating, and then suddenly there was nobody there.

"Then you'll get another car tomorrow?"

"I've got enough bad cards to clean out the airport. Of course I can't drive them all myself — we'll have to get started a little earlier. That makes four — the van, the dummy, the Toyota, and this one. I'll give you the Toyota. We may as well keep the one that already belongs to us." He nodded at Hula.

Liberty glanced into the lot. "Where'd you pick up that guy? He looks like a stiff — are you sure we need him?"

"He's better than you think."

"Well —"

"He's just another body — he doesn't have to do anything."

"Then what's he here for?"

Cruz's voice betrayed a little irritation. "Look — we never could've gotten this far without him. We owe it to him. And he won't make problems — he might seem a little unsteady, but he's not. He's a rock." Michael seemed eager to change the subject. "Speaking of unsteady, I hope you're a little cooler tomorrow. What happened? Forget to beat your wife this morning?"

"I still can't believe you wanted to go all the way back in one car."

"I would've seen it in time. I'm not stupid. And to tell you the truth, I don't think it improves your chances — having the car — if we do get held up over here. If they know you, you'd be better off in a cab. They'll try and plug the entrances."

"Whatever you say." For the second time, the idea that Cruz had anticipated his complaint troubled Liberty. Had he left out the other car just to see how he would react? It couldn't be more simple, more essential. He didn't know which was worse — guile or neglect. "I want to see the back lot here," he said. "I also want to see the place across the highway."

"Definitely. One more thing — I can tell you're used to making your own plans, doing everything yourself. Just because that's not possible here is no reason to get paranoid. I didn't go to all this trouble because I wanted to hand you to the feds. Help me out — I'm going to need it." He put his hand on Liberty's shoulder; a professional gesture, borrowed from a salesman or a priest.

Wally was starting to feel a little sick to his stomach. It wasn't the same thing as fear. His perceptions were dulled, not sharpened; he had to work to keep his eyes trained. Left to itself, his mind began to associate sensations in an arbitrary manner — for instance, it connected Cruz's touch with this feeling of nausea, and tied them both to the curious muffled clicking going on behind his back — it sounded like gravel on plastic — he had forgotten about the ice machine.

"At least it's simple," Liberty said. "That's what I like about it."

Cruz didn't answer. He stepped down into the sun and started off towards the car. Liberty clapped his hands once, waited for Cruz to turn, and pointed to the flower store. He was going to walk through.

In a minute he was standing under the portico in back. The door opened behind him and there was Hula, blinking in the light. It seemed very quiet without the noise of the highway. Hula stuffed his fingers in his pockets; he looked relieved, sheepish, ingratiating.

"Pretty dark in there — I nearly got a mouthful of roses."

Liberty nodded and looked away.

"By the way, the fat lady had a plant stand in the box. She didn't return it — she just got a smaller box."

Another nod.

I'm asking for it, Hula told himself. Why should he talk to me? Who the hell cares? "I'm not a native," he said. "I came down when I was six years old. I wanted to know why the leaves didn't turn brown. They just don't, everybody said. So why am I standing here with you? Same reason. Might as well enjoy it while it lasts, right?"

"If I'd stayed any longer in this city it would've destroyed me." Hula felt thick, top-heavy. "It's not so bad," he said.

Something bubbled up in Liberty's eyes. "What the fuck do you know about it! Huh? Tell me that! Who the hell are you? You think Michael's going to put you to bed every night? He's right at home — watch this, he says, I'll step on the snake! He wants to go out like a comet — he's going to show us all how to die!"

Ray allowed his chin to drop down onto his chest, so that he was talking into his collar "I trust Michael," he said.

"Huh." Liberty clenched his fists and spread his fingers. "Huh." It was a cough, a reflex, with a pause for breath in between. "You never left. You've been here too long. You're just right for each other."

Hula wanted to ask the young man why he'd agreed to participate, if he thought the scheme was hopeless. It was just the sort of question a clear-headed, reasonable person might ask. That was the image Hula desired for himself — balanced, unhurried maturity fully in touch with circumstance; each decision, each act, flowing naturally from the one preceding it. "We'll get there — you'll see." Hula said it with all the tenderness of which his large heart was capable. What else could he feel? The young man still lived in the shadow — therefore he had to battle with shadows.

So they stood there and waited, like islands in a sea of dollars; shopping carts banging together, electric doors jerking open and shut, women balancing packages on their hips while they dug through their pocketbooks, and cars in search of parking spaces hovering in the lot like bees around their nest. Any other pair of men, recently acquainted, might have felt uncomfortable about the silence that had so quickly fallen between them. Not these two; they were in no shape to be embarrassed. There was nothing ironic or absurd about their situation, as far as they could see. They were fishing in a sea of troubles and could be thankful for a little patience. When the Toyota inched around the far side of the building it was as if no time at all had passed.

The three men spent the rest of the morning together. They drove out the narrow rear entrance and timed themselves across the highway. For the purposes of comparision they went back and did it again. Cruz talked, pointed, cautioned, predicted, and admonished like a natural pedagogue; he drove the car like a grandmother. They walked through Jefferson's as quickly as possible, and the muzak, the bold graphics, and the shudder of the ventilators made Liberty claustrophobic, even though the space enclosed was as large as he had ever seen. Cruz mentioned that the floorwalkers wore tiny blue lapel pins.

They retraced their steps, brought the car around front, parked, and sat watching the doors. No one, it seemed, emerged without carrying something; it was a civilized and legally approved form of pillage. The girl in the Fotomat saw Liberty come out and she searched for him again after she finished with her customer — she was always interested in handsome young men — and the complicity and apprehension in his face surprised her when he glanced her way. Blank stares were what she had become accustomed to.

The three men were starting to feel the heat and the fine nervous mood of the morning was gone. Liberty indulged no further outbursts; he seemed to have made up his mind about something. When Cruz told him that the coke might be damaged by high temperatures and that he should park the van in shade, Liberty didn't reply, even though he knew the shadow was going to be on the wrong side of the building in the afternoon. He didn't see that it mattered. He knew that Cruz would feel the collapse of his resistance and it worried him a little. But Michael didn't mention it; he just kept talking. And Hula managed to preserve the semblance of a dialogue by asking a question now and then. There was just no way they could handle all the possibilities — the plan itself was straightforward enough, but it could veer off toward disaster in a thousand different ways. At the end Hula was left with a dull sense of enervation and an impatience for the moment of crisis.

» » »

All day long, from Marathon to Lauderdale — over a hundred miles of coastline — men got out of their cars, walked to the edge of the water, shaded their eyes, and tried to match what they saw against a drawing, an idea. They took snapshots and visited telephone booths. They stood beside the pumps at fuel docks, they talked to managers at charter marinas, and their own inability to define exactly what they were looking for made them irritable. Although the boat they wanted was unique in the area, the little information they possessed failed to distinguish it from hundreds of others similar in materials and design. Prices for new fiberglass hulls had generated a thriving market in antiques, exotics, and just about anything that would float. So when these men, who were not especially knowledgeable to start with, began inquiring about a thirty-foot mahogany sloop recently arrived from the south, they were often told about three or four boats answering that description, one or more of which they were unable to inspect because it was out cruising or because it was moored behind a wall of mangrove.

It was a job the police could have pursued much more effectively. They were out on the water every day. They had hundreds of contacts. They had access to the entire staff at the Port. Most importantly, they could work without the threat of interference. Though Jack was determined to find the boat, he was also resolved to keep the urgency of the search concealed from the police. The department already knew that the traders were looking for Michael Cruz, duplicating their own efforts. If they learned that the same people were conducting a large-scale campaign to find a certain yacht, they'd become intrigued with it too, and, given their abilities, they were much more likely to track it down. Jack didn't think the coke was still on the boat, but he wasn't willing to endanger the transfer by putting the cops a few days behind Cruz. So he insisted that the search be executed anonymously; no calling in favors, no promises, and no bargaining with public employees. No one was to intimate that he was anything other than an average citizen with some money to burn.

Jamie didn't like to have his hands tied. Whatever status he had in the city was due to his widespread connections; he could carry a message a long way. If he couldn't pretend to speak for people more powerful than himself, no one was going to listen to him. And if he couldn't make contact with any of the officials he had so deliberately cultivated, then all his skills were useless.

He wasn't the type to argue. When Jack passed out the drawing the night before and defined the limits within which he wanted all of them to work, he stared at Jamie for a particularly long time. It was as if he thought the heat of his gaze would sterilize any germ of independent action that might be stirring behind Jamie's eyes. When Jamie squirmed and looked away most of the men present assumed that Jack had got the job done.

Had he succeeded? No. In the morning Jamie went directly to the Port. The guard wouldn't let him through to the dock area, where Rawden's office was. Jamie tried to talk his way in. "What's this 'authorization'? I'm always on the list. I'm the boss's son, didn't you know that?"

"You're not on it today."

"Did you check the master for the week?"

"The first place I looked — not there either."

"Rob, wait a minute — you waved me through yesterday, right? Was I on the list then?"

"You got scratched this morning."

Jamie rocked on his heels and whistled. "Well, would you mind calling up Rawden and telling him I'm here? I'll be your best friend."

"Sorry — can't do that."

"Rob, the phone's right there. Save me a dime."

"I'd do it for you, except Rawden's not in. He got scratched this morning too."

"What?"

"That's right. It's a fact."

"Why?"

"Don't know — just got here. Guess I'll find out at lunch."

"Who took over for him?"

"You're asking the wrong person — they don't tell me anything."

"Shit." Jamie stood aside and looked through the fence. The flag was limp on the pole in the courtyard and the two small-windowed detention trucks waited, as usual, in front of the processing center. He turned to the guard. "Rob, this is important. I have to talk to some-one — could you let me in? I can't do anything out here."

"Not a chance."

"I'll take responsibility — I'll get you something better."

The guard was smiling. "Right. You can always swim, you know — float around from the bridge."

"Then call up whoever's in charge and let me talk to him. On sec-ond thought, don't bother." He looked at the striped track shoes on the guard's feet. "I'll see you later. By the way, take Soldier of Mercy in the fifth — Gulfstream." He winked and walked away slowly, as if he didn't know what to do next.

Jamie got through to the house on the first try. He was glad that he'd brought his book with him. He couldn't memorize them all.

"Rawden?"

"Yeah."

"I went down to see you this morning, but you weren't there. Do you know who I am?"

"Uh-huh."

"What're you doing at home?"

"I'm on vacation."

"Oh." He let the dead air speak for him. "Well, I was a little wor-ried, because they scratched me at the same time they scratched you."

"That's standard — who's going to watch you if I'm not around?"

"What about you? Just because you're on a break they cross you off?"

"Makes sense to me."

"You're going to take a cruise? Fly to Acapulco?"

"Jamie — tell me what you've got for me."

"Nothing. I called because I'm looking for a boat and I thought maybe you could help."

"Go on."

"Between thirty and forty feet — mahogany sloop built as a fishing boat. Came in recently."

"How recently?"

"Three weeks max, I'd say."

"What else?"

"You know it?"

"I'm thinking — can't you be more specific?"

"Probably made in South America."

"Mahogany — that's obvious."

"Well — that's all I know."

"No name? Nobody on board?"

"Sorry."

"We get a dozen like that a week. I could go over the register with you, but I don't think I could pick them out. There's no coding for age or materials."

"You'd remember this one. It was nearly coming apart."

Rawden paused. "Does this have anything to do with Michael Cruz?"

"Who?" Jamie kicked himself; it was the worst, the absolute worst thing he could have said.

"'Who,' you say? Wake up, would you please?"

"Michael Cruz."

"That's right. You never heard of him?"

Jamie was better at uncovering secrets than keeping them. He needed time to think. He was standing in a phone booth outside the public cafeteria at the Port. There were two quarters on the shelf in front of him; he flicked them forward, one at a time, so that they bounced against the glass and ricocheted back. "I tell you what," he said. "If you listen closely, you might pick up a couple of interesting facts — for your information. But only if you agree to ignore them for at least two weeks."

"I'm on vacation, remember?"

"Two weeks."

"Fine."

"If this gets out I'm down the tube. That means nothing more for you. You want to kill the golden goose?"

"I can handle it."

"All right. Michael Cruz is in Miami. The Colombians from New York are here and they're looking for him." Jamie wished he could see Rawden's face. As the silence lengthened he began to think he had accomplished something. In a moment Rawden disabused him.

"You call that news? Are you kidding?"

"Hell yes."

"You can pick that up in any bar in town."

"You can't believe that stuff — you can believe me."

"Why do they want him?"

"They don't — they want what he has."

"What's that?"

Jamie lowered his voice for emphasis. "I've said enough. Besides, you can't do anything with it, remember? When you get back, don't forget to put me on the list."

"Don't hang up. I might be able to help you."

If Jamie had cut it off there, he wouldn't have had to make apologies. He had told Rawden about the boat, but that was an acceptable risk. Although he would have come away empty-handed, he would have a little capital for next time, and he could consider himself lucky to get off so easily. He had known from the start that it wasn't such a good idea.

But the fascination of the unknown, the possibility of becoming that one man at the center who could see the entire distance in either direction, and whose cooperation is therefore indispensable, was more than he could resist. In the future they'd come to him to give gifts and display their wounds, like pilgrims before an oracle.

"You can help me?" he said. "How?" It was hot in the booth and the receiver was getting slippery. A tiny muscle in his forearm began to twitch, bumping the skin like a bird under cheesecloth.

" 'How'? What's this 'how'? How do you think? I can find the boat for you."

"Why? What does that do for you?" Jamie was amazed at himself. He was saying exactly what he thought.

"That's my business. Chew on this — it would be useful to me if you had that information."

"Look — I've got my own ass to watch out for here. If the police or your goons get into this it'll fuck it up something awful, and I'll take the blame."

"They're already in it — they want Cruz, remember?"

"You know what I mean."

"What do you want to do, hold a gun to my head?"

"I'll take your word for it. Tell me that you won't interfere — tell me that your only involvement will be what you say to me."

"I don't care about your buddies — I'm interested in Cruz."

"Why?"

"Curiosity. I just want to understand what happened when it's all over."

"Well?"

"I won't interfere. I'll do better than that — I promise I won't interfere."

"That's just words — that doesn't mean anything." Jamie had an idea.

"Do you want to talk to me or don't you?"

"You have to give me something else — something I can hurt you with."

"Like what?"

"That case coming up in Merritt Island — one of the men charged was a plant from way back. Which one — and I want evidence to prove it."

"You're talking about his life."

"No — I'm talking about yours."

Jamie was pleased that Rawden took a while to answer. "I'll give you something better — something you can hang me with."

"What?"

"I'll show you when you get here — do you know where I live?"

"Forget it. There's no way I'm coming to your place — not now."

"OK. I'll meet you at the parking lot outside Vizcaya. Three o'clock all right?"

"I'll see you there." Jamie hung up and stayed in the booth for a little while. If he found the boat, nothing else would matter. He wasn't prepared to examine Rawden's motives; there just wasn't enough time. And he couldn't wait to tell someone.

» » »

When Lisa came back to the city on Sunday night after a weekend at her retreat in the Glades, she stood in front of the double row of steel mailboxes, under the yellow bulb and its attendant swarm of tiny moths, and wished she could remove Ray Hula as easily as she might might pull his name out of the panel. In the days that followed, her anger crumbled away and she imagined that she could look back on what had happened clearly and without bias. And she was surprised to find how easy it was to delete him from her life. They hadn't shared anything but each other; no property, no pets, and very few friends to divide. All she had to do, she learned, was to stay away from his doorbell.

190

Her own rang at about nine in the evening on Wednesday night. She looked out the kitchen window; it was Hula.

When she opened the door she saw his boxy, chrome-fitted suitcase standing beside him. "I was hoping you wouldn't be here," he said.

"But you came anyway."

"I was going to let myself in." Hula had a key to her apartment that she had given him some months previously in a box with a red ribbon and a live orchid.

She looked at his jeans, his sneakers, his watchful, jowl-heavy face. She kept her hand on the doorknob. "Why?" she asked.

"I wanted to leave this." He didn't take his eyes from hers.

"Are you leaving town?"

"I don't know yet."

"What about that job you were doing for your brother? Is that finished?"

"Not quite." He wasn't lying; she could tell by the way he cleared his throat.

"How much longer?"

"A couple of days, maybe."

"Are you glad you went in with him?"

She'd hit a nerve. It was as if he hadn't heard the question. He rolled his head on his shoulders and glanced at the suitcase. "A favor to me," he said. "I'll pick it up in a day or two."

"When you do," she said, "make sure I'm not home, and leave the key."

They looked at each other for a moment. When he reached for the handle she said, "No, I'll do it."

He stopped halfway through his motion and straightened up. "OK," he said. He turned, walked to the end of the balcony, and went down the stairs. The suitcase was heavier than it looked and she had to drag it in.

She didn't leave the apartment again that night. Since Ray didn't come back — she didn't think he would — she spent the time alone. She changed into her robe, washed her face, and sat down in front of the TV. The drink she made for herself tasted awful; she couldn't even stand to look at it, so she got up and poured it out.

She had planned to spend the next couple of weekends in the Glades, closing the house up for summer, when the high water and the mosquitoes made it uninhabitable. There were rugs to roll up, cabinets to seal, and appliances to wrap in plastic. Now she couldn't wait for Friday. She didn't want to be around when Ray came for his suitcase. He'd already proved that he could turn her upside down just by showing his face, and she didn't trust herself to go through it again. So why bother? Wherever he was going, he could get there without her.

After a few hours the glow of the TV soothed her. Before she went to bed she packed up some extra clothes with her toilet kit, so she wouldn't have to return to the apartment after work. The office could do without her on Thursday, and maybe Friday; she had no personal commitments until next week. The raincoat he'd given her last Christmas went into the bag with everything else. It seemed to her that she'd started her life over again so many times that there was no need to be sentimental.

By the time she fell asleep she'd decided that her desire to get out of town wasn't really as admirable as she'd thought at first; if she had a little more courage she wouldn't have to run away. But she didn't change her mind about leaving. The look on Ray's face when she asked him about his brother had nearly unstrung her. That was when she knew he was out of reach, that he had already turned a corner somewhere and wasn't coming back. Later she tried to persuade herself otherwise, but she wasn't successful. She wished it had never happened. The last time she looked at the lighted dial of her clock-radio it was 3:00 A.M.

» » »

Cruz dropped Wally Liberty at the Seahorse Motel early in the afternoon. Before he got out of the car Liberty turned and took a good look at Michael. The dry odor of baked concrete rose off the sidewalk and was dragged in the passenger door by the suction of the traffic on the boulevard.

"I hope it's a little cooler tomorrow," Liberty said.

"I can't fix everything."

Liberty couldn't see behind Cruz's shiny, rapacious stare. "Smile for the cameras," he said, and got out and walked away. It was like leaving an open grave. By this time tomorrow he'd be in the Bahamas and Cruz, most likely, would be dead.

Inside his room, he dropped the key on the chair, pinched off his sneakers, and lay down on the bed, his hands under his neck. Wednesday afternoon. He had been in this motel since Sunday and it seemed like a lot longer than three days.

The original idea had been that he would stay until the coke was off the boat, so that any official interest his departure might arouse wouldn't immediately endanger the hoard. That was over by yesterday, when Cruz told him so, adding that Liberty could leave whenever he pleased, unless he might be interested in taking part in the transfer and picking up some extra cash. Liberty had given up trying to figure out why he had called Michael back to say yes. Now he'd changed his mind again. Although his sense of professional ethics amounted to little more than the belief that he owed it to himself to pursue his own best interests, he knew that his disappearance would look like betrayal to Cruz, and he was glad that his decision had drawn partly on Michael for inspiration.

Liberty didn't know anything about cocaine. He was a dope smuggler, and had got his start in the early seventies, when Mexican grass still dominated the market, and Colombian and Jamaican varieties were comparatively rare in the United States. Miami was a backwater then and most of the traders were amateurs like himself, young men with little capital and an unreasonable fear of the law, since the modest resources of the customs office were entirely inadequate for the job at hand — patrolling approximately two thousand miles of south Florida coastline. The pioneers relied on chance and improvisation — a typical deal might begin on the beach outside a Caribbean resort hotel, with a tentative sampling of some local product, and some talk about somebody who knew somebody who had a yacht down the way; a few extra traveler's checks were cashed at the front desk, a small skiff rowed out one night with a plastic bag in the bow, and eventually the dope might wind up sitting in a closet in Coral Gables for eighteen months, because the owner didn't have any cousins he could sell it to.

More efficient systems of distribution inevitably appeared after the success of these early ventures. American brokers developed permanent contacts abroad and the scale of the deals increased steadily, although the volume of small transactions remained an important part of the market. Most of the buyers and sellers were also consumers; they were as likely to be arrested for smoking their product as for exchanging it with acquaintances or moving it from place to place. The most intractable problem many of them faced was the need to explain their sudden wealth to friends and relatives.

In spite of the real atmosphere of serendipity, which showered good fortune in all directions, those years had had their share of casualties; weekend pilots going down at night, long jail terms for seventeen-year-olds, and foolish gestures in the presence of armed policemen. It hadn't taken Liberty long to observe that the lucky ones were almost invariably the ones who got out early, and that those who didn't often had an exit arranged for them by forces they didn't understand. He worried about it.

A few years later Miami emerged as the most important point of entry for marijuana in the United States. Nixon's DEA, pumped full of dollars by a Congress sensitive to public demands — which were in part created by the scare tactics so dear to the department's forerunner, the treasury — moved into the area with a strength and determination that eventually matured into a sophisticated effort. Agents no longer jumped whenever they saw a joint change hands and dozens of small operators were quickly exposed and warned of severe penalities if caught again. The crucial element was the institution of regional marine and air patrols that could track and intercept any blip they might find intriguing. Where complete concealment had once been a matter of a few obvious precautions, now evasive tactics only invited attention, and success depended on the ability to mimic legitimate travel as convincingly as possible.

In the early years Liberty had sailed back and forth around Cuba to Jamaica in a yacht he borrowed from his family. He took a lot of photographs, experimented with sail design, and told people he wanted to run a charter service. While in Miami he took tourists out on day or weekend cruises and investigated the local waters. He sold his cargoes to a friend from high school, though they never saw each other, and exchanged news with a few people he had met. Assuming nothing, he never allowed himself to trust anybody whose stake in the business was smaller than his own, but he soon learned from the experience of others that there was ultimately no protection against associates trapped by the DEA; he found it useful to believe that the agency knew exactly what he was doing and that his only safety lay in preventing them from catching him at it. He lost his taste for marijuana. He invited systems for jettisoning large cargoes in seconds and he favored the deep water. The drug-associated violence and killings that appeared in Miami didn't surprise him; he'd seen it coming. He took steps to defend himself and hoped it wouldn't be necessary.

He often considered getting out altogether. After seven years of intermittent activity he had $200,000 scattered in various investment accounts, nearly enough to start that charter service he was always talking about. He'd looked into it more closely and discovered that most of the outfits in existence had long waiting lists; there was no question that he could make it work. But for reasons not clear to himself he never took the necessary steps to get started, even though he was gradually withdrawing from the trade and spending more and more time just cruising around, fishing and making minor, fastidious improvements on his boat. At one point he considered entering college at the age of twenty-five. There was something holding him back; he wasn't sure what it was.

The drain on his resources eventually convinced him that some kind of decision was necessary. He made up his mind that his choice, whatever it was, must involve the activity that he enjoyed most — sailing among the reefs and holes of the Antilles and setting anchors in coral rock. It was this that had originally attracted him to smuggling and he wasn't willing to give it up. And when he concluded that the only way to do it profitably was to return to the trade, in a modified and less hazardous role, he threw himself into the task of creating that niche with an enthusiasm and alacrity that amazed him, because he'd never admitted to himself that it wasn't just the sea and sky that had exhilarated him in those first few voyages for profit; it was also the knowledge that the stakes were large and that any errors would result in a lot more than a quick overhaul and a few extra bills. He couldn't perform unless he had a long drop under him. Running a charter, in comparison, seemed about as exciting as sending model sailboats across a tide pool.

There were only two ways to avoid an eventual collision with the DEA and its associated powers. He could either sign up as an agent or never set foot on U.S. soil again. He chose the latter, probably because there was more money in being an outlaw, and immediately began looking for a place in the business that would allow him both comparative safety and a solid income. His strongest assets were his knowledge of the area and his familiarity with current methods of interdiction; no one was more skilled in bringing boats through shoal waters at night. The difficulty was that offloading marijuana on land involved risks which just couldn't be trimmed beyond a certain point; if you were discovered in the act there was no escape, not to mention the likelihood that the people you were selling to would just as soon take it for free and leave you where they found you. Therefore Liberty made two rules for himself: first, he would base himself in the islands and stay off the continent entirely; and second, he would hire out his services to others and never allow himself to own a shipment again, thus removing the need to find buyers on the mainland. In practice, these rules meant that anyone using Liberty had to set up an offshore rendezvous for the transfer and allow Liberty to bring the boat back to the Bahamas. The new high-speed Formula hulls, able to streak out twenty miles and back in an hour or two, made this kind of arrangement more secure than nearly any other, and he soon had more requests for his expensive talents than he could handle. His circumspection and accuracy gave him a reputation for professionalism that protected him in those instances when he got all the way across, within sight of the Florida coast, and suddenly decided that something wasn't right. He'd turn around and bring the whole cargo back to the islands. When a patrol appeared out of nowhere and pounced on the returning Formula boat, still empty, his employers learned to trust the wisdom of his intuition. The move was still intact; they could try again in a day or two. Once in a while Liberty heard that one of his shipments had been seized as it was coming ashore. It didn't disturb him unduly. It was bound to happen now and then; nobody could bat 1.000. The important point was that by the time the arrests occurred he was already well out in the stream and out of reach. He often wondered how many of his former clients had tried to appease the DEA by describing his activities. There wasn't much they could say. Liberty took all his messages through a friend in Nassau, a permanent resident, and doubted that any of these losers could identify him. If the agency really wanted him, he'd concluded, their best shot would be to play traffickers themselves, handing him a full boat in the Bahamas and later appearing at the transfer point with smiles and handcuffs. So he was very careful about who he did business with. He hadn't taken on any newcomers for years.

Because marijuana could be grown nearly anywhere, and the market for it was so large and diffuse, none of the big operators had been able to keep young men of talent from trying their luck at the trade.

Easy to raise, easy to sell; the only really difficult aspect of smuggling dope was the actual shift across the borders. In order for it to be worth the effort, the move had to be at least a hundred pounds — a hundred pounds of a dried plant as bulky and redolent as sawdust. Lots of beginners had come to grief simply because of the physical labor involved. For instance, they might breeze through the Port, tie up the yacht in the canal outside their Miami home, and find that their neighbor had watched them unload a dozen swollen garbage bags at 10:00 P.M. and thought it curious enough to call the police. Nobody with any sense tried to take marijuana through the airport in a suitcase, or even smuggle it through the mails. It just wasn't worth the effort. The best way was to float it in, and since transport by sea into Florida's shallow, overgrown coastline required skills similar to Liberty's, he did very well.

He'd never carried cocaine until he met Cruz. It was the difference between coal and diamonds. Cocaine was light, easy to conceal, and absurdly precious. Like oil or uranium, its production was geographically limited and liable to political control; the entire world supply originated in the damp and remote highlands of Colombia, Bolivia, and Peru. The prime market was the United States, where laws against importation and sale, along with an apparently insatiable demand, kept prices so high that the chief hazard of the trade was the willingness of the participants to rob and murder each other; moving cocaine was like walking around with $10,000 in cash. Liberty had heard that the Colombians had managed to gain control over the export business and were now trying to take over distribution in the United States. He didn't see how they could fail. As long as they continued to monopolize production, and as long as legitimate traffic continued between north and south, the market naturally belonged to them. At any rate, he didn't bother to concern himself with it, because the mechanics of smuggling coke were too simple to require skills like his own—most of it traveled by air, on regular flights — and the problem of sources was nearly insurmountable. Ninety-nine percent of the Americans who went to Colombia looking for coke came back empty-handed. The only people interested in them were the local police, who would sell them a few grams and force them to buy their way out.

Liberty had originally thought Cruz was a Colombian operative who'd been ordered to settle a cache in the Bahamas. From there it would be easy to take advantage of the heavy resort traffic between Miami, New York, and the larger islands, laying off the drug in small and numerous doses. The supply could be safely insulated from any upheavals in Colombia. It was just a guess; Cruz didn't tell Liberty anything about himself. In early May, when Cruz contacted Liberty's agent in Nassau, he said he'd gotten Liberty's name from one of Liberty's oldest and most reliable connections in Miami, a claim that stood up under investigation. Liberty's friend in the city said that Cruz was associated with the leading coke interests in New York and that he had recently traveled to Colombia. In a moment of pride and weakness, Liberty agreed to help Cruz, though not because of the sizable fee he offered; he signed on because he was curious about the trade in cocaine and it appeared to be the safest way he could find out something about it. Since he'd be working for the bosses there'd be nothing to fear from the Colombian authorities. The only danger was the possibility that his employers might want to keep him quiet when the job was finished. But by then he'd have returned to the islands, where he knew how to protect himself. When a check for $20,000 from Aurora Northern, Inc., appeared in his mail three days after his first conversation with Cruz, along with a first-class Pan Am ticket to Cartagena, he decided that they could have murdered him a lot more cheaply than that, and that these were people who could genuinely appreciate his talents.

So it seemed a little odd to him that he spent his first ten days in Colombia finding and repairing a leaky and decrepit fishing boat with an old Dutch diesel in it that ran strictly on memories. The sails hadn't been hung out for years. When Liberty found worms in the base of the mast he told Cruz that they would lose it in the first puff that was strong enough to move the boat. That's why I hired you, Cruz said. On his next run for supplies Liberty bought a life raft, some water bottles, and a good radio. By the time he was done he felt as if he had built the whole thing from scratch.

Nothing up to that point had prepared him for his first sight of the cargo. The little he knew about values for cocaine was enough to convince him that just one of the forty-odd waterproof cases they stacked in the hold was more valuable than anything he had ever carried, and the sheer economic mass they represented — probably a sizable portion of the entire Colombian annual product — shocked him into acquiescence.

By noon the next day they were well offshore and headed north. Cruz was down in the hold with a hand drill, bolting the cases to the underside of the deck, now and then lurching up to lean over the gunwale to leeward in a futile attempt to separate himself from whatever remained in his stomach. Liberty had known for over a week that Cruz wasn't a Colombian; he dropped consonants like a Puerto Rican and his English was too supple to have been learned after the age of ten. Now he was obliged to conclude that Cruz wasn't working for the Colombians either, since they would never have been so stupid as to put all this coke in one place. Then where had he gotten it? Either he had stolen it himself, or someone had stolen it for him. It didn't matter. Liberty didn't try to imagine the circumstances that would allow an outsider to make off, under doubtful conditions, with the chief source of foreign exchange for some of the wealthiest men in Colombia. It was sufficient to know that nobody with any real money or power was involved, nobody who could have prevented the absurd concentration of value that lay under their feet.

Looking back on it now, on the night before the transfer, Liberty understood that although suicide and insanity were still the only words for Cruz, he had a quality of vision that shone through all he said and did; an inspired consistency that demanded respect, even awe. For instance, Liberty would never have thought of trying to bring the coke into the United States, much less announce that it was for sale. In his view the only salvation lay in total concealment in a place as remote from the action as possible; Europe, maybe, or Japan. The coke would have to be leaked into the market through a long string of intermediaries, and over a period of years, with corollary precautions as complete as if the merchandise involved were nuclear bombs. But Cruz, surrounded by palpable impossibilities, didn't calculate odds or consider alternatives. His own survival had to wait upon his instinct for symmetry. He saw beyond his own position; nothing was more obvious to him than the fact that any material interest thrived on exchange, and that rapid and direct contact was the most efficient way to discharge the tension of the market. The most satisfying irony of the entire scheme, Liberty decided, was that Cruz was proposing to sell the coke to the domestic traders for a price well below what it would have cost them to import it themselves.

Liberty now realized that his long paralysis, his inability to resist the vigor of Cruz's obsession — through the long reach southwest of

Jamaica, through the solitary passage across the straits of Florida, through the grounding on Otter Reef, through his own, now incredible, demand to be included at the end — was not due to any supernatural persuasive power attributable to Michael. It was a limitation, not a susceptibility, on Liberty's part. He simply couldn't visualize the end of the journey. Now that he'd examined, with his own eyes, the stage where all these forces would meet at last, he knew that the momentum of the weeks of preparation, drawing strength from two continents, was about to break, and that he would shortly find himself at the center of the storm. It was time to get out. The last doors to the outside were freezing shut.

He planned to be on the first flight to Nassau in the morning. Michael's reaction didn't particularly matter. The traders would murder him in a day or two. If, before he died, they learned the whole story from him, they wouldn't see any need to follow Liberty to the Bahamas.

Liberty didn't hate Michael. If he had it wouldn't have made any difference. He was perfectly willing to be called a traitor; he wasn't at all willing to get himself killed for no discernible reason — certainly not in order to maintain a doubtful and troublesome notion of moral integrity. Let Cruz worry about that — Cruz, who had already upset every convention in a business not noted for its ethical imperatives. Cruz's chief goal seemed to be to arrange for himself the most colorful funeral he could manage.

For the first time in days Liberty felt at peace with himself. Miami, the city of his youth, surrounded him with the shield of its massive indifference — the idea that only a handful of people among these millions cared who he was or what he was doing soothed his nerves and reminded him of the comforting immensity of his adopted parents, the ocean and the sky, who expressed their love for him through a similar unwillingness to interrupt their mighty collaboration for his sake. It's precisely because Miami doesn't need me, Liberty thought, that I can feel at home here; it has already forgotten the first two-thirds of my life, which it supported, and if it struck me down today we would still be strangers to each other.

All the changes — the Cuban invasion, the beanstalk growth of the suburbs, the billion-dollar row of condominiums on Brickell Avenue — were proof of a vitality he had never recognized while he lived here. Now that he had seen it, he was ready to leave. He wouldn't return again for a long time. The next time I'll come here, he decided, will be when I'm ready to stay.

He must have dozed for a while. At eight o'clock, when the light in the room had faded into grayness and the square of heaven outside the window had deepened into a blue so rich and unworldly that he nearly forgot where he was, Liberty got up from the bed and decided to go out in the street. He wasn't hungry, but he hoped a little exercise might awaken his appetite.

He was gone for nearly two hours. When he got back, his feet, unaccustomed to sidewalks, were balancing tenderly on their arches. If he couldn't sleep, he knew he'd at least be able to lie quietly until morning.

He'd been in the room about ten minutes when the door to the room opposite his own swung inward and a middle-aged man in a brick-red suit stepped into the hall. He went down the stairs and gave his key to the manager. But instead of leaving the hotel, he went back up to the second floor, stopped outside Liberty's door, and rapped twice on the shutter.

He caught Liberty in his underwear, about to hang his pants over the towel rod in the bathroom. Liberty stopped and listened. The ensuing quiet emphasized the monstrous nature of the interruption. It was the sign he'd been waiting for, the evidence that his success thus far had been too good to be true.

There was no way he was going to answer the knock. If the person outside really knew he was in there, and wanted to talk to him, he was going to have to do a little more.

Another brittle rap on the shutter; Liberty hung his pants over the rod and waited. There was no harmless explanation for this. He knew it wasn't the manager, and there was no reason why any of the other guests should want to see him; he'd ignored them all from the day he'd arrived.

The only window in the room overlooked the parking lot of the adjacent hotel. The drop from the sill was about twelve feet. He could get out very quickly with a lot of noise or take his time and still make plenty of noise; the screen in the window was rusted and didn't slide easily.

The man in the hall didn't give Liberty a chance to decide. He moved off and tramped heavily down the stairs. Liberty didn't allow himself to draw any conclusions. Since silence was no longer essential, he dressed quickly, snatching his wallet and passport off the table by the bed and shoving them into his pockets. That was all he would need. He turned off the light in the bathroom — the only one he'd had on — and went to the window.

There was a police cruiser parked down the lot about fifty yards away. The nose pointed at the spot under Liberty's window. Although the windshield reflected the Seahorse's outside lights and was therefore opaque, the passenger door was open and a pale oval was clearly visible just under the edge of the roof. That's somebody's face, Liberty thought, and he's looking at this window. Not only is he looking at it, but he wants me to know he is. The man in the crusier couldn't possibly be the same man who had knocked on the door; no one could move that fast. Liberty dropped the idea of exiting through the window. So I'm trapped, he told himself. There was no need to get excited about it. It was a fact. The next few hours, days, even years, were all going to follow naturally from this moment. The process was likely to be tedious in the extreme. He sat down on the bed and covered his face with his hands. What might happen, he thought, if I went out the window head first?

He had never heard the phone beside him ring before. It sounded more like a rattle than a bell. He let it buzz a little, just to make whoever was calling wait a while for his reward. When he finally picked it up it wasn't necessary to say anything.

"Mr. Richmond, this is Arthur Rawden, from the Port. We met a few days ago. When I knock on your door this time, kindly open it."

Ten minutes later Liberty was sitting in the passenger seat of Rawden's dusky blue sedan. Rawden was driving east on the Julia Tuttle Causeway, which crosses the bay at Forty-first Street and is the primary connector between the airport and the beach. Since they were headed away from both the Port and the central city, Liberty had been so bold as to ask where they were going. "Nowhere in particular," Rawden said. The police car that had been at the Seahorse was following about two hundred yards behind. Its high beams were on; their glare lit up the interior of the car. Rawden had Liberty's passport and wallet in his breast pocket. He didn't seem worried about an attempt to retrieve them. And Liberty was not about to do anything until he had a better opinion of his prospects. At the moment, they appeared to be nil.

The Tuttle Causeway was already completed when Liberty was

last in the city. Although it's over two miles long, and crosses the bay at one of its widest points, it bears little resemblance to a bridge — the road surface is only five or six feet above mean high water. Six lanes, split into bundles of three, travel on a level straight across the bay, interrupted at either end by a pair of abrupt forty-foot humps that arch over the channels and allow the tides and the waterborne traffic to pass through unimpeded. The long central section of the causeway forms a narrow island dense with coconut palms and salt-resistant scrub, much frequented by pelicans and men with slimy plastic bait buckets. It was to this island that Rawden was taking Liberty.

As they rolled down the steep eastern side of the hump nearest to the city, Rawden stepped on the brake and rumbled onto the shoulder at the bottom, eventually dipping off the road onto a sandy, uneven lane that curved through the palms to the water's edge. The police car followed and stopped about twenty yards back. When his lights went out it was quite dark; the intervening brush shielded them from the causeway. It was a lonely place at night, a place where authority might exert itself without let or hindrance; Liberty suddenly thought of some of the objects a police officer might carry on his belt: a nightstick, a revolver, handcuffs, and so forth.

Rawden turned to him. His scratchy voice was rapid and subdued. "The first thing I want to say is that I don't want to sit in this cramped seat all night, so if it's all right with you we'll get out and make ourselves comfortable. When I say 'all right,' what I mean is, can I count on you not to bolt away if I blink twice?" He glanced at the police car. "My associate back there would like nothing better than to call up his friends and beat the bushes for you for the next six hours. Are you with me?"

"Whatever you say."

"Good." He opened the door, stood up, and shut it behind him. Liberty did the same. He heard feet crunching toward the rear of the car, then the jingle of keys, and suddenly Rawden's solid midsection shone yellow in the glow of the trunklight. Rawden reached in and pulled out two clinking aluminum beach chairs, sparsely upholstered in flat strips of woven plastic. He shut the trunk and made his way to where a faint rippling sound and the continual shattering of dim reflections indicated the edge of the bay. Liberty followed him.

They unfolded the chairs and grounded them in the rubble at their feet. As they sat down Liberty noticed that the arc of lights across the water allowed him to place himself exactly — to the right, a few miles away, the high mosaic of the downtown office buildings; directly ahead, even farther away, the private docks of the bay islands; and to the left, separated from their inverted reflections by the dark mass of vegetation shielding the private shorefront, the neon ambers and turquoises of the old hotels on the south beach. There was a warm, humid breeze in his face. A few coconut husks bobbed quietly against the rocks. The air seemed to pick up and present to him every odd odor that the wide expanse of the bay could produce: diesel oil, old fish, matted algae, and the oxygen-rich tang of the deep ocean. He could see a long, white-hulled yacht drifting out from the Miamarina, turning south, probably headed for Government Cut. "I've got nothing to say," he said.

"Wait a minute." Rawden was fumbling with a pipe. He sucked the flame of his lighter into the bowl and puffed noisily. Satisfied, he cradled it in his lap and settled himself; the chair creaked. "You've got every reason to be concerned, Mr. . . . . uh . . . uh . . . ."

"Richmond."

"That's right. Liberty could see him well enough to see that he was nodding. "So you've got nothing to say. Nothing to say about what?"

They sat there in silence for a while. At first Liberty was grateful for the opportunity to steady himself, to think, but he had nothing to go on and he found it more and more difficult to concentrate. The cop in the cruiser behind them was like a foot on the back of his neck. The dense air clotted in his throat. His hearing was unnaturally acute; he could hear the rock crabs dragging their hard shells over the coral. He wasn't prepared to sit there all night. "What do you want from me?" he said.

Rawden stirred suddenly, as if he'd been dozing. "I just want to ask you some questions. Number one, why are you still staying in that cardboard hotel? Is this your idea of a vacation?"

Listening to the bay mutter at his feet, Liberty thought: this is the same water that flows around the Biminis and the Greater Bahamas. "You were the one who recommended it, as I remember," he said.

"Did I? Oh yes, you're right — why would I do that? And why would you stay there three nights in a row?"

"Am I under arrest?"

"Arrest? For what?"

"Just tell me yes or no."

204

"If you want, I could fix it for you. But right now I'd have to say no, you aren't."

"Good. Then would you mind taking me back to the hotel now?"

"Detention without arrest — that's it, right? If it's the law that's bothering you, Mr. Richmond, why don't you go talk to it — he's sitting in the car over there."

Liberty didn't answer.

Rawden took the pipe out of his mouth and cleared his throat. "Look, I'm not interested in you. If I was, I could get you a lot of different ways. False papers. Illegal entry. Conspiracy. Taxes. Eighteen dozen smuggling charges. I've got a file on you an inch thick. As a matter of fact, Mr. Richmond, you've been in the business for so long that you're practically immune to prosecution — you've got more lives than a cat. If you exchanged a little damaging testimony for every one of those charges, you'd still have enough left to put half the city in jail — you're a walking almanac of the dope trade. I'll tell you something — you've been on top of a lot of lists for years, and no one's been able to get close to you. Hell, nobody even knows your Christian name. That's how good you are. And that's why I can't understand why you're mixed up in a half-assed operation like this. It doesn't make any sense. Cocaine — you don't need that kind of trouble."

"I don't know what you're talking about." Although Rawden's approach was completely different tonight, Liberty reminded himself that this was the same man who had questioned him at the Port, with the same irritable tone, the same self-indulgent garrulousness, the same mask of eccentric and distracted self-absorption. There was something Rawden wanted; what was it? I can't say the wrong thing, Liberty told himself, if I don't say anything at all.

Rawden went on. "Michael Cruz is an idiot." When he waved his hand a little smoke wafted under Liberty's nose. "You must know that by now. Granted, he's got some imagination, but that just makes it worse. I still don't see how he could've pulled you into this — he's the last guy I would've thought could pressure somebody like you. How did he do it?"

Liberty's eyes were now sufficiently accustomed to the dark to pick out the rows of short pilings surrounding the shoals in the middle of the bay. It was painful — he remembered how he used to pole along those same piles in a dinghy with a shrimp gig and a flashlight on

205

moonless nights just like this, and how he had once dropped the light and watched it burn on the bottom for another ten minutes, attracting shadowy, milky-clear squid to its round-eyed glow. It had nothing to do with Cruz, or Rawden, or the last ten years, and so it hurt to think of it.

"That idea — to have Ray Hula drag the boat off Otter Reef and pull it up the river — that wasn't bad. Was that yours? Ray Hula is not and never will be a smuggler. It's just not the way he thinks. He was perfect for it. If I'd had to trace it through him, I never would've known. That's another thing that amazes me. He would've had to be hung by his toenails before he'd do something like this — I mean literally hung."

He's telling me what he knows to prove what he can do to me, Liberty thought. Don't interrupt; let him get it all out. The only piece left, the piece he wanted to know, was the location of the coke. It was pretty funny, actually; here was a DEA agent trying to get him to drop Michael when he'd already decided to do it himself.

Rawden knocked out his pipe on the arm of his chair. "I don't like to admit it, but I really feel for you guys. You're on your own. So far you've been entirely successful, which is just about the worst thing that could possibly happen to you. Even a professional survivor like yourself — even you, Mr. Richmond—you're going to have a hell of a time walking away when this is over."

He wants me to hate him, Liberty thought.

"Everybody knows about you," Rawden said. "They know everything except who you are. First the coke dried up, then all the traders came to town, and suddenly everybody's looking for Michael Cruz. It's like a fumble on the one yard line—all the players are stacked up like sardines, but no one can see what's going on at the bottom of the pile, where the coke is. You're the only one who knows that, but you don't care anymore — all you're trying to do is keep from getting suffocated. You ought to hear some of the numbers that are flying around. A half ton of coke, ten million dollars. I make forty-five thousand a year, and Washington takes most of it back, but for once I'm glad that I don't have any stake in the game, because this time everybody's going to lose. In fact, I'm surprised that I had to go and get you — I'm, surprised that you didn't turn yourself in. If I wanted to help you I'd arrest you right now. I couldn't do you a bigger favor."

206

Liberty had been over this ground too many times; he was tired of it. "What makes you think I've got anything to do with this?" He didn't expect an answer.

However, Rawden was in a voluble mood. "Listen," he said. "The traders traced Cruz back to Colombia. They got a description of the boat. It's not good enough — they've been tearing up the coast looking for it, but they really don't know what they're after. But I managed to squeeze it out of one of their newsboys — that shows how anxious they are, that they'd be willing to give it to this guy — and somehow it just happened to click for me. I'll tell you something. When I talked to you on Sunday, you had me guessing. I didn't really think you were what you said you were, but I didn't think you were a trader either. You were lucky there — it would've taken a while to check out your paper and I didn't have the time. There was nothing to pressure you with, and I could tell I wouldn't get very far just talking to you. And I thought that if there was anything on the boat, which I doubted, then Hula would find it. When I went to his yard the next day and saw that the boat weighed about half as much as it did when it came in, I said to myself, 'Well, you got fooled pretty good all right, but if you keep quiet maybe you'll catch him next time.' I didn't push it with Hula. That was what really got to me — I knew he was lying, and he'd never lied to me before. He was good at what he did. It's too bad.

"That's the way it happened — I saw you, then I saw the boat, then I heard about the boat and how it was linked to Cruz. All that was missing was your ID. I got that the hard way — I cracked the file for a physical and I ran down everybody but you. This is a first, you know — the first time you've ever been located in the United States."

Liberty was looking straight ahead, out over the dim, light-collecting surface of the bay. My future, he told himself, belongs to this man. What right did he have? In the darkness it was hard to tell the difference between his own thoughts and the sound of Rawden's voice. "It had to happen sometime," he said. "By the way, you've got nothing on me — no drugs, no evidence, no conviction. You jumped too soon."

"Who said I wanted to take you in?"

"You've got the bad paper — that's it. That doesn't count for much."

"Maybe not." Rawden laughed gently. "You think all anybody

wants to do is to put you away somewhere. I'll tell you something, friend — you've already done it for us. You've got a wall around you a mile high. You're your own man — that's what's in it for you, right? Well, just don't ask me to threaten you. I don't feel like it right now." He undid his tie and massaged his neck briefly. "Tell me about Cruz — how did he get the coke?"

"I don't know. He didn't say."

"The traders seem to think it belongs to them. You ever heard of Jack Parko?"

"No."

"He works for a Colombian in New York named Escobar. I hear he's pretty vicious. Well, he's down here now and he's running the search operation. The guy who told me about the boat — I sent him back with a story about one I'd seen at Dinner Key. I made it up on the spot. I hope he had the sense to check it out himself before he brought it to Parko. But they don't need my help. So — is Cruz ready to sell?"

"Why don't you ask him?"

"You don't know?"

"I don't know anything."

Rawden sighed; a bit of phlegm fluttered in his throat. "I don't see why I should have to carry all the weight in this conversation." He pulled on his nose. "Let me make it a little clearer. The worst thing I could do, I suppose, would be to tell Parko about you. Think about that."

"It's all over. You decided — you walked in and dragged me out of the place. You think Cruz didn't notice?"

"He's got the coke — he's stuck with it. He's got to work it out somehow."

"This is boring as hell. I'm tired — I want to go to bed."

Rawden cleared his throat. "You're my nigger and you'll do what I tell you do do."

That was about the size of it, Liberty decided. He could predict, in an abstract sort of way, what the traders would do to him if they thought he could lead them to their precious cocaine, and he also believed that Rawden's conscience was so spotted and leprous already — thanks to many years' professional attandance on the theater of greed, suspicion, and law — that any chance the inspector got to test his inhibitions wouldn't suffer from the arguments of mercy. "Let them kill each other off" — this was the coy sentiment behind those curiously bland, back-page accounts of unexplained murders on Calle Ocho. "Police sources believe the deaths may have been drug-related. The victims have been tentatively identified as . . ." Was it such a long step from this pious indifference to an insouciance just as hypocritical and only slightly less passive?

Another tropical low was moving in; to the west Liberty saw the dim yellow ghost of the city flattened against the vague undercarriage of a mass of invisible cloud, a mass that blotted the weak stars like ink as it slid towards the zenith. Maybe it would rain on Michael tomorrow after all. The breeze on his face, he noticed, had shifted to the right, and a wet wind rattled the old palms back by the police cruiser. The man beside him was quiet; he was waiting for his answer. Liberty turned to him. A kinship based on fear, coercion, and the pure exercise of will precipitated out of the darkness between them. "What do you want to know?" he said.

Within an hour Arthur Rawden knew everything about Cruz that Liberty could tell him. He knew how Cruz had initially reached Liberty. He knew how much money was offered. He knew where the cocaine had been hidden on the *Dart* and was able to guess how it had been removed. He knew the time and location of the transfer and all the plans associated with it. After having Liberty describe the third partner, he correctly identified him as Ray Hula and digressed for a moment on the fertility and intransigence of life as it unfolded; the amazing thing, he said, was the tenacity of the human talent for being surprised. Liberty couldn't tell him about Cruz's origins or how Michael had acquired the cargo. "I believe you," Rawden said. "We'll probably never know, and it wouldn't make any difference if we did. What matters is where the coke is right now. That's the only secret Cruz has — when he loses that, he'll be nobody all over again. It's the same for all of us — it's the cocaine that makes us what we are. We'd have nothing to say to each other without it. It's a little sad, I think — we may never come near it, but we need this pile of white powder to make us come alive. By the way, do you use any drugs? Pills? Dope? Anything?"

"No. Not like I used to."

"I didn't think so. I'll bet you eat seaweed and go jogging every morning too." He stuffed his pipe again, rooting in a plastic pouch and tamping down the bowl with his thumb. "These days people think they're surrounded by all these poisons that are trying to get inside them, but that everything'll be all right if they just keep themselves clean — and the hell with the rest of the world. Their own purity — that's what matters to them. 'Get away from me!' they say, 'I'm healthy! I feel good!' They think disease is a sin — they think any meat that's got blood in it is going to make them sick. What they don't know is that life is always dirty."

"Why don't you tell me what you're going to do with me."

"Not yet. I want to discuss this some more. I don't often get a chance to talk to somebody like you, Mr. Richmond. And you've got to admit we have a lot of common interests. What do you think, for instance, about the federal drug laws? Do they make sense?"

"I didn't vote for them."

"Hell, nobody did. But they're here, and they make you into what the papers call a 'dealer,' and they make you, Cruz, and Hula into a 'narcotics ring.' They've also made you rich."

"I earned whatever I've got, and I've been paying for it ever since."

"But especially right now — I get it." Rawden started to laugh and activated a gritty cough that he had trouble suppressing, in the process alarming some baitfish; they jumped away from his feet and spattered across the shallows. "Anyway," he said, "what about America's youth — twelve-year-olds smoking your Colombian buds? And what about the poor suckers you sell to who wind up dead or in jail? What about them?"

"I don't think about it."

"I know — thinking is bad for you, right?"

"You can't expect me to sit here like this — I've got no sense of humor. I've already decided that I would much rather bash your head in than listen to you talk, and I could use a good beating myself. Do you hear me? I could hurt you very easily."

"Yes," Rawden answered, inclining his head, as if replying to an extremely weighty and deeply-held conviction. He didn't say anything for a few minutes. How nice, Liberty thought — sympathy for the condemned. Rawden had the truth, the entire truth, for nothing. So what if he knew it already? Now there was nothing, nothing even to bluff with. All that was left to do was to hate himself in silence. If I'm bitter now, Liberty told himself, think about ten years in prison — enough bile to rot me away altogether.

"OK," Rawden said, "tell me about the *Cimmerian.*"

If Liberty was surprised by this new line of inquiry, it didn't divert him from his prepared response, which was no response at all.

Rawden hadn't yet abandoned irony. "Did I say something?"

The idea that he still had a card or two to play revived Liberty, even as he rejected it. He didn't answer.

"Tell me about the *Cimmerian* and I'll let you go."

"What?"

"That's right. I'll forget all about you. I'll give you back your paper and drop you wherever you like. Just don't lie to me — that's all I ask."

Liberty started shamming in earnest. "I left my watch at the hotel."

"Did you hear what I said?"

"I left it at the hotel. I want my watch back, I want an audience with the Pope, and I want you to blow me right now. Otherwise I'm through talking."

"You had better listen to me." Rawden took Liberty's passport out of his jacket, sparked his lighter, and held the thin flame to one corner. The polymer case that held it began to stink. Liberty reached out and snatched it away. "Now give me my wallet," he said.

Rawden put the lighter away and handed him the wallet. "There's no reason for you to believe me. But I'll tell you anyway. I could care less about you, or Cruz, or all that cocaine. I'm on leave from the agency — that's a nice way of saying that I got kicked out. They don't know what I'm doing, and I don't think I'm going to tell them. I've got more important ways to spend my time. Tell me about the *Cimmerian,* tell me everything you know, and you'll never see me again. This I promise to you — trust me. What've you got to lose? You can make me an honest man, right now, and it'll change both our lives."

Liberty tottered between disgust and bewilderment. "Why do you want to know?" The lights across the water winked at him. He'd never been seasick, ever.

"Because it matters to me more than anything else in the world. Because all the other questions, all the facts, all the accusations and denials, are meaningless without it. Because I have to know."

"I don't believe you."

"That isn't necessary. It's not relevant — I'm giving you a choice, a real choice, and I'm not going to make it for you. All night you've been telling me that your loyalties lie only with yourself, with your own safety — your own right and duty to put yourself first. OK, so prove it to me."

"I told you all about it on Sunday, remember? I wasn't lying."

Rawden shook his head in frustration. "Don't tell me about truth and lies — I don't want your assurances. You don't understand what I'm looking for — you know nothing about it. I'm not going to explain it to you. So just forget it and listen to me."

For the first time in their acquaintance Liberty thought he heard Rawden's own voice speaking, and for a moment the shadow of hopelessness and futility, which he had lived under ever since that moment at the hotel, fell away from him, because of the shock of this perception—that Rawden sounded like no one more than Michael Cruz. The same private, obsessed, and impenetrable vanity; Liberty suddenly knew that Rawden really didn't care whether he, Liberty, escaped the judgment of the law — he had other things on his mind. The feeling vanished immediately, but it left a painful residue of doubt in the frazzled remains of his ego — painful because he was once more forced to consider the possibility of release. His faith in his own powers, which had been badly wounded in the trap at the hotel, and which had expired utterly under the assault of Rawden's poisonous knowledge, was now stirring and groaning in a wretched imitation of life, like the spasms he had once seen induced in a dead frog by a weak electric current. He relaxed his will and tried to leach away into his surroundings. It might be necessary to think. If he could absorb some of the composure of the wide, noiseless bay and its dark ceiling of cloud . . .

"Well?" It was Rawden; he wanted something.

"Well what?"

"Will you listen to me?"

"Of course."

It was that simple.

Liberty spent the next hour dredging up and wiping clean everything he remembered about the *Cimmerian*. Rawden didn't have to tell him not to theorize or speculate; it never occurred to him. Instead, he emphasized what he had actually seen and heard, a task made easier by the silence, the darkness, and the deep, relaxed slumber of the city around them; that night on the reef returned to him with the immediacy of a dream — all that was missing was a sense of his own participation. The stiff canvas of the officer's features, the preoccupied boredom of the crew, the cool electronic hysteria of a trillion microscopic switches, all informed by an awareness, a collective presence, that surged through bone and steel with the ease of pure energy and set everyone and everything aboard vibrating with the same inaudible hum; Rawden followed him down those dim corridors with an imaginative sympathy so powerful that Liberty felt as lifeless and infallible as one of those cathode screens the officer had demonstrated for him.

Liberty hadn't drawn any conclusions about the *Cimmerian.* It was just another feature of the landscape; more ambiguous than most, and therefore to be avoided. Like most successful traders, he was not in the habit of inquiring into matters that didn't directly concern him. The most significant aspect of his night aboard the ship, in his opinion, was that he'd been taken off the next day with no apparent harm.

But Rawden's fascination was obvious. Liberty continued, dwelling on the most minor physical details, in the hope that Rawden, if he had not already made up his mind, might be persuaded by Liberty's active cooperation to honor his promise of noninterference. He knew that there was nothing else he could do. The Bahamas seemed hopelessly distant.

"OK," Rawden said, "I've heard enough." He threw his chin back and stretched his arms over his head; Liberty could see each black finger silhouetted against the faint glow of the clouds. "Everything you said—it shows how little you actually know." He sounded relaxed, confident, and pleased with himself, like a man who's just finished something difficult. Liberty's pulse jumped. "I'm sorry if I had to be a little hard on you," Rawden said. "I had to — I've got no reason to dislike you. In fact, I wish we had time to talk about a lot of other things — it's too bad that our natural antagonism, so to speak, prevents us from enjoying each other's company more often — in a better world we might have been friends. Yes, I think that goes without saying. I admire you tremendously and I know that, in time to come, you'll succeed at whatever you do. That's not so much to ask, is it? Anyway, I'm not going to make any more trouble for you. I'll take you back to the hotel and let you sleep. I won't touch the transfer tomorrow — I don't want anything to do with it. If you don't believe me, that's your business. And if I were you, I'd put as much distance between myself and Michael Cruz as possible."

213

"What about you? What're you going to do?"

Rawden laughed. "What kind of question is that?"

"All this crap about the *Cimmerian* — what did you want it for?"

Rawden, who'd been shifting around in his seat and adjusting his jacket as if preparing to get up, was suddenly still. The highs and lows dropped out of his voice; his answer was flat and unweighted. "I don't know. No. I didn't know until now. I might change my mind. I do know that I will never — I said never — return to the agency. I'm through taking sides. That part of my life is over."

"Why?"

"Because I'm a different man than I was a week ago."

Liberty fell easily into the role of inquisitor. "Tell me now," he said. "You owe it to me."

"Because?"

"You fucked me over royally tonight. I don't have a choice anymore. You took it away."

"I didn't play fair, is that it? I've got a lot of respect for you, Mr. Richmond — why spoil it?"

"I never tortured anybody. I never put anyone in jail, or took money for what I could do to people."

"It's amazing how self-righteous you jerks can be — you young guys especially. You get in trouble and suddenly you're all moralists. It's not as funny as it seems."

Liberty felt his edge slipping away. "So what now? What do you do now?"

Rawden nearly slapped him down, but thought better of it. He was quiet as he prepared his answer. Then, after a minute, he said "Listen — all my life — all my life I've tried to maintain the law — it was more than a job for me, I really believed in it — not in the law itself, actually, but in my own responsibility as its guardian, because I thought — I thought I had a real, necessary function in the government — and the country — as a whole. Why else would anybody do what I did? I knew what was required of me, and I thought that if I did this one thing well, as well as I could, then my contribution could help to support all of it." His throat whistled as he sighed; he laughed gently.

"Shit, I knew better — I knew when I was doing my job and when I was just fucking around with people. We all loved it, the power we had — a lot of us were nothing without it. If you got a name for let-

ting people off easy, then everybody asked you who it was that'd gotten to you and when you were going to take your millions and retire
in Mexico.

"Well, I'm not saying it was wrong, but I don't see it like I used to.
Because I moved up through the grades so fast I always had to prove
I was a bigger son of a bitch than the next guy, and maybe that's why
I stepped back from it a little — I could crack the whip without even
thinking about it, and half the time I was laughing at myself. Every-
one thought I was just getting meaner.

"What I discovered — and what led to my break with the leadership — was that all my authority in the agency, all the big busts I had
under my name, didn't necessarily add up to anything in particular — it was all in the past, all behind me, and every day I had to face
another set of decisions that weren't nearly as routine as they looked,
because there was always somebody's head on the block, and no matter how hard I tried to stick to the procedures I'd developed over the
years, I knew — though oftentimes I didn't want to know — that
what actually happened had less to do with the code I was supposedly
enforcing than with certain unquantifiable factors which I couldn't
control — somebody else's scheduling, the way I'd slept the night before, a private whim, maybe. And when, once in a while, one of my
men came in from the field with his face shot away it seemed to me
that what I did was worse than nothing." He coughed harshly; the
chair creaked.

"So I knew I had to get out. I told you I'm not going back to the
agency — that doesn't mean I'm going to retire. As a matter of fact,
sometimes I think I'm just getting started — I'm going after the
Cimmerian."

Liberty waited for him to continue, but that was all he had to say.
In a minute or so Liberty opened his mouth, hesitated, and said, "You
lost me."

"That's all right. You wouldn't know. You couldn't know — you
haven't seen what I've seen." He heaved a big, noisy sigh. "I'm tired.
I'm very, very tired. I'll take you back now — I'm sure you'll want to
get up early tomorrow."

Rawden stood up and collapsed his chair with his foot. Somewhere
in the scrub a heron croaked and gobbled. Liberty stared across the
bay. Far to the south, a motor cruiser was crossing in front of
the harbor islands; its bow wave made the needlelike reflections of the

dock lights quiver in succession. "Are you coming?" Rawden said.

You tell me, Liberty thought. What bothered him was the fact that it would be quite a while before he knew without doubt that Rawden didn't intend to collar him; the man could wait, if he wanted, right up until the moment Liberty stepped aboard an outbound plane. He felt drained and weak, stripped of any ability to resist.

They trudged across the uneven limestone towards the car, Rawden leading. He shielded his face with one hand and swept the other in a short arc in front of him at eye level, pushing aside the new webs the spiders had strung across the path since their arrival. The police car started up and the headlights suddenly blinded them. "We'll leave my car here," Rawden said. "I don't need it any more." He got in the back seat of the cruiser with Liberty.

"Where to?" the cop said. He was examining Liberty through the steel divider, his face fleshy, suspicious, and bored.

"The city," Rawden said. "No hurry."

The cop cut straight across the eastbound lanes of the causeway — there was no traffic — nosed through the shallow ditch in the median, and leaped onto the wide, empty, well-lit feeder to the city. "Take it easy," Rawden said. As they climbed the symmetrical hump over the channel the acceleration forced Liberty back into his seat. Nobody moves this fast in the islands, he thought. He turned to Rawden. "Are you married?" he asked.

It might have been a joke, but Rawden didn't hear it that way. "No, never have been. No kids — don't even own a home. It's too late to regret it now. You could say, I suppose, that all my children are in prison." He started to laugh. "Some of them are nice enough to send me a card at Christmas." The laugh died away. "Lucky for you I'm getting soft in my old age. Incidentally, our file on you doesn't mention any wife — I would guess, though, that there isn't any. Am I right?"

"She said no," Liberty said. "I didn't ask her twice."

"Uh-huh." Rawden rolled the window down an inch. The cop in the front seat snickered.

They dropped Liberty in front of his hotel on the boulevard. Liberty stood on the sidewalk and watched them drive away, the gleam of the streetlights sliding over the roof, one after another. He was marooned once more.

There was plenty to think about. There were a hundred ways to

216

get out of Florida; Rawden couldn't anticipate them all. In his brief
visit to Bayfront Park, Liberty had seen dozens of small, speedy boats
that could get him across the straits in a few hours. The difference
between the Seahorse Motel and his place in the Bahamas was the difference between the night and the following day — not much. There
was nothing he could do in advance; he wouldn't know what might
work until he tried it. An impartial observer might assert that Liberty
had been extremely lucky to hang this close to the fire for so long and
remain untouched, but as far as Liberty was concerned, luck had
nothing to do with it. He laid the responsibility entirely on himself.
It's easy to talk about probability and accident in the lives of others;
it's not so easy to bear the judgment of mathematics on your own
head.

In the end, the hundreds of arguments pro and con, reservations,
cavils, rhetorical asides, appeals to reason and precedent, linked factors, and conflicting bits of evidence that Liberty introduced into the
furious debate with himself he arbitrated during the rest of the night
didn't particularly matter, because the answer came to him in a dream
he had shortly before morning — a dream in which Michael Cruz
approached him in this same room with an open shoebox full of cocaine under one arm and one full of coral sand under the other.
"Which one belongs to you?" He didn't answer. "Which one is
yours?" When Liberty's eyes split open and he saw the bare gray
walls exactly where they'd stood in the dream, and the empty space
where Cruz had stood, he knew that the choice no longer existed —
nobody was going to get an opportunity to ask him again — and
some hours later he was waiting beside the Fotomat in front of Jefferson's department store, feeling the edge of a key in his pocket and
watching a small figure in black dodging towards him through the
traffic crawling down Dixie Highway some four hundred yards away.

The Transfer

IT WAS FIVE IN THE AFTERNOON. Jack Parko hadn't eaten any-thing all day except for half a bag of potato chips and his stomach had shrunk to the size of a wad of chewing gum. He normally ate a lot when he was nervous; today he was so nervous that he could barely get a gulp of air between his teeth. He was responsible for twenty-six armed men and ten million dollars in cash. He knew that the fact that he was nervous was going to make everyone else nervous also. Ac-cording to the people who were in a position to know, one of the rea-sons that Jack was so valuable to Escobar was his ability to stay cool under pressure, but, as Jack himself was so poignantly aware, his out-ward appearance had more to do with catatonia than inner peace. All week long Jack had thought he was nervous; today he'd discovered what nervous was.

His personal safety wasn't at issue, or at least not immediately. Mi-chael Cruz was in no position to threaten anyone. As tense and uneasy as he was, Jack could at least take comfort in the fact that he was not Michael Cruz.

It was a normal weekday afternoon on Dixie Highway, which is to say it was about as quiet as an air raid on a munitions plant. The con-stant, reverberating rumble of hundreds of gas engines deadened the more random interjections of horns, brakes, shopping carts, and com-mercial aircraft. There were sparrows and grackles fighting over crumbs under the promenade, but no one could hear them. The few human figures visible in all this noise and activity — mostly people moving from their cars into the stores and back — walked quickly with their heads down, bent slightly forward, as if prolonged exposure to open air, without the insulating barrier of a building or a windshield, might freeze them where they stood — actually, they were just all in a hurry. Jack was reminded of the Long Island Expressway on Labor Day weekend. We could shoot the whole place to pieces, he thought, and no one would notice.

Ramón, Escobar's favorite, was still sitting in the car beside him. Jack watched his other men occupy the corners of the narrow lot, positioning their front wheels for a quick exit. Jack didn't worry about looking at them directly; Cruz must know who they were, wherever he was.

Neither Jack nor any of the men under his command had ever been to this particular address before. When Michael gave it to him over the phone Jack had pulled out a map and inked a small circle around it, visualizing a country roadside where the dust of a passing truck hung in the air for twenty minutes and a gas station with a produce stand attached was the only sign of commercial life; he had worried about the attention the arrival of ten large sedans full of men might attract. The old housekeeper had told him that there was a lot of new construction down there and that they'd run into some commuter traffic on the way.

All the cars had radios. Jack and Ramón had left about fifteen minutes before everyone else, so they'd have a chance to feel around a little and decide where to put the others.

There was no sign of Cruz when they arrived. "He's here," Jack said. "He'll show himself when he's ready." They sat in the car for a few minutes while Jack alerted the other drivers to the location and assigned them their initial places, although anyone not familiar with his terms wouldn't have known what he was talking about. He put two cars at the liquor store just up the road, two cars in the lot itself, and ordered the rest to choke points in the surrounding area, some of which had been plotted in advance back at the house. Then he told Ramón to get out of the car, look around, and jot down the plates, color, and model of every car in the lot.

When Ramón returned the others were starting to arrive. Ramón had walked through the hardware store in the center of the block and had seen the lot in back, with the rear entrance leading away from the highway; it was the first thing he mentioned. Jack had already deduced its existence by watching cars disappear around either end of the row of shops. He decided to take a team off the liquor store and put it back there. Could Cruz have actually hoped that it wouldn't be noticed? Impossible.

He told Ramón to make the change himself and went out for a walk. The sun was still high; as he moved he could feel exactly which portions of his skin were exposed and which were in shadow. He stepped onto the sidewalk under the promenade, with its flat roof supported by a row of round steel posts painted bright red, and he strolled up and down a few times. If Cruz was here he was probably watching from inside one of the stores. Shoppers pushed in and out of the glass doors and a few young teenage kids were standing in a loose group around their bicycles and splashing soda on each other. In his dust-colored suit and agate cuff links Jack looked like a prosperous salesman and attracted no notice.

He went around to the rear and looked at the series of thickly planted half-acre lots that lay about fifty yards back from the building, straddling the exit in the middle. Solid walls of eucalyptus screened them from the shopping center. Here and there he could see patches of chain-link fencing buried in the tangle of shadows and shiny, bobbing leaves. A hole in that wall might make it possible for Cruz to escape on foot; Jack decided that two of the men back here would have to be out of their car. They could slow him down if he ran for the trees.

He walked through a stationery store, emerged at the front, and looked across the highway. The near, northbound lanes were moving at about thirty miles an hour. The far lanes — solid machinery. The light bouncing off all that glossy sheet metal made it difficult to see. When he'd first arrived, Jack had thought Cruz might try to get away by dodging the action in the near lanes, hopping the median, and jumping into a car on the other side. Not likely; it would take him an hour to go ten feet. However, there was plenty of free space beyond the highway — a parking lot of a size Jack usually associated with airports and sports arenas, fronting a gigantic building looming over the flat, brilliant horizon like an artificial thunderhead. It had to be a department store. A car over there, beside the highway, would spoil any attempt to make off in that direction.

The bankers had come; there were three of them and a driver, all sitting in a blue Cadillac drawn up between a half-rotted VW bus and an ageless Corvair. Nobody had told Jack who they were or what they would look like. They were supposed to make their appearance on a signal from Ramón. But how often do you see four well-dressed middle-aged men sitting in a parked car? Jack guessed that, with the exception of the driver, they each had a valise between their knees. They were all old enemies; they'd have a lot of unpleasant things to say to each other if they could just bring themselves to open their mouths and talk. There was too much money, too close at hand, for that.

Cruz's problem, as Jack saw it, was to get hold of that money and disappear. However, Jack wouldn't let it go unless he was absolutely sure that the cocaine was safe in his possession. The difficulty Cruz faced, then, was to provide Jack with that assurance without giving him an opportunity to retrieve the cash immediately.

So Cruz had to have some kind of scheme to insure that both goods and payment changed hands nearly simultaneously and that he could vanish forthwith. Something nobody could anticipate, something that made full use of his only advantage, surprise — an advantage that would dissipate as soon as it was employed. For all his nervousness, Jack didn't really believe that Michael could bring it off. Stealing the cocaine and taking it into Florida were simple operations in comparison. If Cruz thought that the presence of all these straight characters with shopping bags was going to slow anything down he was the one who was in for a surprise. Today was the first day Jack had worn a gun in nearly two years. He was already being blamed for the failure of the search effort, an effort that he thought misconceived from the start; he was glad it hadn't scared Cruz away. Now Michael was going to do his work for him. It was much easier, in Jack's humble opinion, to let Cruz lead them to the coke than to try and find it for themselves. And once they knew where it was there were no risks in mistreating the owner. The value of Michael's life would drop so rapidly that his actual death would be anticlimactic; just the same, Jack wanted the honor for himself. It was no less than his due. Michael Cruz was never going to embarrass him again.

He got back in the car with Ramón and made the last changes. The preparation was over; from now on it was stroke and counterstroke. For the first time since he'd arrived in Miami Jack knew that he was where he wanted to be.

Ramón touched him on the shoulder. "Look." Michael was standing on the sidewalk in front of the hardware store. An array of

224

steel rakes, garden tools, and power mowers crowded the window behind him.

Michael had dressed for the occasion. He wore the dark, gray black synthetic business suit he'd worn on his first visit to Hula; it was freshly cleaned and might have created an impression of moneyed conservatism if it hadn't been a little too small, even for him. He wore it over a pale blue shirt and a silk tie. His black buckle wingtips shone, his hair was brushed back, and his hands were white and clean, with red spots around the knuckles and wrists, as if he had scrubbed them too hard. He didn't look much different from the way Jack remembered him; a little more stiff and scrawny maybe, a little less young. A pair of sunglasses stuck out of his breast pocket and a small bulge below and to the left of it betrayed a pistol. He nodded when he saw Jack sitting in the maroon Seville. That was the first time his eyes had stopped to look at anything in particular; they jerked back and forth over the parking lot like a chaperone's at a high-school dance.

There was nothing to think about. Jack got out of the car and walked across the lot.

He touched Cruz on the sleeve. "Michael — where've you been? I've been looking for you."

"No kidding. Did you bring the cash?"

"Sure I did."

"Let's see it."

"OK — take it easy." He took a step back and ran his eyes up and down the younger man. "You look good — you look all right. It's been a while hasn't it? So." He laid his palms together and turned away from Cruz, gazing out, like him, over the lot and across the highway. "You're about to become a millionaire — how does it feel?"

"Like shit."

"Michael, this is your day to shine. Every toot in New York is dancing in the streets — they're singing your name. Why not enjoy it?"

"You're still with Escobar, right?"

Jack shook his head. "No — right now I'm working for you. We all are. The president of Colombia is watching you on a satellite hookup. The Knicks and the Yankees want to talk contracts. Here it is, Michael — all that hard work — this is where you come to collect. Are you ready?"

"Show me the money and then we'll talk."

225

"Sure." Jack smiled. "Always the businessman — I like it. You've got balls, Michael, I'll give you that. Will you take a personal check?"

A red flush rose out of Cruz's collar and spread toward his ears. "Sorry," Jack said. He lifted one leg and glanced at the sole of his shoe. Ramón rolled down his window. The driver in the blue Cadillac got out of the car, keys in hand, and looked at Jack, who turned to Michael. "The blue boat," he said. "Get in the driver's seat and they'll show it to you. It's not coming out until we see the stuff."

Cruz didn't move. "No," he said. "I want it out of the car."

Here we go, Jack said to himself. "What?"

"You heard me."

"Yes, I heard you." He turned and tapped gently on the plate glass behind him with one doubled knuckle, his face knotted in thought. "Michael, the problem is —"

"What was that for?" Michael had moved a step closer and was staring at him intently.

Jack stared right back. "What was what for?"

"That knock on the window, just now."

"You saw that? You don't miss anything, do you?" He smiled. "It was a message in code." He reached up and rapped again. "See?"

Cruz turned away. "Don't fuck with me. I could kill you right now and nobody would care — they'd just send somebody else in to do what I say."

Jack pushed out his lower lip and rocked his head from side to side. "You know, I think you're right."

"I want the money out of the car."

They both watched an overweight dog walk up, sniff Cruz on the leg, wag his tail tentatively, and rush off to lap up an ice-cream sandwich he'd spotted a few yards away.

"Why?" Jack said.

"Because if it's still in there when I hand over the coke I don't think I'll be able to get it out."

"So what do you want me to do?"

"Stuff it in a couple of paper bags, like groceries, and bring it up here."

"Suppose a cop shows up, sees your gun, and wants to know what's in the bags?"

"I'll think of something."

"It's too risky. Do you have a car?"

226

Cruz didn't take his eyes off Jack's face. "I've got dozens of them — why?"

"We could put the cash in your trunk, right now. What do you think about that?"

He considered it for a moment, rubbing his forehead with the heel of his palm, and said, "I'd rather do it my way."

"Of course. The idea is to make it as difficult as possible. Should I fuck your mother, too?" Jack had spoken too quickly; he regretted it. "Look, why don't you go and look at the money now. We'll talk about it some more when you get back." It was important to create the impression that they were making progress.

Cruz looked at the hard-faced man, already starting to wilt a little, standing by the blue Cadillac. "All right," he said. "I just go over there and say hello, right?"

"That's it."

Jack watched him step off the curb, into the sun, and walk away. Cruz got into the Cadillac and shut the door. The dark tinted glass didn't allow Jack to see what was happening inside. He hadn't seen the money himself; he hoped it was all there.

If anything, the activity in the lot had increased. There was a backlog at the entrance, nearly on the point of spilling onto the highway. Once inside, the cars were trapped — they had to wait for the jam to break ahead of them before they could move. There was only one person in each car. Whatever passengers had arrived with them had already gotten out and disappeared into the stores. A long-haired boy with a white apron over a T-shirt was banging together a string of shopping carts, jerking his hands away deftly at the moment of impact. Did he know that he was on film? One man in each of Jack's cars had a camera and was clicking the shutter at anything that moved.

Jack couldn't believe that Cruz was alone. There had to be someone to take the cash as soon as Cruz unveiled the coke — doing it alone was like trying to let a tiger out of its cage and get in the door at the same time. Right now, the second man was either sitting in a nearby car or waiting inside one of the stores. From where he was standing Jack could see five or six likely prospects behind the wheels of parked cars; most of them were probably waiting for friends or relatives to finish their shopping. They all had their eyes open and were watching the world go by. None of them seemed to be following Cruz more closely than the others.

227

Michael was still in the car with the bankers. Jack was sorry he couldn't be in on their deliberations; four men, none of whom were especially fond of each other, with ten million dollars to count between them. It would probably take a little while. He decided to see what Ramón had to say and returned to the car. The air inside was still cool and Ramón was leaning over the radio, finishing a conversation in Spanish.

"What was that?" Jack said, perhaps a little too pointedly.

Ramón picked up the map and showed him the car stationed at the closest turnpike entrance, a few miles to the west. "They were listening to the news. There's a big storm coming in tonight — a lot of rain."

"Right now?" A minute earlier Jack had observed that there was nothing in the sky to interrupt the increasing brilliance of the sun as it descended.

"Two or three hours."

"We're not going to the beach."

Ramón hung up the mike and lit a cigarette. The sealed car started to fill up with smoke. "He looks like his picture."

"That was him, all right. What do you think — is he alone?"

"No — I think he's with that guy in the rented car. The gold Mercury."

Jack leaned forward and looked to his right, toward the center of the row of stores. Through the glass of the intervening cars he could see a heavy middle-aged man slouching behind the wheel with a soft tennis hat down over his ears. The man felt Jack's gaze and looked back. There were too many windows in between to see his features. "I was standing right in front of him — I didn't notice anything."

"He was there when we got here. It's a rented car. The hat hides his face."

"Well, everybody rents a car down here. He doesn't look like a wise guy to me. There's some more people that you can't see from here."

"He's been staring at the door of the flower shop. How long does it take to buy flowers? What's he waiting for?"

"Maybe his wife works inside."

Ramón shrugged. "I can find out. I'll knock on his window and ask him if he knows Michael Cruz."

Jack thought it was a lousy idea, but decided not to object unless

228

Ramón started to move. He didn't. Jack tapped the radio. "Did you check in with everybody?"

"Yes. What did he say to you?"

"He wanted to see the money. He also wanted it out of the car."

"You said?"

"I said we'd discuss it. I'll do it if I have to — I don't think it'll be a problem."

"Where is it?"

"The coke? Do you think I'd be sitting here if I knew that?"

Ramón waved his cigarette; an ash fell on the carpet. "I don't see where he could put it around here. It has to be somewhere where we can look at it in private. If it's in one of these cars than he's more stupid than I thought he was."

"There's a Salvation Army box and some dumpsters in back — maybe he put it in one of them."

The younger man stared at Jack for a moment and picked up the mike. "I'll tell them to check," he said, waiting.

"All right. Do it fast."

Jack looked up and saw that Cruz was on the promenade again in front of the hardware store, displaying his figure for the curious. When Ramón shut off the radio Jack pointed at Cruz. "He's back. If you have to talk to me, lay your hand flat against the windshield, just under the mirror. I'll see it." Ramón nodded. Jack pushed open the door and got out. The heat surprised him; he waited for his head to clear.

When he got to the sidewalk Michael had nothing to say. Jack smiled. "Satisfied?" Michael didn't answer. "You know, we could easily have brought along just half of what you asked for and said take it or leave it. But we didn't because we wanted to make you happy. OK, your turn."

Cruz hadn't taken his eyes off the squat Cadillac, as if he were still listening to something he'd heard inside. He didn't look at Jack as he spoke. "You get some paper bags from the store, put the money in them — leave the cases in the car — put the bags in a shopping cart, and bring it up here. Then I'll show you where it is."

"It's not going to be enough to show it to me. You'll stay right here until I have it in my hands."

"Same thing."

"We'll see." Michael's obdurate, expressionless intensity was be-

229

ginning to erode Jack's confidence. "Where are you going to be while I'm doing all this?"

"Right here."

"All right — don't get excited. You realize this is a personal favor I'm doing for you."

"Just do it."

It took Jack a few minutes to convince the bankers. At first he was surprised that Cruz was willing to have the cash packed up without his supervision. He immediately discovered that the bankers could be relied upon to discipline each other.

The money went into three large black plastic bags. Jack tied the openings and put them in the cart. He chose a route across the lot that took him past the gold Mercury; as he rattled by he looked down at the man in the driver's seat. He was a big man, dressed lightly in a white shirt and khakis and his hands were in his lap. He wasn't wearing a gun. Jack looked up quickly, to catch Cruz's reaction — there wasn't any. He bumped the cart onto the sidewalk and parked it against the window. Michael glanced down at it briefly and returned to looking at Jack.

"OK," he said. "That money belongs to me." He stepped in front of Jack and turned around, so that he partially blocked Jack's view of the lot and his face was hidden from the men in the cars. "The first rule is that you don't leave this spot until we're done. If you want to talk to any of your people, call them up here. But the minute you step off this sidewalk I don't owe you anything any more, and I'll do whatever I like."

Jack moved out from behind Cruz, like a chessman fleeing to an adjacent square, and put his hand on the shopping cart. "Where's the coke?" he said.

"You heard what I said — remember it."

"This isn't the kind of situation where promises mean anything."

"I know. Just keep it in mind." He stopped to let it sink in. "The second rule is that once we get started here I don't want any arguments from you. Questions, fine — but no arguments. If you do what I say you'll get your stuff quickly and you'll get it before you give up the cash. So there's no risk in it for you."

"That's good," Jack said. "I hate risks."

"I'm just warning you."

"OK, go on."

230

Cruz stepped to the edge of the sidewalk and turned to face him, so that he was talking at the window. "Listen carefully," he said. A little girl in a pink flounce pushed open the door of the hardware store and ran down the sidewalk between them, shrieking with laughter. A small boy burst out of the same door and gave chase. Cruz's eyes didn't leave Jack's face. He's turned this way, Jack thought, because he's worried about a directional microphone. There was too much racket for a conventional bug to work. Jack wasn't wearing one anyway.

"The coke is about a half mile from here, across the highway. It's in front of that big department store. I have some men over there who're going to hold onto it unless they receive certain signals from me."

Jack remembered the car he had put in the lot across the road. He shaded his eyes; there it was, parked on the far side of the creeping wall of traffic, windshield darkened by the blaze of sun behind it, which also blackened the distant facade of the store. Close to the building the cars made a dense undifferentiated carpet. "I don't see any coke," he said.

"It's there — but unless they hear from me soon it'll be gone. What I want you to do is choose one of your men to go over there and see it. Someone who's qualified to identify it. Someone you can trust, because right after he calls you back and tells you about it he's going to take possession. Then I'll be on my way. They can see me right now, and they can see the money — they've got good eyes over there. Unless I'm seen leaving quietly, at my own speed, your man won't be allowed to keep the coke. That's what I want you to remember. I either give it to you my way or you don't get it at all."

"Where is it exactly?" Jack needed time to absorb the news; a little thought could make a big difference here.

"You'll find that out when your man calls."

"Calls where?"

"The pay phone." There was a phone mounted on the short stretch of stucco between the hardware store and the flower shop. Jack lifted his arm high and pointed at it. "That one?"

"Yeah, that's it." Cruz seemed a little annoyed by the gesture.

Jack let his arm slap against his side. "Let me get this straight. You expect me to give you the cash on the basis of a phone call from someone I can't see and who may have a gun in his ribs, for all I know — a call concerning a pile of coke which could easily disappear before I get to it, because you'll already have the money and won't need — and just might want to sell it again — that's if the coke really exists to start with." He puffed out his cheeks and sighed; a series of small, slightly converging lines appeared on his upper lip. "You know what this means, don't you? Your career is over. We'll have to take the money back and take you home with us. We'll have to start looking for the coke all over again. But you'll never know if we find it or not, because you'll be gone." He shook his head. "I've put a lot of time into this operation and now it's all going to waste. You booted it, Michael — I'm sorry for both of us."

"You'll be able to see the coke when your man gets over there and you'll be able to see him after he makes the call. Anybody who tries to take it away will be doing it right in front of you."

"See it — from here?"

"That's right."

Jack noticed that the heavy man in the gold Mercury had a curiously flattened nose, as if he had a stocking tied over his head. He couldn't be sure. The man was slouched down and his white hat was low over his face. "Is he a friend of yours?" he asked, pointing.

"None of your business. There's over a thousand pounds of coke over there, and it's yours if you treat me right."

Jack looked at his feet and brushed at a spot on the skirt of his jacket. "Most of the choices I have to make are difficult, but this one is just too easy. You didn't even come close, Michael. I came here prepared to make a deal with you, and look what happened. You ask me to take your word against ten million dollars. Is it really worth that much? No, it's not."

"You're all talk — you must be getting old."

Jack groaned.

"If you're so anxious to put an end to this thing, why don't you get going? I'm ready."

"Right." Jack waved to Ramón. "I'm calling him up here. The hell with this one-on-one crap."

"Think about what you're doing. Think about it carefully."

Jack was thinking about what Ramón could do with the radio and the car across the highway.

Ramón was a large, handsome man with long, well-tended black hair, yellow brown skin, and bad teeth. He was wearing a loose cotton

232

suit and a gold watch. He bounded onto the sidewalk and looked at Jack, then at Michael. He cultivated a profound silence drawing from equally deep reservoirs of pride and contempt; he looked at Michael as he might have looked at something he'd shaken out of his shoe.

"Ramón, this is Michael Cruz. Michael, tell Ramón what you just told me."

Cruz quickly repeated the terms of his proposition. When he finished, Jack said, "What about it — do we thank him or kick his ass?" Ramón's lower jaw worked forward a couple of times. He turned and spat on the sidewalk. Jack crossed his arms on his chest. "It's too bad we can't start all over again. So" — he poked his chin at Ramón — "would you like to be the guy who goes over there and gets knocked on the head?"

Michael suddenly looked bored. "I don't know what you're so worried about. You've got this money sitting here, you've got forty dozen soldiers standing around, and you've got a half ton of cocaine waiting for you across the street. I thought it was what you wanted."

Ramón also knew about the car on the other side. "I'll go," he said. "Tell me what to do."

"Take our car," Jack said. "Keep an eye —"

"Wait." Cruz didn't look at Ramón; he spoke only to Jack. "Nobody's going over there in a car. The man who goes will go unarmed and on foot."

They listened to the traffic for about fifteen seconds. A jet crawled high overhead; the declining sun gave its underside a bronze gleam. Jack finally thought of something to say. "That's worse, Michael — that's just stupid. Excuse me a minute — don't worry, I'm not going anywhere."

He touched Ramón on the shoulder and escorted him down the sidewalk a few yards. He glanced back; Michael was leaning against the plate glass and surveying the lot. Jack turned to Ramón and spoke softly and rapidly. "I think we should do what he says. He's obviously counting on the fact that a man on foot will get over there way before anyone in a car — so they can make the trade and get out before anyone else shows up. OK. We've got a car on the other side. We'll send Johnny over. You'll stay up here while Cruz tells him what to do, then you'll go back to the car, get on the box, and tell the men over there to move immediately to the front of the store — or wherever Cruz tells Johnny to go — and wait there. Tell them to watch for him — somebody's going to show him the coke — they should see where it is. Tell them to keep an eye on it, but not to do anything else, unless someone tries to take it away. I think Cruz is ready to sell. I'm going to play it straight with him. The coke may be wired — we have to make him think it's all going his way. While you're getting Johnny take one car off the liquor store and send it over, but that's all. I don't want anybody else off station. You can fill in the details. Cruz is going to make a dash from here, somehow. If we don't stop him right away I'll come back to the car and we'll go. I'll take the first shot. Nobody moves until I move." Jack stopped to catch his breath. He could feel his heart accelerating unmercifully; it convinced him of the need to continue. "All right — is that clear? You heard it all?"

"We should take the coke right away. We shouldn't wait for Cruz to run."

"No — let it go like he wants. We don't know what he can do."

"If we surprise him it won't matter."

"Don't argue. Just do what I say."

Ramón was trained to obedience, like all of Escobar's lieutenants, and though the tightness around his mouth and the dull fire in his eyes made it obvious that he wasn't happy with Jack's strategic acquiescence, he didn't dispute it further.

"We have to do it the easy way," Jack said. "Now go get Johnny."

Ramón returned to the car and Jack rejoined Cruz by the shopping cart. "You're on," he said. "Ramón is getting someone right now."

Cruz looked at his watch. "It's five-thirty. I'm giving your man ten minutes to get over there and look over the stuff — any longer than that, and it's gone."

Jack nodded. "Right." He saw Johnny get out of a car near the end of the lot and start in their direction, in response to Ramón's call. The kid kept his head down and was nearly run over by a red pickup that backed out suddenly; he jumped to one side and looked around wildly. You poor shit, Jack thought, I don't blame you. Johnny was Ramón's younger brother. Jack had chosen him in order to pacify Cruz; Johnny was clearly not a threat as an individual; his simplicity was evident in the pale transparency of his face. He wasn't very bright and he had never learned malice. Jack also knew that the choice would rein in Ramón for the time being.

When he reached them he immediately tried to explain himself, as

234

if he had a lot to apologize for. "Ramón — Ramón said you wanted to talk to me."

"That's right, Johnny," Jack said. "You're going to see the cocaine and you're going to tell me if it's all there — all twelve hundred pounds. This is Michael Cruz — he'll tell you exactly what to do."

"Take off your jacket," Cruz said.

"It's OK," Jack said.

Johnny hung it over the edge of the shopping cart. He was wearing a white long-sleeved shirt and beltless black slacks. He was no bigger than Cruz.

"He's not armed," Jack said.

Michael was satisfied. "All right — you're going to walk across the highway and go up to the Fotomat in front of the department store — do you know what that is, a Fotomat?" It didn't take him long to finish. In the meantime Jack looked up and saw that the car on the other side had already moved; apparently Ramón wanted to get close right away.

Johnny seemed to think his job would be easy enough. He was smiling. Jack could see the turquoise roof of the Fotomat in the distant shadow of the building, like a jewel in a box. He put his hand on Johnny's shoulder. "Just do exactly what Michael told you," he said. "Watch your step crossing the road. Don't waste any time, but don't finish with the coke until you're sure it's all there. We'll be watching you from here." He let his hand fall. "OK, get going. You want to take your jacket?"

Johnny couldn't make up his mind. He touched the collar, ran his finger down the sleeve, and chewed his lip. Suddenly he pointed at the three plastic bags at the bottom of the cart. "Is that the money?" he asked.

"That's right," Jack said.

Johnny took a step toward Michael and cocked his head to one side, like a robin eyeing a worm. "Can I have some?"

Jack started to laugh. "Get the fuck out of here," Michael said.

"I'm gone," Johnny said, and went off across the lot towards the highway.

Cruz put a dime into the phone, dialed, and cupped his hand over his ear. "Yeah, he's coming — white shirt, black pants — he's clean. it looks OK over here. . . . That's right, but do it fast. They've got some radio cars, and they're coming after you. They could be there in fifteen minutes." He stepped away from the phone and raised his arm in the air. "Can you see me? . . . Good . . . right. . . . Tell the other guys where we stand. That's it." He hung up. Jack was close enough to hear the coin drop down.

Michael touched his forehead. "I want to put the money in the car. Is that all right?"

"What car?"

"Right here." He looked at the gold Mercury.

"That guy's a friend of yours?"

"Uh-huh."

"I haven't seen any cocaine yet. Why should I let you?"

"To keep me happy. You know I'm not going anywhere right now — I wouldn't get very far."

"Sorry — I gave you a chance before. Now I want it where I can see it. You can do it as soon as the coke is ours."

Michael shrugged and looked across the highway. Jack found his apparent ease and tranquility very irritating. "So you think you're just going to cruise right out of here, is that it?"

Johnny had found a break in the near lanes, bolted through, and squeezed between the barely moving cars on the other side. He was now walking briskly across the empty expanse of the lot. Only his legs moved; he shrunk to a dark silhouette indistinguishable from his shadow. The sun was declining more rapidly now, reaching under the promenade and lighting up the white stucco behind the two men. It made Johnny look as if he were swimming across a sea of gold.

Cruz's answer was quiet and unhurried. "I told you before. If you try and stop me while I'm leaving here then you'll never see that coke. It's that simple."

"No, it's not simple. If you can take it away while you're on your way out, what keeps you from taking it away no matter what happens?"

"I'm not that stupid."

"Hell, you could wait a week and sell it to us again. You've got it on a string."

"Do you think I need another ten million dollars?"

"Everybody thinks you're crazy, Michael — that's all."

Cruz turned to face Jack. "All I'm trying to tell you is that I'm not going to give it away for free."

236

A middle-aged man in a sport shirt, narrow belt, and loafers stepped onto the sidewalk. He was digging in his pocket and headed for the phone. Jack had to stifle an impulse to put out his arm and bar the man's way. The fact that his reflexes were acting in Michael's behalf was unsettling.

"Excuse me," Cruz said. The man had picked up the receiver and was holding the dime poised above the slot. "Excuse me, I'm expecting an important call on this phone — would you mind using the one in the stationery store? It'd be a big help to me."

The man stopped and looked at Cruz. The sullen resentment and distrust he showed didn't make his ordinary face any less ordinary. His shirt was tan, with a pattern of little brown violins. "I was just there," he said. "It's being used."

"There's another one down at the end of the row, by the ice machine. Could you use that? I'm traveling on business and my wife is in the hospital — it means a lot to me."

The man's gaze turned to Jack, who was looking out towards the highway, as if he had no particular reason for being there. "I don't believe you for a minute," he said, and pushed the dime into the machine.

Cruz slapped a five-dollar bill against the dial. "Do you believe me now?" There was no trace of a threat in his voice; it was bright and pleasant.

The man roughly brushed Cruz's hand away and started dialing. He and his friends had often discussed the strange brand of people you ran into just about anywhere nowadays; in his opinion, the thing to remember was that you had rights and not to let them get away with anything.

Cruz was rapidly losing color. He swung around and stared across the highway, barely squinting, even though the sun was in his face. Jack was worried; the call meant a lot to him also. "Michael," he said.

The man had started talking. "Henry, this is Bob. . . . Hey, how are you? . . . Listen, they don't have it here either. . . . I know, you see these things in the catalog and they don't bother to put them in the stores. We'll just have to go with the other. . . . He won't know the difference, you know him. . . . So how'd your game go this afternoon? . . . Only nine? . . . Well, you've got more sense than I ever did. . . . Yeah. . . . OK, I'm going to beat my way out of here now, I've had enough for one afternoon. . . . Saturday, that's right. And don't forget to bring that lovely wife of yours. . . . She did, did she? . . . Well, tell her I said so. . . . All right, I'll see you later."

The receiver was a switch on the current of his enthusiasm; as soon as he replaced it he was instantly morose once more, ready to expect the worst. He moved away with that slightly teetering stiffness a lot of weight can impose on a small frame. When he stepped off the curb his whole body jolted from the impact, as if he expected the drop to be smaller than it was.

Michael was still looking across the road.

"That was close," Jack said.

Cruz returned to a spot next to the phone. "It won't happen again." He reached inside his jacket, causing Jack to immediately do the same. Cruz smiled; he let his hand drop. "Sorry — I should have warned you. I'll do it again — watch carefully." He reached for the same pocket and drew out a long white envelope and a felt-tip pen. Flattening the envelope against the wall behind him, he wrote *Out of Order* in large black letters on the face and hung it on the phone by folding the flap over the dial.

"I feel like we're on stage, or something," Jack said.

Michael stepped away from the phone and surveyed his work. "It'll be over very quickly," he said.

Jack wasn't normally inclined to talk without purpose. He was, if anything, overly quiet; the sound of his own voice was an unwelcome intruder in the relationship between himself and pure silence, a relationship that he found useful in both a personal and a professional sense; it discouraged complaints from his subordinates and allowed him to examine his own thoughts more carefully. At this moment, however, the lull was too much for him. "So how do you feel?" he said.

Cruz kept his eyes fixed on the building across the highway. "I'm ready."

"I feel lousy. You've made nothing but trouble for me ever since you first showed up. This time I'm not going to let you go."

"You'll do what you have to, same as me."

"How would you like to die? Gunshot? Coke overdose? Maybe we could drag you around for a while under the car."

"I feel sorry for you, Jack — if this is so hard for you, why don't you join my team? I could use you right now."

"You should have asked me sooner — like ten years ago."

238

"No — I take it back. You're not good enough. I could tell — I knew it right away."

"Knew what?"

"That you didn't have it — that you weren't hungry enough. I promised myself I wasn't going to wind up like you, no matter what happened."

"You don't like the way I live?"

"Look at what you're doing now — you're putting your ass on the line again, like always. For what? For Escobar? For me?

"I don't see it that way."

"You're the guy Escobar sets loose whenever he gets mad at someone. Why should he get his hands dirty? Let Jack do it."

"It's my job — I enjoy it."

"Yeah, right. I think I hear him whistling for you right now."

"I worked hard to bring you here, Michael. I've been looking forward to it. If you had any class you'd thank me."

Cruz plucked at the skin below his Adam's apple and grimaced. The biggest day of his life hadn't transformed him; he looked tired and a little uncomfortable, as if he knew he'd forgotten something but couldn't remember what it was. The strain of gazing into the glare across the highway was making his eyes water. "Listen," he said, "I'm not here because I wanted the attention. You and your friends made it happen this way. Don't make it any worse."

"You have to write your own insurance."

"I know."

"You broke the rules — you have to suffer for it. If it wasn't me it'd be someone else."

"I'm not complaining."

"But I'm glad it was me. I wanted to see you. It's not going to be easy to kill you, but . . . it never is. You can depend on my judgment."

"Where'd you learn to talk like that?" Cruz sighed; he didn't want to know.

Johnny had been gone for five minutes. Jack could see Ramón sitting up in the Cadillac, obviously not pleased with the way things were going. He was too young; he didn't have any patience. All around them people were rushing in and out of their cars, since the reddening sunlight reminded them of a drink on the terrace, the evening news, a hungry child. A tow-headed kid leaned out of the window of an import wagon and waved a bubble wand; a miniature white poodle watched him from the next car, fascinated. Jack had given up trying to see what was going on in the shadow of the department store. All he could see was the lighted foyer and the roof of the Foto-mat. It was like looking into a tunnel. Every time Cruz glanced at his watch Jack wanted to ask him what time it was. The overheated air collected under the promenade and reminded him of a sauna; he hated saunas. He hated everything about Miami. He couldn't understand why he hated it so much.

Ramón was talking into the microphone. The man in the gold Mercury had all the windows up and the engine turned off; Jack thought about how hot it must be inside. He turned to Michael. "Why don't you give it up now? Tell me where it is, leave the money, and I'll forget about you. It's hopeless — you'll never make it."

Cruz answered so promptly that he might have been considering the same choice. "If you touch me here you'll never see the cocaine."

"You said that already. Do you want to die?"

"You can have me or you can have the coke. You can't have both."

"I understand that. But things have changed, Michael. We don't take chances anymore. Do you think that a group that can pull to-gether ten million in cash in a couple of days won't be able to track you down? The world's not big enough."

"Did you plan this or are you just making it up now?"

"Think about it."

"Suppose I said yes. Suppose — just suppose — that you left me alone for good. What could I do? Go back to the city and ask Diego for some work?"

"Anything you can think of that we might have done to make sure you don't get very far — anything — we've done it."

"Good for you — I'll send you a postcard."

Jack was comfortable with Cruz's intransigence; it was what he ex-pected. "That's all right with me. By the way, where did you find all this coke? Tell me now and save yourself trouble later."

Cruz took his eyes off the distance long enough to glance at Jack. "You don't know?"

"Of course not — why should I? I don't think anybody else does, either."

"It's no secret. It was a gift from a friend."

"Who?"

"He's dead — you can't touch him."

"You killed him, I guess."

"I said he was a friend."

Jack leaned against the glass behind him. His hands were so wet that they slid down it without resistance. "What about that girl on Alton Road? Was she a friend? According to the cops, you murdered her."

"They're wrong. I know who it was."

"Tell me."

"You never used to be like this. What are you so worried about?"

Jack's knees were beginning to ache, but the ledge at the base of the window was too narrow to sit on. "I'll tell you, Michael — I don't like to do things this way. It's not the risk, it's just that there's no opportunity to come to an understanding. We shouldn't have to settle this violently, but that's the way it's going to be. It's a waste."

"All you have to do is trust me."

"It's not up to me. But I can see why they wouldn't — they trusted you in Colombia, and look what happened."

Cruz's face, with its starved, whitish nose, shallow eye sockets, and floating jaw, looked empty for a moment. "That's the difference between you and me. I don't need anybody else to tell me what to do." He twisted his mouth and sniffed. "That's why you're losing it, right now. You're thinking about what they're going to say afterwards. Here's some advice — don't think about that. If you let somebody else tell you who you are, then you start to hate them after a while. You already do — I can feel it. When it's time to get rid of you it'll be that much easier."

Jack reached out and picked a hair off Cruz's lapel. "That's very nice, Michael. The day I'm really in trouble is the day I start listening to you." He examined the hair and dropped it at Cruz's feet. "Just don't bleed on the money."

The phone rang beside them. Cruz lifted it carefully and pressed it against his ear. His eyes turned inward; he was across the highway, with the cocaine. "Uh-huh. . . . Uh-huh. . . . I'll call you right after — don't let it go until you see me leave. . . . OK, put him on." He stepped away and offered the receiver to Jack, his face closed and unconcerned.

Jack stayed where he was and looked at Michael. He brought up

241

his wrist and tapped his watch. "You're running a little behind." He wanted to humble Cruz; he couldn't resist. Michael started to smile. Jack decided he'd made his point and took the phone from him.

Johnny tried to tell him everything at once. "Wait a minute, wait a minute," Jack said. "Where are you right now? . . . Uh-huh. Where's the stuff? . . . How do you know it's all there?" Now that Jack knew what to look for, his vision was improved. "Yeah, I see a blue panel van, to the right of the doors." He demanded and received a full description of Michael's partner.

Cruz stood a few steps to one side, patient and impassive, as if he were a stranger waiting to use the phone.

"Listen, Johnny, I recognize your voice, but I just want to make sure — who'd you ride down with this morning? . . . OK. You saw the stuff and it's all there — this isn't something you're telling me because you've got a gun in your back. . . . No, I understand. . . . When you hang up, I want you to go over and stand in front of the van so we can see you. Just wait there. We'll be over right away. . . . Do exactly what I said. . . . Good — now I want to talk to your friend with the track shoes. . . . See you later." He flattened the phone against his chest and looked at Michael. "All right so far? Are you happy?" It was obvious that Michael's chief concern was the shrinking buffer of time that separated the pursuit cars from their destination. Jack decided not to push him any further. He returned to the phone.

"Hello? . . . Good morning, asshole, how's the weather over there? What's your name? . . . I'm sorry." The voice was flat and anonymous, deliberately so, and no face to match it appeared in Jack's mind. He wanted to close his fingers around it and drag it through the line with the owner attached. "Listen, I told my man to stand in front of the van until we get there. If he moves, or if the van moves behind him, your friend Michael Cruz is out of luck. Is that simple enough for you? . . . Good. Here he is."

Jack handed the phone back to Cruz. He hated to let go. However, the radio car was right there, watching the man. Jack was beginning to believe that the transfer might work exactly as Michael had planned it; that the tensions of the past week might actually resolve themselves all at once. If he could manage to divide the exchange from the violence that must follow it — if he could get the coke safe and out of the way before retrieving the cash — then the two operations wouldn't suffer from their conflicting purposes and success in one wouldn't mean failure in the other. When he finally confronted Michael he wanted him to be cut off from the source of his strength, the cocaine; that way Jack could indulge his emotions freely. It meant that Ramón and everybody else would have to be content to follow Cruz out quietly, just as he had insisted, and restrain themselves until the coke was secure. Jack knew he would meet a lot of resistance on this; Cruz wouldn't be leaving empty-handed. The deciding factor, for Jack, was the radio car waiting on the other side. It didn't matter if Cruz's contact had noticed it or not. The men inside would watch him go; they would stay with him if he tried to bring the coke along. So the radio car, whose presence across the highway Cruz had gone to such lengths to prevent, was the shield behind which he would be allowed to run. Without it he would have died on the spot.

Jack made his choice in the few seconds it took for Michael to take the phone and put it to his ear. Jack stood so close that Cruz would have had to burrow into the wall to avoid being overheard. He didn't bother; he was more interested in getting his message through.

"You know what to do . . . you have to be out of there in five minutes — if you don't hear from me in four, leave and take the coke with you — I've just got one thing here — I'll call you right back."

Cruz hung up and turned to Jack. "You heard it." Urgency, fear, desperation; these might have been expected. The odd element in Cruz's expression was that of resignation and disappointment, showing in his drooping jaw and half-shut eyes, as if the last card had fallen and the contest was over. "I can't waste any time. I want to put the money in the car, right now. Then I'll call him back. That means the coke is yours unless you try and stop me."

Jack had difficulty answering; his throat was blocked and only air emerged. He tried again. "Go ahead. I'm going to leave now, if that's all right."

The other man nodded once and leaned down into the shopping cart, reaching for the money. Standing over him, Jack used both hands to force Cruz's head down and against the inner side of the cart. Michael's neck was twisted ninety degrees and his left cheek bulged through the wire matrix. Jack's body partly concealed the action from the lot. "Keep your gun," he said. "Keep the cash too." He could feel Michael relaxing, preparing a response. Jack's voice was mild and low, intimate as a whisper. "I just wanted to say good-bye."

He let go and walked away towards Ramón's car. He didn't look back. It was all he could do to keep from running.

Inside the Cadillac, he looked up and saw Cruz swinging the black garbage bags through the passenger window of the Mercury. Ramón was upset; his eyebrows were jerking in several directions and he was asking a dozen questions at once. "Quiet," Jack said. "Call the helicopter down now — tell him not to cross 136th Street until I say so." Ramón wasn't satisfied. He had his knee up on the seat, facing Jack, and one fist was opening and shutting nervously. Jack stared back at him. "Just do it, would you please!" Jack was about to grab the mike himself when Ramón did so at last.

He saw that his other cars were getting ready to go; they were edging a foot or two forward to keep anyone from jamming them in. The Mercury, in the center, would need their connivance to reach the exits. The same in the rear lot. As soon as Ramón had gotten an OK from the copter, Jack took the microphone.

"All cars — this is central. We're ready to move. Cars one through five will escort our man wherever he goes. All others stay in place, except six and ten — six and ten, you already have instructions from Ramón. There will be no action — no action, I said — until you hear from me. That's all. Acknowledge in order."

As the numbers came in, one by one, Jack watched Cruz return to the phone and make his call. The man in the Mercury had his back to the door and was leaning over the seat, probably doing something with the cash. There were still no empty spaces in the lot and a few hungry drivers were cruising down the rows. The sun had reached the windows under the promenade and set them on fire. Cruz had one hand in his pocket and was cradling the receiver with the other while he kicked the wall behind him with his heel, leaving half-moon scuffs on the white stucco. This is the way it should be, Jack thought; all the preparation, all the talk, all the waiting — when the moment comes everything falls away. He couldn't understand why he wasn't getting any more friction from Ramón. It was his last chance to complain.

Cruz hung up the phone, pushed his sleeve back to look at his watch, squinted into the sun, and stepped off the sidewalk. He got in the driver's side of the Mercury and shut the door behind him. OK Michael, Jack thought, run for your life.

It was as if Cruz had read his mind. Both doors of the Mercury bounced open at once; with one hand on the window frame and a gun in the other, Cruz spun around his door and crouched behind it, while the other man stood up, wedged a large green duffel under his arm and rushed, head down, for the sidewalk and the entrance to the florist's shop. Jack snatched the microphone off the radio to tell the men in the rear what was coming through. But as crucial as this message was, he never completed it — he didn't even get past the call signal — because the shock of what happened in the next three seconds unstrung him completely.

Although events followed a sequence at once natural and orderly, it seemed to Jack that they were happening all at once, and that it was only his suddenly expanded vision that allowed him to absorb each of them fully without missing any of the others. For instance, the first thing he noticed was how the wide plate windows of the florist's shop and the near side of the hardware store, which only a moment ago had been reflecting the sun so brilliantly, were now separating into large irregular pieces — bright Halloween mirrors outlined in black and overlapping each other as they fell. But before they hit the sidewalk, shattering into a million starry bits, he saw Ramón jerk suddenly, as if a nerve in his side had contracted. At the same time he saw Ramón's long arm curled around the window post with his hand, holding a pistol, resting on the hood of the car. The barrel pointed in the general direction of the Mercury. A line drawn from Ramón's eyes to the gun differed considerably from the line of the barrel, and so Jack remarked to himself, a little irrelevantly, "How stupid — you can't aim a gun that way." He also saw Cruz's partner lose his tennis hat. As the big, heavy man pushed through the door of the florist's (a glass door, from which the glass was rapidly disappearing) the soft hat slipped off the back of his head, collided with the butt of the duffel, and fluttered down, the circular red lining turning like a wheel. He saw Cruz enter through the same door. He saw a shopping bag full of eggs and leafy vegetables hit the ground and split open. He heard other guns going off in a crackling barrage, and he saw three or four of his men swarming out of their cars and rushing the sidewalk, while the half dozen pedestrians in the area stopped in their tracks. He saw a man appear at the door of the florist's, clutch his face, and fall backwards. He saw Ramón pull his arm back into the car and turn to face him, gun in hand. He saw the small black aperture where the bullets emerged. He saw it because it was aimed at him.

"Out of the car," Ramón said. Jack saw that Ramón was in a genuine rage and the muscles in his hand were tensed and probably not reliable. The threat was revelatory; at least Jack understood. Escobar had cut him out. Ramón had chosen this moment to tell him.

"But why now?" Jack said. "Why did you wait until now?"

"Because I thought I'd give you a chance to finish it here. I thought you could do it — I was wrong." Now Ramón shouted, "You were going to fucking give it away!"

Jack remained calm. "If you'd listened to me none of this would've happened. And you all missed him — where is he? None of you guys can shoot worth shit."

"Out of the car! Just get the fuck out!"

Jack made a quick exit. As soon as he shut the door Ramón jumped the Seville into the lot and roared down to the end of the building, careening around the edge and out of sight. An empty shopping cart that was in his way jumped the curb and crashed into the row of pine trees that hid the next lot down. Jack saw all the other cars racing to the rear of the center. He heard a child start to wail. Realizing that the police would be here very shortly, he walked briskly down the highway a few blocks, stopped at a gas station, called a cab, and took a ride back to the city.

» » »

When Hula stopped halfway through the flower shop and turned to see if Michael was following, he made the mistake of looking straight out the now shattered door behind him. What he saw was the burning yellow ball of the sun spreading down across the sky like a ruptured egg and charring everything but itself. When he shut his eyes he saw another sun, black and smoking, on the inner wall of his eyelids. The pale banks of carnations on either side disappeared; he was blind. He turned and walked ahead, erect and unseeing, following the twin discs of light that hovered in front of his face and hoping that his momentum would carry him out the door. An alarm bell was ringing in his ears. Somebody rushed past him towards the front, banging him in the ribs. He brought the duffel forward onto his chest and wrapped both arms around it.

He was lucky in his sightlessness; it slowed him down and disoriented him, so that when he pushed out the back door and stopped just outside, he didn't look like someone in a hurry, and Jack's men in the rear lot took him for a confused passerby even though, had they looked closely, they would have noticed that his features were distorted by the stocking tied over his head. They had heard the barrage and they were waiting for Cruz.

In the blurry corners of his eyes Hula saw the late-model sedan he and Michael had parked directly behind the store. He got in on the passenger side and settled the duffel on his lap. It was very hot in the car; he rolled down the window. He knew there was a lot of money in the bag and it made him feel conspicuous. He pushed it down between his knees. Although he could still hear the alarm, it was very quiet after all the noise and motion in front.

If he had had eyes for it, he would have seen a couple of men getting out of their cars and rushing for the rear entrances of the stores. They were just about to enter when Cruz burst headlong out of the flower shop, dived into the seat beside Hula, twisted the key waiting in the ignition, and bolted out the rear exit, which was providentially clear at the time. He clapped one hand on the back of Hula's neck and forced his head down under the dash. A bullet nicked through a lower corner of the rear window and gouged a rough furrow in the door panel by Hula's ear.

The car that was supposed to block the rear exit failed because the man behind the wheel was unwilling to knock down a paper-skinned old man who was in the way. Instead, he leaned out the window and fired at the car crossing in front of him; he led it too far and the bullet passed in front of the windshield, traveling a hundred yards in a flat arc before crashing through an ilex hedge and burying itself in the twisted stalk of a philodendron. The second shot destroyed Cruz's left brakelight; the third put another hole in the rear window and would've broken the one beside Hula if it had still been up. Spinning end over end, the bullet flew over one of the playing fields that bordered the exit and passed so close to a twelve-year-old leading off second base that he heard it — it sounded like a tiny balloon popping — and it went on to shatter a pane in a louvered window in a house belonging to an active member of the National Rifle Association. He had lost that same window to a baseball more than once; when he found the bullet on the floor it was shaped like a kidney bean and he didn't recognize it.

The man who fired it didn't get out of the lot until the other radio car was through. Ramón and the second car from the front followed him down the exit. Ninety seconds after Cruz first appeared they were all gone, and a small crowd started to gather in the cloud of white dust that hung over the rear of the center.

A half mile away Cruz was racing down a narrow lane beside a canal and looking in the rearview mirror. The canal was only a few yards wide; it separated the road from a long row of lush surburban backyards, all of equal dimensions, so that as they rocketed by it seemed as if a few basic props — kids, a dog, a badminton net — were being combined and recombined in an interminable variety of positions. The road surface was rough and pebbly, to discourage speeding, and the car buzzed like a bee in a jar. The white underlying sand showed through the short grass beside the canal. Cruz could see the sheet-metal skin of the lead pursuer about a quarter-mile back. The road wasn't intended for through traffic; it had been built, almost as an afterthought, by the men who had dug the canal. It was only wide enough for a single car. There was no one coming the other way.

Hula had recovered his sight and was sitting up again. The sun flashed in the water of the ditch, pacing them effortlessly. The seat under him was bouncing like a trampoline and he kept slipping forward and cracking his knees on the underside of the dash. He saw Cruz studying the mirror and he turned around to have a look for himself.

Since the road was so flat and undeviating, he could see only the lead car, a night blue boat eating up the tar under its wheels and apparently content to remain a good distance behind; it didn't seem to be gaining on them. He had to shout to make himself heard. "I only see one — it's not getting any closer."

Cruz shook his head. "There's at least four. They're not getting closer because you can't move any faster on this fucking sidewalk." He sounded angry — angry at the road, angry at the car he was driving, angry at himself. "I don't know how the hell they stayed with me." He was talking about the circuitous and hair-raising route he'd run through the residential area behind the shopping center. He'd worked it out in advance; it required doubling back once or twice and roaring through a construction site. Now he was improvising. "If we don't lose them when we cross the highway we might as well get out and walk."

There was a bridge coming up on the left. A row of short corrugated iron posts blocked the lane just in front of it, placed to stymie

248

anything larger than a bicycle. By the time Hula could see the small orange reflectors mounted on each post he was no longer capable of speech.

About fifty yards from the end Cruz applied the brakes and swerved right, swinging behind a prefabricated garage and surprising a man with a hose who was standing beside his car. The turn enabled Cruz to cut left onto the low ramp leading to the bridge; as they crossed over Hula looked back and saw four full-sized cars braking down for the same maneuver, while the man with the hose stared back at him, not realizing that his troubles had barely begun. When the fifth car skidded past his garage, smashing his last remaining seedling palm and tearing the bumper halfway off his car, he suffered a feeling of violation not covered in his homeowner's policy, and it was nearly a week before he could bring himself to turn on the sprinkler again.

Neither Hula nor Cruz saw any of this. The bridge over the canal led down to SW 152nd Street — Coral Reef Drive — which was the first road south of the shopping center that crossed the highway. As they tailed around the stop sign and headed west Hula saw a car pull out of a driveway between them and their pursuers, but he said nothing about it to Cruz; he didn't want to give him an excuse to slow down. Hula remembered that he still had the stocking tied over his head and immediately hooked his thumbs under the knot.

Cruz was concentrating on the road. "Look what we got," he said, pounding the dashboard with his fist. "Look at it."

The road ahead of them led straight as a ruler towards a shining yellow wedge of sky resting on the horizon and hemmed in by the mature plantings on either side; the only spot in any direction where earth and heaven made contact. Near the bottom of the wedge hung the traffic light on Dixie Highway. It had just turned green. It was a long way off.

Using all his strength, Hula forced the rolled bottom of the stocking over his chin. After that it was just a matter of yanking on it from above, but the low ceiling of the car interfered. His hands kept slipping on the smooth nylon. He was blind, enraged, and on the verge of panic; he tore at his scalp with his nails and bloodied the rim of his ear. The rough fabric finally lost its grip and come off in a rush. He thrust it out the window, where the wind caught it and snatched it away.

Hula blinked and opened his eyes wide. The light was still green.

There was no one in the lane ahead of them. He turned in his seat and looked out the fractured rear window. Bite-sized crumbs of safety glass danced across the ledge and leaped down onto the seat. He saw a large station wagon about two hundred yards back, steadily shrinking in size, since it was moving at about half their speed. It blocked out everything on the road beyond it. As he watched, the blue Cadillac suddenly shot out from behind and passed it, moving at a rate of at least as great as their own. Another car repeated the maneuver. Now nothing separated them except an empty stretch of pavement. The driver of the station wagon could easily have prevented this disaster. But he didn't, Hula thought, hating him.

The ink-colored Cadillac was steadily growing larger. The sun penetrated the lower half of the windshield and Hula could see two motionless torsos in the front seat. He blinked again. Utility poles, rooftops, and ornamental trees whipped by on either side and quickly dwindled into nothing; the entire world was speeding into a blur. Hula felt as if he were being sucked into a machine. He didn't see any hope of defending himself. He was trapped in the car with Michael while a great anger, like a wave, was approaching from the rear. His throat squeezed shut behind his tongue and he saw everything very clearly, from the traces of dirt under his nails to the golden cast of light the low sun rained on the surrounding landscape, making even the most ordinary cement wall or patch of brown grass gleam like something precious. He felt very calm and alert. He was afraid.

He turned again and looked up the road. The light over the highway was definitely closer now. Somehow it was still green. They were already into the commercial margin; parking lots dominated by plastic signs on stilts swept into view beside them. Cruz pushed the accelerator to the floor. They were going eighty miles an hour in a thirty-five-mile zone, on a two-way street no more than fifteen feet wide. Hula could now see exactly how much distance separated them from the crossing — it was at least another ten seconds away. He started counting. The light turned yellow. Cruz put one hand on the horn and kept it there. They were past the point where the brakes would have been any use.

Solid rows of waiting cars defined the narrow channel in front of them. Hula had counted down to three when the light turned red. Three seconds was way too long. He drew up his knees and shut his eyes; he didn't want to see the rest.

Even though there was no collision Hula wasn't satisfied. As soon as he sensed that they were across he sat up and looked back, ready to cheer their deliverance, and saw that the slot across the highway was still open and the Cadillac was fast approaching it. If he'd had time to think about it he would have realized that the people waiting on the green had just received quite a shock, a shock that would probably keep them from moving right away. However, the thought that drove out all others for Hula was the idea that the Cadillac was about to cross over behind them. They were no better off than when they started. Their recklessness had earned them nothing.

But as he watched the blue car bearing down on the intersection like a missile his view was suddenly blocked. Someone in a tractor-trailer wasn't paying attention. First the cab rolled into the gap, then the long steel wall of the container, as long as a freight car and just as high. Hula was about to witness a horrible accident and he was collapsing with glee. He couldn't look away. He expected to see the side of the trailer buckle outward and the decapitated frame of the car come flying underneath.

Nothing of the kind. By the time the truck geared up and, dragged its entire bulk across the intersection there were other cars crossing on the near side of it and the gap healed itself as completely as if it had never existed. He couldn't understand it; he felt cheated. Now he could see cars moving back and forth in a sluggish, jerky rhythm, all sticking as close to their neighbors as possible and effectively denying him any glimpse of what lay on the other side. He continued staring at the receding spectacle for another few moments and slumped back into his seat. He looked at Cruz. "It's incredible — it's like they just disappeared."

"No — they just bailed out at the last minute. Didn't you see them slowing down after we crossed?"

"No."

"They were smart. They probably tailed into the parking lot and knocked down a few trash cans. Lucky for them."

Cruz had slowed down to about forty and was scratching his upper lip with his fingernail. His eyes flashed from side to side across the road; he could barely contain his excitement. "They made us — now everybody knows where we came over and what he look like." He glanced at Hula. "What'd you do with that nylon, eat it?" He waited until Hula was about to say something and then interrupted him.

"We'll be behind the store in five minutes. If we can make the switch there, without being seen, we'll be all right." His hands opened and closed around the wheel. "Ready for more?"

Michael's exhilaration was contagious and Hula tried to keep from catching it. He expected to see the blue Cadillac pop out again and he didn't want to be taken by surprise. On this side of the highway the homes were even newer and there were still some undeveloped lots scattered among them — stands of spindly slash pine over a spiked carpet of palmetto.

By the time they reached the lot behind Jefferson's the sun was into the tops of the trees and was bumping against something solid; a wall of cloud creeping out of the west and extending from one end of the horizon to the other. It split the light into a radiating fan, a peacock's tail of flattened streamers, buttery and half-transparent, slanting low over the ground and introducing an illusory depth to the unremarkable landscape. As they rolled out the access road into the rear of the lot, the high, chalky scarp of the department store rose up before them like the edge of an iceberg. It was a long way to the doors; they drove for nearly half a minute before they started threading their way down the rows of cars huddled around the entrance.

» » »

The most difficult part of the afternoon for Liberty was the moment after he gave the keys to the loaded van to Johnny, turned his back on the lot, and entered the department store. That was the time when he expected a bullet to smash into him and he had no idea where it might come from. As the doors shut behind him he took a deep gulp of the processed air inside and put into action the plan which he hoped would show him if he was being followed; he walked as rapidly as possible down the middle of the store between a double column of squared pillars sheathed with mirrors and studied the unfolding reflections as he passed. Anyone coming after him, he'd decided, would have to maintain a pace at least as vigorous as his own and so would make himself conspicuous; the alternative was the risk of losing him at the entrance in the rear. He was fishing for trouble and it wasn't long before he found some.

A mountainous man with a face like an old potato pushed through the doors about a half minute behind him. He didn't reach for a shopping cart, consult a list, or glance up at the locator board; he headed straight down the central aisle, weaving in and out of the crowd and fixing his eyes on Liberty. The man was tall and easy to watch. Liberty stepped up his pace, hoping to get a reaction, but the man was so large that all he had to do was stretch his stride a few inches. His head swayed above the intervening bodies like a balloon on a string. He turned abruptly and vanished behind a two-story rack of bicycles. Liberty didn't slow down to investigate. He wasn't willing to let him get any closer.

The man had come out of the car Jack had planted across the highway. Along with two other men he'd watched Liberty alternate between the phone booth and the man named Johnny, and although he'd suggested that it made better sense to grab Liberty and inquire directly than to try to follow him to the money, cooler heads had prevailed and, in accordance with Jack's instructions, two of the men had stayed in the car to watch the cocaine while the third was rewarded for his trouble with the job of tracking Liberty on foot. Help was due any minute; right now it was more important to hang onto the coke. Their decision was probably influenced by the presence of a South Dade police car parked alongside the curb by the doors. By the time the fusillade broke out across the highway, pulling the cop off his station, Liberty was already inside the store. When Ramón called a minute later and told them to seize Cruz's partner immediately he was about sixty seconds too late.

Liberty turned into an aisle full of toys and stopped. High walls of bright cardboard hemmed him in and concealed him completely. He had to find a way to get out of the store and into his car without being seen. At least he knew the face of the man he had to elude; he was grateful for that. Although this spot hid him from sight, it also hid everything from him; for all he knew the other man had seen him turn in and might even now be bearing down at him at a near run. A cart pushed by a tired-looking woman following a wide-eyed small girl wheeled into the aisle from the central passage and headed in his direction. The woman's resistance was nearly gone; the cart was full and her eyes were glazed over. She threw a wan glance at Liberty. He stood aside to let them pass. One wheel of the cart banged against his heel. "I'm sorry," the woman said. "Do you work here?"

"No."

"I'm sorry." They continued down the aisle away from him and he looked in the opposite direction.

He was gazing along a narrow channel, briefly interrupted by the central walkway where he'd entered, and continuing at least another hundred yards to the edge of the store. What interested him, however, was a pair of battered swinging doors with small rectangular windows cut into them at eye level. They were all the way down at the end of the row. He walked over to the edge of the central passage, looked around quickly, and walked swiftly down the aisle opposite and pushed through the doors.

When he turned and looked out the smudged window he was prevented from taking the deep breath he'd finally granted himself because he saw the large man with the corrugated face proceeding rapidly down the aisle he'd just traveled and staring directly back at him. Their eyes held for a moment.

Liberty was standing on the edge of another maze of piled and coded goods, only here the aisles were dark and empty, the merchandise was still in packing boxes, and the air was ten degrees warmer. A few bulbs with tin shades descended from the black murk over his head. He broke left, took a few steps behind a two-story wall of cartons, and stopped beside what seemed to be a plywood phone booth raised high off the ground and built into the skin of the store proper. A dyed burlap curtain hung over the near side. He pushed the curtain aside and boosted himself in.

As soon as he stood up he noticed he was looking out a window into the store. He saw his antagonist lurching down the aisle towards the stockroom entrance. Their eyes met again; Liberty flinched. But there was no sign of recognition on the man's face. Liberty had never looked out a two-way mirror before. He immediately understood that this was the first time.

The man pushed through the doors and stopped. The decision that had led Liberty into the box now seemed to him unbelievably stupid. There was nothing to do but hope he could plant a foot in the man's throat when he reached for the curtain.

A clanking, rolling noise, like bottles in a wagon, started out of the silence and increased gradually as it approached the doors from somewhere in the stockroom. The noise ceased a few feet away. A voice with a wide adolescent gap in it said, "No customers in storage." In

254

the quiet that followed, a pair of voices in argument accompanied footsteps coming from the same direction that the clanking noise had. Someone shouted, "Hey George — where's that lawnmower?"

"Coming up," the first voice answered. Then more evenly, "What can I do for you?"

The man finally responded. "Where do you keep the garden stuff?"

"Right outside here."

In the mirror Liberty saw the big man come out into the store, followed by a tall, bony kid with a hand truck tipped back under a high load of boxes. A moment later two men pushed through — one in jeans, one in a gray suit — waving papers at each other. The boy settled the truck just under the mirror and ripped open the topmost carton; it was filled with clear plastic bags of birdseed.

The big man stood in front of a pegboard loaded with chrome and brass hose fittings and pretended to examine them while he watched the boy and the doors. He picked up a pistol-shaped spray nozzle and squeezed it a few times. There was a round bare spot on top of his head which the light-denying qualities of the mirror made appear a little grayish and dead, like everything else. He glanced at his watch and stared fixedly at the doors for a few seconds, then stood erect, lifted his chin, and scanned as much of the store as he could see.

Success — the big man dropped the nozzle, took one last look at the doors, and strode away towards the front of the store. Liberty eased himself off the platform as quietly as possible, moved along the wall a few steps, and boldly pushed through the doors into the brightly lit interior.

When he got outside Liberty saw that the car he had left there two hours ago was still in place. He was pleased; he was ready for worse. If Cruz was on schedule he would arrive within five minutes. Until then, Liberty told himself, all I have to do is stay out of trouble. As he got into the car on the passenger side he looked approvingly at the hundreds of similar cars forming a rough semicircle around the entrance to the store. There was nothing to distinguish him here. Liberty had always associated freedom with anonymity; a crowd like this, so busy and self-absorbed, had the same sweet spaciousness as the open sea. If the man he had just eluded walked out the doors now it wouldn't make any difference. On the other hand, there was the chance that somebody else had been waiting for him back here and was even now making plans for a gathering in his honor; Liberty didn't concern himself with this possibility because there was nothing he could do about it.

A car pulled up to the space beside him. Inside were Cruz and his slug of a partner. They got out quickly. Cruz walked around and got in behind the wheel of Liberty's car while the other man heaved a green duffel bag into the back seat and settled heavily down beside it. Two doors cracked shut and they drove away.

» » »

The pilot of the helicopter said, "We've got another half hour of daylight and about the same amount of fuel."

The man beside him was leaning over and peering out through the bubble shell near his feet, both hands clamped around the rim of his seat. He was trying to overcome his vertigo by forcing it on himself. He was beginning to succeed. When he sat up again he was able to let go of the chair and adjust his headset. His face had that dim sort of grayishness that a dark complexion assumes when there is no longer any blood behind it.

They were hanging a thousand feet over Kendall. They were alone in the air; the WMSJ traffic copter had veered off towards Perrine ten minutes earlier and they were too far south to see the commercial jets gliding in over the ocean on the approach path for MIA. The sun left a scythelike shimmer on the invisible blades over their heads. The plain below them stretched out green, gold, and white on three sides; a sloppy mosaic of lightly incised roads, sluggish automobiles, low roofs, and blue-floored swimming pools with shadows edging across their bottoms, all set in a ragged mat of vegetation. To the east the sea fell away from its muddy edge and turned dark before it blended into the dust-colored haze on the horizon. They could see a wall of clouds approaching over the land, throwing a shadow ahead that obscured the earth underneath. The passenger pointed at it with his thumb. "Can we fly in that?"

The pilot nodded. "We're OK as long as we stay under the ceiling. You get a lot of turbulence on the edge of the front — all you have to do is duck under it."

The other man suddenly clapped his hands over his ears and bent over. "152nd Street and Dixie Highway — I got it," he said. "Head-

256

ing west — a dark green Datsun. Who is this, Ramón? All right, we're going." He turned to the pilot. "They lost it."

They were already swinging away to the south, the land rushing under them like water. "Everybody has a fucking Japanese car," the pilot said.

For the next ten minutes they flew in a tightening spiral over the area between Dixie Highway and the turnpike, from 136th Street to Quail Roost Drive, often interrupting their progress to take a closer look at a specific car. They followed a clockwise curve because the pilot wanted to watch the outer edge. The passenger noticed a couple of stiff-winged vultures on similar tracks, their horny beaks drooping between their shoulders. He could tell the copter was moving by watching the shadow drift across the ground. Now and then the pilot talked to Ramón. "I said I'll let you know when I find it. . . . I don't know. . . . I can't guarantee anything." The passenger didn't concern himself with the fact that he'd become superfluous. He was here only because there'd been some doubt as to how amenable the hired pilot would be to this kind of activity. He'd been ready to make all kinds of threats and promises. None had been necessary. Now that the pilot was taking orders directly from the ground there was nothing at all for him to do. He adjusted the volume on his headset; he couldn't hear Ramón very clearly. It was odd that Jack wasn't doing any of the talking. Something had obviously gone wrong down there.

The circle they traced as they flew was now so tight that the land rushing along the horizon was starting to make him dizzy. The pilot abruptly abandoned it, moved to a point in the center, and stopped; they hovered motionless, like a dragonfly, over a recently excavated lake with a bare, whitish border — it might have been a rim of brine.

The pilot looked at the passenger. "Any suggestions?"

"Don't ask me — ask him." He pointed down.

The pilot nodded. "Station to base," he said. "We covered the area between the highway, the turnpike, 136th, and Quail Roost. If the car's still in there it's not moving."

Ramón was angry. "Then look harder, would you please! Work in towards the city, and don't bother me unless you find something."

"I can't stay up here much longer."

"Why not?"

"No fuel."

"Don't tell me your troubles. Just find the car."

"Ten or fifteen minutes — that's the best I can do."

"All right — can you call your field and get somebody else down here? I don't care what — hold it a minute, I'll get back to you."

In the ensuing silence the chopper blades sounded very loud, as if someone had opened a window. When Ramón came back on again his voice was rapid and excited. "They switched cars. They're in a sky blue Toyota two-door. They left the parking lot behind Jefferson's department store less than five minutes ago. There's three men in the car. Do you know where that is?"

"Yes, I know." They were already on their way.

"Then find them. Green Florida plates. Stick to the through roads — they're trying to get out of here."

"Right. Keep listening."

The man who lost track of Liberty in the department store had come out the rear doors just as Hula and Cruz arrived in their bullet-damaged car, and he saw the two men get out and jump into the Toyota. He was too far away to recognize Liberty or read the plates, but it was worth a closer look, and when he ran out into the lot to examine the car they had left behind, he saw that it had been shot up; from there it was just a matter of time until he rushed back through the store, got on the radio, and notified Ramón. A dark green Datsun, he said, and a big man with a cloth bag. That settled it.

The pilot guessed, correctly, that the car he was looking for would be in a hurry and would therefore head west, away from the highway and the shoreline suburbs, towards the pinewoods and the flat empty roads that ran through them. They caught up with it on Coral Reef Drive about two miles from the turnpike underpass. Since the helicopter was roaring over the road at a freakish speed they easily over-ran the car and they had to pull up over the turnpike and wait for it to catch up. The men sitting in the radio cars by the ramps saw the helicopter before Ramón relayed its message to them: blue Toyota headed west on 152nd Street and approaching the turnpike entrance.

It's all over, the passenger thought. Through the glass beside his feet he could see the little car sliding easily down the road like a bead on a wire. The white-roofed toll plaza stapled across the turnpike entrance had a parking lot beside it where the radio cars were preparing a welcome. In a moment, he knew, he would see tiny people crawl out of those machines and lay flat on the ground. He'd never met Michael Cruz; now he was going to see him die. He wondered if he'd be able to pick him out from this height. He doubted it. He felt as if they should all be wearing numbered jerseys.

It didn't turn out as he expected. Either the driver of the Toyota saw what was waiting for him, or he never planned to get on the turnpike in the first place, because he slid right past the entrance, ducked through the underpass, and continued down the road on the other side, in the process drawing the radio cars out of the lot and onto the road after him. From this height the action seemed painfully lethargic.

The pilot was talking into his headset. "Continuing west on 152nd. Your guys are about a thousand yards behind. I'm bringing it in — I'm nearly empty."

Ramón didn't want to hear it. "Another five minutes," he said. "We need you."

"Sorry — I've got a long ride home."

The dead air hissed for a few seconds. Then Ramón said one word — "Bobby."

Bobby, the passenger, wasn't so dull that he couldn't see the difficulties in his role, but here he was anyway, holding a gun on the only man who could keep him from crashing to earth. He looked at his watch. "A minute ago you said we had fifteen minutes. He only asked for five. Is that too much?"

The pilot glanced at the gun and made a face. He acted as if he were used to this kind of thing. "Put it away," he said.

"Yes or no?"

"Am I supposed to be afraid of you? Is that the idea?"

"You're stalling — make up your mind." Bobby could see the fuel gauge for himself. The needle had already sliced off the upper right-hand corner of the *E*. It was easier to watch the pilot. "Well?"

"All right. Five minutes."

Bobby put the gun away. He called up Ramón and told him the news. "Very good," Ramón said. "Now let me talk to your friend."

The pilot explained to Ramón, in a testy voice, that the blue Toyota was about to encounter some real problems, because a few miles past the turnpike 152nd Street runs into an army research installation with a big gate across the road and a few dirt tracks leading into the woods around it. Looking down, the passenger could see what he was talking about; a cluster of chunky brick buildings, a flagpole, a curving driveway, and a narrow firebreak surrounding the whole with a fence topped by concertina wire and a sandy path running along the inside. It looked like a prison. Beyond it, to the west, the passenger saw open pinewoods and long bare strips of plowed earth, with a few trailer camps, white churches, and phosphate pits like rain-filled bomb craters scattered among them. The Toyota swerved onto one of the trails running through the woods. The other cars dived in after it. Six or eight more were following each other down 152nd Street.

In a moment they were all plunging and bucking through the scrub, confusing themselves with their quick turns and their hesitations, and slowly spreading across the land; an army of invasion distracted by the lack of resistance. The big machines were at a disadvantage here and the lead car had lost sight of the Toyota. The pilot was trying to keep Ramón in touch with it by referring to compass bearings and the names of roads. It was no use; his instructions were too raw, too precise. The passenger could see it all happening right under his feet and he couldn't stand it any longer; "Shut up and fly," he told the pilot, and slapped up the call switch. "Ramón," he said, "Get everybody onto this channel right now." He waited about five seconds. "All right — red car, you're about to hit a road on the edge of a field — take a right. . . . Tan — go straight across the canal and keep going. . . . Dark blue — turn around, go back to your next left, and head out that way. . . . Dark blue, did you get that?" It didn't take him long to get most of the cars onto through roads where they could outflank the Toyota. A minute later he closed the circle in front of it. There was nowhere it could go. He was absurdly happy. He'd stepped into a disaster and was singlehandedly turning it around.

His triumph didn't last. The Toyota slipped out from under him; the pilot was veering away and heading for the city. The gun appeared with the speed of a reflex. He stuck it in the pilot's ear, knocking his headset awry. "Get back there," he said.

The pilot didn't look at him. "If we don't leave now we won't make it."

"We can land here if we have to." He looked down and saw the ground still retreating under him. Turning his wrist back, he fired. The gun went off one inch from the pilot's head. A small round hole appeared in the glass in front of them. Nothing happened. He did it again, and a second hole appeared a few inches from the first. There was something about the material that isolated the shock; the glass might have been punctured by a high-speed drill.

"OK," the pilot said. "OK, Goddammit! But the next time we go down, it's for real." He reached up and readjusted his headset.

The blue Toyota was still at large, although the circle, thanks to the passenger's coaching, was tightening around it. The car's bright roof glowed like a beacon in the fading light as it scrambled first one way, then another; one of the last spots of color anywhere. The helicopter was only two hundred feet above the ground when the passenger saw a man lean out of the driver's seat, turn, and point a gun at them. He didn't hear any shots. He reached predictably, pulling out his own weapon and banging away out the side window, his anger feeding on the recoil. He couldn't tell if he was hitting anything. Aiming more carefully, with both hands on the butt and his arms extended, he tried again, the explosions sounding hollow and muffled, like firecrackers going off in a sealed box. His ears popped and the engine roared behind him. "Ramón," he said, holding down the call switch, "I'm hanging right over him. Can you see me? Can everybody see me?"

He was about to fire again when his seat suddenly tipped and he lurched against the belt around his waist, his gun cracking against the door hinge as he lost his balance. He managed to hold onto it. The ground below was tilting dangerously, wobbling like a drunk and making rude lunges at the sky. He knew that he'd get sick again if it didn't stop. It took him a few valuable seconds to put the gun away. Then he grabbed the sides of his chair, locked his feet against the inner wall of the glass in front of him, and looked at the pilot — the pilot who, he was sure, was responsible for all this. He tried to block out the distress signals coming from his stomach and the weird movie playing outside the copter. The pilot didn't look back at him. He was making a good show of wrestling with the controls. The passenger opened his mouth. "What the fuck is going on?" he tried to say, but it came out something else. He saw the blue Toyota flash over his head like a bird.

The machine righted itself for a moment. He grabbed the pilot's arm, not in order to get his attention, but just to steady himself. It didn't make him feel any better. He let go.

"That's all," the pilot called out. "Tank's empty."

After that it was a matter for the insurance companies to decide. They didn't find any witnesses. The wreckage, discovered on the following morning, showed that the helicopter had come down in one piece, but the impact had been so violent that there wasn't any hope of learning why the crash had occurred. They paid the claim promptly and two men and a truck were hired to come and haul the scraps away.

» » »

Hula wished that it was himself and not Lisa who was stretched out on the straw mat. When Cruz finally let him in she had a pillow under her head and her hair was pushed back from her temples. "She's OK," Michael said quickly, looking up from the rifle he was examining. "She'll come around in a minute." He couldn't hold Hula's gaze and he glanced away. "It wasn't loaded — I was lucky."

In the ruddy light from the paper-shaded wall lamps Hula crouched down beside her. She was coughing and spitting up bits of dark, sticky blood.

Liberty came in the front door, his shirt plastered to his skin, and looked at the body on the floor. "Oh Christ," he said, and went out into the kitchen.

Hula wasn't angry at Michael. He wasn't even angry at himself. He knew, however, that he would never be comfortable with himself again. So he envied the person who had done this to her — myself, he thought, now gone forever. "There's a mattress in the bedroom," he said. "Let's put her in there."

A minute later he was sitting in a chair beside her bed, watching her chest rise and fall evenly. Cruz had gone out. Hula had been in this room before and he remembered the rough, unfinished walls, the smell of pine, and the worn floorboards.

There was a lot of pain gathering inside him and he was doing his best to head it off. He felt responsible for everything but he didn't see what good it would do to dwell on it. A lot depended, he told himself, on whether or not she was hurt. But right now there was no question of calling a doctor and he knew it.

Lisa was breathing easily and her face was relaxed and tilted back on the pillow. She hadn't moved at all.

He had thought that they would be safe here. When they had bounced out of the woods onto Krome Avenue, with the wind dropping, night coming on, and the first raindrops splashing the windshield, Cruz had said that they had to stop somewhere — the roads were crawling with Parko's soldiers and there was no way they could get back to the city. Liberty had wanted to steal another car. But Ray knew where he was again and when he saw the turnoff for Lisa's place it was all he could do to keep from grabbing the wheel himself.

But it was as if he already knew. After the endless ride along the narrow dike, with nothing visible in the headlights but the road and the rain shooting down on it, they had curved through the trees and into the clearing, where the light from the kitchen window had shone into his eyes. He had roared at them to stop and turn around, but they didn't listen. Cruz had broken out of Hula's grasp and run for the corner of the house, his feet splashing across the flooded limestone. That was the only part Ray hadn't understood. It had taken him a moment to realize that Cruz only wanted to cut the phone line.

So Hula had been standing on the concrete stoop, his hands on the door, the rain battering his neck and shoulders — he was shouting at her not to shoot but not to let anyone in either — when Cruz had slashed through the screened porch, burst through the kitchen, and put an end to her resistance. Michael had opened the door for Hula a moment later.

Lisa swallowed and opened her eyes. He leaned closer; she stared at him thoughtlessly for a moment. Then she scrambled up on her elbows, her eyes darting around the room. "What are you doing here?" She sounded a little unsure of herself, but as her memory returned her question seemed more and more just. "Did you hear me?"

"You passed out when Michael took the gun away from you. It's all right now. How do you feel — are you hurt?"

"Michael? I don't remember any Michael."

"Michael, my brother. There's three of us."

"What time is it?"

Hula looked at his watch. "Eight-thirty. Just relax for a minute, Lisa — I'll tell you whatever you want to know." He successfully kept from reaching out and forcing her shoulders down on the bed. "Are you OK? You got hit pretty hard, I think. Take a minute to see if you're all right — it's important."

"There's nothing wrong with me," she said, almost shouting. "I bit my tongue — that's all. Just forget it! Why did you follow me here?"

"I didn't — I thought the house would be empty." Hula leaned back and looked out the door. "There's nothing to worry about," he said. "It's OK now." He wished he believed it.

She settled back on the pillow as if it were made of stone.

"Look, we'll get out of here as soon as we can. I don't care what the others say. Are you sure you're all right?"

"That was your brother who hit me?"

Hula nodded. "I didn't know about that either. I'm sorry, Lisa, but it's done. I can't start over now. So just take it easy — and we'll see what we can do."

She groaned and looked away, her eyes sliding over the rough pine walls. Her hair was damp and her face shone in the warm light from the table lamp.

Hula rubbed his palms on his knees. "You said you bit your tongue — how bad is it?"

She turned her head on the pillow and stared at him. "It couldn't be worse."

He sat up and was quiet for a minute. The rain pounded the roof like thunder. Now and then a drop of water ran out of his sparse hair and down his temple.

He leaned back again and looked across the dim main room to the kitchen. Liberty was standing in the bright doorway with his back to Hula, one shoulder propped against the frame. He was evidently talking to Michael. There's no way he can hear me, Hula thought. He turned back to Lisa. "Look — can you drive? Do you want to leave now?"

The question aroused her.

"I think you should," he said.

"This is my house! What the hell is going on?"

"I know, I know," he said, shushing her with a finger. "Listen to me." He wiped his forehead with his sleeve. "You're not safe here — you have to get out. The trouble is, they may want your car."

"Why?"

"Because the one we came in has been spotted." He looked around the room. "Where are your keys?"

She studied his face for a moment. "Why should I trust you?"

"I can't answer that. But you saw what happened already." He felt himself trembling and realized that he'd been doing it for some time. "So where are they?"

"What about you?"

"I can't — no way."

"Why not?"

"Do you want me to go with you?"

"Yes."

Hula was having trouble keeping up with himself. "Lisa, I — they're in your pocketbook, right?" He looked around the room.

The keys were in her bag in the leather chair by the hearth. He would go into the kitchen and distract the other two while she went out the front door. It wasn't easy to persuade her; he had to tell her more than he wanted to.

When he walked into the kitchen he found Cruz and Liberty sitting under the back window. They had emptied the gun cabinet by the refrigerator and had two rifles and a shotgun in various states of disassembly on the heavily varnished table in front of them. Hula stopped in the doorway and stared. "What's the matter?" Cruz said. He was hunched, like a jeweler, over the open breech of the shotgun.

"She's all right," Hula said. "What're those for?"

Michael shrugged and sat up. "Just in case." Liberty had taken one of the coralbean pods out of the stoneware bowl on the table and was turning it over in his fingers.

"When are we leaving?" Hula said.

Michael nodded at the chair beside him. "Have a seat."

The rain was so loud on the roof that Hula doubted he would hear Lisa go out. He was listening closely anyway. He decided he'd better not stay in the doorway any longer. When he sat down between Cruz and Liberty he left his chair pulled well away from the table — if I have to, he thought, I can get to the door before either of them.

"Relax," Michael said. "She's not going anywhere."

Hula was still wondering what he meant by this when Lisa appeared at the door, her tan leather pocketbook dangling from one hand. She didn't look at Hula; she was staring at Cruz. Her hair was half in, half out of her collar and her face was tight and drawn. "I want my keys," she said. "Where are they?" She was still staring at Cruz.

Michael sighed and slumped back in his chair.

Hula's arm shot out and grabbed him by the throat, forcing his eyes open. "Answer her!" He had his thumb on Cruz's windpipe; it felt like a piece of hard plastic. Then Liberty drove one of the rifle butts into Hula's side and he buckled at the waist. His arm stiffened and fell away.

"Stop it!" Lisa shouted. "Stop it right now!"

Nobody argued. Cruz's chest rose and fell rapidly as he massaged his larynx; his eyes were focused inward. Ray, with one elbow pinched against his ribs, made a succession of strange faces. "Some water," Michael croaked, "get me some water." Lisa went to the tap, filled a glass, and handed it to him. He drank it all down and coughed violently.

"Where are my keys?" Lisa said.

Cruz looked as if he had just walked away from an auto wreck. He got up carefully, stepped around the table, and opened the heavy door at the top of the stairs leading down to the screened porch. "Follow me — I want to show you something," he said, nodding at Lisa. He went down the steps.

The porch was about the size of a small garage. It had a poured concrete floor, a ribbed green fiberglass roof, and a double layer of nylon mosquito netting stretched around the aluminum supporting members on three sides. By the time Hula, following Lisa, appeared at the top of the steps, Cruz had already settled in one of the chairs surrounding the oval glass table in the center. He switched on the lamp beside him. "Have a seat," he said mildly, and started spooning cocaine out of a plastic bag with a tiny gold wand. Throwing his head back, he tipped it into his nose.

Ray accompanied Lisa down to the porch. They warily placed themselves in seats opposite Cruz. In the corner of his eye Hula saw the long, ragged tear in the netting where Michael had broken through earlier, and it restored his sense of himself. The rain was beating the air, beating the roof, beating the ground; a fine mist drifted in from the surrounding darkness.

"OK," Cruz sniffed, his eyes red and moist. "I'm sorry all of this happened — now, about that car." He rolled up the bag and dropped it in his shirt pocket. "Yes, I have the keys."

Ray glanced at Lisa and found her looking back at him with an intense, thoughtful expression. He had no idea what it might mean. There was almost no chance, in his opinion, that Michael would give her the car. He wondered why Liberty had stayed in the house.

"I can see why you might want to leave," Cruz continued. "I think it's a good idea — it'd be better for all of us." He'd taken his jacket

266

off in the house and his gray silk tie hung loose around his neck. "We won't take off till the morning, at the earliest, and a lot of things could go wrong between now and then."

"Wait a minute," Lisa said, leaning forward, her hands balled in her lap. "Shouldn't you be asking me what *I* want to do? Isn't that the question?"

Cruz smiled. "All right — just let me finish." He stood up wearily, moved over to the edge of the screen, and stroked his bruised throat with one hand. "You can't take our car — they'd pick you up before you went ten miles. And you can't walk either."

"So she takes her own car," Hula said.

"Yes," Cruz continued, still pinching his Adam's apple and staring at the damp concrete floor. "I don't see any other way." His white shirt, narrow belt, and black pants, coupled with his small size and short hair, made him look like a Catholic schoolboy. He glanced at Hula. "Do you want to go with her?"

"No," he said quickly.

"Uh-huh." Cruz wandered over to the steps and sat down. Hula was watching him very closely. From what he'd seen of his brother, he didn't believe he had any reason to be afraid — on the other hand, he thought, I don't know him at all. A bit of ice settled in a tall glass on the table.

"Even if you had the keys," Michael said, "they wouldn't do you any good — I blocked the road out of the clearing with the Toyota. So I'm not going to worry about it." He stood up. "I said I wanted to show you something." He mounted to the top of the stairs and turned at the threshold. Hula now realized that he had no intention of letting her go.

"It's about this door here," Michael added, looking at Lisa and tapping on the heavy wooden slab behind him. "If you'd locked it a little while ago, I would have had a lot more trouble getting in. But you didn't. Anyway, I'm not going to make the same mistake." He turned, went inside, and shut the door behind him; the bolt snapped across the jamb. Ray and Lisa turned and stared at each other for a moment.

» » »

While Cruz was busy on the porch, Liberty sat in the kitchen and waited. He couldn't hear what was going on out there. He knew, however, that Michael wouldn't give away the car, and that was all that concerned him.

He didn't like the feel of this place — isolated, surrounded by water, and with only one road to the outside. He wasn't pleased, either, by the sight of all the hardware Cruz had piled on the table in front of him. It was as if Cruz expected a siege. Liberty sensed that there was some factor besides the need for concealment that had contributed to Michael's willingness to come out here, some undisclosed desire to prolong the ordeal, and it troubled him; he wondered whether he should have taken sides with the other man and demanded to leave immediately. But it was too late now. There were a lot of questions Liberty wanted to ask Cruz, starting with the one he'd heard a moment ago, about the keys to the car. However, he was afraid he might hear the wrong answers.

Michael came up from the porch, locked the door behind him, and went out into the main room. Liberty heard the front door open and shut briefly. He picked up the shotgun and sighted down the barrel at the lamp's reflection in the windows on the other side of the room. The action was stiff and there was rust on the cartridges in the breech; this piece hadn't been used in years. He put it down carefully. It's as if it was waiting for us, he thought.

Cruz came back in a moment later, dragging the heavy green duffel. He shoved it into the corner, turned on the portable black-and-white TV on the counter, and sat down at the table. Liberty watched him dose himself with coke out of the plastic bag while a newsman talked about layoffs in Michigan. It was the Miami station Liberty often turned on in his house in the Bahamas; he was always interested in what was going on in his former home, a foreign country, though less than a hundred miles away.

Michael picked up the guns, one by one, and piled them against the ledge under the window. Then he unfolded the map that he'd brought in with him and smoothed it out with the edge of his hand. It was a new map and the creases were still sharp and stiff. "I haven't had a chance to look at this yet," he said. "Maybe you can show me where we are." Liberty glanced at him once and bent forward.

It was a general street map of south Dade County, the same one Cruz had used to plan the transfer; the shopping center on Dixie Highway was circled in red and the intersections north and south of it were marked and numbered.

"This is Krome Avenue" — Liberty pointed to a long, straight line running parallel to and a few inches from one edge of the paper — "the access road for this place runs off of it along here somewhere between Kendall and Coral Reef — 88th and 152nd Street. That's about what . . . sixty blocks. So we must be in there somewhere." He indicated the area west of Krome Avenue containing nothing but the faintly ruled and numbered county surveyor's plats and the narrow line of Levee 31-N running alongside Krome about a mile deeper into the Glades. Cruz wanted to know if 31-N was another road.

"No — that's the dike and the canal we crossed on our way in."

"So there's no roads out here."

"That's right."

"Can you drive off the roads?"

"No way — the ground is all rotten rock, all spikes and holes. Besides, it's flooded."

"So there's only one way out." Cruz looked at Liberty.

"That's right. We're in the Glades — they stretch all the way to the Gulf."

Cruz rubbed his forehead with the three longest fingers of one hand. "They could lock us up. All it would take is one man at the entrance."

"I thought you knew," Liberty said.

Cruz pulled the map closer. "What's this?" he asked, pointing.

"That's the Tamiami Trail — goes from Miami to the west coast."

"It's only a few miles north of here — hell, we could walk it in a couple of hours."

Liberty had heard lots of nasty stories about people who tried to walk out of the Glades, but he decided not to mention them.

"You don't think so?" Cruz said.

"If you ask me, we either drive out of here or we don't get out at all."

Cruz folded up the map and pushed it aside. "If they find us here, we've had it."

"Who owns this place?"

Cruz nodded in the direction of the porch. "It's hers — he's a friend of hers."

"Some friend."

269

"They won't trace it through him — he hasn't been around."

"No kidding." Liberty looked away briefly and then stared at Cruz. "I don't like it — I think it sucks."

"You're not easy to please."

"Then don't try so hard."

Liberty might have gone further if he hadn't been distracted by Cruz's close attention to the TV. He looked up at the screen and saw a tall, sandy-haired man standing in front of a hardware store with a microphone in his hand. There was no glass in the windows behind him. It was still daytime and he was wearing a double-breasted raincoat; a stiff wind riffled the hair over his forehead. Behind him, in the store, Liberty could see what looked like a few white tags and streamers fluttering among the rakes and hoses. Now and then a kid leaned in from one side and waved at the lens. The newsman ignored him. He had to fight the traffic noise and his voice was a little louder and rougher than usual.

"This small shopping center on Dixie Highway looks like a bomb hit it. All the glass is gone from the windows behind me" — he motioned in their general direction — "and from most of the others up and down the block." The camera turned to the right, following his hand. There were some policemen with push brooms sweeping up the fragments and a small, nervous crowd stood behind a row of plank barricades.

"According to eyewitnesses, at about 5:50 this afternoon at least a dozen armed men appeared in this lot and started shooting. It lasted no more than five minutes and the participants were gone by the time police arrived. Observers said that the men got in their cars and drove out behind the center.

"There was one fatality — Mr. Harold T. Phelan of Kendall, who owned a florist's shop here." They were shown a bloody stain on the floor in a circle of powerful light. Then they saw the sign over Mr. Phelan's window, and then Mr. Phelan, wrapped in white, being lifted on a wheeled carriage into a van by four EMT's in short-sleeved shirts.

"He was shot in the head and died on the way to South Miami Hospital." The newsman appeared again, one point of his collar flapping in the wind. "Police spokesmen have no comment on the shooting. None of the stores were robbed, although merchants estimate the damage at over ten thousand dollars. The department is continuing its investigation. Anyone having information relating to this incident is urged to contact the Dade Metro authorities. Larry Burt, WKSO news, Howard."

"Thank you, Larry." The anchorman turned from the monitor like a runner taking a baton. "Cuban community leaders met today to discuss —"

The picture vanished; Cruz had clicked it off. He came back to the table and sat down. "They were all there today," he said, smiling. "It takes a very special party to get them out of their holes."

"So they opened up on you."

Cruz nodded. "I planned for that. It was still pretty close."

Liberty sat back and spread his hands on his thighs. He looked like he had spent his whole life in the sun; his smooth, red brown skin glowed dark as cinnamon against his bright blond hair. You wouldn't have thought he was the kind of person who had ever wanted, or needed, anything badly. "So what now?" he said.

"We'll leave tomorrow, in that other car."

"All of us?"

"Whoever wants to come."

"I think you should leave those other two behind. I want to have a few hours' lead before they talk to the police."

"Don't worry about it."

"I don't like working with amateurs. I could have told you this was going to happen."

"He's good luck. Look, he found us this place, didn't he?"

"I'm not impressed."

"So go blow their brains out. The stuff's right here." Cruz waved at the rifles.

"You already killed them. As soon as the traders find out where they were today, they're dead."

"Everything's a risk. We got what we came for — what more do you want?"

What I want, Liberty thought, is to be out of here.

» » »

Outside, the rain had slackened. Hundreds of bulb-toed tree frogs whirred and sang in the trees around the porch. A few yards from its edge the black and glassy surface of the sinkhole marked the limit of the clearing; beyond it hung the high, dripping forest. The air was warm and moist. Hula had taken off his shirt and stuffed it in the break in the netting to keep the mosquitoes out. He'd already been bitten a number of times, and he thought he could hear the massed drill-whine of thousands of hungry insects struggling against the screen.

Lisa sat in the chair beside him with her head thrown back and her arms folded in her lap. She stared up at the roof with an alert, collected look, like a woman waiting alone in a public place.

After a long silence Hula cleared his throat and asked her what she wanted to do — in other words, he said, if there was anything she could think of. He was less interested in what she might suggest than in establishing some form of cooperation.

"As long as your brother has my keys there's no way we can leave."

"Maybe we can persuade him to go."

She sat up, turned her head, and gazed levelly at Hula. "Ray — don't you realize he's just using you? He doesn't care what you want. He never did."

"Do you really believe that?"

"Didn't he just lock you out of the house?"

"He was only protecting himself — he didn't have any choice."

She shook her head, confounded.

Hula leaned toward her, his moist shoulders pulling away from the back of the chair. "Lisa — all I want is for all of us to get out of here safely. That's what Michael wants, believe me."

"Then what was he doing with those guns?"

"You tell me." She didn't answer, and he went on. "Whatever else he is, he's not a murderer. We'll all be out of here tomorrow, I promise you."

"It's as simple as that."

"Yes."

She shut her eyes and listened to the rain spit weakly on the fiberglass; a hollow sound, punctuated by occasional larger drops falling from the trees. She wanted to hurt him, now. "I've been thinking about your brother. He never would have gotten to you if he was a stranger."

"Maybe not."

"You hated him — you thought that made it all right. So you went along with him just so you could feel how noble and spotless you were — so you could remind him of what he'd done. He read you perfectly."

"I won't argue with you." There was a part of Hula that welcomed this abuse; he wanted all the blame for himself. "It would be ridiculous to say I'm sorry."

"Don't, then. Don't say a word."

They sat there, not speaking, for another twenty minutes. The rain stopped and water beaded along the edge of the roof. The surrounding forest squeaked, rustled, and chirped at the two figures frozen in the circle of light behind the screens. In the sinkhole a pair of small turtles floated at the surface — their heads poked high out of the water, their round eyes watching the house. They ducked under when the door at the top of the of the steps opened suddenly. Michael Cruz looked out at the porch for a moment and went back inside. A few seconds later Lisa followed him in. Hula was glad to be alone.

» » »

At 2:00 A.M. no one was moving around anymore. Hula sat sprawled in a chair on the porch with his feet on the table and a light blue blanket pulled up over his shoulders. When he had gone into the house to get it he had found Cruz and Liberty sitting in the stout, high-backed chairs in front of the fire, the glow from a few slow-burning mangrove logs shining in their faces. Lisa was lying in the bedroom, her head to the wall; she didn't look up when he leaned in.

The chair was uncomfortable; his knees and lower back ached whenever he moved and the pain gave him the impression, only intermittently true, that he was still awake. In a little while he noticed Cruz sitting in the chair beside him, learning forward, his elbows on his knees. It was four in the morning.

"Don't get up," Michael whispered. "I want to talk to you."

He was just a voice. Ray couldn't see anything of his face. He heard a mosquito humming somewhere above them.

"This is only for you — if you tell the others they won't believe you anyway." He paused. "Are you listening?"

Hula pushed the blanket into his lap and sat up.

"We're not going to leave right away in the morning," Cruz said. "We're waiting for someone."

273

In rousing himself Hula kicked one leg of the table; a tall glass sitting on top fell over and shattered on the concrete. Now he was awake.

Cruz ignored it. "We'll wait all day if we have to," he said. "But I don't think we'll have to — he won't waste any time."

Hula cleared his throat. "Waiting for who?"

"For that guy you saw in your office — the bald-headed guy."

Ray had no trouble remembering him. "Are you crazy?"

"We don't have any choice."

Maybe he is crazy, Hula thought.

Cruz went on. "Look, I know you're worried about your friend. You want her out of here as soon as possible. But unless I take care of this none of us will be safe."

"Wait a minute," Hula said. "You better start over."

"The only reason I'm telling you this is to warn you — if he kills me, you'll be next. He's going to try it tomorrow."

Hula had become accustomed to the sound of gunfire by this time and the news didn't shock him. "So?"

"This isn't the traders I'm talking about now — this is different. He knows us. He'll find us here and he could find us anywhere else."

"Who is he?"

"You don't have to know. But he'll be here tomorrow, because it's the last time you and I will be together."

When this conversation began Hula had hoped he would learn something. Now he knew otherwise. "This is shit," he said, waving at the dark. "This is the umpteenth time around. What do you want from me?"

Cruz refused to be shaken. "Nothing. I just wanted you to be ready. Right now I'm standing between you and him, and when I'm gone, it'll be all up to you. That's all."

"But why is he doing this? What's he got against us?"

Cruz pushed back into his chair and kicked some broken glass away from his feet. "There's always some things you have to take for themselves." Ray heard the rustle of soft plastic followed by a sharp inhalation — cocaine again.

"What do you think of me, Michael?" Hula's tone was aggrieved. "Do you think I'm an idiot?"

Cruz laughed easily. "First you tell me what I am."

Hula felt his anger rising inside him and did nothing to restrain it.

274

"I don't know a goddamn thing about you, except that you're a crook and a liar and you've got nothing on your mind but your own bullshit tightrope act."

"A crook and a liar." He laughed again. "Like you, maybe? I'm listening — go on."

"You're the son of a fucking dead Portugee sailor and you hate it — you hate it so bad you couldn't even stick around for his funeral — you had to leave home and go to New York where she couldn't reach you and where you could tell the cops whatever you wanted."

"Is that what she told you?"

"She didn't know anything about it — you just disappeared."

"What else?"

"But it wasn't enough to wreck her life — you had to come down here and go to work on mine."

"That's right," Cruz said. "Any more?"

Hula felt his anger begin to subside. He was breathing heavily, his fingers lashed tight to the arms of the chair. His mouth tasted like a stack of pennies.

"OK," Cruz said. "Now I'm going to talk about you." He paused deliberately, waiting. The swampy, full-throated night sang in Hula's ears.

"You're a fat, lazy old cow with your balls in hock and not enough brains to count to three."

This wasn't enough; Hula wanted more. "I'm bleeding — I'm sinking fast."

"You got a picture in your head of what you are and what other people are and you haven't touched it for thirty years, because all you do is pour beer down your throat, fuck like a dead whale, and bitch about people you don't know."

"Is that the best you can do?"

"Your father was a smiling, pussy-whipped Polack drunk who couldn't do anything but lick sawdust off a barroom floor." Cruz lingered over each word. "Your mother — my mother — was a lonely, crazy old cunt who made one mistake and spent the rest of her life trying to pretend she hadn't."

Hula reached out deliberately and caught a handful of Cruz's shirt. He tightened it in his fist, waiting.

"I'm not finished," Michael whispered.

275

For reasons unclear to him, Ray's grip loosened and he took his arm away.

"But the only thing that matters," Cruz said, "is that you're my brother. That's why I'm here right now and that's why I love you."

That was all. Michael got up abruptly and vanished; Hula heard his sneakers going up the steps.

Perhaps it was his imagination, but in a little while Ray thought he could see the first milky light of day floating out of the night and blackness around him. It wasn't enough to see by. He watched his mother dying once more in her musty bedroom in Providence, a yellow snapshot of Cruz at seven in a frame on the table beside her.

Michael had been trying to tell him something, something important, and hadn't been able to do it. That fact meant more to Ray than the message, whatever it was — something about their mother, who hadn't seen Cruz since he was fifteen. So she also had failed to get a message across; she died before she could reach him. It seemed that nobody, not even Michael, could find that last bit of strength.

However, if Hula had been paying more attention on his last visit to Providence he might have had a better idea of what Cruz was talking about.

If he had looked up as he mounted the iron-plated stoop into his mother's house, the house where she had died two days earlier and where she was now laid out in a casket in the front room downstairs, he might have noticed the tall man in a charcoal overcoat and brown, narrow-brimmed hat standing halfway down the block and watching him. It was the same man who would fall asleep in a car outside Hula's yard in Miami, the same man who later visited him to talk about Michael. Like Cruz, he hadn't been inside his mother's house for years.

Victor Hula was born in Providence eight months after Ray and his father had left for Miami. He was out of the house before Cruz was born, out at fourteen because the state had decided he was too dangerous to do without medical supervision. After he left, his mother never said another word about him. It was as if everyone had agreed that he no longer existed.

So it was up to Cruz to find out who he was, after the man had shot at him twice and killed two of his friends and announced, by letter, that he was going to kill Ray too. The doctors said that narcolepsy — sudden, involuntary sleeping — is not usually associated with psychosis but that the two can occur together, the onset of one triggering the other. They also said that Victor had always claimed that he had no relatives. His caseworker had lost track of him shortly after he was discharged; he didn't like the drugs and never came back for them.

It became clear to Cruz that Victor blamed certain individuals, his family in particular, for whatever had gone wrong inside his head. The last person he had killed — the girl on Alton Road — was just another proxy. Cruz had arrived at the funeral hoping to find him there, but when the moment came he couldn't bring himself to do what he had planned to do. So he stopped at the top of the stoop, looking back at Victor and praying for something to happen, and finally he said, "Are you coming inside?" and Victor said no, and after they had stared at each other for a moment there was nothing left except to turn and go in, knowing that he had failed and might fail again.

He couldn't tell Ray about it — not then and not any time later. They were his brothers; they were all that was left of a past he had rejected; one of them was cursed in life and marked for death and the other, an innocent, would be required to participate in his destruction.

Outside the hammock the night hung over the rustling, water-bright plain like dark, clinging smoke. An alligator bellowed far off in the sawgrass. Hula got up and felt his way to the steps. In the quiet, darkened main room he glimpsed Cruz and Liberty in the chairs by the hearth, their heads outlined against the dying fire. He went into Lisa's bedroom and settled in the rail-back chair by the window. You might think there was nothing really going on. But most of life will hide itself from strange eyes. Emptiness, solitude, and peace are names of false ideas that can lull a single heart; they're never found outside one.

Crawler

O N THE MORNING AFTER THE TRANSFER Jack Parko woke up early and had three cigarettes in bed. There was no ashtray in the room and he used the glass he'd left on the floor. A quarter inch of water — melted ice from the scotch the housekeeper had given him the night before — drowned the butts and added a foul stink to the air, sharper and more penetrating than the smoke itself.

A lot of people had looked in during the night, seen him, and shut the door. He remembered thinking that there were too many of them to be accounted for by those in search of rest; no, they all wanted a peek at their former leader, now in disgrace. He felt like the prize bear at the zoo.

Jack was still wondering why Ramón hadn't killed him. It was the obvious solution. Once you'd gotten as far as Jack had, you couldn't be eased out; you had to be retired in a hurry. And Ramón was always ready for whatever was needed. He did what he had to do; that's why he was running things now.

Maybe, Jack thought, this was Ramón's idea of a joke. If Jack couldn't bring himself to hate Ramón, it might have been because he felt older this morning than he ever had in his life.

There was enough noise coming from the rest of the house to keep him in his room. He heard doors opening and shutting, cars pulling into the driveway, footsteps in the hall, and muffled conversations from which he could pick out a few weary obscenities. There was a lot more Spanish than yesterday. Nothing surprising about that — nobody had to talk to Jack anymore.

Jack didn't go out of the room because he didn't want to see anything dry up as soon as he showed his face. He had nothing to fear;

281

Ramón had made the decision and nobody was going to spoil the new man's first day on the job. What waited for him out there, instead, was a kind of slow freeze made out of fish-eye stares, sudden silences, and muttered remarks about his clothes and the shape of his head. Jack had known for years that his odd appearance was the subject of much discussion. Now he'd hear all the nicknames for the first time. He was a ghost, a spectre, a sunburned and unwelcome reminder of his former power and legitimacy; he belonged with Nixon and Idi Amin in a home for junked tyrants.

By 9:00 A.M. he judged that the activity in the house had quieted as much as was necessary for him to leave his cell.

The main room looked like a just-emptied encampment. There were sheets and pillows scattered over the couches, telephone cords looped on the floor, pencils, maps, and crumpled cigarette packages on every level surface, and tiny paper coffee cups littering the carpet. The housekeeper had fried some eggs for breakfast and their smeared yellow remains were hardening on a half dozen paper plates. A few men sat around in small groups and talked quietly or dozed. The central air had been humming all night and the house smelled like Freon and cracked vinyl.

Jack toured all the larger rooms. Ramón was gone, Arthur was gone; they'd left Mario in charge. He was sitting on a stool in the kitchen. When he saw Jack he turned, hiked up his elbows on the counter behind him, and looked away. He was right next to the pressurized coffee machine. While Jack looked for a cup Mario turned over the lined pad beside the phone. Jack gave him plenty of time to settle himself; he didn't want any trouble. Mario was wearing a pink shirt and a narrow black tie. Everybody got promoted this morning, Jack thought, as he squirted a puddle of the thick black liquid into the clay mug he'd found. He added about a pint of milk from the refrigerator.

He left the kitchen and stopped by the glass doors overlooking the terrace. Three men in gym shorts were sitting in the sun near the brick wall on the far side of the pool. They didn't look cold; it was warming up already. Their hardware was piled up in a fourth chair and their clothes were strewn around them. Ramón left all the trash behind, Jack thought. They were stretched out and their faces were turned toward the sun. One of them looked up, shaded his eyes, and gazed in Jack's direction. Then the other two sat up and did the same. Jack stared back at them for a while and moved on.

He'd managed to pick up a few things through his skin, so to speak. The bankers were gone and nobody was much concerned with security, so the cocaine must be safely on its way to New York. Nobody was here but Escobar's men — therefore they'd finished the job without drawing any interference from the other partners. They ought to have been grateful. For ten million dollars they'd gotten enough coke to float the market for the next six months and starve all the other brokers into retirement. I should be proud of myself, Jack thought. It was the toughest, biggest, and most sensitive buy of his career, and he'd brought it off exactly the way experience had showed it must be handled. A straight business deal — no tricks, no promises, nothing special — nobody tried anything that they might have had to regret later. Escobar didn't understand that; none of the Colombians did.

So they dumped me, Jack thought, because I was too careful. Maybe they were right, he told himself; times had changed. Maybe it didn't make sense anymore to cover your tracks when there was so much shit flying around that nobody could see in front of his face. It was getting harder to tell what things meant — Michael Cruz, for instance, had gotten out of Colombia with a ton of cocaine. A few years ago that would have proved there was a new and powerful group breaking into the system, but now no one was sure. Apparently it was some kind of accident.

They hadn't gotten Cruz; Jack was certain of that. That's what they were doing this morning. They were all out looking for him. No other job would have eaten up all the men so quickly. If Cruz tried to walk into any bank in Miami this morning and deposit so much as a pair of twenty-dollar bills, that would be the end of it. Jack knew that Cruz wasn't that stupid, and he took comfort from the fact, because he wanted to find Michael himself.

He didn't know where to start. He couldn't go anywhere without a car, and no one here would give him one.

He was standing by the windows in the dining room with his hands joined behind his back, looking out over the lush, close-cropped back lawn streaked by the retreating shadows of dozens of palms and paperbarks and still sparkling with the night's dew. A pair of mockingbirds dipped from tree to tree, wing spots flashing. It looks like a private park, he thought, or a golf course. The house belonged to Escobar's wife, though he doubted she'd ever been allowed to see it. Jack himself had never met her. She probably had another place like this of her own, with a few coffee trees and a row of bananas — a little bit of Colombia in the U.S.A. One thing Jack had learned in life was that women always knew what to do with money. What did Cruz plan to do with ten million dollars? Open a club in Hong Kong? Buy some new clothes? Buy another chance to die?

Calling a taxi and renting a car at the airport seemed like a needlessly tedious and time-consuming way to get started, but Jack had nearly made up his mind that there was no alternative when the old housekeeper appeared just outside the window and caught his eye. The man was in thin cotton pajamas and slippers and had a heavy brown robe draped over his shoulders; the tie for the waist had come loose on one side and trailed through the grass behind him. He had his head down, as if the movement of his feet required constant attention. The skin on his neck and under his thinning white hair was soft and tender as a child's. He was moving past the window from right to left and Jack would have thought he was just out for a stroll if the old man hadn't swung his head toward the house just as he passed the window and looked directly into Jack's eyes with an ancient, knowledgeable, and half-vacant expression on his face. At the same time the hand hanging from his thick sleeve flipped over once, as if he were trying to shake some water off of it. Then he turned slowly and shuffled wearily off towards the rear hedge over a hundred yards away.

Jack knew that he'd been summoned. A few minutes earlier he'd considered asking the housekeeper to intercede with someone to get him a car. He'd dropped the idea, not because he didn't think the old man would do it, but since he didn't believe Mario or anyone else would go along. The housekeeper was flawlessly neutral; in the few days Jack had been here he'd found himself repeatedly assuming that the man was deaf and dumb, even though he'd heard him speak and had talked to him himself more than once.

But there couldn't be any doubt about what had just happened and Jack was ready to try anything. He waited, giving the old man a chance to make a little more distance into the yard, then walked down the hall to the back door and followed him out.

284

Jack found him standing outside a clump of red-blossomed ixora bushes shielded from the house by a short hedge of bougainvillea. He was mumbling to himself and pulling apart a waxy orange flower in his hands. His ankles were wet; there was water beaded on his leather slippers. When he looked up and saw Jack the remains of the flower fell to the ground.

"You wanted me?" Jack said.

The housekeeper nodded gravely. Jack turned and glanced back towards the house. All he could see was the crown of the low roof. He wondered if anyone would come out after them.

The old man tilted his head back and peered serenely at the cluster of lofty coconut palms on the other side of the hedge. He remained staring at them for so long that Jack began to think there was a message here he was missing; he followed the man's gaze and looked up at the trees himself. All he saw were the heavy male fruit hugging the crowns and the ribbony fronds hanging nearly motionless above them. The old man just wouldn't be rushed.

Out of the corner of his eye Jack saw the housekeeper's hand straying towards the deep pocket in his robe. It didn't make any sense; this man was just too old to be required to kill anybody. He also noticed that there was nothing in that pocket as substantial as a gun. Take it easy, he told himself — you've got enough problems.

When the housekeeper brought his hand out again he was clutching a white paper napkin crumpled into a wad. He held it cupped in one hand while he laboriously unfolded it with the other. Inside was a single shiny metal key. He held it out; Jack took it from him. "What's this?" he said.

The old man had lost interest. He was trying to put the napkin back in his pocket but his fingers kept slipping over the opening. He didn't look to see what he was doing. His white, wrinkled hand just kept sliding across his hip and coming back again.

Jack persisted. "This is a car key, right? Which car? Did Ramón give it to you?" He stooped and held the key in front of the man's face. He wanted to reach out and shake him.

The housekeeper wouldn't look at Jack. "Don't give me this shit," Jack said. "It was Ramón, right?" He shoved the key in his pants. "Don't tempt me, old man. I know who you are." Jack picked up the trailing end of the man's waist strap and strung it through the empty loop in his robe. As he did it he could feel the man's warm breath on the side of his face. He straightened up. "OK, so who gave it to you? It wasn't your idea."

Jack didn't know how many cars were left in the driveway; he hadn't looked. He was excited and impatient. "I don't have time for this," he said. "You'll never see me again. That's right. I'm out of here — I'm gone."

There was nothing in those eyes to suggest that he'd heard what Jack said. Jack was about to leave when the old man started to say something. His lips were moving but there was no sound coming out. He coughed feebly and tried again. "Go on," he whispered. "Don't come back. Look — is this who you are?" He brushed at his speckled chest with one hand. "You can go on too long and you won't even know it. Don't come back."

He was out of breath. When he tried to suck in a big gulp of air he started coughing again; his mouth shook as he bent over.

Jack watched him for a few seconds. He didn't feel any pity for him. He's a fake, he thought — he loves it. Then he said "All right. It's between me and Cruz. But thanks anyway." He turned and started purposefully for the back of the house.

There was no problem with the car. Nobody paid him any attention as he walked through the quiet rooms and out the front door. They're glad to get rid of me, he thought.

He burned a few gallons of gas before he was able to think clearly again. They'd given him a radio car and he listened to some of the men reporting in to Ramón at various times, but there was obviously very little happening. It sounded like they were all over the city. There wasn't much chance that he'd learn anything useful. But he didn't turn it off because he wanted to have some idea of what was going on. If they found Cruz he didn't know what he'd do.

Jack was used to having a lot of people wait on his orders. That was where his power lay; he could translate his will into collective action. Now he was stuck with a habit of thought that was no longer appropriate. All of the schemes that took shape in his head required capabilities far beyond his own. He had to keep reminding himself that no plan or idea was any use unless he could accomplish it by himself.

For a while he just drove around aimlessly, looking hard at the people he saw on the street and in other cars, and hoping for a miracle. In fact, he kept telling himself, if Cruz had any sense he would have been out of the city hours ago, and he probably was. If Escobar was patient, and did all the groundwork carefully and thoroughly, Jack didn't doubt that he could catch up with Cruz within a year or two. Jack himself believed he could do the same thing on his own, though it might take a little longer. It was just a question of reconstructing what had already happened. But he didn't want to think about it; it was too easy to see himself doing it. He wanted Michael, immediately, right now, without delay. Therefore Cruz was still here somewhere, just out of sight. It was necessary to believe that before anything else.

Cruz had to stay somewhere last night, somewhere where the money would also be safe; it wasn't likely that he'd let it out of his sight. He obviously couldn't afford to go anywhere where he might be known. Half the city must have heard about him by now. That eliminated the hotels and all the houses associated with the trade. Even if Cruz had a few connections in Miami, he couldn't let himself rely on them. He was poison now; he could kill people in bunches.

What did that leave? An apartment he'd rented under another name, a place belonging to one of his partners, or a ticket out of town. None of these possibilities brought Jack any closer to him, and the third was painful to think about. He pushed it aside. These partners — where had Cruz gotten them? The big man who ran in with the money definitely wasn't hispanic. Maybe Cruz brought him down from New York, or recruited him right here. The guy had shared the worst moments with him, so Cruz must have thought he was worth his trust. He looked like one of those cement salesmen or truck drivers who became local brokers — the workhorses of the dope trade. He could have come from anywhere. And the third man was just a voice on the phone. Jack was once more forced to admit that everything he knew about Michael Cruz could be collected on the back of a business card. It was as if Cruz had been planning a move like this all his life. He had less substance, less positive identity, than a three-month-old child. And this was the man that had starred for the Knapp Commission.

The more Jack thought about it, the bleaker his prospects appeared. No amount of sweat was going to squeeze any useful conclusions out of the facts. Cruz had brought him face to face with his own impotence, and Jack's celebrated patience, caution, and tenacity now clung to him as heavily as an old man's accumulation of years.

He stopped for a drink downtown at noon. The bar was full of Cubans, laughing and talking and jumping in and out of their seats. Jack felt crowded on all sides. He refused to use his Spanish; he wanted to be left alone. The era of the solitary drinker, he thought, is over. He drank gin and stared at the painted mirrors above the bar.

The liquor didn't do him any good. He couldn't stop thinking about Michael Cruz, the author of all his disasters. Although his experience this morning had proved how little reason there was to continue, he still felt as if he owed it to himself to go on; Jack had no affection for lost causes, but there was simply nothing else he could do. He'd already decided that this would be his last day in Miami. Why not use it to exhaust himself? Why not go back north knowing that he'd done all he could, even when further effort was demonstrably pointless? How else, in fact, could he make it through the next few hours? He didn't allow himself to consider it further. He paid his bill, pushed his stool back, and walked out into the bright, blinding street. For the next half hour he drove around and around the splintering center of Miami, noticing nothing, thinking about nothing, matching his rhythm to the city's own fast-scurrying agitation.

There was nothing about the boat to identify it with Cruz. And it didn't bear much resemblance, either, to the mental image based on the Colombian drawing that Jack had studied so assiduously a few days ago. Jack had never had much interest in boats and couldn't tell you why one was different from another. They were big or small, power or sail, wood or metal — his knowledge of taxonomy extended no further than these crude antitheses, which were more than sufficient for someone who hadn't been afloat for over twenty years. Jack crossed water in cars, trains, and aircraft.

So Jack wasn't relying on any native expertise when he crossed the Twelfth Avenue bridge, parked at a small motel on the other side, and walked back up the hot sidewalk to the summit, about forty feet over the greasy surface of the Miami River. He shaded his eyes and looked down the channel toward the boat that had caught his eye momentarily as he drove over the hump a minute earlier. He didn't know what he'd expected to find. It didn't have a Colombian flag dangling from the mast, for instance.

The sun beat down on his head with such force that he had to lean against the rail. The heavy stream of traffic crossing behind him fouled the small breeze; he could feel the heat of the exhaust. I must

288

be in bad shape, he told himself, if I can get this excited over nothing.

The boat was about two or three hundred yards down the river, tied up alongside a plank-faced embankment. Behind it a row of metal-roofed sheds wavered in the heat. Nothing was moving anywhere nearby. He could see the tops of a few dusty and opaque trees poking up between the buildings. From this height it seemed as if everything — the river, the sheds, the flat roofs beyond, the pale towers in the distance downtown — had half-buried itself in the ground to escape the heated air.

The only aspect of the boat that had led him back up the bridge was its singularity; even Jack's naive eye could see that it was different. It was old, dirty, thick-waisted, and roughly constructed. Beside the sleek, white-hulled factory yachts in the marina opposite it looked like an abandoned sofa. It didn't match the boat in the drawing, which had been a lot more narrow and graceful. Jack had fixed the drawing in his memory and was able to recreate it without effort. He went over the major features and compared them against what he saw, finding to his surprise that although the overall appearance of the boat was greatly dissimilar, some of the individual points were exactly the same — the mast grew right out of the forward wall of the cabin, for instance, and the hinge-shaped rudder rose up to a height nearly flush with the deck in the rear. Jack looked down at the foul water below him, broken here and there by sodden clumps of floating garbage — plastic bottles, bits of wood, chunks of tarred Styrofoam — and rested his eyes for a minute. He had plenty of time. The silence in his head seemed particularly heavy and expectant. There was a tendency, he knew, to find only those things he was looking for.

What if it was Cruz's boat? Michael was long gone anyway. It was just a museum piece now. With this thought and others Jack tried to prepare himself for disappointment. It was a necessary exercise because he'd known as soon as he saw the boat that it would be fatal to his aimlessness. It didn't particularly matter that there was probably hundreds of hulks like it all over the city. What excited him was the process of forgetting now available to him through direct action; in this respect the boat might be as effective as a quart of bourbon. He'd been thinking too hard all morning and he badly needed something to do. Taking a minute to fix the location of the boat in his mind, he walked back down to his car and recrossed the bridge.

He couldn't get anywhere near the river. All the streets leading down to it were heavily fenced some distance away, protecting a series of contractors' depots, municipal garages, and concrete warehouses. The gate he decided was closest to his goal was in the center of a long chain-link fence fronting an unpaved courtyard surrounded by low cinder-block sheds. It was locked. The large metal sign on the fence said "Miami Salvage, Inc." and included a phone number. One car, a late-model Ford, was parked inside. There was no sign of life.

Jack, a curious yachtsman interested in buying the boat, didn't even consider climbing the fence. He looked through the wire for a little while, returned to his car, and leaned on the horn. When a second blast produced no result he decided to try the number. He wasn't really surprised to find no one around. It was barely past noon; the city was stunned by the sun overhead.

He walked back towards Flagler Street, the hot concrete burning through his soles, and found a phone under the awning of a small market. The crates on the table beside him held unruly piles of mangoes, guavas, papayas, red plantains, and other mysterious vegetables; he stared at them stupidly as he waited for an answer. After ten rings a small, suspicious voice growled hello. Jack tried to sound breezy and cheerful and failed miserably.

"Is this Miami Salvage? . . . I was just over the bridge at Twelfth Avenue and I saw that old wreck you've got tied up in the river. Is it for sale?"

"I don't know. You'll have to ask the boss." The man on the other end sounded sullen and tired, as if he'd been hoping for someone else.

"Is he around?"

"No — I don't know where he is."

Sounds good, Jack thought, sounds very good. "Is he going to be back later?"

"Don't know — you could try."

"Uh, tonight, maybe? Do you have his home number?"

He didn't get it immediately. In fact, he didn't get it at all. "What do you want with that piece of shit?"

It was a question but it sounded like a challenge. "I'm — I don't know, I think I could do something with it."

"He's not around."

"Do you have his home number?"

"It's in the book."

Jack could tell he was about to hang up. "What's his name?"

"Ray Hula." The line clicked. Jack replaced the phone; the dime fell into the coinbox.

The boat had served its purpose. Jack no longer had any interest in it. He'd thrown everything into the smelter — the boat, the drawing, ten million dollars, the housekeeper's key — and all of it had boiled away except this precious bit of metal at the bottom: Ray Hula. Jack felt a little sorry for him, whoever he was. The man probably had no connection at all to Cruz, and yet he'd have plenty to answer for. In certain situations one victim was as good as another.

A half hour later he was back at square one again. Ray Hula didn't answer his doorbell. Jack had tried to pick the lock with a piece of wire, but his skills had atrophied over the years and it defeated him. He nearly took out his gun and started shooting; he was that frustrated. But there were people around the pool under the balcony and he might need a little time once he got inside.

He walked back down the stairway and went around to the rear of the apartment block. It was a long, rectangular, two-story building overlooking a narrow strip of common lawn, a few palms, and Biscayne Bay. There was a balcony here also, divided into short porches by a row of masonry walls. If he could get onto one of the adjacent porches it would be easy enough to swing over to Hula's. Those sliding doors might give him trouble, but he'd worry about them later. He returned through the breezeway to the front of the building, climbed the stairs, and knocked on the door of the apartment next to Hula's on the left. I'll have to do this very quickly, he thought.

A tall, bleary-eyed young man in a T-shirt and gym shorts answered the door. Sleep still clung to his face. It was Hula's friend Norton, the cabdriver. Jack was pleased. The man didn't look as if he was capable of much resistance.

"You don't know me, but I'm a friend of Ray Hula's," Jack said. "Can I come in?"

There was no response. It wasn't so much hesitation as complete incomprehension; Norton just wasn't yet prepared for waking life. Jack saw his chance and took it.

"This is very important," he said, stepping over the threshold and moving past him into the living room. "Wait here," he said, calling over his shoulder. "I'll explain everything."

At the rear of the apartment he pushed the glass door aside, stepped onto the balcony, put one leg over the rail, reached up for the top of the barrier wall, and swung himself around it to Hula's porch.

Hula had left his screen unlocked and Jack walked right in. He had two objects in mind; to find something that tied Hula to Cruz and to discover where Hula was at this moment. The man next door would probably call the police, so he didn't have much time.

The living room was dark and stuffy. Jack turned on the overhead light and looked around him. A sagging couch, a pile of newspapers, a small round dining table, a TV set, an easy chair, a framed color photograph of a tugboat on the wall — Ray Hula obviously lived here, but what else could you say? The wastebasket was filled with peanut shells and junk mail. Jack could feel a little panic coming on. His momentum was fading rapidly.

In the bedroom he yanked out the drawer in the night table and dumped it on the mattress. He found old utility bills, spare shoelaces, bottles of aspirin, a rusty belt buckle, sufficient change to clean out a vending machine, and a list of names and phone numbers, which he pocketed. A manila mailing envelope held open over the bed dropped a thin swatch of faded clippings. Jack's heart leaped when he looked at them. They were all about Michael Cruz — Cruz and the Knapp Commission, Cruz and the lawyers, Cruz the informant. Jack was one of the few people who knew that the testimony Michael had given — the testimony the police had been so proud of — was actually a shrewd invention of certain individuals eager to divert attention from themselves. The men who'd gone to jail were doomed anyway. Jack had a collection of these same clippings himself; one of the pictures was the one he'd handed out to Escobar's group. So what was Ray Hula doing with them? A rhetorical question. And where was Ray Hula now? Where indeed? Jack couldn't help smiling as he opened the closet and dragged a cardboard box down from the upper shelf. It held a heavy pair of service-issue binoculars and a bundle of old papers. Among them he found a large black-and-white studio photo of a navy recruit in his dress whites, sitting on a stool with crossed arms, as young and raw and resolute as any of Escobar's fresh trainees from Bogotá. He was blocky, thick-necked, and already going to fat. This is the man, Jack thought, that I saw bulling his way into the flower store. This is Ray Hula.

The other papers were just as old — a high-school diploma from

1948, a map of the south Florida coast with an uneven row of tiny crosses inked in just offshore ("Merchant traffic sunk by U-boats July–December 1942"), a handbook of aircraft silhouettes, some yellowed letters, a picture of a girl in a bathing suit standing awkwardly on a beach — Jack pushed it all aside in disgust and stalked into the main room. There was nothing here. Hula obviously kept all his papers at his office.

Jack banged his way around the kitchen, wrenching open the cabinets and slapping them shut, shoving his hands under the flatware trays, and assessing Hula's tastes in liquor. He couldn't stay here any longer. In the living room he pulled up the corners of the rug and dug into the seams of the couch. He didn't know what he was looking for. A fine desperation expressed itself in his sudden, jerky movements; it took a lot of work to keep his mind clear. Maybe Ray Hula is already dead, he thought — maybe Michael killed him.

There was only one thing left to do. He didn't like the idea, but he needed results. He went back out onto the porch, carefully climbed the rail, and swung himself around the wall. The man who'd let him in was going to answer a few questions.

Jack found him sitting in a chair staring at the blank tube of the TV set. He jumped up when Jack pushed the curtains aside. He was wide awake now. Jack looked quickly around the room and walked in. "Hula wasn't there," he said, pulling his gun. "Tell me where he is or you're dead — right now." He held the gun out at arm's length and pointed it at the man's narrow curly-haired head, drawing back the hammer for effect. He was well aware that this person might not know a thing. He was determined, however, to find out all he knew.

The tall man didn't react properly. He set his long-fingered hands on his hips and stared back at Jack. "Fucking asshole," he said. "Weird fucking bullshit." As far as Jack could tell he was totally without fear.

Burdened with a sense of mounting futility, Jack turned the gun and fired. The TV exploded outwards, scattering glass and metal over the carpet. He took a deep breath. "You're next," he said. "Where is he?" He would've liked to use his hands but he didn't want to get that close.

The man glared bitterly at the TV and chewed his lip.

Jack cocked the hammer again. "Now," he said.

Norton shook his head. "I don't know — he doesn't tell me a thing,

293

like all you fucks." He looked at the floor and scratched his cheek.

He's hiding something, Jack thought. All of a sudden he's hiding something. Jack didn't feel good about it at all.

He had his back to the short hall leading to the bedroom. By the time he turned and looked it was too late. A short, heavy, and muscular man with a battered old face and a Hawaiian shirt was reaching out for him in midair. Jack tried to bring the gun around. The man's head crashed into his chest, driving him backward off his feet. Norton ducked aside and Jack fell clumsily into the stuffed chair, knocking it straight back into the wall. His head bounced against the plaster. He wasn't thinking about the man who'd attacked him — Norton's friend, the former prizefighter and ice-cream salesman. He was worried about the gun in his hand. It was necessary to hold onto it without accidentally shooting himself. Jack had a well-justified fear of bullet wounds and he'd momentarily lost his sense of which way the barrel was pointing. He only knew that it was in the general region of his stomach.

When he hit the wall in the chair the other man's body followed shortly after and smashed him into it. By this time Jack had gotten his finger out from behind the trigger and was ready to maneuver.

He soon learned that he couldn't move. The old boxer had locked his wrists in a ring around Jack's arms, binding them down from behind. He was a lot stronger than Jack.

"Don't let go!" Norton shouted, dancing and waving his hands.

The old man was enjoying himself. His weight alone was enough to keep Jack from stirring. Meanwhile he slowly tightened his grip, squeezing Jack's wind out of him with the patience of a starfish. Jack couldn't do anything with the gun. Although his wrist was free now, his lower arm was wedged tight, pointing down towards his hip, and his own body lay between the weapon and the other man.

He'd fallen forward into the chair, his collarbone driven into the headrest and his upper thighs jammed against the edge of the seat, and there was nothing supporting the middle of his body except the natural strength of his spine. Jack, who was thinking very clearly, had just started to dwell on this fact when he realized that his attacker had noticed it also. Careful not to relax his hold, the man was gradually sliding one knee up towards the small of Jack's back. When he got it there all he'd have to do was put his weight on it. Jack's old backbone would bow inward and crack like a twig.

He reacted to this new knowledge with a furious, twisting struggle to turn himself over. He didn't move an inch. Norton saw it, however, and sat down on Jack's ankles. The boxer's knee had reached the top of Jack's hip and was boring up and in. Jack briefly considered shooting a hole through himself just to get at him. But he never found out if the old man would actually have broken him in two, because he somehow discovered the necessary motion. Dropping his shoulder, Jack drove his hand straight down towards his crotch, forcing his rigid fingers between his legs and both under and well into the boxer's pants, gathering the man's testes in his fist, pulling them back, and driving his nails into them. One of them either burst or slipped away; he flattened the other.

The man's whole body turned stiff and nerveless. He didn't make a sound. Jack managed to turn half over and the man's bulk slid into the chair beside him. There wasn't really enough room for both of them. Norton was still sitting on Jack's ankles. He looked surprised when he saw Jack staring back at him. He should have realized that his friend the boxer was out of action and that he'd better change his tactics. But he just bore down harder on Jack's feet.

Jack grabbed one arm of the chair for leverage, sat up, bent forward, and slammed the gun against Norton's head just above his ear. The man slumped gently onto the carpet. Jack struggled out from under the boxer, who was starting to make soft choking noises, and wobbled to his feet. One of his ankles gave way; he'd twisted it badly when he wrenched himself around to swing at Norton. Swearing bitterly, he fell over the prostrate man and bloodied his elbow on a piece of a vacuum tube that had blown out of the TV set. He was able to stand up again by putting all his weight on his good leg. The pain enraged him. His face was a clotted purple and his dentures had come loose. These two clowns, he thought, nearly killed me. He was out of breath and his ribs shrieked in protest when he tried to fill his lungs. All he wanted to do was get out of there. He took a last look at the two men on the floor and put his gun away under his coat. He shut the door behind him as he left. He took the elevator down; he could barely walk.

His car was in a shady corner of the lot facing Hula's block. He sat in the dim interior and fingered his injuries, pressing hard on the worst bruises. He was taking vengeance on his own stupidity. Nobody had come to his aid as he dragged himself across the hot asphalt. Nobody seemed to have noticed anything unusual. There were children playing on the terrace and a few people sitting under umbrellas around the pool. He started the car and turned on the air conditioning. If Norton had called the police they would be here in a minute or two. Jack could see the heat shimmering above all the parked cars in the sun and wished they would all melt away.

What had just happened? What did it mean? He'd identified Cruz's partner — it was the first real breakthrough since he'd arrived. If he called Ramón and told him about it, it would blow open the whole search effort. Dozens of men would interest themselves in Ray Hula. Hula, unlike Cruz, was a real person; he had a history, a permanent residence, and a public identity based on what he did rather than what he was rumored to have done. Ramón could go a long way with him — Hula might even lead him straight to Cruz.

Jack pushed the idea aside. If he turned Hula over to Ramón there was a good chance they'd reach Cruz a lot sooner, but Jack himself would lose his chance to play. No, it was more than that — if Ramón thought Jack was holding anything back for his own use, then he'd kill him for it. The only advantage in telling Ramón about Hula was that Jack would know his work hadn't gone to waste. He probably wouldn't be around to enjoy the results.

He looked up at the whitewashed balcony across the lot. Hula wasn't likely to come back here within the next half hour. By that time the two men in the next apartment would be making some noise. It was time, Jack knew, to give it up. He'd done all he could, and he'd come a lot closer than he'd had any right to expect, but he'd fallen short even at the moment he'd come nearest. What he needed now was a doctor.

He turned on the radio and listened. They'd switched channels and he had to flip around for a while before he heard Ramón's weary voice acknowledging their reports. They were still looking for Cruz. There was no hope, no excitement, in those brief negatives. Everyone was getting tired.

So this is the end of the road, Jack thought — sitting in a parking lot in Miami with a couple of cracked ribs. Michael had beaten him. He was in no hurry to leave — where could he go? If I was twenty years younger, he thought, I wouldn't give up so easily. I'd drive back to Miami Salvage and turn over the whole neighborhood — in a day or two I might come up with something. But the experience of the last twenty-four hours had coarsened his tastes. He wouldn't settle for anything less than immediate satisfaction. His power was gone, leaving behind only a sort of anemic brutality.

The pain was getting worse in his chest, a spear digging into his side whenever he took a breath, and he realized he'd have to do something about it. But the car was so dark and quiet that he couldn't bring himself to turn the key and rejoin the world. Though he hadn't yet admitted it to himself, there was a part of him that was glad he had failed. A burden was gone from his shoulders, a burden he'd carried so long that he'd forgotten it was there.

It came back in a hurry. Through the window he saw a big man come up the stairs from the breezeway and turn down the balcony toward Hula's apartment. He'd been watching him for a few seconds before he realized it was Hula.

The solid, meaty neck, the bald head, the flattened ears, and the thick, columnar legs belonged to the man he'd seen on Dixie Highway running into the flower store. Any remaining doubt fled when Jack saw him let himself into the apartment. Hula's broad back filled the threshold for a moment and the door shut behind him.

Jack touched the gun under his jacket. He took out his handkerchief and dried his hands. Hula must have noticed as soon as he walked in that the place had been turned over. It didn't make that much difference. Jack found a pair of sunglasses in the glove compartment and put them on.

What had Hula come back for? Why was he so reckless? Either Hula has no sense at all, Jack thought, or there's a few things I don't know. The pain in his side had become minor; his strength crept back to him. "Ramón," he said to himself, smiling, "You think I'll call you now? You think so?" He had a good view of the door to Hula's apartment. Behind the door, he thought, is Ray Hula, and behind Ray Hula is — guess who? — Michael Cruz. So Jack had found himself connected once more, his will brought into focus, and his mood improved considerably.

The door darkened inward and Hula stepped out. He turned and locked it behind him. The solid whitewashed balcony cut him off at the waist. He didn't seem to be in any hurry. He pocketed the keys and started down the walkway towards the stairs, apparently carrying nothing more than he'd gone in with. Jack was afraid Hula might call on the two men next door, but he went right past them. He was a big man with an erect, balanced stride, his belt buckle leading the way. He didn't study his surroundings. His light blue, short-sleeved knit shirt and white cotton pants fit too snugly to conceal a gun. He turned into the stairs and Jack saw his wide shoulders bobbing down a step at a time.

Jack had already tried threatening someone today, without success, and he sensed that Hula might not respond to that type of pressure either. He decided to follow him instead. It might be hard to keep from being noticed, since he'd have to escort Hula out, but it didn't make that much difference. Hula wouldn't know that there was only one man behind him. One way or another, they were going to come face to face.

Jack prepared to get out quickly in case Hula ducked behind the apartments. It wasn't necessary. Hula emerged from the breezeway at the bottom of the stairs, turned left, and walked down the sidewalk under the balcony. He stopped outside another white apartment door in the brushed, sand-colored plaster. The trees hid his upper body; Jack could only see the backs of his legs. He was just standing there. Then he drew one hand up and out of sight for about five seconds. He's knocking on the door, Jack thought.

Up above, on the balcony, Norton emerged from the apartment next to Hula's holding an orange towel against his head. He staggered drunkenly against the railing, found his legs, and stood up straight. The towel, heavy and wet, slipped away from him and fell over the edge, catching on one of the trees and hanging there about eight feet off the ground. He peered over the wall and looked for it, his shoulders swaying. The event spoiled Jack's concentration. Hula was only a few yards away; he couldn't help but notice.

No one answered Hula's knock. He turned away and came back down the walk under the balcony, passing right below the orange towel. He ignored it. When he stepped out from behind the trees and cut into the parking lot Jack thought for a moment that he was coming right for the car. As he reached inside his jacket he got his first good look at Hula. His face was broad, smooth, fleshy, and hairless, as if it had been boiled for an hour or two. The eyes were large and set a little too far apart. He looked absolutely dry and cool; the heat couldn't touch him. Although he weighed at least 250, most of it in his chest and shoulders, he was as light on his feet as a man half his size. He could've been anywhere between thirty and sixty. He didn't look like a young man, but his heavy body showed none of that puddling effect, that pull towards the earth that comes with age, and his skin was as thick and creaseless as an orange rind. He didn't have any eyebrows. Jack guessed he was older simply because he was bald. He was an imposing sight, bulk and quickness combined, and Jack wasn't completely disappointed when he turned away from the car and walked straight back along the curb of the terrace, passing about ten yards distant and vanishing behind the hedge that ran down the center of the lot. He had never looked at Jack. He hadn't glanced back at Norton either, who was still on the balcony, now leaning against the wall with his eyes shut. Hula was clearly intent on his own business. Nothing else concerned him. Jack felt like a child on the floor watching a giant go by. He cradled the gun in his lap, waited a minute, put the car in gear, and followed him around the hedge. It was about one in the afternoon.

Jack couldn't understand why the car was so hot even though the air conditioner was going full blast. He had two broken ribs and was developing a fever. The wheel felt light and brittle under his hands. With every minute, he thought, I am more lucid, sensitive, and aware. All the malice had gone out of him; he was becoming an extremely dangerous individual.

» » »

At 7:00 A.M., while Jack was debating whether or not to leave his room at the big house in Miami Springs, a wet breeze rattled the vines outside Lisa Bishop's window. She was awake. She hadn't been asleep long enough to forget anything.

The body on the floor by the window belonged to Ray Hula. He was on his back with a pillow under his head, his eyes shut, the air whistling through his nostrils. She sat up and looked at him. He filled most of the space between the bed and the wall, his shirt hiked up above his pants and the pale flesh of his belly billowing out to one side like a soft-boiled egg. The hair around his navel was thick and grizzled. Sleep lay swollen on his wide and ignorant face. His hands were dirty; he'd left a few smudged fingerprints on his cheek. The battle against unconsciousness had left him sullen and restless in defeat. When he reached up to scratch his nose he banged his hand against the wall and groaned through his shut lips, as if he'd expected no better, and turned onto his side.

Lisa got out on the other side of the bed and dressed quickly, reaching over Hula to pull some underwear out of the dresser, and putting on the jeans and the red-purple long-sleeved shirt she'd laid out for herself the afternoon before. She was careful not to make any noise, not for Hula's sake, but because she was listening. The house was quiet. All she heard was a small wind filtering through the trees.

She sat down on the bed and put on her sneakers. The floorboards were cool under her feet. The spots of light shining through the side window had a washed, liquid quality imparted by the leaves they passed through; they wavered and flickered agreeably on the far wall. Lisa had always liked to be up early in the morning, while most of the world was asleep — she felt fresh, privileged, and unencumbered — and she had some of that feeling even today. But she knew how fragile it was. It depended on whether the other two men had left during the night. The silence allowed her to hope.

She didn't rush herself; she went into the bathroom off the bedroom and brushed her hair. Examining the edge of her tongue in the mirror, she found a dark, painful streak where she'd bitten a piece of it cleanly off. The inside of her cheek opposite was ragged and inflamed.

When she was ready she walked around the bed and out into the living room, glancing at Hula's dingy white-stockinged feet on the way.

There was no one in the living room, although the large green canvas bag was now leaning against the hearth, and no one in the kitchen either. She walked across the tiles and pulled back the door to the porch. Michael Cruz was smoking a cigarette in one of the chairs by the glass table. He had his shoes and socks off and his black jacket lay across another chair. His face was white and drawn. He looked up at her in surprise, pulling his legs in over the rough concrete.

"You're still here," she said.

He nodded after a few seconds. He had one arm locked against his waist, the hand cupping his other elbow and the forearm holding the cigarette straight up in the air. He looked as if he were cold.

"Where's your friend?"

"He went for a walk." There was an aerosol can of insect repellant on the table beside him. "Take it easy." He turned away, looking into the bright, sunlit clearing.

300

She didn't know how to express her frustration. "When are you going?"

He didn't answer immediately. The ash on his cigarette was at least an inch long. "Tonight, I think."

"If you take my car, how am I going to get out?"

The ash fell and crumbled on the floor. A turtle scrambled off a rock in the sinkhole. It was very quiet at this time of day, before the insects had warmed to their buzzing.

Cruz didn't answer her.

She walked down the steps, across the porch, and stopped in front of his chair, turning to face him.

Leaning his head to one side, his eyes half-shut against the smoke, he studied her up and down. "How long have you known Ray?"

"What does that have to do with anything?"

"If you have to blame somebody for this, you can blame me. It wasn't his idea."

She groaned, laid her palms on her sides, and pushed them down toward her hips.

Cruz sat up quickly, tossing the cigarette away. "Listen," he said. "We'll be out of here today, I promise you." He was staring up at her from under his tangled dark eyebrows.

She started to go, then turned back again, picking up the can of insect spray. She showed him the label. "Does this stuff work on you?" She dropped it on the floor; it clattered around her feet. "Just stay away from me." She stalked up the steps into the house.

In the kitchen she made coffee in the scarred tin pot that had been there for years, scattering grounds on the counter and sweeping them up with a dishtowel. While she waited for the coffee she cleaned up the kitchen, rinsing out the tumblers she found on the table and refilling one of the ice trays. There wasn't much to do. She tried the phone; it was still dead.

Already the air felt thick and sluggish. As the sun heated it, it would soak up even more water until, like long grass after a heavy dew, it would shed moisture at a touch. Lisa went around the house letting down all the blinds. The coolness trapped inside should last until the early afternoon.

In the now very dim living room she stopped beside the heavy green duffel pushed up beside the fireplace, listened for a moment, and undid it. She couldn't see inside. When she stuck her hand in she immediately came up against a solid layer of small, flat, loose-ended packages. She pulled one out. It was a bundle of hundred-dollar bills held together by a wide strip of brown paper wrapped around the middle, the whole no thicker than a slice of bread. The money itself felt soft and worn. She fanned one end; the bills had no stiffness and wouldn't riffle. Tossing the package back inside, she tried to lift the whole bag. It was too heavy for her. She felt a little sweat dry on her wrists as she caught her breath. They actually did it, she thought.

Straightening up, she put her hand on her forehead and leaned against the cool brick of the chimney. There was at least a million dollars in that bag, she guessed. That's why they had come here — not to harass the owner, not to play with guns, not to fight among themselves, not to recuperate after a difficult performance — no, they were here to protect this money from the people they'd taken it from, and therefore they'd chosen a place as lonely and isolated as they could find. They'd turned her house into a bank vault; she was locked inside with the gold.

The threat this money represented made her own complaints seem trivial, even ridiculous. Her anger was only an expression of her powerlessness — a fly buzzing between windowpanes. But she knew, at a basic, anatomical level, that she was right and that they were wrong. What did it matter if the money was real, if the bullets were real? The things that were important in life had nothing to do with illegal drugs and large canvas sacks of cash. And their situation was a choice, not a judgment. That was the real horror of it.

Turning from the hearth, she fell into one of the big oak chairs, crooking her elbows on the high arms. She felt restless and exhausted. Ray started snoring in the bedroom. She was glad he was asleep; she could do without his solicitude. He was a clod — he was all flesh and choked feelings. Never in his life, not once, she reminded herself, had he thought clearly about who he was or what he was doing. He just drifted along from day to day, watching the world swim around him, foolishly trusting in his own inconsequentiality. He wasn't even graceful in this thoughtlessness. He made love like a mole — his eyes half-shut, his body heaving, his tongue wandering over her like a warm sponge. She hoped he would sleep all day; she didn't want to hear his apologies.

302

She heard the coffee boiling and went into the kitchen. After she poured her cup she added a little water to cool it off. It's not even 8:00 A.M., she thought, and I already feel as if the day is over. Ray sleeping in her bedroom, his brother Michael brooding on the porch, and who knows how much money sitting in the living room — the house was full of obstacles and the prospect of a long, murderous afternoon. She felt weak, too weak even to think. She decided to take a walk.

It was a beautiful morning; the sun was just over the trees on the far side of the clearing — not the intense, hard-edged ball of colorless light that it would become later, but a sort of messy golden smear without a discernible center, an illuminated haze that awakened a reciprocal glow in everything it shone on, lengthening and clarifying the air in between. Every pebble in the clearing had its own texture, and each trailing root in the tough grass had a rhyming shadow. There was no obscuring heat in the air. The dark, tea-colored water in the sinkhole was quiet and still, its surface puckered now and then by rising fish.

Lisa stepped down onto the stoop and shut the door carefully behind her, the bare wood dry and warm against her hand. She forgot her troubles for a moment; something across the white clearing had attracted her. It was in the shade of the forest near the spot where the track ran into the hammock. From where she stood it looked like a pile of brush pushed up by a bulldozer, nearly as tall as herself, the leaves on the outer branches already curled and withering.

She walked across the open space, getting a little sand in the heels of her sneakers, and discovered that there was a car at the bottom of the pile — a small foreign car with a shattered rear window — Ray's car. It was easy to see it once her eyes adjusted to the shade. Someone had twisted a number of leaf-heavy branches from the nearby trees and laid them over the roof and hood, tying them down with a few pieces of woody vine. A heap of dead leaves near the bottom hid the wheels. Her own car was drawn up in its usual place, a nearby patch of bare rock under the dense overhanging limb of a ficus. She couldn't understand why anyone would go to all this work to hide the car. Who was going to see it here? Did they expect somebody?

Turning, she started down the narrow road through the forest. From here it was about two hundred yards, through a couple of shallow bends, to the edge of the hammock. As she walked, not hurrying, squinting against the sun, Lisa briefly wondered what had happened to the third man — the young, good-looking one she'd seen in the kitchen the night before.

He was sitting on a bundle of exposed roots near the spot where the track emerged from the hammock, but she didn't notice him right away. As she rounded the last turn her gaze suddenly stretched to meet the horizon; she could easily see five miles across the plain.

Motionless in the shade, his legs stretched out in front of him, his head resting against the smooth gray trunk of a wild tamarind, Liberty faced out towards the road, his hands in his lap. It was a good vantage point. The road cut through the border of thorny, waist-high scrub that surrounded the hammock everywhere else, allowing him to look out over the Glades even though he was sitting down. A fly landed on his shoulder, hopped onto his chin, and crawled up the side of his face.

The road dipped lightly as it left the hammock, flattening out at a level about even with the tops of the flooded sawgrass. It pulled the eye a long way into the marsh; a bright, magnesium white ridge pushing out of the drowned landscape like a strip of caulking forced into a crack. The grass had finished its swiftest growth of the season and the new green shone through last year's straw. The road ran due east past a small, elongated hammock on the right and lost itself in the pooled light of the sun. Right now Lisa Bishop was in the way and the dark, vertical outline of the leg she was resting on interrupted his view of the road.

He looked like he'd been out all night. A number of mosquitoes — or, more likely, a poisonous insect — had bitten him on his left eyelid and it was swollen half-shut. Soil and leaf litter had smudged his white jeans. There was a brown wool blanket with a satin edge bunched up on the ground beside him. Two creases, suggesting lack of sleep, slanted down from the flanks of his nose. But these signs were deceptive; Liberty had spent most of the night at the house. He'd arrived here not much more than an hour ago.

Lisa knew about the dry spot under the old, heavy tree. It was the best place to sit on this side of the hammock. Liberty had scratched up a few of her old gum wrappers soon after he got there. When she turned away from the light, intending to climb into the same place herself, she saw his legs and feet lying in the shade of the lowest branches. Startled, she slopped a little coffee on her sneakers.

Liberty saw her body twitch but he didn't see her face — a stout horizontal limb hid it from him. In a moment she squatted on her ankles and peered in. "You scared me," she said. He glanced at her and looked back at the road.

Lisa didn't see any reason to be afraid. She immediately ducked under the limb and sat down in the hollow beside him. It was a few minutes before she said anything.

In the meantime she took the opportunity to study him. He'd collected a little pile of spiral-striped snail shells on the ground by his hip. He looked no older than thirty and his skin was deeply and evenly tanned. His shirt hung loosely on his shoulders; he probably weighed no more than herself. His hands were small and well-kept and he had tiny blond hairs on the shanks between his knuckles. He hadn't moved since she'd noticed him and he was still looking out under the tree and across the Glades, his eyes relaxed, focused a long way off. But although he looked capable, self-contained, aware, healthy, and thoughtful — like someone she might want to know, not at all like she imagined a drug trader, rubbed raw and brutalized by paranoia and violence, should look — she still sensed that he was a different person than he was the night before, not only because of his reticence, or his drawn, weary face, or the defeated look in his eyes. It was none of these, although they all contributed, but instead an aura of transparency about him, of absence, as if he'd lost, or sent away, some necessary part of himself. He was there, but he wasn't there; he was somewhere else also.

"I'm Lisa Bishop," she said. "Who are you?"

Liberty turned his head carefully and looked at her. His face was a little moist. He spoke slowly and tonelessly, as if he'd been dosed with tranquilizers. "Wallace Price Liberty," he said. "Wally Liberty. Twenty-nine years old this morning."

"Happy birthday," she said, smiling. For some reason she felt safe with him, even comfortable. "You're up early."

He turned back to the road. "So are you."

"I couldn't sleep." She said it without irony. "I was thinking."

"This is a beautiful tree — a *Lysiloma.*" He bumped the back of his head deliberately against the massive trunk, twice as wide as an oil drum. "It must be a hundred years old." He arched his neck and looked up at the thousands of tiny, delicate leaves over their heads.

"I thought it was a tamarind."

305

"Same thing."

Lisa looked at his thick, pumice-colored hair, his shirt open at the neck, his shoulders banked against the gray bark. "Do you live around here?"

"I was born here. Now I live in the Bahamas."

She sat back and followed his gaze into the Glades. "I like the islands. I used to go all the time."

He didn't answer.

"There's always a breeze, even in summer."

More silence. He had nothing to offer or accomplish in this conversation. In fact, he seemed to have lost any will or desire of his own. Watching the road — that was all that concerned him. "Why did you move over there?" she asked.

"It was safer. I was afraid of being locked away."

"For what?"

"For breaking the law — for not living the life that was prepared for me."

"Oh," she said, as if she understood. "Then you're a smuggler, I guess."

"I'm not anything — I'm nothing. It took me a long time to see that."

"Excuse me?"

"I always wanted to be anonymous. I wanted to be able to go anywhere, to be anybody. Now I'm getting my wish. All these years I knew I couldn't come back to Miami, but I did it, and here I am." He tried to settle himself more comfortably, his neck and back peculiarly stiff. "I had plenty of chances to get out."

"Then you're not going back?"

He glanced at her briefly; it was the first time he'd really looked at her. "They'll come right down this road. We'll see them a long time before they get here, and we'll sit and watch them come."

"Who's coming?"

"The Colombians — the big traders. Or the cops. The Colombians will get here first, I think."

"Wait a minute," she said, her voice climbing. "How do you know?"

"I just do. I knew it the moment I woke up this morning."

"You didn't know last night?"

He shook his head. As far as he was concerned, it was over.

"Everybody gets those feelings now and then," she said, pulling back.

He didn't respond. She wasn't satisfied; she couldn't drop it, not now. "When are they coming?"

"Before nightfall. I don't know exactly."

"So why don't you leave?"

"It's one of those things you can't change. So the question is, can I prepare myself?"

She had wanted to touch him before, and now she turned and laid one hand on his shoulder. "But how will they know where to look for you?"

"I have no idea."

She bowed her head, leaned forward, shut her eyes, and clasped her ankles in her hands. "You're lying, I know it. Either that or you're crazy."

Liberty lifted his chin high and rubbed the back of his head against the tree. "If you want to live you'd better walk out of here right now. The sun will keep the mosquitoes down — you could be out on Krome Avenue by late afternoon."

"It's a long way."

"If you're here when they get here they'll kill you too."

She sat up and pushed her hair back from her face. "No," she said. "Absolutely not," briefly pressing her palms over her ears. "You and the other two are going to drive away and that'll be the end of it. I belong here — you don't. None of you do." It made her feel better to say it. She sat quietly for a moment. "Why did you pile all that trash on top of the car?"

"That was Cruz."

"But why?"

"So it can't be spotted from the air."

"From the air?" She put her hands flat together and looked at her thumbs. From the air, she thought — thin air.

She had talked Liberty nearly out of his daze. He picked up a twig, scored it along its length with his fingernail, and began peeling off the bark. "Dade County is a battleground," he said.

Lisa brushed her hands on her knees. "I just can't absorb all this. It's so pretty here in the morning, with the sun on the water — " She pointed to the pile of snails beside him; some of them had started to crawl away. "What are those?"

He reached down and picked one from the side of the root it had started climbing. Its eyes waved dizzily on their narrow stalks; its soft body twisted and rippled. The shell itself, nearly two inches long, was a high conical spiral ringed with rounded, glossy bands of pearl, chocolate, and slate blue, with a barely visible pattern of engraved lines running across the grain. Lisa had never seen one like it.

"These are some of the most beautiful snails in the world," Liberty said. Holding it in front of Lisa, he touched one of its tiny spherical eyes with the twig. Eye and stalk rapidly shrunk back into the body of the animal. "Here, take it."

He passed the shell carefully, Lisa holding it by its pointed tip. "I've never seen one like this," she said, "or like any of these. Where'd you find them?"

"They're tree snails — they scrape fungi off the bark. You don't see them because they spend most of the dry season hiding high up in the crooks between branches. The best time to look is on a morning after a rainy night in spring, like today. As a matter of fact, I've never seen so many in the same place."

She looked down at the dozen or so remaining on the ground between them. Against the dark, sandy soil they were bone, ocher, sulfurous red, emerald, butterscotch, charcoal, and tourmaline. "It's amazing," she said. "They're all different."

"Not really — in Cuba, where they can interbreed easily, they all look pretty much alike. You only see these different varieties in the Keys and the Glades."

She put the shell down and picked up another one. "Oh?"

"It's because they're isolated. This hammock isn't any more than what, twenty or thirty acres? But the snails can't cross the grass to the next one, so they've been stranded here for hundreds of years. That means they've had a chance to develop separately. That hammock over there, for instance" — he pointed to a heavily wooded island across the plain — "probably has its own collection of types, and none of them are anything like these." He looked down and saw one of the snails topple over as it tried to crawl up a loose piece of bark. "The scientists who first noticed these things went crazy trying to name all the different kinds." He took a deep breath and blew it out slowly. A puff of wind pushed through the leaves over their heads.

Lisa looked suspicious. "How do you know all this?"

"I told you — I used to collect them."

308

"You don't seem like the kind of person to be doing what you're doing."

"Maybe not. That doesn't change anything, does it?" He looked at her, smiling.

She gazed back at him for a moment, examining the flat, blue, and unmarked clarity of his irises, and said, "How did you get into this — this business — in the first place?"

"Like anybody else. I saw an opportunity and I took advantage of it. That's the American way, right?" He smiled.

She nodded. "No — I mean how did you get mixed up with Michael Cruz?"

"That's a good question." He dropped the snail he was holding, leaned back, and shut his eyes. "I guess he just reached me at the right moment — it had to happen sometime. You know how you get the urge to do something really stupid, just for the hell of it." He swallowed once, with difficulty. "When you get older, it's hard to stay fresh — you see more and more lousy things happen to people — and after a while you start to expect everything to turn out wrong. You get cautious — you get reasonable. Basically, you get pretty cold. You don't want to hear from anybody. I saw that happening to myself, and I didn't like it. So I took a chance." His eyes sprung open, suddenly empty of thought or feeling. "It was a mistake. They're coming, right now — I know it." He reached around the tree behind him; his hand returned holding a pistol. He held it tightly, his fingers whitening under the nails.

He'd frightened her. "There's nothing out there," she said. "I don't see anything."

Liberty apparently did. He didn't hear her. Spots of light trickling through the tree mingled on his face. "I could use this on myself as well as them," he said. "I'll do it if I have to. I could die right here, on the ground, under this tree. I'm not moving."

The sun was emerging from its fiery, bloodshot placenta on the horizon. The numerous dragonflies, swooping over the sawgrass and across the road, appeared black against the glow. Lisa heard heavy running footsteps coming down the road through the woods. Liberty's eyes were shut again, his hand resting on the ground with the pistol under it. The sharp shells of the tree snails swayed and bucked in the air as they moved off.

Ray Hula stumbled around the last bend in the trail and stopped at the edge of the sawgrass just a few yards from the base of the tree. He was silhouetted against the light, facing the road, his shoulders heaving, his breath emerging in great coughing rasps. "Lisa!" he bellowed, his voice flying away across the shallow water. He cupped his hands and shouted again.

Ray Hula was the last person Lisa wanted to see. She pulled her feet under her and stood up, stooping low to get out from under the tamarind, one arm in front of her face, small branches catching at her hair and clothes. Ray heard her and turned around. She came out with the clumsy momentum of a large animal, blindly pushing her way into the light and air. She didn't stop to look at him. Before she had fully straightened up she was already walking quickly down the trail into the hammock, her sneakers crunching on the loose rock, a few stray leaves clinging to her red shirt. Hula took a couple of flat-footed steps after her and stopped, gasping for breath. She vanished around the first turn.

While he waited to catch his wind, his eyes bulging with each stroke of his diaphragm, he looked at the spot where she'd stepped out onto the road and saw a pair of straight, white-sheathed legs lying together in the shade. His eyebrows glistened. He'd run only a couple of hundred yards and the strain had nearly undone him.

Although there was no sign on his face that he knew what he was looking at, or even that he was thinking about anything whatever, in a moment he lurched forward over his toes and dove headfirst under the tree. He landed in the dirt in the spot where Lisa had sat and the first thing he saw was the gun lying under Liberty's fingers. Scrambling onto his knees, he fell back on his hands. "What the fuck is going on?" he said, a short twig adhering to his lower lip. He left behind a few tree snails that he'd crushed when he landed, and their fat, colorless bodies oozed out from between the fragments of their shells.

Lisa didn't turn around to see if Ray was following her. She walked down one side of the trail, avoiding the soft sand in the middle. The air was buzzing around her. Her legs felt numb and she had little sensation of movement. This is what happens, she thought, when you get angry too quickly.

It was a long morning. Lisa, needing something to occupy herself, spent most of it preparing a midday meal. As soon as she got back to the house she took the machete off the hook in the kitchen and vanished into the woods on the far side of the sinkhole. She hacked her way to the edge of the hammock and cut open a cabbage palm. When she reemerged twenty minutes later she had the heavy white bud cradled against her stomach.

She went into the house, leaving the bud on the kitchen counter and wiping off the blade of the machete with a dishtowel before hanging it up. It took a while for her eyes to adjust to the relative darkness. Glancing out the door to the porch, she saw that Cruz was still down there and that Hula had joined him. They weren't talking or looking at each other. The small light coming through the fiberglass made their skin green. She was glad that they were here, in the house, where she could see them. She felt a little dizzy and she sat down at the table to rest.

She heard someone on the steps and looked up to see Ray coming through the door. He swung the handle shut behind him and turned to her, although he didn't move any closer. His face was heavy and his arms hung limp at his sides. He looked cold and dour, almost menacing, but she wasn't at all afraid. "Where'd you go?" he asked roughly.

"None of your business." It felt good to stare back at him.

"I'd feel better," he said, "if you'd let me know where you're going when you take off. Not that I can do anything for you. But it makes a difference to me."

She held his gaze for a moment and then looked out the window. The white sand in the clearing burned as bright as a snowfield.

"I'm not asking you to forgive me," she heard him say. "Just to make things easier. As long as I'm here I'm going to do what I can to keep you from suffering for — for what's happened already."

How noble, she thought, examining the soft webbing between her fingers.

"There's nothing you can do about it, so you might as well enjoy it. I don't mind telling you that I've got no idea what's going on here, but I promise you that Michael and I and the other guy will be out of here today. I can't make them go now. If you've got any bright ideas, tell me about them. I'll do what I can."

His words had weight but no meaning; they collided pointlessly against the back of her neck. She turned to him again. "I appreciate your concern."

He crossed his arms on his chest and leaned against the door frame. "You might not want to hear any of this, but so what?" He paused. "You want me to leave? Is that it?" His voice was loud and bullying.

"You can do whatever you want — it makes no difference to me."

He turned and started down the steps. She blinked; he was gone. She felt better immediately.

In the next few hours Cruz and Hula were in and out of the kitchen on their way to the main room and back. She barely noticed them. She couldn't have said with any certainty where they were at a particular time. At one point Cruz went outside and returned with a pair of heavy black plastic garbage bags over his arm, recrossing a moment later to get the green duffel. She had just finished slicing up the palm bud and was drying her hands on a paper towel.

Curious, she went to the door and looked out. She saw Cruz upending the sack in the center of the porch; the bills slid out in a rush, burying his shoes. He extracted himself carefully and backed away. They're going to divide it up, she thought. She couldn't see any notes except hundreds. There was something profoundly unserious about it; it both fascinated and disturbed her. She stood there, staring at it, until Ray glanced up at her. Then she turned and went inside.

It was nearly two o'clock before she was ready. The table was set for four. Cruz and Hula were still on the porch, sitting quietly, their faces slick as ice. "Where's your friend," she asked, standing at the top of the steps.

"He won't come," Cruz said. "He's not hungry."

"Did you ask him?"

"No."

Hula had his nose in Cruz's bag of cocaine and was sniffing it warily, like a dog at a garbage dump.

Liberty was under the same tree at the edge of the hammock. Most of the snails had crawled away. The Glades simmered in the distance. She asked him if he wanted to come back to the house and have some dinner. No thanks, he said. He wasn't sweating at all. He was very pleasant about it.

So there were three at the table that afternoon. Lisa was the last to sit down. The food rested on platters between them — the chicken on a bed of rice, the palm salad in a white plastic bowl. There was cold beer all around. She felt limited by her company; she had nothing to say to them. But they all submitted without complaint to the discipline of the meal.

Using his knife and fork as pincers, Cruz lifted a second joint off the platter and laid it on his plate, returning to the serving dish for some of the tomatoes, rice, and onions that accompanied it. Hula followed with a thigh and a drumstick. They handed the salad around. The food had turned out well and they all discovered, after a few mouthfuls, that they were hungry. The silence filled with the busy clinking of metal against china and the neutral sound of the glass mugs meeting the table.

Hula laid down his fork, finished chewing, took a swallow of beer, and said, "Where's Liberty?"

Lisa answered without looking at him. "He didn't want to come."

Cruz flourished his knife over his plate. "He's doing us a favor." He turned to Lisa. "How long have you owned this place?" Apparently he didn't want to talk about Liberty.

She had told this story a hundred times — her former husband's hunting cronies, her efforts to sell after his death, her fumbling apprenticeship in maintenance, the discovery that she liked the quiet and the isolation, and her decision to keep the house. She was surprised at how easy it was to tell it now.

Hula had nothing to say; he was concentrating on his eating.

"Lucky for us, I guess," Cruz said.

She found herself looking back at him a moment too long. "I was just getting ready to close it up for the summer."

Ray had emptied his plate and was treating himself to more chicken, his forearms tanned and massive over the table. "This dinner is easily worth a good hundred thousand," he remarked, still chewing. Lisa glanced at him and looked away.

Cruz had caught the odor or her disgust and reacted to it. "We'll be out of here by sundown, at the latest — that's about three or four hours from now."

"Fine," she said.

Hula swallowed and cleared his throat. "I don't know about you, but I feel a little better knowing he's there — if you know what I mean."

"This is nice, whatever it is," Cruz remarked, crunching a water chestnut in one side of his mouth.

"That's heart of palm salad — from a cabbage palm. They grow wild here." Every time she looked at him she felt as if she were saying more than she intended.

"You should open a restaurant — in the city, I mean."

"I don't know if I like Miami anymore."

"There's a lot of crap floating around," Cruz said.

She noticed that he held his fork like Ray did, with the tines pointing down. "What do you mean?"

"People used to come down here just to spend their money, but now they're not happy unless they go back with more. They see all this money and they think all they have to do is reach out and take it." He returned to his food.

"Isn't that what you're doing?" she asked.

Cruz put down his fork and looked at her. "No — I'm a businessman. Five years ago I could've finished this in two days. But now everybody's greedy, and there's just not enough to go around."

"You're talking about the drug trade," she said. "That's part of the problem."

He leaned forward and pointed a finger at her; he'd abandoned his manners. "There's nothing wrong with making money. The only people who complain are the ones that already have it."

"Would you like some more?" she said, pushing the salad bowl towards him. Cruz sat back. His smile was sudden and relaxed, and she had more trouble with it than she did with his aggression.

Hula sat back and daubed at his mouth with a paper napkin. "You and I," he said, looking at Lisa, "have been here a while and we've seen some changes. We're old enough to get sentimental. But nothing ever holds still."

She turned to him with surprising fury, her jaw set, her words rapid and distinct. "You used to say that all you had to do was mind your own business. That's what I did, and look what happened." She immediately regretted it; she'd lost her head. Not that she didn't mean it.

Hula tossed the napkin on the table. "So write your congressman."

Cruz looked stiff, almost embarrassed, as if he'd intruded on a domestic crisis. It was very quiet in the room. All you could hear was a fry pan simmering gently on the stove. Lisa thought the moment had been blown all out of proportion. She rose to her feet and began clearing away the dishes. She splashed some water on them and turned on the percolator. Ray and Michael were neither talking nor looking at one another. They're brothers, she thought — that's why they trust each other. She'd known as much when she watched them dividing up the money. So here I am, she told herself, interrupting their great adventure with my lime marinade and my tender conscience. It was the same way she'd felt when she came out here with her husband on his hunting weekends — out of place, denied entry, a pebble in their shoes. But why should I feel excluded, she asked herself, if I never wanted them here to begin with?

There were three bananas in the pan, halved the long way and cooking in butter. She turned off the heat, took down the bottle of rum from over the sink, and slopped an ounce or so over the fruit. Quickly, but without hurrying, she brought the pan to the table, lit a match, and set it on fire. A noiseless blue flame leaped up around the rim of the skillet. She pulled her chair out and sat down. When the last glow consumed itself and vanished she pulled the pan towards her and picked up a serving spoon.

No one said anything as she handed out the portions. As they started eating Lisa noticed that the bananas had come out exactly right, but her success didn't seem nearly so important to her as it had a short while earlier. The silence gathered authority in the cool, curtained room; the kind of quiet that is considered disastrous at any normal social occasion, but she didn't try to fill the gap, even though the weight of each passing minute made it more and more likely that the first words that attempted to break the pall would sound false and self-conscious. When she finished her dessert she looked across the table at Ray and Michael and studied their faces. There was almost no family resemblance. Ray had a broad wedge of a forehead that duplicated the slope of his nose, while Cruz's thin, vertical, olive-skinned face barely had room for his small features. The only similarity, obvious once she'd noticed it, was a full, rounded, and outward-rolled lower lip pinched slightly at the middle. It made Ray look sensual and his brother look sullen. It struck her as funny and she smiled. By this time the men had finished their fruit and were looking back at her blankly. "The two of you have the same lip," she said.

They turned to face each other. Lisa started giggling and looked away. Something had snapped inside her; she didn't want to laugh but she couldn't help herself. Neither of the men saw the humor. She tried to keep a straight face. "I'm sorry," she said, covering her mouth with her hand. "I'm sorry. It's just that — it's just — " and away she went again. She sat back and settled one arm over the chair behind her. Tears glamed at the corners of her eyes. "Coffee for anybody?" she said, when she finally began to recover.

It was only after Cruz had jumped out of his chair, grabbed the rifle out of the case, and bolted out of the house, his light footsteps clearly audible as he ran across the clearing, that Lisa had a chance to forget herself for a moment and realize that his disappearance was no result of anything she'd said or done, and as her eyes flickered from Hula's astonished face — he had stood up suddenly, as she had — to the crumpled yellow paper napkin that still lay in the doorway to the main room where it had fallen in Cruz's rush, she remembered hearing a muffled bang, like a balloon popping inside a closet, in the direction of the road; a noise which had preceded his exit by an instant. A gun, she thought, makes a sound like that. Liberty was out there under the tree. There couldn't be any hunters wandering around in this weather. Ray kept looking to one side and then another, as if he expected, at any moment, to be attacked by a piece of furniture. Well, she said to herself as calmly as possible, I knew something had to go wrong. She was listening very carefully but there was nothing more to hear.

» » »

The bald-headed man Jack had followed away from Hula's apartment earlier that day wasn't Ray Hula, although Jack didn't know it. And there was no one to tell him that the other door the man had visited belonged to Lisa Bishop. He never did figure it out.

The pain in his side made it necessary for him to drive the car with one hand. Even then he felt as if someone was continuously limning two or three of his ribs with a blowtorch. That was when he thought about it; he tried not to think about it. At a stoplight he pulled up his shirt and noticed a large and irregular purple stain on his white skin about midway between his hip and shoulder. At first he thought it was blood, but it was dry to the touch. Must be a bruise, he decided. Somebody honked and he drove away.

Jack suspected that he'd broken a couple of ribs. He was only partly right. What he didn't know was that one of those ribs, at the moment it gave way, had sheared off like a splinter, following the grain, and had sliced inward, tearing the peritoneum and severing a group of blood vessels before its natural tension brought it back into place. So Jack had a slow internal leak, and the mulberry blotch he'd noticed represented only a fraction of the blood he'd lost, the greater part of which had spread into his body cavity. The frenzied response of his immune system to this destruction of barricades had generated

316

his fever, which he saw no reason to question; he would have been more concerned if he felt perfectly normal. Jack believed he was closing in on Michael Cruz. He expected to feel light and speedy. He had no idea how badly he was hurt, and when he nearly blacked out behind the wheel he mistook the darkness for the shadow of a cloud overhead.

He didn't have much sense of time passing. He was driving on elevated freeways and it seemed as if he'd been doing it for quite a while, but he couldn't be sure. The sun was still climbing; he could stare directly at it through the tinted glass. There wasn't much traffic and he hung well back of the car he was following, a Japanese compact with California plates. He realized, rather dimly and without attaching much importance to it, that he was heading down the Palmetto Expressway towards SW Dade and Dixie Highway along the same route he'd taken to meet Cruz the day before.

As he rolled down into the streets at Kendall he sat up and took notice. There were signal lights here, and parking lots, and dozens of exits on either side; he would have to stick closer to Michael. To Michael, he thought — but I'm not following Michael, I'm following someone else. Who was it then? A big guy — a big guy with a bald head. Now he remembered. Ray Hula. You better pay attention, he told himself. You better watch where you're going. Maybe you had too much to drink and maybe you'll blow the whole thing right here.

He needed the pain to keep himself alert, and he deliberately associated the jagged fire in his side with the sky blue roof off the car he was following, so that the agony itself would pilot him through those moments when the strain overcame him and his thoughts went their own way. At times it seemed as if his conscious mind was just a bubble on a deep yellow ocean, and at other times the pain ebbed back, leaving a dark, muttering hole in his chest. Nothing frightened him more than the idea that he would lose track of his goal. He took his photo of Cruz out of his wallet and stuck it on the sun visor.

He made a point of establishing his location as he traveled, telling himself that as long as he could remember where he was he could be sure of maintaining some connection to reality. There were so many signs on Dixie Highway, so many printed messages hanging in the air, that he had trouble picking out the ones that mattered — they were small, narrow, and inconspicuous, mounted on short poles on the side of the road, with white lettering on a green background — but he persisted, and by the time he forgot the last one there was usually another coming up in front of him. Meanwhile, he watched the sky blue compact float about two hundred yards ahead. The man inside was so large that his shoulders blocked out half the windshield. Jack read the license plate again. He didn't ask himself why Ray Hula should have a California number. What difference did it make?

The pain in his side had reached that level of intensity where it couldn't increase further without losing its coherence, and it suddenly decayed into two parts — the stimulus, still buried in his ribs, and the response, which was exclusively mental. As the fire spread throughout his midsection, it was less and less able to make the journey to his head, so that he felt it as an advancing nullity, a black fungus growing over his innards and relaxing them as it traveled. The pain had anesthetized him. He felt cool and aware. At times he was driving; at times he was lying on his back in an open field.

They had left the city and were rolling between long rows of fruit trees and pole beans. There was nothing to look at out here. It reminded him of parts of New Jersey, or the flat tidewater of Delaware. Jack had given up trying to conceal himself from Hula. What was possible in the city or on the highway didn't make much sense when you could go five minutes without seeing another car. But he wasn't troubled by his increased visibility; Hula could make what he wanted of it. Certain unnamed forces had guaranteed a reckoning between them. Jack didn't believe in surprises. If Hula had time to prepare himself, their encounter would probably go a lot more smoothly.

The radio was still on and Jack could hear Ramón blowing off a little steam now and then when somebody didn't report on time. Jack had sent in a few messages of his own — without the microphone, of course. He reminded everybody that Michael Cruz and Jack Parko had known each other for quite a while and that if anyone was likely to find him, it was himself. The ten million, he said, didn't mean anything to him, and Ramón could have it provided Jack got to keep Cruz's personal effects. He asked why he'd been given a radio car and whether they'd like to hear a live interview with Cruz. It was Ramón's Colombian pride, he said, that kept him from answering any of these questions. Jack understood; it was always difficult to step into someone else's shoes. He explained who Ray Hula was and what he looked like. He described his own wounds and how he had suffered them, not ignoring the mistakes he had made. Up the road, Ray Hula's rounded silhouette was never out of sight, and Jack felt as if he were speaking to him also. After a while he noticed that he was repeating himself and he stopped talking. He was getting drowsy and he hoped they didn't have to go much further. Jack had fallen asleep at the wheel only once, when he was eighteen, and he still remembered it quite clearly.

The car bucked beneath him; he had turned off the asphalt onto a gravel road. The tires crackled under his feet. There was nothing growing in the gray-earthed fields on either side. He looked in the rearview mirror and saw a large olive green switchbox, about the size of a refrigerator, planted in the weeds by the phone pole at the entrance. It had smooth corners and a series of horizontal vents on the near face. It wasn't much of a landmark, but it would have to do.

The road wasn't any wider than the car. Hula stirred up a cloud of thin white dust behind him that hung close to the ground. Jack turned the radio off; he knew he wouldn't have to wait much longer.

The last cultivated fields dropped away behind them and the road became a low dike traveling across a grassy plain that sparkled in the heat because it lay under a few inches of water. Where the grass was low Jack could see clouds reflected in its surface. A few dense clumps of trees sailed by. When Jack took his eyes off the road for a moment to look around he felt one of his front wheels start to slip off the shoulder, and it carved its way along the rim for a few yards before he wrenched it back on. He forced himself to steer with both hands and he pulled up close behind Hula.

The blue compact stopped and Jack nearly ran into it. He left the engine in neutral and reached for his gun, watching the dust slowly drift away from between them. Hula hadn't turned around; Jack could see the outline of his ears on either side of his head. He didn't want to get out of the car. There wasn't much feeling in his legs and he didn't know if he could trust them. Although there was no question in his mind that he could do whatever he had to do, it would be easier if Hula came to him.

At various times in his life Jack had needed to get information from men who didn't want to give it to him. These experiences had convinced him that people are basically weak, that there are certain forms of persuasion that will work every time. Once you'd established that you meant to do what you said you'd do, the job was nearly finished. It could take as little as five minutes.

In a way Jack's knowledge worked against him at this moment, because it gave him a confidence in himself that allowed him to expect success without making any plans. Although he believed he was thinking very clearly, the fact was he had barely a thought in his head, which was as vacant and undisturbed as the wide blue dome of air or the topographical wasteland all around. When Hula got out of the car, shut the door, and started walking back towards him, Jack felt nothing more than a mild and pleasant anticipation. There was no way the man could conceal a gun in the clothes he was wearing. Jack raised his own in full view and held it trained on Hula's chest. He let down the window an inch. The door was already locked.

Hula had to stand very close to the car in order to stay on the road. He stopped by the window, facing Jack, his tooled leather belt at the level of Jack's eyes. The barrel of the gun was only inches from his navel. When Jack tilted his head to look up at the man's face, a dark lid came down over his vision; there was a bad connection somewhere. He stared at the blankness for a moment and dropped his chin. His sight returned immediately. He saw Hula's arms, which were very large and had an almost feminine roundness, hanging free at his sides. The man was just too big to see all at once. His voice came from a place high over Jack's head. He spoke very clearly, as if each word was crucial to his meaning. "You were following me, right?"

Jack nodded.

"Why?"

Jack didn't see any harm in telling him. "I'm looking for Michael Cruz."

"Michael Cruz."

Jack reached up and turned off the car. He tapped on the window with the gun barrel. "I know some people who thought you could tell me, that's all." It was very quiet out here. The whole world was silent for them.

"I wish you wouldn't point that at me. It's hard to relax."

"It's just a habit," Jack said. "So where's Cruz?"

"If I told you I think you might use that thing, and then where would I be?"

"I got nothing against you." It felt strange speaking into the man's

320

stomach. "Why don't you come around to the other side and get in? We'll talk."

"I like it better this way."

Jack shrugged. "Suit yourself." Although he was quickly tiring of this conversation, he wasn't sure how he should force the issue. Since he'd expected that the answer would be available at about this time, the lack irritated him and he had trouble concentrating. He was stalled for no apparent reason, and his resentment focused itself on the man outside. "I'm falling asleep," he said. "Let's get this over with."

"Michael really did a number on you and your friends, didn't he? He made you look bad."

"Look, there's a lot of questions I'd like to ask you, but I'll settle for just one. Am I making sense? I mean, you look like you'd take a long time to die."

Hula suddenly crouched down beside the car. Surprised, Jack accidentally bumped the gun against the window. Hula had put his face as close to the glass as he could without actually touching it. He resembled one of those big, moon-faced fish staring out of a tank at Coney Island. The barrel was pointing at his forehead. "Do you know who I am?" he said.

"If you move again you're dead." Jack wasn't prepared for the bare, meaty skull, the level gaze, the jaw wide as a mailbox. The sight offended him. He decided that he'd kill the man no matter what happened.

"You don't like me — I can see that," Hula said. "By the way, I'm not Ray Hula — but you might say I'm responsible for him." He smiled. "So here we are. This is what they call the howling wilderness — seems pretty quiet to me. I'm going to rest my elbows on the ledge here, is that OK?" He brought up his arms without waiting for a reply. "So you and I are both looking for Michael." He scratched his nose vigorously, screwing up his face as he did so. "We want him for different reasons. Can he accommodate both of us? I don't see why not. He owes us, right?" Leaning his ear toward the window, he tapped on the glass with his knuckles, as if testing it for weak spots. "But you've got to admit that I deserve the first crack at him, since I know where he is and you don't — that's assuming you don't blow my head off first, of course." He looked up and stared at Jack for a moment. "That's what they call a basis for negotiation."

Jack couldn't think of anything to say. He had made the mistake of listening and was now trying to shake out a few contradictions in his assumptions. He hadn't gotten very far. In fact, he still hadn't decided whether this man was Ray Hula or not. Pulling the trigger would immediately simplify matters, but he didn't feel right about it. He was disappointed in himself. This sort of thing had never been a problem.

The man examined him critically, his head tilted to one side. He was squinting, as if it was difficult to see through the dark glass. "So," he said, "you're one of those big-time drug traders that Michael does business with — a pimp for the forces of oblivion. It's a war, a secret war — almost invisible, except for the blood running down the streets and into the courtrooms." He pointed at the gun. "But it makes life serious for you. You have real choices. How often do you get a chance to kill somebody if you're working for the IRS?" He let the question hang for a minute, as if he expected an answer. But the pause was only rhetorical; he went on.

"A sense of mission in life — I speak from experience now — is a dangerous thing. You hide it from the light — you broadcast it from the rooftops — it chews away your heart, your lungs, your brains, and you still think you're doing yourself a favor. You know what I mean? Every setback is turned to advantage. You retreat so far into your imagination that you see yourself reflected in everything you touch, and you might even shut your eyes and go for all of it, for everything, like Michael did. And you might even convince yourself that you've succeeded, when all you've actually done is destroyed yourself and set the furies loose."

He laughed. "Understand me now — this isn't my situation. I have very limited goals."

Jack was feeling groggy. His backbone had somehow gotten hooked onto his left hip and he couldn't sit up straight. Although he didn't know it, his blood pressure had dropped steeply in the last few minutes. He concentrated on keeping the gun pointed at the bald-headed man's face. Where was Cruz?

"You don't look so good," the man said. "Maybe you weren't much to start with, but really, you look like a home abortion. Where's the old fire? Shape up! Pull yourself together! There's no room for weaklings on my team!" He leaned back and looked down the road behind them. "By the way," he said, with a knowing, conspiratorial glance, "you didn't invite any of your friends to this party, did you?

You wanted it all for yourself? I thought so. Nobody wants to share Michael with anyone. It's that sense of mission, right? He means a lot to you."

Jack was glad that there was a quarter inch of heavy glass between him and this man. "So where is he?" he croaked, happy that he'd at last come back to his purpose. He had made up his mind. If the goon didn't answer, right now, he was dead.

"I'll show you. I'm going to get up — don't get excited."

What's he going to do, Jack thought, point him out to me? Be careful, he told himself.

Jack didn't know that while the man had been talking to him, kneeling on the ground, he had patted the road around him with his hands and had located, on the shoulder, a loose chunk of coral rock about the size of a small cabbage, which he had placed carefully by his side. It was in his hand when he stood up. Jack got his first look at it when he saw the man's arm swing out from behind him, palm behind the rock and fingers wrapped underneath, the hand gaining force from a rhyming motion of his whole upper body. That's a rock, Jack thought, too logey to shut his eyes. He didn't doubt that it would come through the window. The important thing was to squeeze the trigger. He could feel his knuckle pulling it down but it seemed to be moving through an arc ten times as wide as usual. The subtle release, and the nearly simultaneous recoil, arrived long after the moment when he first expected them.

The rock hit the glass before the bullet and the window fell into Jack's lap in hundreds of tiny, pattering chunks, like the pieces of a jigsaw puzzle, leaving only a few small bits in the bottom of the frame. Jack's shot had missed the man by a good six inches because his hand had wobbled with the effort of pulling the trigger. He didn't get another chance. The stranger dropped the rock, grabbed Jack's forearm at the wrist, pulled it out of the car, and broke it easily over the edge of the door. Jack was dumbfounded; he now had two elbows on the same arm.

"This won't hurt a bit," the man said as he reached in and grabbed Jack's other arm, breaking it in the same place and with the same motion. "I'm not a very nice person," he explained. Jack stared down stupidly at his hands — the man had flung them back into his lap — and realized that he would never see Michael Cruz again.

He looked up to see the man standing by the door, turning over the gun in his fingers and muttering to himself. "Goddamn machine pistols," he said. Stepping away from the car, he brought his arm back around his waist and heaved the gun away like a discus. It shone high in the air, turning end over end, and hovered there for a moment before it splashed into the marsh a long distance away, raising a brief, glittering swarm of water droplets in the green sawgrass. The sound reached them a fraction of a second later. That was quite a throw, Jack thought. The quantity of blood now pooled around his intestines made him feel heavy and torpid. He shut his eyes.

The door opened and he found himself being rudely shoved into the passenger seat. He finished the move of his own accord, drawing his crippled arms in toward his stomach. The man got in after him and started the engine. "A real luxury liner," he said.

He shifted into drive, spun the wheel all the way to the right, and dropped the right front tire over the edge of the road. Then he switched to reverse and did the same with the left rear one, so that the car lay diagonally across the dike with only two wheels still on the surface. "That's the best I can do," he said.

He got out of the car, walked up the road, and ducked into the Japanese compact. It made a squalling, tinny noise when it started. He drove it up the track about fifty yards, popped it into reverse, and rammed it backwards into the big car, hitting it on the front left quarter and punching in the driver's door. Jack wasn't touched. His head sank onto his chest.

When he looked up again the stranger had poked his face in the shattered window and was staring at him, the sun bleaching the back of his neck. "I'm going now," he said. "I've got a long walk ahead of me. Is there anything I can do for you?"

Jack just wished he would go away. The man drew his head out a small distance so he could squeeze his arm in alongside it. Then he took Jack's chin in his palm and turned it first one way and then the other. He pulled Jack's lower eyelids down with his thumb and peered critically into his pupils.

"You're in bad shape, old man. I don't like to be around sick people — it depresses me." He extracted himself from the car and crouched down beside it, his thick stubby hands curled over the window ledge. His skull looked like a soft, leathery, and misshapen hen's egg. The stranger shook his finger and clucked at the dying man.

"You're a long way from home, grandpa." He winked once and stood up.

Jack watched him walk around the sky blue compact and start down the road, stopping once to wet his handkerchief in the marsh and spread it over his smooth head. There was no sense of impatience in his stride, no leaning forward from the hips, no pumping of the long arms. He was perfectly balanced and he put one foot directly in front of the other. Before long he looked very small on the narrow road, the vanishing road, between the two half-planes that went on forever.

Jack had never won any awards for grace, and the virtual uselessness of his hands made his next and final act as clumsy and pitiful as any human effort, but he ignored the numerous arguments against success — even scraping off his shoe at one point and using his two largest toes as a pair of tweezers — and eventually he unburdened himself. He called Ramón, told him where he was and stated his belief that Cruz might be found there also. He didn't say anything about Ray Hula. He didn't have time. Before he got to it he was no longer capable of speech.

Jack knew that he was dying. That knowledge, in itself, might not have been unwelcome — he was an old man and had seen enough of life — if Cruz hadn't cheated him of a peaceful leavetaking. Jack wasn't ready to go. He had an important message for Cruz that hadn't been delivered. The message was crucial to Jack's sense of himself; he saw around him a corrupt world made habitable only by a constant dedication to private notions of justice and dignity. The essential pride, the life-giving pride, would wither unless all those who challenged it were quite cut off. Strange morals for a killer! But Jack, unlike the vengeful gods he impersonated, was made of flesh and couldn't guarantee punishment to those who offended him. It seemed grossly unfair that he should be taught this lesson on the last day of his life. Michael Cruz was still at large — free, unregenerate, rolling in wealth. This was the only certainty Jack's quickly deteriorating mind could carry, and it shed a reddish, stinging haze over his last thoughts. The strength of the feeling kept his aged heart beating a few minutes longer than it might have if he was at rest. Would it have been different if he had been allowed to go another few miles down the road, to see Cruz again, face to face? He never found out.

The sun was high and the wide, island-spotted prairie slept in the heat. The sky was no longer empty; the warming air had started to people itself, as it did every day, with a scattering of small, distant, and shadowless clouds.

» » »

The shot that interrupted Lisa's dinner wasn't the one that Jack fired at the bald-headed man. It came from Liberty's gun. They found him under the tree, on his back, with the pistol lying in the leaf litter beside him. There were black powder smudges on his lips, as if he'd just had a meal of ashes. The back of his head was gone, but you couldn't tell by looking at him; the wound was hidden against the ground.

When Hula and Lisa arrived at the edge of the hammock Cruz was nowhere in sight, although they'd left the house no more than a half minute after him. Before they had a chance to think about it the undergrowth scraped open at the side of the road and Cruz pushed his way out, squirming away from a vine that had caught on his shoulder. "Liberty's dead," he said. "Stay right here — there's nothing you can do about it." Then he crossed the road and fought his way into the brush on the other side.

Hula and Lisa turned to look at each other. Neither had anything to say. Then Hula carefully laid down the shotgun he'd brought with him, got down on his knees, and crawled under the tree where Liberty was. It didn't take him long to agree with Cruz. When he stumbled out he was wiping his hands on his khakis. He nodded vigorously, his mouth working through a series of strange grimaces.

"Is he dead?" Lisa asked. Hula kept nodding. He was walking around in circles and nearly tripped over the shotgun. "Why?" Lisa said.

Hula stopped at the place where Cruz had vanished and peered into the tangle, his temples sweating freely. He reached out with both hands and closed his fingers on a couple of insubstantial, leaf-cluttered twigs, trying to steady himself. "I think he shot himself," he said.

There was a narrow margin of shade on the edge of the road. Lisa sat down carelessly in the dust, cross-legged, her head drooping and her eyes shut. A few tiny grasshoppers leaped away from her.

Cruz suddenly appeared on the road a few feet from Hula. There were fresh scratches on his forearms. He was staring at Lisa, waiting for her to notice him, and when she looked up he said, "I need some rope — maybe some clothesline. Do you have any?"

She didn't answer quickly enough for him. He walked over to her, reached down, lifted her to her feet, and planted his hands solidly on her shoulders. "Think," he said. "Yes or no?"

Awakening, her face hardened and she flung his hands away. He didn't react. "I've got some," she said.

"Go get it. It's very important."

She stared back at him; they were only inches apart. "Would you mind telling me why?"

"I will, later."

She looked at Hula, standing and watching a few yards away, and started back towards the house. Michael turned to Ray. "Come on," he said, and ducked into the woods at the spot where he'd emerged. Hula went in after him, his thick arms crooked over his head.

Three steps and he could go no further; he was caught in a net of vines, spiky creepers, and aerial roots. When he leaned against it the thorns cut into him. Cruz's light-colored shirt retreated into the dark a short distance ahead. Afraid that he might lose him, Hula kicked and flailed at the vines, breaking some and tangling himself in others. He made a lot of noise to no purpose. Bits of torn leaves and stems found their way down his collar. Before long he was close to panic and he might have ripped his clothes to shreds if Cruz hadn't returned, his voice coming out of the dimness with a hollowness like Hula's own hoarse breathing. "All right!" he said. "Don't move." Hula watched, arms at his sides, as Cruz slashed away the tangle with a pocketknife in his fist, the blade slicing alarmingly near at times. The green and yellow vines fell in heaps at his feet. Cruz turned, crouching, and went off again. Hula scuttled after him, banging into trees, catching his toes on high roots, and blinking the hot salt out of his eyes.

Cruz traveled about ten yards farther into the gloom and stopped, sitting on his ankles. He looked as if he was digging into the ground with his hands, scratching at the edge of a rounded white limestone outcrop. Hula stooped down beside him and put his palm on the rock to steady himself. As soon as he touched it he lost his small composure. The rock was warm, soft, and moist; he'd put his hand on the chin of the bald-headed man, who was stretched out full-length on the shallow, root-clogged soil. Hula quickly got his feet under himself again and took another look. Very little light penetrated the canopy overhead and he didn't immediately recognize him. He saw a large man lying on his back, either dead or unconscious. Hula had already discovered one corpse in the last five minutes and expected the worst.

"Take his shoulders," Cruz said. "We'll carry him out."

Ray was in no hurry to touch him again. "Who is this guy?"

"Just do it!" Cruz pushed the man's legs apart and grabbed him under the knees. Hula tried lifting him with his hands flat under the man's shoulder blades, but it didn't work; there was nothing to hold onto. Instead he buried his fingers in the armpits. The man weighed well over two hundred and they couldn't lift him entirely off the ground. "We'll drag him," Cruz said. "Back out the way you came." Facing each other, staggering and grunting, they pulled him off his bed in the leaves and started towards the road.

By the time they got there Hula had realized that the man had probably suffered one of his sleeping fits and might wake up any moment. They stretched him out in the shade on the road's edge. Cruz stepped back, pulled a gun out of his shirt, looked it over, and replaced it. Then he leaned over the stranger and started going through his pockets. "Where the fuck is she?" he said.

Hula stood with his arms crossed, leaning back on one leg, one hand scratching his cheek, still breathing hard and staring down at the man in a common attitude of thought. "So he killed him, you think?"

"Don't know," Cruz said. He patted down the man's entire body and found nothing. Then he pulled his knife open and measured the blade against the man's throat, pressing the blunt side into the skin before drawing it away. He looked as if he was having some trouble restraining himself. He stood up. Gently, almost affectionately, he laid his toe on the man's ear and gave his head a shove. "Sweet dreams, asshole."

Hula looked up and saw Lisa coming around the bend in the road with a coil of clothesline dangling from her hand. She stopped when she saw the body. Cruz rushed over to her and snatched the line away. "Who's that?" she said. No one answered her.

She watched silently as Cruz roughly rolled the man onto his stomach, bound his wrists together behind his back, cut the cord, and used the remainder to wrap his ankles. Then he righted him again and brushed the dust off his face. Just as he was finishing the man's eyes popped open, throwing off unconsciousness so quickly and completely that it seemed less a process of awakening than a sudden release. "So you found me," he said, looking at Cruz and grinning broadly. "You saved me the trouble." He didn't struggle at all; he might have been paralyzed from the neck down. When Cruz backed away the man didn't turn his head but only followed him with his eyes.

Cruz looked at Hula and Lisa. "That's it. There's nobody else. That's all."

"That's one too many," the stranger said. "Come and talk to me, Ray — and you too, Lisa." He couldn't see either of them from where he was lying — he would have had to lift his chin and look backwards — but he seemed to know they were there.

"Don't listen to him," Cruz said. "There's nothing we can do for Liberty — we'll leave him here. I'm going back for the car — are you ready to go?"

In the hot, buzzing silence, with the heavy burden of the sun bearing down on them, it was hard to believe in any sort of finality.

"What happened?" Lisa said.

Cruz didn't explain. "I'll be back with the car. Anyone who's coming can get in then." He started down the road towards the house.

"Wait a minute," Hula shouted. Cruz stopped and turned around. "What about him?" Hula pointed to the man on the ground.

"I'm taking him with me." Cruz didn't stay to discuss it further. In a moment he was around the first bend and out of sight.

Hula and Lisa were left standing bewildered in the heat with the bound stranger. Lisa's sense of resentment, of personal violation, which had kept her going all day, didn't seem relevant anymore now that Liberty was dead. So without making any conscious decision about it, she no longer thought of Ray as her opponent, her persecutor. She'd known him a long time. They were in trouble. It was only natural that they'd turn to each other.

She put her hand on his arm. "What're we going to do?"

He was quiet for a moment; he felt the change in her. "I think we should go with him — both of us."

She glanced at the stranger and found him peering fixedly back at her, his mouth open, his chin high in the air. "I don't want to stay here any longer."

Hula nodded once. Saliva pooled under his tongue. He was still thinking about the body under the tree — how it looked, how he had touched it.

329

Lisa pulled him a few yards farther down the track into the woods, away from the stranger. "Who is he?" she said, standing on her toes, whispering, and looking back at him. "What's he doing here?"

"I don't know — Michael said he might come. I think that's what he was waiting for."

"He's the guy I saw at the pool that day — the guy who wanted to know about you."

"I know."

She shuddered and let go. "That's enough — I'm OK. I don't want to hear any more." She took a step away, wrapped her hands around her ears, and stared at the ground. "I liked that other man — I felt as if I knew him." She swung wildly at a mosquito. In this atmosphere any large motion became unnatural.

But there was no somnolence or forgetfulness in the whitened air or in the black green rim of the woods. The sun was a bludgeon hanging over the landscape, poised to smash whatever might attempt to set itself above the level, and nothing larger than a dragonfly dared to venture into its sight; not from lassitude, but out of a strict fear. Even the vultures had left the sky.

Hula heard wheels on gravel and looked up to see Cruz coming down the track behind the wheel of Lisa's old station wagon.

Ten minutes later they were all sitting in the front seat of the car. Hula was in the middle and Cruz was driving. The bald-headed man had the backseat to himself, except for the two well-stuffed garbage bags on the floor. His wrists were still bound behind him and he had a gag in his mouth. His blocky head bounced against the roof now and then. Nobody was talking. They had agreed to drop Lisa off somewhere on Krome Avenue.

Whatever else can be said about their experience at Lisa's house, at least they had been free there to act without interference from the normal constraints of their daily lives. There was no one to observe what they did, no one to compare their performance against conventional models. Now that they were going back to the city they had to consider how they might reenter the sublunary world. For Hula it was a sobering prospect, and he was in no mood for conversation. Lisa was twisting a strand of hair around her finger and looking out the window; he guessed that she felt the same way.

Before they left Cruz had insisted on dividing Liberty's share of the money between himself and Hula. Ray didn't help him with it.

330

The difference between three and five million dollars seemed to him a meaningless sort of quantity. "Liberty died for this money," Cruz said. He was sniffing coke off the blade of his knife as he worked.

Hula didn't want to go near the cash; it was tainted. Giving it up, on the other hand, would be the same as admitting that this whole scheme had been a mistake. A mistake? That was too mild. It was an incredibly inept combination of bad judgment, fantasy, and blindness. What had he lost? Lisa Bishop's respect, his own peace of mind, and quite possibly his safety and personal freedom. He'd never known that he had so much to lose.

In compensation he had become one of the wealthier men in the city. He could remember some nervous moments in the past when a few extra dollars might have made life much more pleasant. Now he had five million in cash. He would have to put it somewhere; there was nothing else left to do. And it was necessary to finish the job before the police picked him up; in other words, before they acted on Lisa's story. He wondered what Silva and the rest of his employees would think when they read about him in the papers. If they knew about the money they'd probably envy him. As a millionaire, Hula thought, other people's envy is something I'll have to learn to enjoy, because there won't be much else left.

So he wasn't that eager to get back to Krome Avenue. He looked through the windshield at the narrow white road running up ahead straight as a plumbline. There were no landmarks to watch for. The water was as high as he had ever seen it; it filled all the space between the woody hammocks and there were spots where it drowned the grass completely.

After today, he thought, I just might never see her again. He didn't doubt her intentions in this respect. It might have been easier to bear if he really believed there was no other way. But Hula, in spite of all that had happened, still clung to his childish Floridian optimism, his refusal to turn his back on the future, and so his certain knowledge that he had lost her for good was made more painful by a groundless feeling that it was, in some unfathomable way, completely unnecessary.

He couldn't blame Michael for it. And although he regretted nearly every breath he had drawn in the past two weeks, he couldn't blame himself either. Disasters of this magnitude were not attributable to human error. His own contributions — stupidity, cowardice, and negligence, which were responsible for the hollow feeling in his chest — had definitely added their flavor to the result, but he was convinced that even if he had taken an entirely different approach the same outcome would have forced its way into being.

He could tell by the way she was sitting — stiff-legged, feet braced against the engine wall, one hand pinching the denim over her knee — that she was worried also. She's shown me a lot in the past few hours, he thought. Now he was empty and she was — well, he didn't know what she was. He would never find out because she was vanishing right in front of his eyes.

Hula was so wrapped up in himself that he was the last to notice why Cruz had stopped. He looked up; far off in the distance he saw two cars strung together like bright beads on the road — a small blue one and a larger black one behind it. Cruz whipped around in his seat and tore the gag out of his prisoner's mouth. "One of them's yours. What about the other one?" Hula squinted and bent forward. Neither of the cars were moving.

"I don't know who he was — I didn't ask him," the stranger said.

"How'd he get here?"

"He followed me."

"From where?"

"From Ray's apartment — he was sitting in the parking lot."

"How'd he get there? Don't lie to me!"

"I was in a hurry. I didn't ask him."

Cruz fell back behind the wheel. "Lisa," he said. "How far from here to the road?"

"Two or three miles — we're about halfway there."

He muttered something in Spanish and stamped on the accelerator. Hula had nothing to grab onto; he started bouncing all over the seat. Lisa put up her elbow to fend him off. They hit a flat stretch and Hula succeeded in locking his knees under the dashboard. Two vultures clawed their way into the air from the roof of the big black car and flapped away.

They all sat still for a moment after Cruz braked to a halt a few yards from the nearest car. "I'm sorry, Michael," the stranger said. "I thought you'd be dead by now."

Cruz ignored him. He got out, boosted himself onto the hood of the blue compact, and walked over the roof to get to the other car.

He went in the passenger door. The glass was so heavily tinted that they couldn't see what he was doing inside.

He must have found the keys to the Fleetwood, because it shortly started bucking and heaving like a boat on a short anchor. He was trying to straighten it out. But the smaller car was jammed into the arc he was turning on and he couldn't budge it; he had only two wheels on the road.

"We can walk," Lisa said. "It's not that far."

Cruz leaned out of the car and motioned Hula over. He looked at Lisa; he didn't want to leave her alone with the stranger. She knew what he was thinking. "Go ahead," she said, getting out to let him by.

He made the mistake of scrambling across the compact's hood and he burned his hands on the hot metal. He was swearing and squeezing them under his arms when he met Cruz, who was now standing between the cars. "If we can push the small one back a few yards," he said, "I might be able to jerk the other onto the road. Let's try it." He reached inside the compact and put it in neutral; the two cars weren't joined and they had no trouble pushing it away. "All right," Cruz said. Hula went back and stood beside Lisa while his brother tried again.

It was no use. Even with the compact out of the way, the right rear wheel couldn't drag the right front one over the shoulder. Cruz tried going forward with the same result.

Next they attempted to roll the Cadillac off the road. Cruz and Hula put their shoulders to the fender and pushed, rocking the car like a three-ton porch swing, but the wheels had dug themselves into the gravel and they couldn't budge it.

So they were stuck. The two cars jammed in the throat of the road rendered Lisa's car absolutely useless. If they wanted to go any farther they would have to walk. Hula had already worn himself out trying to move the Cadillac and he didn't want to discuss it; he just wanted to get started. Cruz wasn't in any mood for conversation either; they just backed away from the machine and returned to Lisa's car, edging their way alongside the blue compact. Hula was very careful about where he put his hands. They hurt worse than he was willing to admit.

Cruz opened the rear door and dragged the two garbage bags onto the road. Hula pulled them both forward and left them leaning against the grill. By this time Lisa was standing beside them, her soft leather pocketbook over her shoulder. "Are we walking?" she asked, as if she already knew the answer. Hula nodded. "What about him?" she said, glancing into the back seat.

"He's staying here," Cruz said, his arms resting on top of the open door. "You go ahead — I'll catch up in a minute."

Don't argue, Hula thought, watching Lisa. Just this once, don't argue. The sun beat down on him like a hammer. It bounced into his face from the hood of the car, the chalky road, and the flooded plain all around him.

"Michael's got plans for me." It was the stranger's voice, coy and teasing. "He wants a little privacy. Don't you, Michael? You know, privacy is just about all they got out here."

Lisa didn't argue. She didn't look at Hula. She turned and picked her way past the blue compact, grabbing the door handles for balance. Hula was relieved. He didn't know what Cruz planned to do. He didn't want to know. He slung one of the bags over his shoulder and followed her.

They had to climb over the rear corner of the Cadillac. As he stood behind Lisa and helped her up he glanced back into the driver's window, which didn't have any glass on it. Jack's corpse was inside, lying on its back on the seat, both arms hanging over the edge. His mouth was open; he looked like he was preparing to take a bite out of the steering wheel. One of his eyes had collapsed inward and there was a small runnel of clear fluid running out of it and across his temple. Hula had guessed that there might be someone in there but it was still a shock. It was the same man he had seen standing under the promenade on Dixie Highway with Michael the day before. He felt uncomfortable staring at him. The man was obviously dead. One look was enough; he lifted his knee onto the hot metal of the hood and boosted himself over.

She had already started down the road and he didn't try to catch up with her. The bag was heavy and bumped against his kidneys as he walked, nearly knocking him off stride. His skin spun a wet cocoon of steamy air around him. He was watching Lisa's flat hips work inside her jeans and waiting for the sound of Cruz's pistol. Hula didn't want the stranger dead so much as he wanted the waiting to be over. So he didn't slow down or look to either side as his feet crunched across the limestone. It seemed as if the silence was pouring into his ears so fast,

334

like water swirling down a drain, that if something didn't happen soon his head would crack from the pressure. He imagined that Michael was taking all this time for the pleasure of torturing him; he couldn't have been more sensitive if the bullet was aimed at the back of his own skull.

He knew he was listening much too hard and he tried to stiffen his eardrums against the shock, humming tonelessly to drown it out in advance. Lisa wasn't stopping or turning either. He came no closer to her and neither of them made any ground on the grayish, heat-faded clumps of trees that clung to the track where it ended in the center of the horizon.

Then Lisa halted and dropped her forearm off the top of her handbag. She shaded her eyes and looked up the road. So you noticed them too, he thought. There were three or four hard-shelled beetles jostling in a narrow space where the trail met the sky at the limit of his vision. The sun glittered on their polished wings. He knew that they weren't really beetles but he didn't want to admit it to himself.

He had almost overtaken Lisa now. When he stopped beside her and looked in her face, his hands still tightened around the neck of the bag over his shoulder, he was startled to find no aggrieved reserve, no testament of undeserved wrong, but instead a gentle, despairing, hopeless sliding away of her features toward her chin and the line of her jaw, as if they were in full retreat from an untenable position. A loud noise blared in his ears; it was the horn of the car. He turned and saw Cruz standing beside the driver's door and waving at them, his head just visible above the two cars in between. "Those aren't the police," Hula said. "We ought to go." He nodded towards Michael. If his hands had been free he would have touched her. Still looking at the cars on the horizon, she reached out and laid her fingers on his chest, as if to keep him from moving. Her expression hadn't changed. The cars hadn't gotten any closer. Out here, any kind of movement was tremendously difficult.

The stranger was still alive when they got back to Lisa's car. Cruz had retied the gag around his mouth.

"It's Escobar," Cruz said. "They found us."

Hula was out of breath. He had lifted the garbage bag onto the hood and was resting his hands on it. "We'll leave the money here. They'll be so worried about it that they'll leave us alone."

"Forget it," Cruz said. "It wouldn't even slow them down."

335

"Then what the fuck are we going to do!"

Lisa was looking down the road. The glassy sparks didn't seem to be getting any closer, but there was now a small, whitish cloud of dust hanging over them. Hundreds of frogs trilled obliviously in the shallow water. "I count four cars," she said.

Michael didn't look up. He was examining the creases in one of his palms, cradling it in the other and running his thumb across it. "That's just the beginning. But it'll take them a while to clear the road." He pushed out his heavy lower lip, curled it down, and drew it back in.

"A fire," Hula said. "We'll light a fire. Maybe someone will see it from the air."

He finally got a rise out of Cruz. "Listen," he said, pointing a finger at Ray, "nobody's going to get us out of this but ourselves. Remember that."

"So what're we going to do?" Hula couldn't understand why no one was interested in this question. He wanted an answer, right now.

Using the bumper as a bottom step, Cruz climbed onto the hood and walked up the windshield to the roof. It didn't buckle under his weight. At nine feet he was the tallest thing for a half mile. He cupped his hand and held it up between his eyes and the sun; an oval shadow wrapped itself around the side of his head. "More like six. Six big ones." His cheeks were drawn up under his eyes. "We sure as hell can't stay here." His shirt hung slack from his pinched shoulders and the sun shone right through the sweat-darkened bight under his lifted arm.

When Hula followed his gaze down the road he saw the chrome grill of the first car raised off the ground by the heat mirage and glittering in the pale air. It trembled, was swallowed up, and popped into view again. He couldn't hear the engines, although he thought he felt the ground vibrating under his feet. His vision wasn't that sharp; it seemed to him that there was only one car, which kept splitting sideways into multiple images and coming together again.

Lisa had recovered. "I think Ray is right," she said evenly. "You should leave them the money."

"Not a chance," Cruz said. He sounded bright, almost cheerful. He jumped lightly down from the roof, grabbed the bag Hula had left on the hood, and slung it into the back seat.

She watched him, her arms crossed on her waist, moving only her

336

eyes. "We could make it look like we were never here — leave it in one of the cars, for instance."

Cruz had one leg behind the wheel. "They already saw us," he said. "Let's get the fuck out. Ray!"

"OK — I just want to see something," Hula called back. He had wandered up the road, past the blue compact, and was standing beside Jack's sepulchre, the black Fleetwood. He had his hands in his pockets and didn't seem to have any specific purpose in mind, although he now and then glanced back at Cruz, as if he was considering some business that he would rather perform unobserved.

The reason for this poor show of diffidence was curled inside his fingers in his pocket. If I do this, he thought, it will quite possibly be the most stupid and ill-conceived act I have ever committed. On the other hand, he thought, it just might work.

When in doubt Hula generally preferred to do nothing and hope for the best. He could quite easily have turned around and walked back to Lisa's car, never really admitting to himself that he had abandoned his idea — although he would have — and telling himself that he would be sure to do it at the next opportunity, or that he really ought to think about it a while longer. And this result might have been more likely if Cruz, who seemed to sense that something very odd was happening, hadn't stepped out of the car, shouted at Hula again, and taken a few rapid steps in his direction. In doing so he gave Hula the necessary boost. By the time Cruz shouted "No!" it no longer mattered.

Lisa was watching from inside the car. The man in the back seat was grinning, with difficulty, in the rearview mirror. She saw Ray yank one hand out of his pocket, unscrew the Cadillac's gas cap with the other, lean down over the car, bringing his hands together on the side of the fender, and cup them together for a moment. She couldn't see the match but she knew it was there. Cruz was running towards Hula. He hadn't yet reached the blue compact.

Hula didn't see the flame; the sun was too bright. He just saw the pink orange head of the paper match whiten after he struck it, the stem blackening and curling as he held it upside down. He dropped it when it started to burn his thumb. It fell noiselessly into the dark mouth of the pipe. It happened so quickly that he couldn't be sure what he'd seen. One moment the match was still in his fingers; the next it was gone.

337

Turning, he bent low over his toes, ready to dive away. If this doesn't work, he thought, I give up.

The concussion instantly blew all four tires of the Cadillac; it staggered in a cloud of pulverized glass and dropped onto its rims like a ponderous hoofed animal killed by a bullet in the head. The bright, blood-wreathed muffin of flame that rolled out from underneath curled back and cradled the car in a basket of dark fire, while a single oily glob of black smoke floated rapidly towards the zenith, following the trail of Jack's departed soul. Jack's body burned like a torch. The whole car burned. When it was through burning, a few minutes later, it was as fireproof as a brick oven.

The shock threw Hula off the road and into the water. He landed face up, on his back, with his arms raised over his head. A few drops of burning gasoline hissed into the grass around him, but nearly all of it had ignited in the initial fireball.

Lisa saw him go over the edge. She jumped out of the car and ran up the road. Cruz, who had been sheltered from the explosion by the blue compact, grabbed her around the belt and dragged her back. It took all of his strength. He hustled her into the car, slammed the door, pounded on the hood with his fist, and waved his arm in a broad arc towards the rear. "Back it up! Back it up! The other one's gonna go!" She stared at him with her mouth half open, wondering what she had done to upset him.

She did what she was told, not for anything he had said, but simply because he was making so much noise. In her confusion she mangled the proper sequence; she floored the accelerator while the car was still in park and only then switched it to reverse. It shot away backwards as if it had been stung by a bee. She cracked her forehead against the steering wheel. The man in the backseat was thrown on the floor. Luckily the car stayed on the road until she regained control some distance away. She looked up the raised track and waited for the blue compact to explode. She was disappointed; it never did. Then she remembered Hula.

Meanwhile Cruz had slid down the white rubble embankment and was over his knees in the grass-choked water, slogging toward Hula. He held his arms up for balance and he lifted his feet high at each step. Lisa could see Ray floating like an inflatable beach toy at the edge of the road. The wreck of the Cadillac smoked and cooked above him. He wasn't moving at all.

But all he required was Cruz's touch. Michael grabbed him roughly under the neck and tried to sit him up, stepping back when he started to thrash around. A few gentle waves spread out through the grass in a rainbow arc. Cruz was shouting at him. "It's only me, you fuck!" and something else that Lisa didn't catch.

In the mirror she saw the man in the backseat struggle off the floor and sit up, his arms still crossed behind his back. His lower lip was split but not bleeding. He smiled at her and she got out of the car. She couldn't stand to be close to him; he looked like Ray might look if he had been pumped full of formaldehyde.

The first time Hula got to his feet he leaned the wrong way and fell over again. There was nothing to stand on; beneath the flat surface of the water, beneath the thin layer of muck and roots and yellowed skeletons of last year's growth, the eroded limestone floor was a brittle honeycomb of rock needles, bumps, buckets, and guyots, having all the sharpness of a bed of nails and none of the regularity. Every step was a balancing act. He got up again and proceeded more carefully; it took them over a minute to wade a few yards along the road, away from the fire, and up the shoulder.

The sawgrass had ripped Hula's shirt to pieces and he had long angry cuts on the soft flesh of his back. The remnants of his shirt looked like they had been dipped in a weak red dye. More serious were the deep slices in his palms and fingers, where the horny teeth of the stiff green blades had torn through the outer skin. But he was happy; his plan had worked. It must have been quite a bang. He thought all the cuts he had suffered were from the explosion. If someone had draped a medal around his shoulders he would have understood perfectly.

He was an appalling sight and Lisa put the back of her hand over her mouth as he lumbered out of the water with a sly grin on his face. On his shoulder a couple of leeches waved their blind, questing snouts. Coming up behind him, Cruz looked grim and drained, his lips clamped together. His shoes were full of water and his pants were torn at the knee. He immediately turned and looked up the road past the burning Cadillac. The cars were half again as close as when they had first seen them, but they were still a long way off. They could just hear them now; a steady, weak rumbling behind the crackle of the fire. The frogs and insects had shut up for the time being, as if they also were threatened. But the air was full of movement. Perhaps attracted by the heat and noise, hundreds of bronze-winged locusts were zipping and flitting around the cars. They were clumsy and their bodies rattled as they flew. Many of them smashed into the cars and fell to the ground, where they lay on their backs with their stiff legs waving.

"Let's go," Cruz said.

Lisa took Hula's arm and led him around to the passenger side. He walked very slowly, his elbows out from his body. He felt the sun on his skin, which was just starting to sting and burn. Blood and water dripped off his fingertips. Lisa got in first and he followed her.

Nobody even suggested turning the car around. They had to back up all the way. Hula sat and watched the blackened wreck shrink away through the windshield, the flames colorless in the glare, their heat rippling the white road. Soon the Cadillac was just a small lump in the distance at the end of a thin strip of bleached rock that rolled out from underneath them like the hull-wide wake of a ship crossing a green ocean. They were traveling backwards into the future, looking at the hole Hula had blown in the bridge to the past. There was nowhere else to go.

The only thing Cruz said between the time they left and the time they reached the clearing in the hammock was, "I could've killed you back there. If you tempt me again, I will."

Hula and Lisa agreed that someone must have seen the explosion and that help was on the way. They wanted to believe it too badly to admit any doubts. But they also agreed that if the Colombians arrived first, they would walk through the Glades to the dike on the boundary of the national park. Neither of them knew how far away it was. All they knew was that it was in the opposite direction from Krome Avenue. Hula had given up worrying about what he would say to the police.

They ran out of things to talk about long before they reached the hammock. Hula looked out the window at the sawgrass prairie stretching away to the horizon — the same sawgrass, he realized, that had laid his hands open almost as soon as he touched it. He now understood why no one lived out here, and why Liberty hadn't wanted to come. The sun was already beginning its long slide into the west; when it's down, he thought, it will all be over. He avoided looking at the hands lying useless in his lap. They felt as if all the skin had been ripped away; each individual nerve writhed in a bath of pure oxygen.

340

They would hurt much worse, he thought, if I had nothing else to think about. The blood drying on Lisa's hands was his own.

They rolled backwards past the tamarind, down the short track through the woods, and pulled up by the front door. Cruz stayed at the house just long enough to grab the rifle and the shotgun out of the cabinet in the kitchen. When he came out Hula and Lisa were standing by the car. "I'll be at the entrance," he said. "If anything happens, you'll hear it." He jumped into the front seat and jerked away, taking the stranger with him. After a moment Lisa took Hula by the elbow and brought him into the house. "Don't rush," she said, "We've got time."

He stood in the middle of the kitchen while she cut away his shirt with a pair of scissors. Then she sat him down at a stool under the window. To dress his wounds she had to touch his bare skin, and it was difficult to forget how well she knew every contour of his arms and shoulders — not only how they looked, but how hard she had to press to feel the bones underneath, how securely his muscles lay over each other. Sitting behind him at the table, she leaned close and curled one palm over the base of his neck, which was free from scratches, while she ran a wet sponge over his back. Under the rank smell of the swamp on his clothes she thought she could detect his own heavy, slightly sweet odor. She was glad he couldn't see her face. The broad and firm spread of his back was one of his features that had first attracted her to him; she had felt as if it could absorb a lot of emotional heat. It seemed to her, at this moment, that she had a very clear idea of what parts of her life were valuable to her, and Ray was one of them. But it didn't change anything at all.

"We can do it if we have to," he said. "You'll need the heaviest shoes you've got."

"What about your brother?"

"If he wanted to come with us, he would have said so."

Her hands were trembling as she pulled a clean undershirt over his upraised arms. "I'm afraid," she said. "I don't think I've ever been so afraid."

She swaddled his hands in a pair of splints made from white gauze and cardboard. It took her about ten minutes in all. Then she pushed her materials into the center of the table and sat back.

The kitchen was darker than it had been earlier in the afternoon. The sun had passed over the house and the roof was half in shadow.

Across the clearing a powerful brightness spread along the ground into the woods of the far side, lighting up the red bark of the trees. Ray heaved himself to his feet and walked tentatively up and down the room, like a man trying on a new pair of shoes. "Thanks," he said. He stopped and leaned against the refrigerator.

She chose this moment to pull the band off her hair, push it back, and retie it. Her hands dropped into her lap. "I'm not sorry, Ray," she said, "about all this. No, that's wrong." She shook her head. "I mean I'm glad you're here — that's all. I like to think it could've been different, but . . ." She shut her eyes for a couple of seconds and then looked back at him. It didn't seem to have cost her anything to say it, and she wasn't waiting for an answer.

"Yeah." Hula knew better than to continue. The quiet was already full to overflowing. A few weeks ago they might have passed this hour on the terrace by the pool at the apartments, drinking and watching their ice melt, a little bored with themselves and each other but not imagining it could be any different. Right now that time seemed inaccessible, nearly fantastic. He didn't want it back so much as he wished there was more to remember.

She stood up suddenly. "I'm going to get some things together."

He nodded. "I think we should go back to the entrance, so we'll know who's coming ahead of time."

"All right."

A few minutes later they stepped out of the front door. Tiny lizards danced away from their feet. Hula's shadow plunged over the sand ahead of him; now that the sun had lost much of its force, it felt merely warm on the back of his neck. They walked past Hula's car, still buried under thorns and brush, and into the track leading away from the clearing. Lisa took three steps for his two. A flock of swallows swooped and sailed high up under the now burgeoning gold clouds. The birds' thin frenzied shrieks were nearly inaudible. Lisa walked with her head bowed, arms crossed on her chest, pushing off her toes like a skater. As they went they passed a soft plastic bottle of insect repellant between them. A retinue of excited mosquitoes followed low in their wake.

They found Cruz huddled on the road at the edge of the hammock, facing the sawgrass prairie, his elbows hooked around his knees. He looked small and forlorn. When he heard their feet on the gravel he jerked his head around, saw them, and snapped it back. The road into the Glades was empty for as far as they could see.

Cruz had left Lisa's car at the edge of the track, the outer wheels sunk in the underbrush. As Hula came closer he noticed the rifle and the shotgun lying beside Michael in the sparse grass in the center of the road, the two garbage bags piled up behind the car, and the bald-headed man stretched out under the tree, next to Liberty's corpse. Hula assumed that the man was dead. He also saw the bag of cocaine in the sand by Michael's knee. Cruz was slapping at his wrists and neck; the mosquitoes had discovered him.

When Hula reached him he noticed that Lisa was hanging back a few steps. He didn't blame her. He turned to her and silently pointed to the bottle of bug repellant in her hand; a propitiatory gift. She dropped it in his gauzy, outstretched mitt. When he leaned over to hand it to him, his brother looked up at him for the first time. The ironic, self-contained wariness was gone from his black eyes, and they were even more penetrating without it. The face around them however, looked like it belonged in a hospital bed. It was gray, toneless, and no longer acknowledged any relationship to the man who owned it, as if it was sloughing away from the inside. Cruz had aged rapidly in the last few hours.

He didn't have any messages for Hula. He took the bottle, nodded, and looked away, smearing the clear liquid on his wrists and ankles.

"Nothing happening, I guess," Hula said.

"See for yourself." He tossed the bottle on the ground. The remark didn't invite further discussion and Hula didn't know what more he could say. He had a feeling that he'd better be careful.

Stooping, he picked up the bottle clumsily and shoved it in his pocket with his thumb. "We tried," he said. "It just didn't work out."

"You don't sound too disappointed." Michael pushed one hand across his face, his palm digging into his cheek.

Hula took a few steps forward and talked to Cruz over his shoulder. "Well — we thought we'd wait up here, so we'd know who's coming a little ahead of time." He couldn't be any more studiedly casual than that. As the silence lengthened behind him he started to worry. The old Cruz would have laughed at him.

"If you know any way to get out of here you better do it now."

"What do you mean by that?"

It was Lisa; when Hula turned around she was standing beside Cruz, towering over him. Cruz glanced at her white canvas sneakers next to the bag of cocaine. "I mean Escobar is already overdue."

"Then what are you hanging around for?"

He tilted his head back and squinted up at her. "I wouldn't want to disappoint him."

For a moment Lisa looked as if she might laugh, but she didn't. "You might miss him anyway."

Hula decided it was time to intervene. He came up beside them, words bubbling out of his mouth. He wanted everyone to understand one another. "Michael — what she means is the cops might get here instead — that's what we're waiting for. If they don't then we're going to leave. That's all. Maybe it's not the best way, but it's all we could come up with. I don't see any other choices. So that's how it stands."

Cruz had stopped watching him after the first sentence, as if he didn't expect to hear any more of interest. "So you're going to walk," he said, "through the swamp."

"Not unless we have to." Hula had come this far; he couldn't stop. "So you don't mind, then, if we go over to the cops." It made sense, in his opinion, to maintain the fiction of their partnership for as long as possible.

"There won't be any cops," Cruz said.

Lisa had heard enough. "I'm going to sit down," she said, not waiting for comments. She didn't like standing so close to the bodies under the tree. Her car was on the other side of the road and a few yards deeper into the hammock. She got in and sat on the edge of the blue vinyl seat with her feet out the door, lifting one hand and pushing back her hair.

She was the first to notice the sound. It was a bit like a small outboard engine running at high speed. She sat up and held her head still. In a few seconds Cruz and Hula heard it too.

It came in low over the road from the east, moving directly toward them and swelling in the air; a light helicopter with the sun shining on its bubble head. They heard the blades whipping and the engine roaring underneath. The sky quivered at its approach, the sawgrass flattened under it, and a light pillow of dust followed along the road. At about five hundred yards it swerved and climbed away, coming around in a smooth arc to hover, motionless, over the edge of the hammock, like a hummingbird over a bank of flowers. Two distinct faces peered down at them. Cruz started coughing and got to his feet, picking up the cocaine and the two guns. He remained stooped over as he ducked into the shelter of the trees. Dropping everything in the weedy grass, he sat down again, still coughing, turning his face from the road. He didn't have any advice for Hula. Lisa had pulled her legs into the car, shut the door, and rolled up the window. Hula felt left behind. Slowly, almost reluctantly, he trudged across the short distance to the cover of the trees. He didn't feel any more or less secure. Someone had noticed them, someone who appeared to have a particular interest. A shower of tiny leaves rained down on his head.

As soon as the helicopter moved off Cruz stood up and walked down the road into the sawgrass a few yards, turning to watch its progress, his figure dwarfed against the horizon. The machine traced a few large circles over the hammock, cut to the center and hung over the clearing for a short while, and wandered off into the surrounding prairie as if it had lost its purpose, turning one way and another, the sun flashing on its white body. But it didn't abandon them; it only withdrew to a respectful distance, like a dog at a barbecue. There was no need for Cruz to interpret the event. No one mistook it for good news.

Hula studied Lisa's profile in the dusty window of the car while Cruz sniffed cocaine off his pocketknife. The road into the sawgrass was still empty. They could all relax; the aircraft had shown them what to expect.

The bald-headed man groaned and started coughing violently. So he's alive, Hula thought. He didn't attach any particular importance to the fact. Cruz turned around and hiked back up the road to the spot where he had left the guns and sat down, falling back on one hand. A few feet of chalky soil separated him from the prone figures under the tree. He looked dull and irritated.

Hula watched the man on the ground lift his head awkwardly and blink. "What's that noise?" he said. He looked at Hula, his expression open and curious.

Hula walked away. He got into the car in the seat in front of Lisa. Now he wished that Cruz had killed the man, if only because he didn't want to listen to him. The aircraft droned somewhere out of sight. He reached over the seat and put his hand in Lisa's lap. When she looked back at him he knew that there was no point in saying anything; she understood perfectly. There was no false sympathy here, no chance to blur your eyes with tears and fall away. He envisioned the two of them struggling through the sawgrass, the sun flaming on the horizon and the helicopter hanging over them like an aroused tern over a school of baitfish. He wondered why Cruz hadn't fired at it.

"Michael — what's wrong with you?" The stranger was taunting him. "You've been dogging around all day. Why don't you get it over with?'

Since Cruz didn't answer, the man was left to make his own conversation. Cross-legged on the ground, Michael rested his elbows on his knees and scratched at the dust with one fingernail. Now and then he looked up and checked the road. His apparent indifference didn't discourage the man under the tree, who seemed to thrive on the sound of his own voice, which was clear, unhurried, and powerful. Ray and Lisa heard every word.

"Michael's got a lot on his mind. All these years he's been disappearing at the last moment, as if he just got bored and needed a little air, while everybody watches the roof fall in. Where's Cruz, they'd say, and then the lights go out. He thinks he was running from me. That's your excuse, right? That's why you couldn't sit still? Well, here I am, Michael. It's time for you to collect."

He coughed roughly and went on. "You know what I'm talking about? That girl out on Alton Road on the beach — you knew as soon as you went out the front I'd come in the back. She was so young and fresh I had to put a pillow over her face. It's not that hard, you know, once you realize that you're just as human as anyone else — the problem is that most people don't have any confidence in their own feelings.

"Well I'm beyond that now. I don't need any excuses. I've given up supposing I can tell the difference between the friendlies and the hostiles — all I do is try to keep myself in shape."

He was just like this, Hula thought, that day in my office. Cruz didn't seem to be paying any attention. He sat huddled over the bag of cocaine, occasionally throwing back his head and sneezing.

"Michael, are you listening? Just because you've got the upper hand here doesn't mean I'm going to let you off." He arched his neck and rolled his eyes back at Cruz. "There you are." Then he brought his chin forward again and settled himself, staring up into the airy leaves of the tamarind. "All right, suit yourself. As I was saying, I'm

346

getting a little tired of waiting for you to finish with me. You stretch me out next to this corpse here and then you lose your nerve. I didn't make your friend go through this. What's the matter? This is what you wanted, right? You were waiting for me out here — you wouldn't leave until I showed up. I took the bait and I got caught. But you don't have much else to be thankful for — those cowboys are on their way and they'll take care of all of us at once. So you're not going to get any satisfaction out of this unless you act now. You put this whole thing together and I'm all you've got to show for it. You won't have me much longer."

His voice wore on and on, rising and falling like the spiraling buzz of the helicopter. The man refused to let Michael's silence quiet him; he seemed to feed on it. He asked Cruz dozens of questions and answered them all for him. Hula learned about numerous other occasions when he had nearly caught up with Cruz, only to lose him at the last minute; an apartment block in Jersey City, an incident in a crowded bar in Manhattan, another girl dead in a hotel room, somebody named Dunn who had gotten in the way. It seemed to Hula that the really interesting points were being ignored and he sharply regretted not knowing who the man was or what he was doing here. But not so much that he would ask him; he was obviously losing his grip.

"Listen, I'm talking to you," the stranger said. "If you'd blow my brains out right now I'd be forever in your debt. Wouldn't you rather do it yourself than have those other creeps do it for you? They're not looking for me and they won't treat you any better than I would. That's why I'm going to die happy, Michael. Because they're on their way."

Cruz wilted under his barrage. Once in a while he got up to stretch, his bony wrists poking out of his shirt, but he never gave any sign that he was listening; he just got more and more limp and haggard. Hula thought it might be the cocaine. Cruz had been bending over his knife all afternoon. Now and then he dipped his finger into the bag and rubbed the tip on his gums. There was dust in his hair and his hands were a whitish gray. He looked as nervous, hunched, and querulous as a laboratory monkey. Earlier Hula had hoped that Cruz might think of something, anything, that could do to improve their chances. He had given up on it. His own thoughts yielded no better.

Lisa asked Ray, without any great urgency, if he knew what the man was talking about.

"No," he said. "It has nothing to do with us."

"Who is he?"

"I don't know."

The man heard them. " 'Who is he?' she asks. Michael, why don't you tell her? Why the big secret?"

Cruz stopped scratching his ribs and sat very still. The man continued. "Go on, do it. I won't stop you. Let's understand each other."

For the first time in over an hour he was quiet. The helicopter mumbled somewhere out of sight. Hula stared at the prostrate figure under the tree. A minute ago he had told Lisa that the man's ramblings had nothing to do with them, but he'd known it was a lie as soon as he said it. He had seen too much of Cruz to believe that physical fear alone could make him fold up like this, and he had long been aware of the high wall of threats and silence Cruz had thrown up around his relationship with the stranger, as if it was the one aspect of himself that he couldn't allow Hula to see, even though everything he had done had brought Hula and the other man closer together. Now they were face to face, with Cruz in the middle. Hula was certain that this was the cause of Michael's collapse. Cruz couldn't meet the situation; it required more of him than he could give. The thought that he might be overestimating his own significance never occurred to Hula. It is because I am here, he thought, that Michael can't lift a finger. He wanted to know why, very badly, and for the first time he thought Cruz might be ready to tell him.

He was wrong. In the coarse sand at the edge of the road Michael had lined up all the bullets and shotgun shells, tips upward, within easy reach. He plucked out a few rounds, grabbed the rifle, and started quickly down the track into the Glades, pushing the cartridges into the magazine as he went. When he was clear of the hammock he stopped and turned around. He laid his cheek on the stock and squinted down the barrel. Each time he pulled the trigger his shoulder jerked back and he stood up straight, dropping the gun across his waist, to see what he'd done. He fired three times.

Hula had expected something much more conclusive and couldn't figure out why Cruz was aiming over their heads. But he wasn't firing blindly; before each shot he swung the barrel a little to one side, as if he was leading a target. The yielding silence swallowed the explosions. Then Hula remembered the helicopter.

The sun shone low over the hammock into Cruz's face. After the third shot he shaded his eyes and bobbed his head momentarily as he peered into the glare. The sound of the machine faded and leveled off; he had neither brought it down nor driven it away. He walked stiff-legged back into the hammock, looking at the ground in front of him, and tossed the rifle into the weeds. He sat down abruptly in the spot he had just vacated. Long shadows streaked the edge of the road. He reached back and vigorously scratched the base of his skull.

The man under the tree didn't lose any time taking up where he had left off. "So you wasted three bullets," he said. "We're all still here. Why don't you tell them who I am?" Hula believed without question that Cruz had picked up the rifle and started shooting for no other reason than to avoid confronting this demand. Ray wanted him to answer. Right now nothing else seemed as important. In the seat behind him Lisa was also wide awake and listening. The man's voice hung in the still air with the solidity and force of the silence around it.

"You don't have any choice. If you don't tell them, I will."

Cruz pushed a chunk of coral a few inches with his toe.

"Michael, I'm not kidding, for once. This is the real thing."

The new element in his voice startled Hula. It was fear, and it made him sound almost human. He doesn't want to say it either, Hula thought. He wants Michael to stop him.

"It's not a long story. I could tell all of it before the Colombians get here. Even the parts you never heard."

Cruz ran his hand along the upright row of shells, knocking them over one by one.

"Michael — don't let me down. Do it for me." Hula knew exactly what the man wanted.

Cruz fell back on one hand and slowly drew his knees under him. He got up on one leg and swayed gently, a fragile plant in an underwater garden. It took all his strength to get to his feet. He didn't touch the firearms and he didn't look back at Ray and Lisa in the car. He couldn't have done it with his own energies; he was getting help from elsewhere. The sweat had dried in dirty smears on his face and the slanting light, golden in the late afternoon, nearly succeeded in giving color to his grayish skin. Judging from the line of his shoulders, what he had suffered already was nothing beside what he was about to feel. The man under the tree waited patiently for his approach, and it seemed to Hula as if the entire landscape — the hardened, oily leaves, the thin road running into nothing, the drowned sawgrass, and the cloud-heavy sky — was also awake and breathing. Cruz's feet scratched along the rough surface of the track. He was bent over and he had his arms crossed in front of him. Whatever transformation had overtaken him was complete.

Hula got out of the car and shut the door behind him. He glanced once at Lisa and followed Cruz up the road. The thought of interfering didn't even occur to him. He was certain, however, that his place was beside the other two men — as a witness, as proof of his commitment to their seriousness. He couldn't endure any confusion about the details. That was his role, his contribution; he was utterly faithful to himself in this respect.

He came up beside Cruz. The spreading branches of the tamarind shaded the two bodies at their feet. Michael didn't acknowledge his presence; he stood with his head bowed, looking down at the man beneath him, who gazed back with a quiet, patient confidence in his eyes, as if he had known all along that this moment was coming. A few mosquitoes struggled on the stranger's face; they had plunged their needles into his thick skin and couldn't retract them. Unable to stop the flow of blood into their bodies, some of them had burst and now lay tangled in their own gore. Cruz took out his handkerchief, stooped down, and brushed them away. His motions had none of their characteristic abruptness.

Hula couldn't help noticing Liberty's body a little farther under the tree. His face had swelled since the morning and he was barely recognizable. Even his skin was darker, making his blond hair very bright in the shadow over his forehead. Hula felt as if the body didn't belong here anymore. His mouth tasted funny and he turned aside, looking up the road into the Glades, trying to clear away the unpleasant pictures that floated into his head — spoiled fruit, gorged mosquitoes, Liberty's soft and discolored face. The road was empty. He had thought it would be easier than this.

Now Cruz was talking to the bald-headed man. His voice was all air; it had no bottom to it. He got down on his knees and leaned over the man, his hands balled at his waist. Hula couldn't hear him very well. There wasn't much. Something about having to wait a little longer, but until then maybe he'd settle for this. Michael looked as if he was about to fall over. Hula squatted on his heels in the weeds and white rubble. He didn't want to be excluded.

So they were all huddled there under the trees in the dead leaves and the bits of dry bark and the still, close air that smelled as if it had been breathed in and out so many times that it had a rind on it. The man's face was pale as a mushroom. Only his eyes had color. They watched Cruz and nothing else. There was no fear in them, no feeling of any kind beyond an intense, concentrated attentiveness maintained without effort. They were no more likely to blink than glass eyes, and Cruz was near enough to frost them with his breath.

"Right," he said. "I'm supposed to finish it for you now." Hula could barely hear him.

Cruz reached inside his shirt and pulled out his gun, a .45 with white facing on the handle. It wobbled in his hand. "But not yet, and maybe never, because I'm different from you. But I'll give you a taste." He put the gun away and worked his hands under the man's body, one at the shoulder and one at the hip. Cruz's eyes squeezed shut and his lower jaw slid to one side as he lifted. It wasn't enough. He stopped and rested, his shallow chest heaving.

When Hula realized what Michael was trying to do he didn't offer any help. But he didn't look away either. In these circumstances he could tolerate almost anything, even this.

"Go ahead!" the man shouted, at once raging and exultant. "Try it again! I'm ready! Show me all of it!"

On his next attempt Cruz succeeded. He dug in his heels, lifted, pushed, struggled, groaned, and found that extra strength; the man tilted on one side and suddenly rolled over, coming down heavily on top of Liberty's ripe corpse, nearly burying it, cheek to cheek, and forcing an evil muttering noise out of his dead lungs. The stranger's face came up sticky with a filmy gray jam from the back of Liberty's head. He was oblivious; he had no thought for himself. His mouth stretched open in a wide frozen smile and his eyes shone above Liberty's mottled face. "That's not enough! I want more!"

By this time Hula had retreated to the road. He knew that if he looked under the tree again he would probably be sick, so the man's voice broke against the back of his skull.

One of his bandages was coming loose. He stood up and tried to tuck it back together, poking at it with his puffy fingers. Lisa was out of the car and right beside him with both hands wrapped around the meaty part of his arm. He wondered if she was trying to get his attention. The helicopter suddenly roared by overhead, followed by a brief blast of air.

Hula glanced up at her. She was staring under the tamarind and digging her fingers into his biceps. Her expression blended shock and revulsion in an absolute rigidity. He heard a smacking noise and someone grunting nasally, like a string of soggy, muffled sneezes. They were just the sort of noises you might expect, given the circumtances. He turned and looked.

In the deepening shadow under the tree Hula saw Cruz sitting astride the two bodies, one dead, one living, and energetically packing the bald-headed man's nose and mouth with dusty handfuls of raw cocaine, ramming it into his nostrils with his thumbs and forcing it past his teeth by prying them open with the blade of his knife. Some of the excess sifted down and whitened Liberty's face. The man's body kicked and bucked as he snapped at Cruz's hands, spitting out half-moistened lumps of bleached powder and choking on the rest. Hula had to look away, and his eyes fell, out of habit, on the spot where the arrow-straight road split the horizon. He saw at least six or eight of those hard-backed beetles that were actually cars crawling interminably towards him, as if they had all the time in the world.

Fool's Night

Y EARS LATER Escobar considered himself fortunate for having been kept out of the last stages of the Michael Cruz business.

Escobar was in New York on the day Jack Parko was killed. Even though the coke was safely on its way north by then, the other traders still held Escobar hostage to the outcome in Miami, where his lieutenant, Ramón Galdos, was in charge of the effort to locate Cruz and retrieve their investment. Until that money was recovered or otherwise accounted for, Escobar endured house arrest in his three-story brownstone in Jackson Heights. He watched TV, drank coffee, and answered the phone in person. In the months to follow he often complained that he had suffered most from what had happened in Miami since his own people were chiefly involved, but he once remarked in private that the one thing he'd learned from Michael Cruz was that there are situations in which everybody loses, hinting that the lesson might have been much more expensive. Within a year he had reclaimed his Colombian citizenship and was managing his family's estates near the border with Ecuador. Escobar still maintained an apartment in Miami but he rarely visited it, and then only to see his banker and take his family shopping. He was a wealthy man, much respected in his circle, and he lived to see his grandchildren married.

None of this made any difference for Michael Cruz. He was fighting for his life.

The Colombians failed miserably in their first rush for the hammock. Their lead car was still over two hundred yards away when Cruz, ignoring the driver crouched under the wheel, shot out a front tire with the rifle. The Seville leaned to one side and caught a rim on the edge of the dike. A smaller car might have bolted all the way over, but the Cadillac just rammed its nose into the rock under the sawgrass and stopped, leaving its flat tail hanging over the road. At the moment of impact a small figure in a black T-shirt and lemon-colored pants popped through the windshield and fell into the water. When he got to his feet Cruz fired again. Disconsolate, the man sat down quickly and laid one hand flat against his ear. A few minutes later he slumped over into the grass, but by that time no one was watching him any longer.

The next car stopped a few yards behind the first and didn't move again until the remaining three or four had come up behind it. There was no shooting in the interim.

Ramón sat in the front seat of the second car. The sun hung just above the black clump of trees where the track apparently ended. He'd spent over an hour clearing a burnt-out wreck and a blue Toyota off another section of this road and he didn't feel at all sorry for the man in the lemon-colored pants.

Michael Cruz and a few others were camped out at the edge of that line of trees. The helicopter had reported that there were only three of them altogether, one of them a woman, but Ramón was naturally pessimistic and couldn't accept that figure as any more than an estimate. He would agree, however, that there was at least one person there with good eyes and a rifle. Picking up the microphone, he ordered everyone to sit tight.

You could see a long way out here. The plain between the hammocks was as flat as a parking lot and offered no better opportunities for concealment. Ramón had discovered the properties of sawgrass a few miles back while clearing the road and he had no intention of sending any of his men squirming through it, their heads bobbing above the water — the water was so high that the densest patches of grass extended only inches higher. They'd be easy targets, but he wasn't thinking about their lives. What worried him was the embarrassment.

It would take about thirty seconds, he guessed, to charge up the road from the cover of the lead car to the edge of the trees. He had about twenty men in all. Therefore Cruz would have to kill two men every three seconds in order to stop them. Ramón knew that his soldiers would balk at anything so stupid unless he was leading the way, and that was definitely out of the question; he valued his own life much too highly.

356

The pilot had said that there was a clearing he could put down in at the center of the hammock. The safest way to get the money out was by air. Although he had heard nothing yet from the car he'd left by the entrance on Krome Avenue, Ramón thought it unlikely that his traveling circus hadn't been noticed by now and he expected that someone would be waiting for him at the end of the long crawl back. In fact, he had nearly decided to leave in the helicopter himself. So it had to come down in the clearing as soon as possible.

He wondered what Parko would have done here if he hadn't been dumped, dumped and burned and tossed into the swamp, his roasted body cramped up against the door and tangled in the charred springs of the upholstery. When Ramón saw what was left of Jack he chose to understand it as a personal message from Cruz.

Five minutes; he would give himself five more minutes to decide. What he needed was a machine gun or even a half dozen carbines. What he had was a gang of kids with .38s and soft heads. Some would die. He didn't have time to wait around for help and his pride wouldn't allow it anyway. Night was just a short while distant.

Cruz, Hula, and Lisa looked back at Ramón from the edge of the hammock. They saw a row of cars, one in front of the other, each windshield a lozenge of opaque fire in the setting sun, like a string of open furnaces in the fading heat. Nothing was happening. They crouched uncomfortably under the edge of the trees and watched. Hula put the shotgun down, slid his feet out from under himself, settled heavily on his rear, laid the gun across his lap. Michael had tried to give Lisa a handgun but she had refused it.

"What the fuck are they waiting for?" Cruz said.

What the fuck are *we* waiting for, Hula asked himself. His hands were worse than useless. The helicopter buzzed in his ears.

"You don't need me," Lisa said. "I'm going back to the house for a minute." She got up and left, walking evenly down the center of the track.

"Get down!" Hula shouted. She ignored him. She didn't draw any fire from the men in the cars. They were looking into the sun; they didn't even see her.

Hula didn't want her to go but he didn't say anything more. They had talked about trekking out of the hammock into the Glades. Now that the helicopter was here the idea seemed even less attractive. If they could just wait until nightfall, or if Cruz could bring it down —

357

at any rate, Hula didn't intend to sit here until the Colombians stumbled over him. He planned to keep running until he couldn't run any farther. It made perfect sense. In the meantime he tried to keep from shaking too violently.

Cruz stood up and fired once at the helicopter with no apparent effect. He hadn't said much since he'd killed the bald-headed man; just a few abrupt and half-audible commands. Now he busied himself with the guns, stuffing the chambers and wiping off the stocks with his handkerchief. Hula almost envied him.

He sat beside Cruz and watched the swelling, blue-shadowed clouds roll towards them over the level vastness of the landscape turning gold in the sun. The cars looked very small out there. It was hard to believe in the threat they represented. He knew that time had nearly run out for him, knew it without having to know why, but he failed to see how those six cars could participate in any crucial way since they were so tiny and insignificant in the distance, hedged in by the water and nearly flat against the ground. He could block them out with one finger. They hung discreetly on the edge of vision; he tried to reduce them further by mere wishing. If they didn't move for another hour it would be dark. Then the helicopter might leave. Then anything could happen.

There were men in the cars, little men in black, and they were leaking backwards out the doors, as if they couldn't open them more than a few inches. They crawled over the fenders like crabs on a rock, scrambling up the row and ducking behind the derailed lead car. Cruz sat cross-legged beside Hula and aimed carefully with his elbow braced on his knee. The shot didn't echo in the open plain and none of the men fell over, although they all froze for a moment. Then they crept forward again, their faces white and indistinct under their dark hair. There were at least a dozen of them. The doors shut and the last ones disappeared behind the lead car. Cruz snapped the bolt back and the empty shell popped out and hit Hula on the thigh.

"This is it," Cruz said, and coughed.

The lead car lay slanted across the road at a rising angle like a sheet of plywood propped against a fence. Suddenly three or four men rushed around and grabbed it under the bumper, lifting the near wheel off the gravel. Cruz fired and one of the men went down. By the time he fired again they had dragged the rear end to the edge of the track and dropped it over. As it fell it exposed a knot of men in front of the second car, like a nest of ants under a rock. Cruz's second shot killed one of them. The rest scuttled back alongside the cars, dragging their casualties after them. They were well disciplined. No one tried to get in the doors of the new lead car until all the men were past it, and the doors stayed open to cover their retreat.

The last barrier was gone and the way was clear. Panic bubbled up in Hula's throat. He discovered his foot was asleep and starting banging it mercilessly against a root. When he looked up again the car in front was already rolling. Cruz shot out a tire and one wheel collapsed onto its rim, but this time the driver maintained control and the car stopped for only a few seconds before resuming its approach, at once tedious and implacable, advancing over the bleached rock like a crippled tortoise. The second car started to move behind it, and then the third. Although it seemed to take forever, they all finally crept into motion.

"The shotgun," Cruz barked. "Now!"

Hula didn't have to be persuaded. Forgetting that his hand was still wrapped in a half yard of white gauze, he reached for the butt and knocked it off his lap, the pain from his lacerated palm squeezing tears from his eyes. Cruz heard the gun fall and reached around to get it himself. He aimed, the barrel boomed, and the windshield of the lead car fell away, revealing an empty rear window frame and nothing in between. The car kept coming. Whoever was driving it was under the dashboard.

"The gas tank," Hula said.

"I can't reach it. It's behind the block." Cruz laid the shotgun down carefully beside him and picked up the rifle. He dug into his pockets for a few more shells and packed them into the magazine. "I can't stop them."

Something drew Hula's eyes to the bodies under the tree on the other side of the road. Streaks of yellow light lay across an elbow, a leaf, a patch of skin. He didn't know what to say. Michael had failed him — Michael, who could make planes fall out of the sky, who could laugh at the DEA, who could rob the drug traders and demand payment for it. "What're you going to do?"

"Kill a few more. I got three already." A few bullets zipped into the road beside them, kicking up bits of sand and rock. Ray was forced to admit that they were shooting at him, shooting in order to do him harm, not caring who he was or why he was here or whether he wanted it. Their indifference infuriated him. Now he could see a few heads edging out the windows of the cars and aiming tiny pistols at him. One of the men wore glasses; he saw the lenses glinting. Another leaned halfway out of a window, his arms hanging limp, his bloody head upside down and bumping against the door. They were coming too slowly for Hula. At this rate it would take them another three days to reach the hammock — time enough to get tired of watching them and plenty of time to do something, if only there was something to do. They were still a long way off, too far for their fire to be really effective. Hula wanted to stand up and make obscene suggestions. Then he had an even better idea. "Let's burn the money," he said. "Dump it in the road and burn it, right in front of them." He thought it was pure genius.

Cruz didn't bother to answer him. He just kept pumping bullets into the caravan, his shoulder jerking from the recoil. The lead car bucked and swayed on its bad wheel, deaf to his harassing fire. The sun was so low that the water on either side of the road had deepened blue as night and the clouds overhead flushed bright conch-pink. Colors faded in the long shadow of the hammock but burned twice as fierce wherever the light hit them. Hula saw the helicopter swing into view way off in the distance and settle gently onto the dike. A bullet sucked past his ear.

Now Cruz was on his stomach and firing with the barrel just a few inches off the ground. The gun leaped in his hands; blood drenched the dyed leather of the first car. Hula saw what Michael was doing and half believed that he would murder them all before they reached the hammock. He flopped onto the thin soil and hiked himself up on his elbows. A mosquito bumbled into his eye and he caught it between his lids when he blinked, flailing at it with his cloth-wrapped mitt. As if in answer, a bullet smashed into the green bark of the tree beside him; the Colombians were finding their range. Turning on his hip and digging into his pockets again, Cruz looked at the ragged splinters of white pulp dangling from the hole. "If you're going, you better go now," he said.

For some time Hula had been planning to follow Lisa to the house. "What about you?"

"I'll wait for Escobar."

Hula got up into a crouch and stopped.

"Stay down or get the fuck out," Cruz said. The rifle jerked again and more blood splashed down the road.

"I'll see you later," Hula said. He didn't move. Now he could hear the cars crunching over the gravel. He wanted Michael to look at him, to answer, since he was well aware that they might never see each other again.

"Yeah, right," Cruz said, still squinting down the barrel.

Hula realized that it was foolish to hope for anything more.

He crawled out from under the tree and stumbled down the trail into the hammock, acutely aware of how conspicuous he must be and waiting for a sharp bullet to cut into him. He heard the guns cracking in protest. Kinetic shocks jolted up his legs as his feet thudded into the sand. He was around the first bend in no time and suddenly there was no sound louder than his own breathing. He slowed to a wobbly, soft-ankled walk.

The overgrown forest crowded the road, its black snags and feelers scratching and clawing at the red sky in the west. Night was only minutes away. Hula picked up his pace; the track seemed longer than it should be. When he reached the clearing the sun was already buried behind the house. Lisa was nowhere in sight. He no longer understood why he had let her disappear. The front door of the house hung open on darkness. Bats tumbled and squeaked over his head in the dusk, their wings making their peculiar rubbery pops and sighs.

She was sitting on the bench by the table in the kitchen. All the lights were off. He didn't see her until she spoke. "Ray."

He froze.

"What happened?"

"Michael is still out there." He heard the shotgun boom. "They'll be here in a minute." She didn't answer right away. "Are you all right?"

He could see her better now; the side of her face, her hand on her knee. "I was about to come looking for you," she said.

He sat down beside her. A shiver lost itself in his bulk. "I'm here now."

"Are you ready to go?"

"I was ready yesterday."

She stood up, reached behind her, and lifted a large and heavy paper bag into his lap. "You'll have to carry this."

361

He pinned it against himself with his forearms.

"I don't see any point in waiting around," she said.

"There's no time."

"So let's go."

He felt dizzy as he stood up. She slipped past him into the main room and out the door. As they came down the steps into the clearing dozens of mosquitoes rose out of the dusk to meet them. The first stars glittered overhead. A battle raged at the edge of the hammock less than a quarter mile away.

They floated along the front of the darkened house, past the screened porch, past the sinkhole and into the intimate and humid face of the night, listening to the guns bite and roar while thousands of hard-shelled insects buzzed and rattled in the trees. They weaved through the coral boulders at the edge of the pool and entered the deep shadow on the far side, a narrow space where the hard roots slithered over the high rock wall and dove into the water. She found the lane of cool sand shining where it climbed into the woods. Hula was right behind her. Smooth limestone outcrops loomed out of the darkness. The forest closed overhead and dry leaves rustled at their feet. When Hula stopped to catch his breath he realized that he couldn't hear her anymore and that he had lost sight of her as soon as they had left the sinkhole. "Here," she said. She was right beside him.

They sat on a low rock and rested. Hula waited for his eyes to adjust. It was no use; this was the highest part of the hammock, dark as a closet in the middle of the day.

Lisa lifted the paper bag off his lap and set it on the ground between her knees. He heard her hands moving inside it. After a minute she told him to stand up and step in front of her, facing away. He felt her touching his hips and guiding him into place. "Now hold still," she said. In the night her voice was more solid than the ground under him.

The bag contained, among other things, eight long strips of canvas about six inches wide, the remnants of the mat that had once covered the porch's concrete floor. She had taken it up when the edges rotted away after years of rain and heat. Starting at the ankle, she wrapped one of the lengths around Hula's leg as high as his crotch and secured it by poking holes in the end with the tip of the machete and fastening them to similar holes in the previous turn with short twists of wire. The fabric was rough and extremely stiff. When she had finished with his other leg he could barely move. He sat with his feet sticking straight out in front of him while she performed the same operation on herself. In the meantime he doused himself with the musky, oil-based bug repellant.

So this was the armor she had prepared for their departure; canvas waders and a thin film of chemicals. They didn't do any talking while she worked. Lisa still had one leg to wrap and pin when the shooting died away.

Hula knew what it meant. He sat in the dark, immediately weakened by the death of his brother; not saddened or grieved, because Cruz had chosen his own end, but as if a part of himself had been moved out of reach. Michael had haunted him in life. Now his ghost had fled away into nothing.

The night had swelled so large around Hula as they left the clearing that he didn't realize he was still only a few yards from the sinkhole, and the noises that suddenly broke out of the dark in that direction seemed so close that he nearly cried out. He reached up and touched Lisa just above the knee; she twitched and moaned. They couldn't see each other but they could still hear it — a soft splashing and gurgling, as if a small whale were paddling around the sinkhole. He felt her hands brush his as she continued wrapping her legs. The splashing stopped before she was finished, but it was shortly followed by excited shouts in Spanish and the rumbling of six cars as they swept into the clearing. Their headlights pierced the woods; tiny scraps of light flickered among the leaves over their heads. There was more shooting and someone yelling for help. Although it all happened just a few steps from where they sat, they didn't see any of it.

The helicopter dropped past them and landed in the center of the clearing, drowning out all the other noises. A blast of air reached across the sinkhole and up the gully. It felt weak and briefly cool against Hula's daubed face and neck. Lisa pulled him to his feet. They were ready to go.

He stuffed the paper bag with the remaining canvas inside his shirt. She grabbed him just above the wrist. "If I let go," she said, "don't move!" He could barely hear her above the roar. She yanked on his arm and he stumbled after her, eyes wide open and seeing nothing, his feet banging among the rocks, each step a last-ditch effort to keep from falling headlong into her. He had no idea where they were going. More shouts filtered through the trees.

The commotion faded with time and eventually the buzz of the insects overpowered it. When Hula stopped she didn't let go of his arm and it brought her up short. "Where are we?" he said. He wanted to hear her voice.

"Near the edge, I think."

"Why don't we just wait here till they leave?"

The Colombians answered for her. More voiced floated out of the night somewhere off to their left. They weren't shouting now. Hula distinctly heard the solid thud of a shoe against a root and the subsequent stifled outburst. Lisa's nails dug into his skin. A beam of light outlined a spiky clump of palmetto; whoever held the lamp was on the other side. The bright ray darted across the open floor of the forest, flashing against the massive, smooth, and widely spaced trees. "They're behind the house," Lisa said. Another beam flickered into life behind them, crossing the first over their heads. It was farther off and not as powerful. Lisa leaned close to him and pulled the machete out of the bag under his shirt. "I know where we are — let's go."

Hula's clumsiness vanished. He drifted after her, slipping through the dark as easily as a puff of smoke. After a minute they headed down a gentle slope and came up against an unyielding wall of cool leaves and sharp branches. They moved a few yards to one side and she waded into the tangle; somehow it gave way before her. When Hula looked back from inside he saw the stronger beam dart into the hollow they had just vacated. He didn't look back again.

She dropped his wrist. The thicket had closed up around them. Solid and elastic walls of needle twigs, wait-a-minute vines, and sticky, clinging webs hemmed him so close that he couldn't have fallen over if he'd tried. It was just this sort of botanist's nightmare that persuaded most people to spend their weekends on the far side of Krome Avenue. But Lisa had found the trail she had hacked out earlier in the day and she slipped through so easily that Hula had to struggle to keep up, lurching after the dry scrape and shake of the twigs as they whipped back at him and listening for all the other sounds he would rather not hear. There was nothing except his own elephantine crashing. The world fell silent to watch him go by.

The trees thinned out over their heads and pools of stagnant water bubbled and stank at their feet. The night had glutted Hula's eyes so completely that he mistook his first high glimpses of open sky for tricks of his imagination, and when he saw Lisa stop and darken into

364

being on a pale, open bank of white sand he walked right into her. She would have fallen over if he hadn't hooked his arm around her belt.

They stood beside the tall nest of cabbage palms where she had cut the bud that morning. Beyond it a narrow scrub margin merged into the sawgrass plain. Behind them, no more than two hundred yards away, the Colombians sniffed along the edge of the thicket, shining their lights in each other's faces and preparing a more thorough search; they had lost too much this afternoon to go away hungry. Before long they would find the hole in the brush and file into it.

Lisa couldn't hear them but she knew they were coming. She led him around the edge of the trees and into the waist-high scrub. "Which way is west?" she said.

He tilted his head back and examined the stars. "Straight ahead."

"All right, you go first."

He nodded and started slogging down through the tough undergrowth. She called after him. "Ray — wait a minute." He turned and looked at her, his head black against the sky. She followed him out and leaned over his waist, tugging and straightening the canvas integuments over his legs. Then she did the same for herself.

Twenty minutes later Ramón burrowed out from behind the cabbage palms and clicked off his flashlight. He had water in his shoes and blood on his clothes. In a moment a few others soundlessly joined him. Against the dark mass of the hammock they loitered, nearly invisible, brushing off their sleeves and slapping at bugs. A warm breeze blew into their faces. The flooded, rock-armored desert beginning at their feet and extending to infinity made them look self-conscious, as if they felt conspicuous here, exposed under the hovering night full of stars, when in fact no one and nothing noticed their emergence except a few hundred mosquitoes. Ramón's eye traced the line Hula and Lisa had followed into the sawgrass and rested momentarily on the spot far off in the distance where their gray silhouettes faded into the horizon. If he saw them he gave no indication. He stood there for another minute or two, softly tapping the butt of his flashlight against his leg. Then he turned and nodded at the other men. They went back the way they had come, hunching their shoulders as they ducked into the woods. Ramón was the last to go. He took his time about it, his dark eyes drifting back and forth under his brow while he looked out over the water. The flashlight's nervous drumming stopped, and a moment later even his eyes fell still.

Some time later the helicopter rose out of the hammock, lights burning bright as phosphorous through the risen dust of the clearing. It circled twice and swung away to the north, passing high over Hula and Lisa, who looked at it without interest or recognition. Then Hula leaned on one foot, raised the other high in the air, and plunged it in the sawgrass a few inches from its original spot. At that point he had to stop and rest.

His ear canals had swollen shut and he couldn't hear the mosquitoes any more, much less feel their bites. The great majority never even lighted on his skin since the repellant turned them away, but even if as few as one in every hundred wasn't, for mysterious reasons, discouraged by the chemical, then this small fraction was more than enough to suck him dry, while the rest danced in a vague swarm around him. They blundered into his eyes, throat, and nostrils like timid medieval mariners.

At midnight, four hours after Lisa had stepped off her property, the hammock still floated in the distance behind them. They had slowed down considerably after the first half hour. They didn't have any choice. If they had continued at their earlier pace the sawgrass would have cut their shoes to bits. Hula tried clearing a path with the machete and had no problem slashing down the flexible upper parts of the grass, but the stiff basal stems were out of reach under the water and their serrated edges had nearly sliced through Lisa's sneakers. Hula's round-toed boots suffered almost as badly. So they had to lower their feet tenderly onto the bottom, not putting any weight on them until they were resting flat on the root-choked limestone, a process that required the patience of a chess player and the balance of a gymnast. They weren't very successful.

Hula was thinking about the dike that supposedly bordered the eastern edge of Everglades Park. Lisa had heard about it from her husband. It was probably no higher than the road that led back from the hammock to Krome Avenue; maybe two or three feet above the water. In all the time Hula had traveled up and down that road he had never realized that it was a bridge over an abyss.

To reach the dike all they had to do was continue west. According to Lisa it was no more than five miles from the hammock. The sky was still partly clear when they started and Hula picked out Polaris low over the horizon, but he had lost it soon afterwards and had been guessing ever since. He couldn't find his way by looking through a few small holes in the overcast, so he just followed the clouds. All afternoon they had drifted east to west. If they had changed direction in the meantime it was too late to worry about it.

Heat lightning flickered noiselessly overhead, too weak to touch the ground. Lisa couldn't lift her feet out of the water anymore. She shuffled after Hula, the sawgrass slicing bits of rubber off her sneakers. She had lost the skin on the side of her heel where the grass had cut through her shoe. Her face felt numb and tight. Once in a while she remembered why she was here and why she had to continue, but most of the time she didn't think about it. She could see well enough to see Hula and there was something about him that was bothering her, but it was only when he stopped and let her catch up with him that she realized what it was. The canvas over his knees had come loose and now hung in shreds down his calf. Reaching around him into his shirt, she pulled out another length of canvas and wrapped his leg in it, fastening it with a crude knot on his thigh. When she finished she remained stooped over, her hands hooked behind his belt, unable to straighten up again. Five mosquitoes tried to puncture her ripe cheek. Nocturnal minnows nipped and tugged at her raw ankles in the shallow water. She didn't feel them at all. Hula pulled her upright, steadied her, turned, and moved away.

Although the coral rock lay just under their feet and free air bathed their heads, the plain compelled them to traverse its most difficult zone, the sawgrass, which like the others had strict horizontal boundaries and nearly limitless vertical ones. A narrow interval of eroded limestone, half-rotted muck, and fresh water, no more than a yard in depth but repeating itself endlessly in length; the soft air pinned them to it and the hard rock held them up.

Hula knew that it shouldn't be this difficult. He gave it all of his attention and it didn't get any easier. They'd been slowing down for hours and before long they wouldn't even be able to stand up. Then what? Lying on their backs in the shallow water, watching the clouds roll solemnly overhead — a little time to rest while their blood leaked away in the dark. But what if nothing happened? What if they got weaker and weaker, too weak to talk, to weak to do anything but breathe, but the end they were waiting for never arrived? Or what if Lisa slipped away and left him alone? He could lie here forever, through the dank summers, the dry winters, the fires, the droughts, the storms, until even his bones bleached and crumbled into the white rock, until he was nothing more than a weightless and invisible skein of memories hanging over this tiny patch of sawgrass, a disembodied nerve, powerless to leave, powerless to sleep, unable even to cry out. What then? What could he wait for then? There was enough water here to float ten Miamis but it was too shallow and nothing could vanish in it.

Lisa's uncertain silhouette was black, as black as the low wall of trees flattened against the horizon, almost as black as the wet mirror of the swamp. Though moonless and overcast, the night was just light enough to see by. The sawgrass looked as pale and soft as an old man's hair and the masses of vapor hiding the stars shed a cold phosphorescence. Hula felt very thin and insubstantial as he slid his feet through the burning water. His toes banged into something hard and shocked him awake. His other shoe was already coming forward. He saw himself lean and fall like an ancient and long-dead tree, snapping limbs and crashing into the undergrowth. As he looked down he noticed that the sawgrass had melted away beneath him and he was falling towards a dark rift that had suddenly opened like a door in the rock. He could hear the water rushing into it. Then the dike cracked against his head and his mouth was full of sand.

» » »

Michael Cruz sat beside the waxy oak table under the window in the kitchen. It was late at night and the only light in the room was the hanging globe over his head. His hands were bound behind his back.

Three young men with drawn faces, black hair, and black eyes stood along the edges of the room, as if they didn't want to get too close to the light or to Cruz — one by the sink, another smoking in the doorway to the porch, and the third, with a short knife, by the entrance to the main room, gouging splinters out of the frame with the tip of the blade. The third man went out and came back several times. Each time he reappeared the other two looked at him expectantly, but he never said anything. He just glanced at them once, his face heavy and blank, glanced at Cruz, and went back to work on the frame.

The man by the sink spat over his shoulder into the drain and walked up to Cruz. He came so close that Michael would have had to tilt his head back and look straight up to see him. He didn't bother; he stared at the ochre floor tiles and the row of pine cabinet doors under the counter opposite.

After a long moment in which he did nothing but study the top of Cruz's head, the man stepped back, reached across himself, and slammed the back of his hand into Cruz's cheekbone. Cruz's face turned but his chin didn't fall onto his chest. The man returned to the sink, rested his palms on the edge, and crossed his feet at the ankles. An angry red blotch darkened on his right hand just behind the knuckles.

Outside, in the clearing, the helicopter rested in a half circle defined by the cars drawn up under the rim of the woods. All the lights were off. Two men leaned against the grill of one of the cars and looked at the house. One of them nervously stretched his arms over his head.

The three men standing in the kitchen pushed away from the walls when they heard footsteps in the main room. Ramón came in and stopped just inside the door. He shook his head almost imperceptibly and ran both hands through his long blue black hair, pulling it away from his face and revealing the ink-colored stain on his temple. He was taller than the others, though not necessarily any older, and was dressed severely, in a white silk shirt and black tie under his dark suit.

He walked into the middle of the room and pulled a chair away from the table so that it rested opposite Cruz. When he sat down he immediately fixed his eyes on Michael's face. He noticed the dry, brownish cigarette burns on Cruz's hands and neck and took a deep breath.

The man behind him at the sink cleared his throat and said that they couldn't get anything out of Cruz but that maybe he just needed a little more work. Ramón's face tightened at the sound of his voice. Without turning around, he raised one hand above his shoulder in a half-fist and made a flicking motion with his thumb. The man lit a cigarette and handed it to him.

Ramón took a long drag and blew it out his nostrils. His eyes never left Cruz's face. Then he leaned forward, deeply absorbed in himself, and touched the glowing end to a spot just under Cruz's ear. Bits of gray ash drifted down and speckled Cruz's shirt.

All Cruz had to do was lean his head to one side. Maybe he had tried that before and had discovered it didn't work. But he just

369

screwed up his face a little. The cigarette started to hiss and Ramón took it away. The burn it left looked exactly like the others.

Ramón flicked the butt out the door to the porch and reached back for another. Then he straightened his arm, rolled up his sleeve, and pressed the burning end against the smooth olive skin under his wrist until it made that same hissing sound. But he couldn't be as casual about it as Cruz. His eyes flared open and he swallowed deliberately. When he took the coal away there were bright drops of sweat on his forehead. Michael had no reaction.

Ramón tossed the second butt out the door and signaled for another. Amazed, the man behind him reacted too quickly and nearly fumbled it. Ramón was still staring at Cruz and smoked the first half inch before he told the other men to leave the room. They looked as if they were happy to go.

The day hadn't been a complete success for Ramón. His determination to run down Cruz had cost him considerably in blood and exposure. Now he was nearly finished, but there were certain things he wanted to learn from Cruz before he left; things so important to him that if he didn't learn them soon he would have to regard all his work today as a personal failure. This absolute seriousness of purpose was partly to blame for his absurd gesture, but if he thought he could make Michael talk by roasting himself further he would have done it in a moment.

He sat bent forward in the chair, his knees nearly touching Cruz, searching his face for a sign that might tell him how to proceed. Cruz's features were as thick and static as a Mayan deity's. Even though Ramón had never seen him before he knew that this couldn't be Cruz's normal appearance. The uniform swelling of his ashy purple skin had erased the creases around his nose and mouth and made him look young and chubby, as if he had been raised on sweets. His puffy, half-shut eyes, the slight backward tilt of his head, and his slack expression combined to give him a look of contemptuous and invulnerable superiority.

As Ramón sat opposite Cruz and leaned forward to study his face he had a strong apprehension of a separate awareness inhabiting the man in front of him, an awareness completely disguised and hidden behind the numb masklike face and the shiny marble eyes; a consciousness, a self, even the volatile elixir of a soul trapped inside the small figure who had killed so many of his men tonight, and he knew

370

that this inner spirit was retreating even further, shrinking and evaporating invisibly and out of reach in spite of all his efforts to contain it. He felt just as helpless as his victim. It was as if Cruz had gathered his remaining strength and willed an end to himself.

Ramón wanted to reach out and murder Cruz right there just to bring him back for a moment from wherever he was going. He didn't do it because he didn't want to see himself doing it. So he just sat there and sweated, knowing that he was waiting too long and that he had other responsibilities even if no one would dare remind him of them. The night pressed in on the house. Gnats swarmed around the lamp over his head. He got up, went to the sink, and drew himself a glass of water. When he turned around he saw that Cruz was still looking at him, completely enclosed in the sharp circle of light over the table. Ramón lifted the glass and drained it all at once. Then he placed it gently on the counter and strode out the door to the main room.

When the long blades of the helicopter began to turn in the clearing Ramón had already given instructions to the men on the ground. He climbed into the machine beside the pilot and shut the door behind him. The engine worked itself into a roar. As they rose out of the dust and above the trees he saw a few small figures crouching in the shelter of the cars. From five hundred feet the sandy clearing looked like a patch of misplaced snow. The Glades stretched away forever beneath him. Twenty minutes later Michael Cruz was dead.

» » »

That same night, miles to the east, a man was drowned when his small speedboat capsized in the backwash created when the three-ton screws of the converted destroyer *Cimmerian* spun into full throttle.

The man was Arthur Rawden, former inspector at the Port of Miami. A launch from the *Cimmerian* recovered his body and brought it ashore next day. The subsequent investigation determined that Rawden had stolen the boat from the impoundment basin at the Port sometime between ten and midnight and had taken it ten miles outside the Government Cut to a spot on the edge of the Gulf Stream, where he intercepted the *Cimmerian* as it cruised up from the south at ten knots. Heavy cloud cover reduced incipient light to almost zero.

The captain of the Coast Guard cutter *Argus* reported that he had been trailing the *Cimmerian* at a thousand yards on the port quarter since sundown, and his deck officer testified that if Rawden's boat had been carrying proper running lights he would have seen it long before he did, when the *Cimmerian*'s spotlight caught it drifting under the hull and into the heaving chaos of the backwash. "No," he said, "I couldn't tell if anyone was on the boat — at a thousand yards I was lucky to see it at all. No sir, all I saw was the sharp bow of the speedboat pointing up in the air and turning half over before something seemed to grab it by the stern and pull it straight under. A couple of seconds later it nosed out of the wake and floated there, swamped, while the water quieted around it."

The question that most interested the bench concerned the *Cimmerian*'s reasons for tripling engine speed at the moment Rawden approached the dangerous area over the screws. A state attorney described the likely sequence of events: "A man on the bridge throws the throttle to full. The twin propellers respond to the increased power and gain speed. The large volumes of water displaced backwards create a temporary surface eddy near the stern which pulls the light hull of the boat toward the area over the screws. It drifts back in the wake a few yards and suddenly the powerful double vortex spinning out from the propellers erupts underneath it, throwing tons of water in the air and possibly developing a downward suction also. The small boat, only fourteen feet long, is tossed around until the sea pours into the stern and drags it under. A few seconds later it passes out of the turbulence and its buoyant hull resurfaces in the wake. Similarly Rawden's body."

The judge was also curious about the outfit worn by the commander of the *Cimmerian* at the inquest. "Is that a uniform?" she asked.

"Yes, your honor, if you mean am I required to wear it."

"Then you're a member of the armed services?"

"No."

"Then who requires you to wear it?"

"My superior."

The commander wore khaki fatigues, a woven green belt, white socks, and black shoes. He stood before the bench as stiffly as a recruit at attention, but his tone and the set of his shoulders made it clear to everyone in the room that his posture was a deliberate mockery of his situation. He was tall, spare, and angular, and he had at least ten years on the judge.

"And who is your superior?" she asked.

"I'd prefer not to answer that."

"Why not?" Her voice had a harsh, cautionary edge. He took a few moments to compose his answer.

"I was in command of the ship at the time in question and I assume full responsibility."

She didn't get much further with him. He said he took orders from the owner's agent in Miami and that he didn't know the owner's name. "Then who signs your paycheck?" she asked. He said that it was an unsigned draft on an account in a Bahamian bank. He added that he never had any trouble cashing it.

As for the time in question, he hadn't been on the bridge and his second in command had given the order to increase speed. It was a daily drill intended to test the engines and other systems. The small boat wasn't noticed until it was too late.

Rawden's three-inch obituary in the *Herald*, which was overshadowed by the accounts of his death, eulogized him as a "pioneer in law enforcement" in the Miami area and mentioned a citation he had received from President Ford for his work with the DEA. Understandably enough, there were certain members of the community who read it with great satisfaction.

He had no immediate family and no suits were brought against the government for his benefits. The state entered no charges against the *Cimmerian*. Opinion at the Port split between those who said he had stayed on too long and had tried to do too much and those who said, a little less forthrightly, that maybe he had noticed something that everyone else was too busy to see. But he was dead and the topic slowly faded from interest. Few serious discussions revolved around the *Cimmerian*; it was too sensitive a subject.

Nobody knew that the commander had lied to the court when he said he had been in his quarters when the accident occurred. Rawden could have enlightened them.

The sea was quiet on the night of his death and he had nothing more to contend with than a low swell out of the southeast as he raced out of Miami to meet the *Cimmerian*. He knew where to look for it. For the last twenty-four hours he had tracked its movements by monitoring the radio reports its shadow, the *Argus*, called in to base. From these Rawden extrapolated the big ship's likely course and decided that it would pass due east of Miami at about eleven on Friday night.

373

He needed a fast boat to reach it. So that evening he called the Port and told them he was coming down to clean out his office. One of the duty officers let him in and followed him to the administration block — standard procedure in off hours, though it would have been ignored if Rawden were still on the clearance list.

After an hour of sorting papers and dumping them into boxes while the officer yawned, strolled the corridor, and made a few phone calls, Rawden said he had to go out to his car to get his pipe. The officer nodded. A recent transfer from Atlanta, he had heard a lot about Rawden and the sight of this large, stooped, and scholarly man, whose name had carried so far, emptying years of his life into a wastebasket so affected him that he was willing to hear any request Rawden might have made. When Rawden didn't come back immediately the officer started digging through the papers himself, leaving the door open and listening for footsteps in the hall. He wasn't looking for anything in particular.

So Rawden had no trouble getting a certain key out of the cage by the dock. There was plenty of gas in the twin-engined Formula he found; it had recently been confiscated by the harbor police. He ghosted out of the basin, throttle damped so low that the muffled churning of the propellers was no louder than the buzzing of the lamps on the piers. Neither the boat nor Rawden was missed for another half hour.

As soon as he passed out of the Cut he unleashed the engines and discovered, to his pleasure, that it didn't matter if anyone came after him because he could easily outrun anything on the water. He stood over the wheel with his feet set apart and his tie beating against his neck while the swells skipped against the tailfin and the hull slowly rose out of the black ocean until it was skimming over the surface like a missile. He knew all this by touch; he hadn't turned on any lights and he couldn't see the boat underneath him.

The *Cimmerian* looked like a group of weak stars swarming on the horizon, distinguished from the wallowing container ships that rode here and there on either side by its cloudy brilliance; the upper decks were lit up like a chandelier. By the time he was close enough to guess at the outline of its white steel hull he had already slowed down considerably.

Now that he was here he suffered a sudden loss of purpose. His conviction that the *Cimmerian* could somehow provide whatever was lacking in himself, could show him why he had junked his career and trampled on his authority — could even tell him why he had grown to despise every sign or vestige of his former life — was a conviction that depended on some distance between himself and the undeniable bulk, the intransigent size, mass, and sweep of his yearning's object, and now that he was face-to-face with it his sense of urgency was stronger than ever but he didn't know how to proceed. And how could he have known? The *Cimmerian* refused to define itself in any terms except the physical. That was what had brought him here.

But there was nothing ambiguous about the way the ship blotted out the tropical sky over his head as he drifted towards it, engines barely muttering; a mosquito homing in on a mammalian body. He could hear the waves crashing against the bows. No one moved along the spotless white railings and companionways. The elaborate cups and ears of its radar complex spun evenly on their metal stalks thrust high into the night. The water around him began to sparkle and turn milky as he approached the circle of the ship's radiance, and he could now see into many of its lighted ports and windows, but he had yet to locate a human figure. Maybe, he thought, a crew is entirely superfluous; maybe all the hollow rooms are empty and I'm the first to approach this power which looks as if it was designed and built by men but which has obviously gone beyond them. It slid through the water like a knife. He didn't doubt that it was aware of his presence. He thought of the man on the *Dart* and the few others who had been plucked out of the sea and forced to tour the ship's interior — was that what he wanted? He was close enough to hear the hull singing and the spray hissing along the waterline.

The Formula pitched and rocked as it met the wake of the big ship. Rawden closed his hands on the rail over the windshield. Not twenty yards away the high and dizzy wall of the destroyer surged past him, its whiteness apparent even in its shadow. It took a long time to go by. A fine cold mist wetted his knuckles. For a moment, but only a moment, he knew he had made a mistake.

He found himself looking at the narrow bucket of the stern as it dragged away from him into the dark, its wake boiling out from the screws and flattening the sea around him, so that the foam fizzed up from below quite audibly, untroubled by any disturbance on the surface and leaving gassy streaks and fingers lying exhausted on the black water. The lights of the Coast Guard cutter trailing the *Cim-*

merian shone sharp and bright in the distance. He woke out of his stupor and jammed the throttle wide open.

The speedboat nearly leaped out from underneath him. He shot past the long ship in seconds and cranked the wheel hard over across its path. The Formula's rear end skidded out to the right, engines roaring as they broke out of the water and finally biting into the next swell, catapulting him under the *Cimmerian*'s bows. He didn't straighten it out until he was racing down the far side. He clung to the wheel like a starfish while he carved a widening spiral of foam around the larger boat, whose gleaming white superstructure leaned, toppled, and snapped back over his head. He wanted to be noticed; he wanted to show what he could do.

Nothing human marred the skewed and fragmentary glimpses he caught of the upper deck. The lights shone back at him in the glossy walls of water he threw up from his gunwales — black mirrors hanging frozen in the air, streaming shapes that didn't even begin to curl and fall until he was long past them. Not a drop touched him at forty knots. The wind smashed into his face and funneled down his collar, pulling his shirt out of his belt and dragging him back from the wheel, but although he had to fight just to fill his lungs he didn't even look at the throttle because he knew that nothing on the water, not even the *Cimmerian,* could stand this kind of harassment.

He was right. But for the moment he had the stage to himself; the glittering hulk cleaved to its course and furnished a steady reference for his acrobatics, which were as reckless as they were exhilarating, so reckless that he imagined he wanted nothing else for his trouble and a short while later was tempted to make believe he hadn't noticed the lone man who had appeared on the shielded balcony under the bridge. But he kept watching him anyway as he roared circles around the *Cimmerian,* mercilessly punishing the hull of the Formula, and with each circuit he tracked the man's progress down the companionways and along the lighted starboard decks to the rear of the ship. The man never looked back at him.

When the figure finally stopped and leaned over the rail on the main deck at the center of the stern, standing over the wake in his officer's cap, Rawden peeled off his orbit and swung away behind the ship, then cut into the backwash at half speed and slowly crept up from the rear. He closed the gap into its shadow. Quieted, the noise of its engines reduced to a thin vibration over the drowned thunder of the *Cimmerian*'s screws, the Formula matched speed and nosed forward.

The deck was about twelve feet above the water. The man stood outlined in black on the rail and looked down on Rawden, who recognized him from Liberty's description — this was the *Cimmerian*'s chief officer, the stark, elegant ironist who claimed not to understand the logic behind his duties — but Rawden knew better, or believed he knew better, and as he stood looking up from the rocking, delicately gimbaled hull of the speedboat he was certain that he had finally reached the end of his long history of denial and renunciation and was about to turn around, to start upward, to extend himself rather than shrink away, but it all depended on the man behind the rail and he didn't dare stir himself or open his mouth for fear of disturbing the precious equipoise he had found here, in the shadow of the *Cimmerian.*

The officer, who had been in command of the ship from the day it was commissioned, was not required on the bridge at this moment. His primary responsibility was the maintenance of certain internal systems that relayed information to a room at the Port. These systems operated automatically; he didn't understand how they worked and no one had informed him of their purpose. However, there were a few facts relevant to his situation that would have appeared conclusive even to a man much less perceptive than himself — namely, that the widespread corruption in the Miami DEA office had prompted numerous calls for an autonomous internal security system; that this system was now in place under the inquiry-proof umbrella of a continuing investigation known only as Special Projects; and that all the tracking systems aboard the *Cimmerian* were focused not on the private traffic coming in from the south and east, but instead on a growing flotilla of official patrol vessels, both those belonging to the department itself and those loaned to it by the Port, the customs office, the Coast Guard, and the U.S. Navy. In short, the *Cimmerian* was consuming nearly half the DEA's regional budget in a determined effort to police the DEA's own operations. The officer was a veteran of two difficult wars and this knowledge did not have a good effect on his state of mind.

The destroyer's engines boomed and shuddered so loudly that Rawden had no chance of hearing anything the officer might say; nor did the officer give any sign that he was making an attempt. He leaned his hips into the rail, both arms staked out like struts on either side, as stiff and rigid as a tripod. Rawden couldn't see his face. But there was no need for words, in his opinion. This confrontation had been too long in the making to depend on any such exchange for its outcome. They already understood one another. Rawden was waiting for a larger, a more meaningful gesture.

So when the officer abruptly turned and walked straight back from the rail, disappearing from view, it took Rawden by surprise. Then a powerful searchlight flashed out of the upper decks and pinned him in place. He heard a deafening rumble shake the water beneath him. Suddenly afraid, he spun the wheel and pushed the throttle to the board. He was too late. The surface exploded into motion; solid mountains of green water shot up on either side of him and a roaring geyser ripped one of the Formula's engines off its mount, spewing gasoline in his eyes. When he turned around the deck fell away from his feet. He felt weightless for a moment. Then he was in the water and the noise was amplified. He reached out for something to grab onto and found nothing. He hadn't planned on this; he couldn't believe it was happening. His eyes stung so badly that he couldn't open them.

Ten minutes later they pulled his body out of the warm ocean and into the launch. The *Cimmerian* drifted at rest a few hundred yards away, all its lights burning. They penetrated into the water and attracted thousands of small nocturnal fish. If you had been sitting on the lowest step of the gangway, just above the gentle slapping of the waves against the hull, you could have seen dozens of needle-tipped, diaphanous fins poking through the surface and twitching this way and that, as if they were moths drawn to the brightness.

Communion

A T ABOUT AN HOUR BEFORE NOON on Sunday morning, two days later, Ray Hula was sitting in a red and white cab parked outside the justice building in downtown Miami. The flag on the meter rested at the nine o'clock — waiting time — for which the driver received only six dollars an hour, and it would take him four more hours like this just to pay back his lease for the day. He was getting impatient. He could usually count on at least five or six airport runs on a Sunday morning and Hula was wasting his time.

"Look," he said, "I can't sit here all fucking day." He pulled a printed card from behind the sun visor and handed it back. "Just call the company when you're ready — the garage is right around the block."

Hula was too busy watching the doors to pay much attention. He dropped a five-dollar bill over the edge of the front seat. The driver shook his head and lit a cigarette.

The few people out on the streets were the kind that generally escape notice during the week, when the parking lots are full and the state and county offices disgorge hungry crowds at lunchtime. A couple of dozen sat on benches under the palms across the avenue or gathered in small groups near the corner, as if they also were waiting for something, but none of them seemed to be in any rush. The hot sun swimming overhead drained the urgency from their faces. Even the white limestone of the public buildings lacked solidity.

Someone with a black-jacketed arm pushed open one of the central doors on the ground floor of the building and let out Lisa Bishop, wearing a seersucker coat over a tan shirtdress, with a rattan pocketbook hooked in her elbow. She started down the broad sidewalk to the right, moving briskly, her face showing that relieved and slightly queasy look people adopt when leaving hospitals or dentist's offices. She had small white bandages taped to her palms. When Ray called to her she nearly stumbled as she stopped to look at him.

He pushed the cab door open on his side and motioned her over. She approached no closer than was necessary to keep from shouting.

"Get in;" he said. "I want to show you something."

She looked at him evenly. "Ray, you have to understand — "

"Have you got a car? Can you drive?" He hopped out of the cab, shut the door, and tossed another five-dollar bill through the window onto the driver's seat. "Thanks buddy," he said. The red and white sedan jerked away from the curb.

"I need a ride," he continued, glancing up at the multistoried pile over their heads. "You can give me a ride, can't you?"

Lisa noticed that the man who had let her out was still standing just inside the doors.

"You don't trust me?" he pleaded. "No? Is that it?"

"Look," she said, turning to him, "I know why you're here. You want to know what I told them. But I've listened to enough questions this morning — and you know the answer anyway." She started down the sidewalk.

"That's not it." He scurried up beside her, twisting at the waist and dropping words in her ear as she marched off, eyes straight ahead, heels clacking on the stone. "That's not it. I know what you said. I was in there myself this morning."

They walked by the three-sided booth where the parking attendant usually sat. There was an old man sleeping on the folding chair inside.

Hula was right next to her when she stopped at the car and reached into her pocketbook for the keys. She pulled them out and turned to look at him. "Ray — I just think we need a little rest from each other, all right?"

He held her gaze, waiting. She broke away and opened the door. As she started to get in he reached behind her and pulled up the locking post on the rear door, swung it open, and stuck his head in, one knee on the cushion, reaching across the interior and yanking up the locking post on the front passenger door. Then he ducked out and hurried around the car.

Lisa saw what was happening and started to lean over to push the button down again. But she hesitated for a moment, her hand poised in the air, and she must have decided she had lost her chance because she didn't complete the motion. Ray didn't waste any time getting in beside her.

The car had been sitting in the sun and was as hot as a sauna. She started it up and backed out so vigorously that Ray had to grab onto the foam heel of the dashboard. He made a face; his hands were taped up also. But he recovered quickly. "You rented a car — good idea," he said. "They told me they've got mine down at the pound — they said I could pick it up later in the week. Did you see the *Herald* this morning?" He turned to face her, sitting on one leg and stretching his arm along the back of the seat. "They found Michael. They dragged him out of a canal — there was a picture."

She didn't answer and he must have listened again to what he had said, because his mood suddenly lost its buoyancy. It was no victory for Lisa. She had wanted to be alone; now they were sharing the silence. When she had opened the heavy Sunday paper beside her coffee that morning the first thing she had seen was the blurred, ashy image of Michael Cruz being pulled headfirst out of the water and up a whitened ridge of spoil by three policemen. His chin rested on his chest and his face was hidden under his dark hair. She had shut the paper and pushed it away. A moment later she got up, went into her kitchen, and washed the shiny newsprint off her fingers.

They rode as far as Biscayne Boulevard without speaking. She turned north, heading for the apartments. There was little traffic and they waited alone at some of the lights.

"I'm leaving," she said. "I'm going to California to stay with my sister."

"Yes." He nodded. "For how long?"

"I don't know."

Hula nodded again and looked out the window. "Then maybe you'll do one favor for me before you go."

"What is it?" she said quickly.

"Turn around and go back down the boulevard."

"That's not much to ask." She didn't want to be sharp or touchy but she couldn't help herself. It was because she knew she would do what he said. Her tone was a warning, a confession of vital interests.

Hula didn't offer at it. "You can take the connector. Jackson Hospital, at the civic center."

She rolled into a parking lot fronting a pharmacy and turned around. She was relieved, actually — by granting him this much she felt she could keep confidence in her right to refuse him anything else. They had found an excuse for being together; they could speak more freely. She was only mildly curious about what he wanted to show her.

They started down again, past the gas stations, the stucco-sided, windowless restaurants, the poster-blocked facades of the airline offices. "We could have waited forever out there," Hula said. "The cops didn't know anything was happening. They didn't go until we told them about it." He coughed into his fist. "They found Liberty's body, too, but the Colombians were long gone."

Lisa wanted to ask him where he had learned all this, but she didn't want to display her ignorance. The men at the justice building hadn't told her anything. The more she thought about it the less glowing, in retrospect, seemed their show of empathy and concern. Tell us all about it, they had said, somehow giving the impression that she could transfer all her doubts and anxieties to their account. There had been soft, fatherly smiles for her when she was finished. But they hadn't told her a thing.

Maybe, she thought, it was because I withheld certain facts that I didn't think of asking any questions.

Hula continued. "I don't know whether Michael's friends blame us for what happened — whether they'll forget about us. So I think your leaving town is a good idea."

It hadn't entered into her decision. She was innocent; what could they want with her? It might be different for Ray, but she had avoided thinking about that. "What're you going to do?"

"Nothing, I guess. A lot depends on whether they bring a case against anyone. Then I might have to testify."

"What about you? Are you going to be charged?"

"I don't know — nobody tried to arrest me. They just said thanks, we'll call you."

Lisa cut around the big banks downtown and climbed the feeder ramp to the connector. She was about to tell Hula precisely that which she had promised herself she would never tell him; her silence concerning this gift to him being the first condition of her decision to make it. She cleared her throat. "Ray — when I talked to them this morning I didn't — I said that I knew you, of course, but I didn't say

384

I knew anything about you and Michael — about what you did before you showed up at my place."

It hadn't been easy for her to sit and talk to those men, pretending to be open with them and all the time wondering what they had heard from Ray and feeling as if nothing was more obvious than the gaping hole in her story. And these were the people she was depending on to reassure her; they represented the world to which she belonged and wanted to return. So she was surprised, even startled, when her admission received little notice from Hula.

"Thanks," he said. "I didn't tell them much either. But they can't touch me — they don't have a prayer." Suddenly restless, he sat up and crossed an ankle over his knee. "What're they going to charge me with? Smuggling? They don't have any coke, they don't have any money that was paid for the coke — all they have is what comes out of my own mouth. I'm not going to hang myself. Let somebody else go to jail. Let 'em open the jails and let everybody out — I don't care. Of course," he said, looking at her, "you could get me for trespassing. If you wanted."

He was grinning. The city rushed by behind his head. She shook free and looked at the road. His breeziness, his whimsical contempt, threatened her somehow; she felt as if she were walking on a wire.

Yesterday morning, after the park ranger had found them sprawling on the dike in the middle of the Glades, he had loaded them into his big orange truck and taken them back to the trail, where they were laid out like corpses on either side of an ambulance, and she remembered looking across at Hula's misshapen, clotted face and seeing him look back at her as they were rushed back to the city — he hadn't been grinning then, and she had known she could close her eyes and he would still be there, still alive, the same person as before, and it helped her to believe the same about herself. Since then she had decided that she didn't want to see him again for a long time, but it was comforting to know that there was someone who had been through all of it with her, and her departure was predicated on the hope that someday she could come back again and talk about it with him. Now that hope seemed deluded. He had changed; he was sly, forceful, ambitious. She found herself checking the speedometer and the rearview mirror for signs of trouble.

"Anyway," he said, "the worst is over. I'm healing up pretty fast. I

385

guess you are too — here you are driving already. I meant to thank you for saving my life." He smiled again. "You didn't think you had it in you, did you?"

After a moment she said, "No, I didn't."

"Well," he said, "neither did I." He turned and looked out the window at the broad, flat expanse of the city visible from the height of the connector. "The cops don't know anything about it, except what you and I told them. They went over the whole place with microscopes."

"How do you know all this?"

"They told me. When I was in there this morning I said I couldn't remember it very well, it was all such a shock, so they kept priming me with new stuff. It was pretty funny."

"But didn't they ask you what you were doing with Michael in the first place?"

"Of course they did — I lied. We were all lying to each other — that's how we passed the time."

When they got to the hospital he was still talking. It wasn't like him at all. He knew it; he kept issuing disclaimers. There were so many times, he said, when the most unlikely circumstances had saved them. Suppose she hadn't gone to cut that palm bud for lunch? They would never have gotten out of the woods. Suppose the stranger hadn't blocked the road? The fingerprints of a benevolent power marked every so-called accident — what had they done to deserve such care? Who wanted them to live? Who could they thank for all this?

In Lisa's opinion, the people who really had the unseen powers on their side rarely needed assistance; they didn't get shot at by strangers or attacked in their own homes. But she didn't argue with Ray; it would have made her feel even more sour and irritable. So she just watched the road while she listened to him ramble, wondering how two people could react so differently to the same ordeal.

The streets around the civic center were full of people in white clothing — laboratory smocks, doctors' coats, nurses' uniforms, and bleached leather shoes. Hula told Lisa where to park and led her across the crowded lot to the main doors of Jackson Hospital. He had become subdued and preoccupied, and he didn't answer any of her questions.

It was a semiprivate room but only one bed was occupied. The bald-headed man lay there on his back with the sheet drawn up to his chin and his upright toes poking up the blanket at the foot. He didn't move at all. When Lisa saw him she drew in a breath with a hiss between her teeth. "Why did you bring me here?" she said, her voice increasingly hurt and bitter as she repeated it, but she was propped against Hula and she had one hand in his collar. Ray stroked her hair without really paying any attention. He stood against the chrome rail of the bed and looked down at the man's blank, pale blue, and large eyes. They floated in their sockets like hollow bearings in heavy oil. Lisa had to look at him again. When she did she knew for certain that he was alive but she couldn't have explained how.

"Do you see it?" Hula said.

She stepped away from him and pulled a Kleenex from her bag; she was finished. "See what?"

"Try again. Do you see it?" He was still staring at the man — breathless, hypnotized.

She thought she understood. "Of course he's alive. They wouldn't keep him here if he wasn't."

"No. Look again. Look at his face."

She couldn't tell whether he was being purposely mysterious; he interested her more than the man on the bed. "I really don't know what you're talking about."

"Once more. Listen to me, Lisa. Please!" His low whisper had turned ferocious. She watched him reach up and pull back the sheet, uncovering the massive chest bulging under the smock, the huge, rounded shoulders. She shuddered when she saw the hands. They were green-purple from the wrists down and still showed the deep ruts left by the clothesline.

"Look at his face!"

Frightened, she did as he asked. She saw the smooth, domed skull, the sloping forehead, the fleshy nose, and the dark, full and almost colorless lips. It was all there in a glance and she didn't know what more to look for. "It's him," she said. "It's the same man."

"Look again! Who is he?"

She turned to Ray's eyes boring into hers. His passion unnerved her. She looked back at the man in the bed. "I — I don't know. I mean I don't know him. I don't think I ever saw him before — before — "

"No! Who does he look like?"

387

Suddenly it was obvious. She didn't have to tell Hula. She just groaned deep in her throat and slumped against him, closing her eyes. His relief was palpable; he put his arms around her. Now that the spell was broken she knew that she had noticed the resemblance before, that she had known about it all along but had refused to countenance it, refused even to think about it, shutting it out of her mind from the moment she first saw him. She hadn't missed the much more subtle likenesses between Ray and Michael. Somehow those had been much easier to acknowledge.

"It's got to be," Hula said. "It's no accident." He was himself again; his voice carefully eased itself back to normal.

Still not quite certain of herself, but feeling a need anyway, Lisa turned her head and looked once more at the figure beside them. He's right, she thought, there can't be any doubt.

Ray dropped his hands to his sides. "Lisa, I'm sorry, but — but I wanted to hear it from someone else. That's all."

She didn't push away, not immediately. "Don't apologize."

"Who else could I ask?"

"It doesn't matter. I already knew, I think."

They were so quiet for a minute that she thought she could hear the man on the bed breathing. She was afraid of him — of his strangeness, his silence, the pain she had heard in his voice just before Michael attacked him. She decided she wouldn't look at him again.

Hula turned away from the bed. "Do you see now? Do you see why Michael couldn't kill him?"

She remembered Cruz sitting huddled in the road while the stranger's voice floated out from under the tree — clear, powerful, taunting. She bit down hard on her thumbnail.

He went on. "I didn't see my mother for forty years. She must have been pregnant when Dad took me away. He didn't tell me, she didn't tell me — Michael knew, but he didn't either."

"But why? What made him come after you?"

"I don't know," he said, turning in on himself. "I think he blamed us for leaving her. My father, Michael, myself — we all left her. There was something wrong with him and he never stopped blaming us."

She shuddered. "It's awful — he was so evil, so weird — I mean, I almost felt sorry for him."

"I think Michael used me to get to him — to force him to act."

She straightened up and made herself take a deep breath. "It's better this way — you have to believe that." Her eyes were full; she looked at the ceiling and blinked.

"Maybe."

There were brisk footsteps in the hall and a white-coated Oriental intern with a clipboard stepped around the door. His face was too wide to be Japanese — Korean, maybe, or Chinese. When he saw them he was startled. "This is private. You can't be in here."

Lisa started to go but Hula held her back. "Why not?"

The intern looked as if he couldn't decide between going for help or arguing further. His command of English was uncertain. "Because," he said. "It is so."

Hula let go of Lisa and leaned over the bed, holding his face near the stranger's. "But I'm his brother. See?"

After another moment of veiled confusion, the intern bobbed his head once and dropped his objections. He moved quickly to the bedside, edging Hula out of the way. He lifted the man's wrist and started counting silently, looking at his watch.

Lisa touched Hula's elbow. "Let's go."

Hula shook his head and nudged the intern. "What's wrong with him?"

The young man finished counting and wrote something on the clipboard. Then he took an empty syringe out of his pocket and tore the plastic off it.

Ray was twice his size and was having trouble keeping his hands to himself. "He's my brother — I have a right to know."

"Who is he?" the intern said, as if trying out the phrase for his vocabulary. "Who is he?" He expertly slipped the needle into the man's arm and drew the plunger back; the cylinder filled with purple blood. Then he produced a small black-capped bottle and transferred the sample to it. His movements were quick and exact.

"Tell me — tell me what's wrong." Hula curled his hands around the bedrail.

Glancing sharply at Hula, the intern pocketed the bottle and pulled out a penlight. He leaned over the man and shone it into his pupils. "He must not be alive. He must not, but he is. I can't explain."

"What?" Hula leaned over him also. His brother's pupils shrank in the light.

The intern sounded as if he had borrowed his tone from his professors. "In cocaine," he said, holding his thumb and forefinger a quarter inch apart, "this much is fatal. We found this much." He spread his fingers wide.

"But when will he wake up?"

"Maybe tomorrow. Maybe never. I can't explain."

"Then he's all right?"

"His health is good. He is awake. There's nothing wrong with him. I can't explain." He snapped the light off and hurried from the room.

Hula didn't try to stop him. He stayed by the high bed, his head bowed, his back to Lisa. The air conditioner made a hollow, rushing sound.

Lisa was no longer so anxious to leave. She felt numb and remote.

When Hula turned around a minute later there were tears in his eyes. He put his palms on his cheeks and pushed his skin back from his face. "He's mine," he said, his voice squeaking through a clogged gullet. "He's all there is. I'm not letting him go." He sounded as if he didn't think he could make a difference, as if he were already too late. Lisa knew he wanted something from her but she didn't know what it was.

"There's no hurry," she said.

Hula dropped his hands and looked over his shoulder at the man on the bed.

Lisa turned away for a moment. "He was sick — he would have killed us."

"Fuck it," Hula said, suddenly emphatic. "It's dead, it's over. Let him sleep on it." He patted his pockets and looked around. He tried, but it didn't quite come off. "We don't belong here—let's go." He waited for her to move.

He'll never change, Lisa thought — and neither will I. It was foolish to think anything else. She watched him turn and pull the sheet up to the man's chin. Seeing them together, she realized that their likeness was absolutely necessary while their differences were arbitrary and accidental; they were the same man seen from separate angles. The stranger was healthier, stronger, more acute, and more self-controlled. He drew life and power from within. He was superior to Ray in every respect but one, she thought — humanity. Somehow he had never become a person. He had come out of the mold too late; he was too perfect and nothing could touch him afterwards.

Hula was leaning over him again. "I'll be back," he said. "Don't worry." He stood up, glanced at Lisa, and followed her out the door. When they were gone it was quiet in the room.

Lisa welcomed the hot blast of bright air as she stepped out the main entrance of the hospital. It made her feel alive again. Her car was a long way across the lot and she started briskly out of the shadow, Ray hurrying alongside her. "There's something I didn't tell you," he said, squinting.

"Yes." She didn't slow down but she was willing to listen. As they walked between the locked cars she felt the heat radiating from their polished surfaces.

"Remember when I came out to the edge of the hammock that morning and found you and Liberty under the tree?"

After a moment she nodded.

"You went back to the house. I sat with him for a while."

"Go on." He seemed to want encouragement.

Hula found his stride and concentrated on what he was saying. "Well, he told me that he was never going to leave that spot. But he also said that you and I might get away somehow. He wasn't specific. And he gave me this." He fished in his pocket and came up with three or four keys on a circular silver ring. He jangled them once and closed his fingers around them. "They go to his place in the Bahamas — it's in Alice Town on North Bimini. He said it was a big house, private, with its own beach and pier. He said it was mine if I wanted it. All I had to do was walk in."

"So?" Lisa knew what was coming next and wanted to get it over with.

"So why don't we nip over there for a few days? No one'll stop us — we can do what we want."

"Forget it." She looked straight ahead.

"Why not? Why the hell not?"

"Do I have to justify my every move to you?"

"But it's perfect!" Hula heard himself shout and lowered his voice. "It's only fifty miles away. No one'll know we're there. We can swim, cook, sleep all morning — stay as long as we like. It's a beautiful place — it's where Ponce found the fountain of youth."

She walked a little more quickly.

"Well?" he asked.

"I said no."

They were still halfway to the car. If you had been standing under the concrete awning that shaded the doors to the hospital you wouldn't have known how the argument ended, because the last thing you would have seen before the two figures melted into the gleaming, foreshortened ranks of the countless automobiles massed in the distance was Hula's arms waving over his head in frustration and Lisa's narrow, sharp-shouldered back suddenly dark before it crumbled into the whitened, blinding glare.

Epilogue

$\mathbf{I}$T WAS A LONG SUMMER IN MIAMI. There was no hurricane that year and the rain never stopped for more than a few hours at a time — washing out the last week in June, hissing through July, streaming down drainpipes and leaching the stiffness out of August and September, until the city floated high on a rising column of weed-choked water and the sea went brackish five miles offshore. Traffic stalled in the low places and headlights shone through curtains of spray at noon. Canals backed up and flooded golf courses. Jet airliners skidded down slick runways at Miami International. The rich moved out to the Keys, the beach hotels cut their rates, and the unseen poor holed up in their mobile homes in the outlying districts and waited. The drug trade, the healthiest sector of the economy, remained violent and untaxable. It was a summer like most others and the city grew in spite of it.

The wet season ended on an afternoon in October and dry air from the northwest swept across the peninsula for the first time in six months. In the evening the crowded Cuban neighborhoods downtown spread into the streets and people sipped coffee out of tiny paper cups well into the small hours.

To the west, the water level dropped through the following weeks in the wide plain of the Glades and patches of white rock showed through the yellowing sawgrass. The explosion of aquatic life — of microbes, minnows, and mosquitoes — that the rains had set off shrank into the deeper sloughs and canals; in the drier areas these asylums sometimes contained more fish than water and functioned as scum-thickened tureens for flapping congresses of herons and egrets. All over the Glades the retreating tides concentrated life where moisture was still available. In a few months' time the plain would transform itself into a sere, rattling desert. Visitors to the national park, touring its boardwalk-ringed oases, would be amazed at the luxuriance of the animal life, not realizing that even the largest alligators are willing to be photographed by strangers in return for a string of deep pools to preside over.

On a mild weekend in November a young man on a bicycle pumped south along the rutted, precarious margin of Krome Avenue. The road demanded most of his attention and he didn't have much opportunity to study the greening fields on either side. There wasn't much to see anyway — just the flat, gray soil and an occasional house or shed beside a long pine windbreak. The strong drafts that the produce trucks tunneled after them as they roared up from behind pulled at his shoulders and boosted his speed. But he wasn't trying to make time. He had never been along this particular stretch of asphalt before; he had seen it only on a map while sitting at the kitchen counter of a tract house in Howard where he was a guest and where he had decided, on Friday night, that it might lead him out of the city.

He wore an old red sweatshirt, a collapsed canvas backpack, khaki go-to-hell pants, and sneakers. It wasn't the type of outfit worn by people who expect to stay clean.

Most of the dirt roads that led off to the west had plastic newspaper boxes on posts at their entrances. Ignoring these, he put his foot down at some of the others, shading his eyes and peering off into the hazy distance, as if he were looking for something at the end of one of them. But he apparently didn't find it, since in each case he pushed off again after a moment and pedaled another mile or so down the avenue. It was about eleven in the morning and the plain was quiet and empty; the still air bred silence out of itself. At times there was nothing moving at all except for the bicycle and a few black-winged vultures easing high over the landscape like bits of ash.

He stopped again at the free-standing switchbox that Jack had noticed on his way to his death. The young man looked at the road that ran off beside it. Unlike some of the others, this one showed no recent tire tracks and didn't look as if it could handle agricultural machinery. It divided two broad fields planted with tomatoes and extended indefinitely towards the horizon. He reached up, readjusted his backpack, and turned in. His wheel wobbled when he came off the short slope into the sand but he managed to stay on his seat. A crop broker passing by in his dusty Pontiac saw him go in.

An hour later he rolled down the last hundred yards to the edge of the hammock. He slid off the bicycle, parked it, hung his backpack on the handlebars, and walked up and down the road while he caught his breath; his legs stiff and clumsy, his hands on his hips, and his mouth hanging open. He had dirty blond hair, wire-rim glasses, and a day-old beard.

Returning to the bike, he pulled a black imitation-leather case from the pack and slid out a pair of binoculars. Then he sat down carefully on the edge of the road, propped his elbows on his knees, and scanned the horizon, one finger twirling the annealed focusing wheel. He soon tired of it. There was nothing to hold his attention. The pale, burnt sawgrass covered the plain for as far as he could see, interrupted only by the low islands of a few other hammocks, each a weary green enclosed in a gray border of leafless scrub. The sky was empty and the only sound was the blurred scratching of a few dozen hidden insects. He put the binoculars down and leaned back on his hands.

He felt uneasy for a moment; the silence of great open spaces is unsettling. On his feet again, he scrambled down the rough shoulder.

All the water was gone and the moldering limestone base of the Glades lay exposed to the sun. He took a few uncertain steps across the bleached, pitted rock and squatted on his ankles, reaching down and running his finger along a dried-out sawgrass shoot. It was papery and nearly colorless, but the sharp spines along its edge were still horny enough to draw blood, as he discovered when he tried to uproot the bundle in his fist. He opened his hand and found a line of beaded scarlet across his palm.

The water had taken everything else with it. The holes and pockets in the stone held a few ounces of desiccated muck, but that was all. He stood up and climbed onto the road, looking around briefly before he hung the binoculars on the bicycle and started down the trail into the hammock, his feet leaving dry tracks in the soft sand.

When he came around the last bend and saw the house he stopped and looked at it for a while. There were no cars in the clearing. No dogs boiled out from under the stoop and the clothesline had been pulled out of its bracket on the wall. All the windows to the left of the front door were broken; it was obvious that no one had lived here for

397

some time. When he stepped forward again a flock of sparrows burst out of the brown grass and whirred into the trees.

He didn't want to find anyone here, not because he had anything illegal in mind, but since he would just as soon not make any excuses. They would want to know what he was doing on their property, and he would have to answer that he was looking for snakes. It generally didn't go down well with strangers even though it was the truth; they either looked at him funny or told him to get the hell out. He rarely knew whether or not he had been believed.

But he wasn't so single-minded in his interests that he wouldn't stop to look at anything else. He circled the house and peered in all the windows. The floors were bare except for a few empty beer bottles and related trash, probably left by other uninvited visitors. Someone with a sense of humor had stretched a pair of nylon panty hose across the one undamaged wall of the screened porch. Heaps of long-dead vines, the wrack of the summer's high water, wreathed the corner foundation supports. He pushed them aside with his foot to see if anything had crawled underneath.

The last tenants had taken their furniture with them and the shell of the house didn't offer much fuel for speculation. If the owners planned to use it this winter they probably would have started fixing it up by now. In a few months, if there were no signs that anyone was making an effort to maintain the place — no chain across the road, no posters on the door — someone would come in with a book of matches and burn it to the ground. A few more years would remove the last visible traces; the Glades have always resisted settlement.

He stepped off the concrete platform of the porch and looked across the clearing, wondering what to do next. The sinkhole was the obvious choice — it was the only water he had seen since he'd left Krome Avenue and it was bound to have attracted a few snakes. He planned to fight his way into the woods sooner or later but he didn't expect to have much success there. The tangle of roots and rocks offered too much concealment. It's no use knowing that what you're looking for is right under your feet if you have no way to get at it. There were some people who would pour gasoline down any likely hole or crevice to force out whatever was inside, but he wasn't one of them. He considered himself an amateur.

He chose the sinkhole; if he checked it now he would get a second chance later on.

In another minute he was crouching at the edge of the water beside a pitted chunk of limestone and staring back at a large, brownish, and heavy-bodied snake that was resting on a mat of vegetation about four feet away. They were aware of one another. When the snake's head had lifted out of the weeds the young man had frozen still, and now the snake couldn't see him anymore and was testing the air with its long, supple, and black-edged tongue. So the two minds lay balanced there in mutual alertness, a common situation in such encounters.

The young man had been bitten often enough by snakes as large as this and would have lunged for it by now if he had any confidence in his opinion that it was only a harmless *Natrix*, a water snake. But an error here could be painful. He knew that cottonmouth moccasins had the same stout body and sable skin. If he could open the animal's jaws and check its teeth he could immediately settle the question. On the other hand, he had no intention of getting poisoned out here in the middle of nowhere just to make a precise identification, and after a minute the tension lapsed; he knew he wouldn't reach for it. And the snake also seemed to know that the crisis was over. Raising its head another inch or so, it slowly stretched itself out and slid away, calm and majestic, its power acknowledged.

The young man stood up, his knees aching, and watched the animal pull its tail into a wet pile of sticks and dead reeds under a coral boulder. He didn't feel cheated; it was what he had come here for.

The reflection of the trees on the far side darkened the water and made a window in the surface. Scaly gars floated stiff and motionless about six inches down, ignoring the blue-tinged fins of sunfish rolling and flashing near the shelter of a patch of fleshy, gourd-stemmed water hyacinths. Something puckered the surface near the center, where the bright overlay of the sky balked his eyes — a turtle, maybe, or a rising fish. He picked his way through the mud and tussocks toward the far side of the sinkhole, his eyes alert for movement. At one point he stooped abruptly and came up with a hatchling alligator in his hands. It whipped its head back and forth, throwing off drops of water and squealing like a puppy. When he put it back it clambered through the weeds for a short distance and stopped, exhausted, its jaws propped open for a threat, its feet splayed out from its sides.

A few minutes later he reached the other end of the sinkhole. There were deer tracks in the soft bank. He raised his eyes and saw the sandy trail climbing into the woods, the trail that Hula and Lisa had stumbled into six months earlier. It offered as easy a passage as he was likely to find. Looking back once into the clearing, he curled one hand around an exposed root and hiked up the sculpted limestone embankment into the forest.

He must have found the drier parts of the hammock more interesting than he had anticipated, because he didn't reappear for over an hour. A green-winged heron took advantage of his absence to do some fishing in the shallows near the house. Surprised, it squawked and leaped into the air when he came back down the trail. It rowed across the clearing, gaining altitude, and slipped over the trees on the far side.

He climbed down onto a wide platform of thick, twining roots and dangled his feet over the water. Fish darted away into pockets in the limestone. It was cool in the full shade of the big trees and he decided to stay for a while.

The autumn afternoon rested easily on the clearing, dry and colorless in the watery sun. The roof of the battered house slanted low over the front windows. The strong contrasts of summer hadn't survived the onset of the drought — the landscape had turned pale and fragile as it died back. The young man tapped his cigarette into the sinkhole and watched the ash break up as it sank through the green water, attracting dusky minnows who spat out bits of it and turned away. He could see a whitish limestone ledge a few feet down. Beyond that the water was too murky.

He stretched out on the wide, tawny root at the edge of the platform and leaned his face over the rim. One arm hung straight down from his shoulder and the smoke from the cigarette drifted up into his eyes. It seemed like a lot of work to raise it to his lips. He started to think about other things and he might have fallen asleep if he hadn't noticed the oddly kinked, thin, and chalky root that lay half concealed behind a screen of more lifelike ones that plunged into the sinkhole at the back of the small, roofed inlet he was lying over. He looked at it for a short time; a bleached thread in a tangle of brown, and decided that it wasn't a root at all — it was a length of rope. He leaned over a little farther and reached for it, but his arm wasn't long enough. Sliding on his stomach, he hooked his heels under a stout root behind him, allowing him to bend at the waist and swing his shoulders under the platform — it was still too distant. Blood pooled in his head, reddening his face. But the attempt wasn't a complete loss. He was able to follow the rope with his eyes to where it ran up the back of the hollow and he saw that it was neatly knotted around a black limb in the deepest part.

This intrigued him. He couldn't see how he could get at the rope without going swimming. While he was considering it he remembered that the ledge he had crossed to reach his perch wasn't solid, but rather an overgrown mass of old roots full of cracks and spaces. Therefore he might be able to get at the line from above.

Leaning over again, he tried to fix the knot's location in respect to the top of the platform. It didn't take long. Satisfied, he swung himself up and crawled over to the likely spot.

People who have any experience with snakes generally know better than to thrust their hands into dark holes in the ground. Before he did it he poked around with a short stick to see if he could scare up any life. Nothing happened. So he got down on his chest and reached into a small break in the surface where a smooth, mottled root split into two. He had to go in up to his shoulder but he found the knot. Somebody, he thought, went to some effort to conceal this.

He was wrong about the material — it was a piece of clothesline, not rope. He managed to undo it by touch without losing his grip. Using both arms and a variety of other holes in the woody shelf, he passed the end hand-over-hand toward the rim over the water and eventually got it free. When he looked over the edge again he saw that the line had worked out from behind the vertical roots in back and now fell directly into the water. It seemed to go down beyond the submerged ledge. He sat up, braced his feet, and started to pull.

It was hard work at first and he wondered if the line was caught on something. He was worried that it might break. He knew that alligators dug burrows in the banks of pools like this and he imagined that he might be tugging on a strong steel hook with an eight-foot reptile on the end.

Suddenly it was much easier; the line went slack. He bent over and saw something like a black bubble large enough to swallow him rolling out from under the drowned ledge and rushing up through the water. As it broke the surface he jerked up his legs and scrambled away. It was a good ten seconds before he was ready to go back to the edge and look over again.

When he did he found a black plastic garbage bag turning slowly in the water like a half-inflated beach ball. The clothesline was knotted around its neck. He stared at it for a moment before he discovered that the other end of the line was still in his hand. Disgusted with his own skittishness, he sat up and hauled the bag, which was heavy in spite of its buoyancy, out of the water and onto the broad root beside him. He tore it open with his fingers. A small chunk of the contents fell out and dropped in the sinkhole.

There was nothing inside but money. He reached in and pulled out a thick sheaf of hundred-dollar bills wrapped in a brown paper collar. They were all hundred-dollar bills. The bag hadn't leaked and all the money was dry.

He didn't know that there were five million dollars in the bag, minus the bundle that had dropped in the water. He didn't know that a Colombian, Ramón Galdos, had found another five million in the house across the clearing on a night in June. And he didn't know that the rightful owners, Ray Hula and Lisa Bishop, had never come back to look for it. He just knew that he had a decision to make.